The DIAMOND HUNTER

Fiona McIntosh is an internationally bestselling author of novels for adults and children. She co-founded an award-winning travel magazine with her husband, which they ran for fifteen years while raising their twin sons before she became a full-time author. Fiona roams the world researching and drawing inspiration for her novels, and runs a series of highly respected fiction masterclasses. She calls South Australia home.

PRAISE FOR FIONA McINTOSH'S BESTSELLERS

'A blockbuster of a book that you
won't want to put down.'
BRYCE COURTENAY

'McIntosh's narrative races across oceans and
dances through ballrooms.'
SUN HERALD

'This book is fast-paced, beautifully haunting and filled
with the excruciating pain of war.'
WEST AUSTRALIAN

'A fine read . . . The moral ambiguity McIntosh
builds into the novel gives it a depth that takes it beyond
a sweeping wartime romantic thriller.'
SUNDAY HERALD SUN

'McIntosh weaves a diverse cast together,
and you gain an appreciation for her depth of research.'
BOOKS+PUBLISHING

'A captivating saga of love, loss, and the
triumph of the human spirit . . . Fiona McIntosh
is an extraordinary storyteller.'
BOOK'D OUT

'A perfect blend of romance, action,
mystery and intrigue by one of our best
known and popular authors.'
NOOSA TODAY

FIONA McINTOSH

The DIAMOND HUNTER

MICHAEL JOSEPH
an imprint of
PENGUIN BOOKS

MICHAEL JOSEPH

UK | USA | Canada | Ireland | Australia
India | New Zealand | South Africa | China

Michael Joseph is part of the Penguin Random House group of companies
whose addresses can be found at global.penguinrandomhouse.com.

Penguin
Random House
Australia

First published by Michael Joseph 2019

Cover photography: girl by © Alexander Vinogradov/Trevillion Images;
street scene © Lee Avison/Trevillion Images; flourish by Rawpixel.com/Shutterstock
Inside front cover photo by Joanna Czogala/Arcangel
Internal design: diamonds by Ikonacolour/Shutterstock and flourish
by Rawpixel.com/Shutterstock
Cover design by Louisa Maggio © Penguin Random House Australia Pty Ltd
Typeset in Sabon by Midland Typesetters, Australia

Printed and bound in Australia by Griffin Press, part of Ovato, an accredited
ISO AS/NZS 14001 Environmental Management Systems printer

A catalogue record for this
book is available from the
National Library of Australia

ISBN 978 0 14378 779 2

penguin.com.au

MIX
Paper from
responsible sources
FSC® C009448

For the first man I ever loved . . . and still do.
Rest now, Dad, after a long, wonderful life.

Frederick Richards 1926–2019

PROLOGUE

September 1871

The air sagged beneath the burden of the day's heat and the African sun felt as pitiless as her mother's gaze upon meeting the man Louisa had chosen to marry.

Louisa Knight understood now that Death had turned its lens on her. She considered it a personal triumph that neither anger nor despair bloomed in her mind at the realisation that she would not recover from this latest bout of fever. It was a killer of many, so why should she be spared?

What Louisa did feel, as she contemplated her own end, was regret for all that she must now leave behind. It wouldn't be long, she grasped, for even as her thoughts finally found clarity as she emerged from the fever that had recently rattled her teeth like dice in a fist, she knew that, in sharp contrast, her body was slumping towards surrender.

Louisa would take her final breath and the two people closest to her wouldn't know that she had slipped away. Somehow that felt easier. She didn't want to see any more guilt in her husband's hooded eyes, or fear in her child's. Instead she allowed the regrets to line up before her. The most important stared back with a wistful smile: she wished she could have lived to see her daughter grow up to fulfil all her early promise. Clementine's language was advanced, her instincts – particularly her empathy – were already well developed, and her thoughts were, at times, so complex Louisa worried for her. *I hope my daughter wants more for her life than just becoming a dutiful wife*, she thought.

How ironic. She had not only settled for marriage as her life's sole achievement but she had outraged her family by falling for someone without pedigree or wealth. Despite her wry thought, no amusement could reach her lips; control over her body had already been ceded. *Just a little longer*, she begged, so she could arrange her thoughts fully and leave this life with a tidy mind.

Yes, she had married a poor man. Leaving him behind was her second regret. In their seven years together, she had known only love with James. Their passion for each other had burned bright, like magnesium. It was so strong it blinded them, obscuring everyone and everything around them in shadow.

She had chosen him instinctively, knowing it would cost her at some point, and the debt was going to be paid sooner than she'd imagined. What a pity. But if she looked at her twenty-seven years, she had never been without love. Her parents lavished her with affection, her half-brother adored her – and she, him – and then her love, James . . . well, he simply worshipped her. On the surface they were mismatched – she could hardly deny it – but in truth they were a perfect fit, finding each other addictive.

Poor, darling James. His boundless desire to impress upon her family that poverty should not define him had guided his capricious decisions. One of those unpredictable choices would now kill her. There was no way out of this.

She turned to her third regret: beloved Reggie. She had never thought of him as a half-sibling. He was her big brother and she loved him unreservedly. She could imagine him in England at this moment, all but shaking a fist at her for being gullible, for being a stupid romantic fool. 'What about your family? What about your life here in England? Woodingdene is yours – it will never be mine; we should be running it together. And if you won't think of yourself, then how about considering Clementine in your foolhardy adventure? My niece is every inch a Grant.'

She couldn't deny it. Their daughter behaved more like his child than James's. She was serious, driven, not at all unreliable. Even now at six she was dependable in her moods, her ways, her promises. And yet the little girl adored her father as much as Louisa did. James could make their serious child laugh in the tightest of situations, and Clementine would have to rely on that now because the grimmest of circumstances was not far off. The youngster's emerging character was about to be tested in the toughest of ways. She hoped her husband would no longer call home this tent in which she now lay prone, but instead would decide to cut his losses and return to England.

What had life come to? Now she ate, slept and made love under canvas. Her family would be appalled. She hoped they would never discover her way of life in Africa. They may reimburse James for the headstone she'd already ordered. He would discover it was ready, waiting for him to tell the undertaker the words he wanted hammered into the stone. Nothing grand. James would keep it simple, but his grief would be hard, complex. A month ago she'd written him a letter, after emerging from her second bout of fever, and then hid it for him to find at the right time. She'd felt she needed to warn him against being selfish in his grief . . . to remember the child in his life. She'd written that letter knowing she would never leave Africa or see the soft, misted greens of the vale at Woodingdene again. This new and surely fatal fever had arrived, cruelly early, in the dark hours prior to dawn, after James had departed to be one of the first at the riverside to dig for his precious diamonds.

She turned inwards again, to contemplate her final regret. Too tiny to matter to anyone else, yet the pain of this loss hurt the most. The baby growing within her had never had a chance, despite her best hopes to live out the year. She hadn't told James that he was to be a father again; the right moment hadn't arisen since they'd alighted from the ship at Cape Town because she'd needed to be sure. She had sickened throughout the voyage from England but had presumed it was simply a lack of sea legs. Unfortunately, her health had taken a darker turn. Her precious boy – she was sure it was a son – would accompany her to the grave. The Little Karoo – this African desert – would take her and her son into its secret, silent depths and keep them until their parched bones became part of its limitless dust. James had never understood why she didn't want him to reach for her in the humble cot they shared. He'd wrongly interpreted her resistance as despair – a sort of punishment for the misery he'd brought her. The truth was she had needed every ounce of strength for the baby, but now it was too late for him. James did not need the torture of knowing that she had taken his child with her.

Louisa pushed that darkness aside and considered the events that had collided to deliver her into the Cape Colony. This whole sorry mess had come down to weather. *How thoroughly British*, she thought with no amusement.

Their ship had foundered around the Cape of Good Hope. They'd been advised in London that the P&O ships were now sailing via the Suez Canal, which had opened almost two years previously, but James, refusing to accept any help from her private funds, had paid for what he could afford. The Shaw, Savill and Co ships still braved the route around the frightening Cape and braced for the roaring forties, which would speed them to the other side of the world and that great continent of Australia.

His determination and pride had impressed her, turning down what her money could so easily have bought for them. It had all sounded like such a grand adventure back home in Northumberland. Nothing could hurt her at Woodingdene Estate. She'd grown up among servants and wealth, indulged by all. In the back of her mind had always been the obligation to make a good marriage – to continue the creation of wealth and their family's name. She knew her father had hoped that through her he would gain the respectability he craved.

'Marry old money,' he'd urged her. 'I want you to enjoy a good name and all that it can offer you.'

'But I like Grant,' she'd insisted on numerous occasions.

'So did your mother when she married me, but even she can see the benefit of our only daughter joining our family strategically to another so our grandchildren will reap the rewards.'

'What about Reggie?'

'Don't start, Louisa. It's hard enough as it is. I am fond of Reggie, but he will always —'

'I regard him as my brother, a true Grant, and not whatever it was you were about to say.'

Her father had smiled. 'He's lucky you're his half-sister, but he won't be the man in your life for much longer, my darling. You're twenty now. I'm afraid we must unleash your mother so she has the freedom to start hunting the best matches.'

'I will marry for love, Father.'

'Indeed you will. I suspect your mother loves me but don't for a moment think she didn't first fall in love with my bank account and how happily I spent its contents on her.'

It was true. Her father was generous with his money; she'd heard as much murmured by jealous women out of her mother's earshot.

'Have you seen how he splashes it around? That monstrous house he's building up north! So garish.'

'New money always is, dear.'

'Look at the way he lavishes it on her. She's like a chandelier, she sparkles so much.' Louisa had liked the image of her mother as a twinkling chandelier, but when she'd heard their cruel accompanying laughter she'd understood that this was not a compliment.

Her father's country manor was indeed a monster, sitting on near one thousand acres of private land, but to her child's eyes Woodingdene Estate was a friendly house with magical gardens. Henry Grant had chosen to mark his worldly standing with bricks, using his ability to generate money from a wide range of overseas investments to fund this gregarious dwelling that reflected all his travels. She grew up to learn that its taste was not so much fashionable as ostentatious. Nevertheless, Woodingdene was well ahead of its time in its design, furnishings, and especially its new-fangled hydroelectric generator that powered the house, which had the whole county talking. Little wonder people spoke about Woodingdene as if it had arrived from beyond the moon to settle on a natural crag just beneath the hill. The sprawling estate plunged gently towards a lake and a slow-moving stream, via rock gardens, a stunning arboretum and valley gardens with gentle waterfalls.

She didn't dare dwell right now on the iron bridge that had her initials romantically wrought into its design. This was James's work, commissioned by her father, thus bringing together the young woman full of uncontrolled passions and the quixotic Scottish engineer with whom she had fallen in love, before falling prey to his adventuring spirit.

So come now, Death whispered in her mind. *Time draws close.*

Louisa Knight felt the lightest of breezes stir her hair, which had once been described by her husband as 'fairy's tresses'. When she had asked why, he explained it was so long and soft that a fairy could snuggle up and go to sleep in one of its darkly golden curls. Today it was moist – dull now, she was sure, but that didn't matter any more.

'Clementine?' she whispered.

'I'm here, Mummy.' She felt a little hand grip hers. So Clementine had never left her side.

'Fetch your father . . . but hug me first.'

She felt the chubby arms reach around her neck and the touch of a soft, warm cheek against her dry, feverish face; heard her daughter remind her that she loved her and say that she would run down to the river to fetch her father.

'Good girl, my darling.' She had just enough strength to steal a kiss of her child's cheek, the skin velvety like a ripe peach. She hoped her daughter saw a smile as she pulled away, for she knew it would be gone on her return . . . and so would she.

———————

James Knight was on the brink of losing everything.

He'd already lost his opportunity in Australia, and his status as a rising young engineer had evaporated too. His wife tended to look at him now in a different way, and her understanding showed not in her eyes but at the edges of her lips, which tugged south in an unspoken message of disappointment. James knew Louisa fought it: she still told him she loved him, and her voice always found that special tenderness despite his failings. But she no longer wanted to feel his hands on her body or the heat of his desire for her. Her recurring illness had diminished her proud frame to a skeletal version of itself. Shoulders that had once been squared were now rounded in resignation. He had admired her idealism when they met, and had fallen in love with the woman who wanted to share his adventures – to be an enthusiastic, romantic wife to her swash-buckling, fortune-hunter husband. But he'd also seen the dismay that had clouded her normally loving gaze when he'd proposed his entrepreneurial idea to leave their ship bound for Australia and remain on this continent. It was an audacious plan, with huge risk but high stakes: everything he responded to and everything she'd been raised to avoid.

His energy and promises had convinced her but she had to set aside the realisation that James had already booked their transport to the diamond diggings in the Cape Colony before he won her assent. He had been confident of his persuasive power. 'We're closer to home,' he'd assured her as they stood on the dock and waved goodbye to the people they'd come to know.

But what James knew now, a year on, was that whether Africa or Australia, it didn't matter – his darling Louisa no longer cared for his wandering spirit and promises of fortune. That latter was especially pointed, given she was a wealthy woman in her own right and several times had offered to pay their passage home as well as fund his exploits, so long as their life became easier. He'd refused both in his usual cavalier manner, claiming that living out of a tent would give them a new appreciation for life when he struck it big. But now he was down to the last few pounds he had to his name. His name! That held no currency either; if anything it was a filthy word to his wife's family, and he knew all too well how much they hated it that their two prized girls, Louisa and Clementine, were forced to bear his name as their own.

James pushed the shovel into the ground and threw its contents into his tray. He took an unhappy breath, already certain that there was no telltale reflection of sunshine lighting on a diamond. Even in the rough, these magnificent stones could make a man's throat tighten. He'd joined the rush with tens of thousands of other opportunists from all over the world, hoping to get rich quick. Few had. But even fewer would give up as long as some were hitting the big time.

'Daddy?'

'Sweet Clementine – what's up, my wee darlin'?'

His daughter was tiptoeing barefoot into the water alongside him, her skirts soaked.

'Mummy's sick again. Can you come?'

'Did she send you?' He hoped so, because then maybe he could avert the blame for Clem's wet clothes.

'Yes.'

'All right, darlin'. I shan't be long.'

'Can I wait with you? I don't like being alone watching her look so sad.'

James frowned. 'Is she sleeping now?'

His little girl, gazing seriously from eyes that looked too large for her head, nodded. 'She just woke up but then she fell asleep again.'

'Just a wee while, then. I'll do a few more panloads.'

'Will you tell me the story of Baby Joseph's Pebble?' she asked. 'I'll help you look.' She peered into the tray as he shook it.

He smiled. Even his little girl had been captured by stories from only a decade or so back that had now become legend. James caught the glance of a fellow labouring not far away from him – certainly within ear's reach. He liked the Zulu man: quiet, stolid, hardworking. They'd become friendly through Clem mostly, who talked to everyone.

'Have you heard the story of the Peculiar Pebble, Joseph?'

'No, sir, Mr Knight.'

'Well, it's one of the reasons we all find ourselves here.'

Joseph One-Shoe nodded but kept his back bent working, and James began as he stirred his pan for that all-important glint in the wet earth. 'A Boer farmer's son found a stone while he was resting beneath a tree not two hundred yards from the banks of the Orange River. According to him, it "blinked".'

'His name is Erasmus,' Clementine said to Joseph.

James grinned. 'And he took it home for his little sister to play with.'

'I wish I had a little sister.'

'Maybe one day you will.'

'Nothing in here, Daddy.'

He gave a sad nod. And there'd been nothing for nearly a month, despite the dozens of trayloads he had shaken in hope. He began to pan a small load, and as muddied water dropped back to its source and splattered their clothes, he returned to his tale for her amusement.

'The children in the family had long ago cast the gleaming pebble aside when a neighbour, enchanted by it, offered to buy it, thinking it was topaz. The family said it was just a pebble that their children no longer wanted and made it a gift for him.'

'Why?' Clem asked, clearly for Joseph's benefit.

'Because they are generous.'

'Didn't they want the money? I thought that they were poor farmers.'

'Poor is relative.'

'What does that mean?'

'Well, we pay the Boer farmers so we can mine their land.'

'So we are poorer than them,' she said.

You're too smart for six brief years, Clem, he thought. 'Anyway, the neighbour gave it to an Irish pedlar.'

'For how much?'

'Well, I can't be sure. Either way, people at the time said O'Reilly – that was the pedlar's name – knew he had a diamond after he used it to cut his name into a windowpane.'

Clementine turned to their neighbour. 'Did you know you can cut glass with a diamond, Joseph?'

Joseph paused from his panning and used his kerchief to wipe the damp from his skin, his large teeth laughing back at her. 'I do now, Miss Clementine.'

She returned his smile as her father finished the tale.

'O'Reilly ended up showing it to a mineral specialist – that's someone who understands things from the earth, Clem – who confirmed, after also scratching it on glass and blunting a knife with it, that it was indeed that rare gem known as a diamond. He guessed its worth at five hundred pounds. The Irish pedlar exchanged the stone for money with glee, selling it to the governor of the Cape, who in turn sent it to the 1867 Great Exhibition in Paris. The people were stunned by the twenty-one and one-quarter carats of perfection.'

'And it was yellow.' She frowned. 'You forgot that bit.'

'Yes, a brownish-yellow, like Vickery's Darjeeling tea not long brewed.' He winked at Joseph and then explained what he had meant by that remark.

'Anyway, it was named "Eureka" and it was, by all accounts, wondrous – it had been cut and polished into a superb cushion-cut diamond of near eleven carats – enough to take anyone's breath away. I swear we are going to find our own Eureka to make us richer than anyone can imagine.'

'And much bigger than twenty-one and one-quarter carats, Daddy.'

'Fifty, you think?' He grinned.

'One hundred,' she said, jumping into the air.

Joseph One-Shoe laughed and James knew that he'd caught their meaning. 'That's it, Clem. I think you should let your petticoats dry out before your mother finds you.'

'I don't think she'll get up today to notice,' she said, sounding far older than she should.

His conscience pricked; he should go and check on Louisa. 'You go back. I'm right behind you, darlin'.'

He watched her wade through the shallows to the bank. 'Bye, Joseph.'

'Goodbye, Miss Clementine.'

James bent back over his work, chafing at the hard-won realisation that this parched, scorched land belonged to the hunters, gatherers and warriors who had endured here for centuries. The Boers farmed but to him all they seemed to do was exist, not live. There was so little joy in the expressions of those he had met: serious, hard Dutch folk who struggled for survival on an unforgiving land where almost every creature that roamed was capable of killing them . . . if the summers didn't get them. It should never have been the domain of the Britisher or any of the other struggling, fortune-hunting whites who had previously only known a couple of months of testing warmth each summer. Yet here he was, part of the greedy mob in one of the most dangerous and challenging places of Her Majesty's Empire in pursuit of hidden treasure.

James Knight, his mouth grimly set, began agitating the pan of mud, trying to convince himself that it was a mild morning by African standards. But he was at the mercy of the elements no matter the season, always ankle-deep in water and so bone-weary and hungry that the mere thought of the approaching African summer depressed him. This was not his normal state of mind; his brother-in-law, Reggie, had once accused him of being an insufferably cheerful individual. But Africa was taking its toll. Was the price too high?

You made your bed, so lie in it, spoke a voice in his mind, using his father's gruff tone. It was true. But what was the point of life without risks? Meanwhile, the person who suffered the most at his decisions was Louisa. He didn't deserve her loyalty, or such faith, for he was yet to reap any dividend for his family.

Should he accept her money to book a berth home and confront the painful disdain of her relatives? It was while he was thinking of Reggie's scorn that the cry went up. It carried across the wilderness towards the river and into the quiet where hot, tired men were unhappily engrossed in their riverside labour. All were hungry, most were likely looking forward to the watery beer or the release of a few shots of liquor in the jumped-up pub once the sun went down.

James, by chance, was the closest white digger to the area of the bank the man was hurtling towards; closer still was Joseph One-Shoe with whom he shared a curious, mostly silent, yet easy relationship at Klipdrift alluvial diggings.

The running man, still quite a distance from them, yelled again. The clarity of his words was lost, yet the hideously still air did not blur their intensity. James pulled off his hat with its jaunty feather and straightened his back, easing the protest of pain his body gave. His shirt clung uncomfortably like a moist flannel to his back, and his trousers were soaked to the knee from standing in the clear shallows of the glittering Vaal River. Louisa had called for him. Clem was waiting for him. But he needed to see what this fuss was about, he reasoned, and let his curiosity win.

The excited man was leaping over small mounds of rough ground as he approached, not looking where he ran, risking a fall that could mean days of difficult work with a twisted, swollen ankle, or potential death from snakebite. He wore the motley attire of the diggers: trousers likely held up with string, boots likely in poor repair. In the early days James had tried to stay neat, mostly for Louisa's sake, yet it was impossible in this environment and with the work he did here, and week by week he had begun to look as ragged and clownish as his fellow workers. Being clean-shaven was no longer practical; nor were white shirts and polished boots. The kerchief soaked up the sweat and the silver-grey raptor feather his daughter had found was his identification. Clementine said their surname suggested his ancestors had worn armour, so he too should wear something silvery. Anything to please Clementine. Nevertheless, James was glad there was no tall mirror in his family's tent to show him just how forsaken he now appeared.

The summoner yelled again, waving his arms to catch more attention. It was clear he was joyously stirred-up and not simply alarmed. More men stood from their toil at the riverbed to make sense of the commotion, but James would surely hear the news first.

He looked to his right where his companion, built like the steam engines James had once designed, worked his claim with relentless energy. Joseph's interest had been captured too and he returned James's glance.

'What he say?' The man's modest but adequate English impressed James, who knew not a single word in Joseph's language – had not even got his tongue around some of the pidgin language the Boers spoke with the locals. He knew the Zulu was a warrior because he wore a leopard-skin headband, which spoke of his courage. He had adapted a pair of baggy, patched trousers, cutting them short to come halfway up his shins, and he would wear a shirt if he was in the presence of women after sundown. Although the African could move effortlessly across the harshest ground, one of his feet was clad with a tattered boot; it was too small, so he'd cut out the toe.

'Can't make it out yet,' James replied, wiping his sleeve across his face, and regretted causing the dirty smudge that Louisa would insist on cleaning.

'Daddy!' He turned to regard his child, back at the bank down-river. Since the day of her birth, he had felt sure that she alone challenged every reason Louisa's family had for hating her choice of useless husband. As graceful in movement as her mother, with similar dark blonde hair and a serious gaze reminiscent of her Uncle Reggie, Clementine was blessed with the Knight analytical mind. To James his daughter was frighteningly precocious for her six years. Full of curiosity, she stored knowledge like a vault. Always talking, forever engaging people with her serious manner and the irresistible charm she'd surely inherited from her mother. Before the child's arrival he couldn't have imagined loving any girl more than Louisa . . . and yet he alone knew that he did. His daughter was the reason he bent his back each morning and clung to the hope that this would be the day he would make them rich and secure her future on his terms. He would return them to England triumphant; his two girls would be lavished with fine clothes, a magnificent home or even two, and invitations to all the best society events. They would be regarded as the couple upon whom the heavens smiled.

His child called again, small hands cupped either side of her mouth so her voice would carry. Her mother had stopped curling her hair into ringlets, letting the child's hair flow free to reflect the sunlight in rich golden glints. No getting away from the satin ribbon, though, that her mother insisted be tied daily atop her daughter's head. Today it matched the colour of the clear dome of sky that was unbroken by cloud or differing hues. A single rich cobalt, like her eyes, like the common blue butterfly of his native Scotland.

He yelled so she could hear him easily. 'Don't come back in the water, Clem. Has your mother woken?' He looked back towards the higgledy-piggledy tented city they called home and tried not to think about the monstrous Woodingdene Estate that his wife had given up in order to be with him.

What had started out as separate straggly communities of little more than canvas stretched over sticks had expanded until the tents were forced to cluster close together, the boundaries lost definition and became covered over with a circus of humanity from all walks of life. So many nationalities were living side by side, eking out just enough to feed themselves. His child was not eating well, she was becoming lean having arrived chubby, her skin browned instead of rosy, her legs skinny like a new calf's. She was not unhappy, though – of this he was sure.

'What?' he called.

She had edged closer to him. 'I said she's very sick. She doesn't want to move.'

He looked over his shoulder at the running man. Joseph had stopped all toil to await him too. He yelled back to his child, 'Just sit with her. I'll be there in a blink.' He blew her a kiss.

She smacked one in return and skipped away once again into the maze of tents. Clementine knew her way around the tent city as well as he did; they both carried a map of it in their minds. But the old question burned like a belly ulcer: what sort of life was this for a child who should be thinking about schooling and pretty petticoats? It was a redundant question. For the time being they were stuck here in the Cape Colony until he could earn their passage back. Success could be today, tomorrow, next week. As it was, he was getting his rights to dig cheaply. Diamonds had been emerging regularly in this river region and syndicates were beginning to acquire farms outright. No doubt this farm would be bought up soon.

'Diamonds?' The African's smooth forehead creased. He stood straight to his full height and shielded his eyes from the slant of the sun. His biceps, outlined by the glimmer of his perspiration, bulged with the action. Joseph made James feel short and runty, even though he was proud to be the tallest in his family at five feet ten inches. Most of the Westerners had little time for the black Africans, interacting more easily with the Indians and Malays known as the Cape Coloureds. It was Clementine who had befriended this man simply because he worked a claim alongside her father's. They shared equipment, looked out for their respective diggings and belongings, and had been known to share food from time to time. Louisa felt safe around him.

'I can't say his name so he let me choose one. I've called him Joseph One-Shoe,' Clementine had explained to her parents one night.

James had laughed. 'That's an odd name. Joseph after your pet rabbit?'

'I suppose. I was going to call him Joseph Tuppence.'

'Why?'

'Because he told me that's all he has in savings.'

'He probably can't speak our language.'

'He can, Daddy. He was taught in a . . . a . . . special school run by a vicar.'

'A mission?'

'Yes, that's the word he used. Mission. He understands everything we say but he speaks slowly because he doesn't have all our words . . . besides, he told me that he only speaks when he has something to say.'

James remembered how he'd laughed at this remark because his daughter never ran out of things to say. 'You make a good pair.'

'I like Joseph – as much as my ragdoll, maybe more.'

'Because he talks back?'

'No, because he's wise.'

'Wise.' He'd grinned. 'Do you even know what that means?'

'It means clever.'

'It's a special sort of clever.'

'Are you wise?'

'I'm afraid not.'

'I am thinking he shouts of a new diamond find,' Joseph said, interrupting James's memories.

James turned his head. 'You're right!' he replied, his pulse leaping. 'It's a fresh dry strike!'

Without further discussion both men waded out of the shallow waters.

'Where?' Joseph asked.

'He's saying the De Beers farm. That's got to be nearly 20 miles from here.' He glanced at his companion. 'If it's a new rush and he seems excited, I'll have to get to my family and move across to that farm. We'll need to tear down the tent, pack up our belongings.'

He groaned. 'A sick wife and a young child move slow. I'll have to grab passage for us on a wagon.' He shook his head. 'I'll never make it. I'll not have the opportunity to peg out a claim.'

'I will make it,' Joseph said. 'I have no packing. I will buy your claim.' He held out his hand.

James stared at the upturned pink palm with its deep network of lines. Wise lines, according to Clem. 'Why would you do that?'

'Your child is kind to me. She has learned me some new English. Today I can count past twenty. I can work money out better. No one will cheat me now. She is going to teach me all the way to one hundred and lots more words.'

'You'll do this for us?'

'If you trust me.'

'I trust my child's heart.' He touched his chest. 'She calls you her friend. She has no others.'

The man nodded. 'I am Zenzele . . .' he said, adding several other names James could not pronounce, and including a click that confounded his listener.

'I am James, but I can't speak your name easily. Clementine —' he pointed to the riverbank — 'she calls you Joseph One-Shoe.'

Joseph nodded with a smile. 'I like this name.' James felt convinced that his companion could make a roomful of glum people smile too when he grinned so brightly.

He shook the man's hand, pointing to his feet. 'Why do you wear only one shoe, by the way? I am sure we can organise another boot.'

Joseph looked thoughtful, pausing to find the right words. 'I am a diamond digger like you, Mr James, but I am a warrior from my tribe. I don't want to forget that.' He lifted his foot – it was the one without the shoe. 'This means I never forget that I ran across miles to kill a lion that killed my friend, that I have fought for my tribe, and that I am here because my chief sent me. It tells me I am Zulu, not a white man.' He tugged at his cut-off trousers to make his point.

James whistled. 'You killed a lion.'

'It is why I keep watch at night. They watch us.'

'We have guns.'

'That is, how you say, for the not-so-brave. A warrior must fight the lion with only his spear and his . . .' He couldn't find the right word so he tapped his temple.

James nodded, smiling with understanding. He dug into his pockets and withdrew a few mangled notes. 'That's the last of my money. It should be enough. If you get there in time, buy the biggest claim you can – we'll work it together. We'll be partners.'

Joseph frowned as he tested the word. 'Partners.'

'You and I.' James pointed to each of their chests. And shook the pan that Joseph held. 'Together.'

'Ah, partner?' he repeated, as if storing the new word away. James gave an encouraging grin. 'Then I will get there in time, Mr James. I leave now. No one will catch me.'

The runner arrived, breathing so hard he could no longer speak. He bent over, hands on his knees to haul in the air. The shallows surged with men arriving from around the diggings and the tents to hear the news. 'It's a new rush!' he ground out. 'They've found diamonds just lying about on the veld at the De Beers farm. Claims are being registered hand over fist. I've just come back for my equipment.'

Joseph caught the gaze that James cut his way. The Zulu's grin was full of knowing. He pointed across the water to the opposite riverbank. James understood but only believed it when he watched Joseph wade out into the wide river and begin to swim across. The African gripped a leather pouch between his teeth, no doubt keeping James's money dry. Few others saw the African slip away from the crowd but a cry went up when a pair of wily Australians pointed him out.

'Hey, look! That black bastard is making a run for it.'

'His claim's as good as any,' James offered.

'Yeah, and he'll make it long before the rest of us. He can go cross-country. Have you seen those tribal blokes run?'

James shook his head, glad Clementine wasn't around, although she was probably used to hearing this sort of language around the camp.

'You watch him, mate. He'll be there before most of us can pack up and hit the road.'

James grinned inwardly and for the first time in nearly a year felt the sense of anticipation and destiny that had urged him to leave their ship and abandon his well-paid job with a major engineering firm on the other side of the world. He had alighted with his child in his arms, holding his wife's trembling hand. Louisa had been full of questions but also faith in their youth and love. 'Go along with this,' he'd pleaded, ignoring her look of disbelief that said, *You promised Australia, not Africa. You promised a home, not a tent. You promised a real city with hotels and theatres and fashion, not the wilderness . . .*

'I will find my fortune here and you will be proud of us . . . and we shall make your family eat humble pie,' he'd promised instead.

So now this was it. His final chance to make good on his promise to beautiful, trusting Louisa.

'I guess we shouldn't waste any more time, then,' he threw at the Aussie.

Men were tripping over one another to get back to the tents, frothing with hope and greed. They looked like a shoal of fish as the water was stirred up, and they clambered over each other to get a yard ahead. James didn't join the hysterical throng. He suspected fights would soon break out. The hottest part of the day was yet to punish them as they prepared the oxen for the wagons that would haul this vile-smelling, dust-ridden tent town away from the river diggings and onto the harsh veld.

He would trust Joseph One-Shoe. He cast a glance across the distant landscape, where he could just make out the loping figure moving fast and fearlessly across country towards their fortune.

———————

As James Knight felt his spirit rise, Louisa Knight's spirit left her. Her final breath sighed farewell as her daughter prattled on about finding a diamond the size of a conker.

Part One

1

THE BIG HOLE, KIMBERLEY, CAPE COLONY

March 1872

They discussed the need to wear gloves to keep it true to the Queensberry Rules, although Joseph preferred what James called 'fisticuffs'. His opponent – John 'Mr Knuckles' Rider – felt a similar kinship for the faster, bloodier version. There was no doubt that the shouting mob wanted the crunch and smash of bare knuckles against nose, jaw and ribs . . . preferably those belonging to Mr Knuckles.

The yelling men had got plenty for their wagers. The resplendent moustache of Mr Knuckles had created a natural platform from which rivulets of blood could run freely from his stupendously damaged nose. Clem had learned this fighter had a pedigree for stunning knockouts and tended to leave his final winning blows for the later rounds.

'You've got 'im, Knuckles. Look at 'im. He's a goner,' Clementine heard his minder say as he rubbed the man's shoulders. Her adeptness at lip-reading had been honed above the relentless noise of the Big Hole, where she'd learned how to work out what her two men communicated from a distance. She took offence at the beating her best friend had taken tonight. Clementine tried to distance herself from the thick air in which the tang of men's sweat combined with a variety of oils. The men in the audience wore a sickly sweet pomade slicked through their hair that gave off a lavender fragrance, while the ropes that mapped out the boxing ring smelled of animal fat, making her feel nauseous. The sweating bodies of the two boxers were both liberally oiled with a mineral-smelling grease to help deflect the blows as they tried to punch each other into unconsciousness. Oil lamps guttered and gave off a pungent, chemical aroma. Onlookers clinked pewter mugs of ale and laughed uproariously at jests and daring wagers. There was no single voice that could be picked out; it was simply a general roar of excitement. It occurred to Clem that she liked everything that was attractive in life – in this she showed every inclination her mother could ever hope for. She didn't wear pretty dresses because they were not practical, but it didn't mean she didn't like them. She didn't play with her two dolls because they got dirty so easily and could break. Her ragdoll could take all the punishment in the world – like Joseph – and still smile back at her no matter how ragged he became.

Her memories of Woodingdene were few but vivid, and someone who had made an impression on her was an old man who worked for her grandfather. He was Scottish and seemed to be in charge of all the fishing and hunting around the property. Everyone called him 'the Ghillie'. She never did know his name, but he once made her a doll from rags when she'd become bored with the grown-ups' conversation and had wandered a few yards away to explore the boating sheds. She'd found the ghillie winding fishing line and neatening up the rods. They'd struck up a conversation of their own and before long he'd begun fashioning some of the clean rags he had in a basket.

'I used to make these dolls for my Meggie when she was a wee lass.'

'Who is Meggie?'

'My beautiful daughter.' She had noted his eyes became misty and, sensing sadness, held back the obvious question.

'Would you like a lad or a lassie?'

'A boy please,' she'd replied.

'Why's that then?'

'Because I'd like a brother. Girls are a bit soppy. The ones who come to play don't want to go climbing or exploring with me. They just want to play with the doll's house and have tea parties.'

She remembered him grinning as he worked. 'I'll give your ragdoll trousers then. You'll have to name him.'

'I'm going to call him Gillie, after you.'

'I'm honoured, Miss Clementine.'

Gillie, made predominantly from calico, still grinned back at her each day from his pencilled-on smile that her mother replenished regularly so it never faded.

A roar went up in the crowd. It no longer mattered to her that Joseph One-Shoe had become a boxing hero for the Kimberley mob and remained unbeaten to this day. 'No more, Daddy,' she tried, forcing her father's attention back from Joseph's face, which was slick with blood.

'He can take him, Clem.'

'Mr Knuckles feels the same way,' she insisted, watching the opponent spit again into the pail.

'That Englishman doesn't have much more but Joseph does, don't you?' Their man nodded through his deep breaths. Silent as always. 'Besides, there's a haul of roughs up for grabs with this final.'

'We've got plenty of those,' she countered.

'And soon we'll have the big one, I promise, and we can go home.'

Go home. Two words her father used as a persuasive phrase whenever he needed her to cooperate. Except England was not home to her. Home was here. And her father's home meant leaving her mother alone in Africa, lying in her grave. No more weekly visits, no more wildflowers gathered to make her cold bed look pretty, no more whispered prayers or long, one-sided conversations about why she had stopped wearing petticoats and was only washing her hair once a fortnight now. Oh, yes, and that she was sorry she was play-ing truant from school because she preferred to watch Daddy and Joseph try to dig up 'the conker', which was how they referred to the elusive massive rough diamond her father was certain was in their path. Going home also meant leaving Joseph One-Shoe.

She leaned in, not at all self-conscious that she was in a place where no other little girls dared to tread. 'Joseph?'

His large head, round as a football, turned towards her. One eyelid was swollen, slanting across his vision, while a deep cut above the other brow bled gleefully despite the grease her father kept slathering over it. 'Yes, lioness?' He sounded weary.

'Did you feel his bone break below his chest?'

He nodded. 'I see him leaning into it.'

'His rib's gone,' she murmured knowingly. 'And his eye is fully closed.'

Her father laughed. 'No one would believe me if I said my fighter was discussing strategy with my seven-year-old. So we go for the ribs.'

'No,' they said together.

'Joseph only pretends to,' Clementine assured. 'Mr Knuckles will protect himself because he can't help it.' Her voice was drowned out as a man rang the bell and Joseph hauled himself to his feet. 'You have to knock him down this round,' she yelled, unable to hide her fear. She mouthed a word in Zulu that only Joseph could understand; it meant 'rising' but they both knew it referred to his upper cut.

'There's a cache of six riding on this final,' he warned Joseph.

'He knows, Daddy.' Her words galloped alongside an accusa-tory glare.

At her full height Clementine could still only look Joseph One-Shoe in the eye providing he sat cross-legged on the ground, as he did now inside their tiny shanty hut. The roar of the bloodthirsty mob was behind them and the sawdust from the boxing ring would be swept up and used again for a future fight.

Clem was cleaning Joseph's face of the blood from his fight. Her father had paused just long enough to stitch the cut near his eye and had then taken off to claim their prize and mark its handover with one or two – or six – shots of whisky at one of the local pubs.

'Am I hurting you?'

He shook his head.

'Are you the strongest man in the world, Joseph?'

He winced as his lip, recently sealed, broke open again as he smiled. 'Maybe.'

She gave him a wad of lint. 'Hold that against it.'

'Your mother would not like to see you doing this.'

'Mummy's dead. She can't stop me.'

'You sound like an old lady talking.'

'And you now sound like an Englishman.'

Joseph shrugged. 'You have taught me well.'

She smiled. 'You can go home to your people and teach them my language. You can go back to your real name of Zenzele and all its other bits and the click.'

'I'm happy with Joseph for now.'

'Will the chief still be angry?'

'Probably. I was only meant to leave the tribe until *intwasah-lobo*.' He frowned. 'I sorry.' He winced as his grin cracked his lip again. 'What is the word for when the leaves appear?'

'Spring.'

He nodded. 'Two springs have been born and I am still here.'

'Do you miss them?'

'Yes.' He was glad now he hadn't confirmed to Thandiwe that they would be man and wife. He had been preparing to sit down with her family to pay the bride price but then the chief had sent him on his important mission. He had told her he would be gone until the next rains. He hadn't known then that he was lying to her. Thandiwe would have taken his friend, Lungani, for her husband by now, he imagined. He wished them prosperity and many children but he rarely let himself dwell on the woman he loved . . . another one much younger needed him here.

'I would hate you to leave.' Clementine suddenly hugged him. 'Please don't ever leave me, Joseph.'

The Zulu was cautious. He was popular with the white folk but the women would not take kindly to seeing him showing affection to this child.

He pulled her gently away. 'You will have to leave me before I leave you,' he assured her.

'I will have to be dragged away, then,' she said.

'Don't dirty your shirt with blood,' he added as an excuse to fully break her embrace.

'Too late. Mrs Carruthers said I should be wearing petticoats like a proper girl and she's going to speak to Daddy about it.' He nodded and made no comment. 'But skirts and petticoats just get in the way,' she continued, sounding vexed. 'Daddy says I'll have to wear them when we go back to England but I'm never going back.' He watched her carefully. She was leading somewhere, he could tell. 'Mrs Carruthers says I'll be sent home soon so I can be properly schooled. She says my mother tried but my father is hopeless and that teaching me about Greek myths and astronomy or the geography of the world is no help to a girl. Sarah Carruthers says her mother thinks I run wild and shouldn't spend so much time with you.'

He nodded, unsurprised. Their conversation was interrupted by drunken singing and Clementine, in spite of her soured mood, giggled.

'Let me get your father before he has a bucket of something nasty thrown at him,' Joseph said, sighing as he hauled himself to standing, yet still slightly bent. He was far too tall for the shanty in which the Knights lived.

Clementine stood at the makeshift door as her companion stepped gingerly out into the night. His slight stoop suggested he was mindful of the cracked rib her father had explained about, as well as his bruising, and she hoped he wouldn't begin bleeding again.

They'd won convincingly with a knockout: a viciously fast upper cut that Joseph had taken a mighty amount of punishment for as he waited for the precise moment to deliver it. She'd seen it in the same moment that Joseph had. *Now!* she'd screamed in her mind.

She'd watched as the boxing hero from England had had his feet lifted from the floor as Joseph's fist, rounding upwards in a tight arc, connected with his chin. She'd heard his teeth crunch and then the crowd's roaring cheer had nearly lifted the roof of the boxing den. Beer had been spilt in frenzied joy that ran as freely as the blood from Mr Knuckles's mouth, and Clem realised he must have bitten through his tongue or lip. The celebrations had become wild.

Clem glanced at her father, who was lifting an arm to empty the dregs of a bottle of liquor. She'd often heard him say he was looking for her mother at the bottom of the glass and she'd never fully grasped his meaning. It seemed to Clementine that he was using the same excuse to search for happiness at their win, and to look for the conker diamond.

He appeared jolly enough when he was bellowing out a ballad, but she couldn't remember the last time he had looked happy. She didn't want him to pick her up and pretend, breathing his ugly whisky fumes over her. It was at times like these, when he'd got to the end of the bottle and hadn't found her mother or his happiness, that he would cry while he hugged her and tell her how sorry he was to have brought such a terrible existence upon her. He would weep real tears, promise to make amends, and try for a few days and then his *shadow* – that's what Joseph One-Shoe called it – would catch up with him again.

She slipped out of their sparse, tiny dwelling, which was little more than a couple of cots and a series of hammered-together shelves. They'd lived through a desert winter in this so-called home and at night she had seen her breath steam before her. She had watched it in fascination, distracted from the chill, as she'd pondered that the mist was the breath of her life and as it dissolved to nothing, so would she . . . like her mother. Joseph One-Shoe had assured her that as long as she could see that steam escaping her mouth, it meant she was capable of achieving everything she set her heart on.

Clementine wished her father would speak to her like that. He used to. Now he lived staring at a black hole of grief into which he had poured his vitality, his hope, his sense of future, his thrill of life. A hollow was what was left for Clementine. She tried to fill it with her chatter and fun, with love and affection, but it gobbled all she gave and didn't return much. A slight twitch of a smile now and then, but she sensed it was only because he was remembering that he *should* – that he had a little girl who needed to see his face express something other than his pain.

The liquor helped veil the sorrow but he was a stranger to her when he was intoxicated, and these drunken nights were happening more often. She found herself tucking her father into his cot in a reversal of normal roles. Tonight Clem helped Joseph to lay him down on his side but not before he'd captured their attention and shaken a little canvas money pouch.

'They're yours,' he said to his Zulu friend. 'I think I've drunk mine.' His head sank onto a pillow that was biscuit-like it was so flat.

She chuckled again like a tolerant wife might. 'He'll sleep it away now.'

By the light of the tin hut's single candle Joseph took the sack and let five small rough stones tumble into his large palm. He glanced at Clem.

She shrugged. 'He wants you to have them. Tomorrow you'll find the conker,' she said, tapping her nose in the way her father did.

'Aren't you sleepy?'

She shook her head. 'Can I sit out with you for a while?' Clem looked around their humble dwelling: not an item of decoration other than the tiny ink pot of wild daisies she herself had gathered. 'I like looking at the stars.'

He nodded and she followed him outside a few moments later, careful not to take his hand, as much as she wanted to . . . just in case.

They edged away from the ramshackle town and strolled towards what was now known as the Big Hole.

It was a cool night. Joseph carried only his tribal blanket, but she was glad she'd bothered to grab her cloak and woollen hat. 'Daddy said this is the largest hole in the world that's been dug by hand,' she remarked.

Sporadically placed lanterns formed a makeshift safety rail lighting its edge. No one was working – the only other people around were men drinking in the distance; they couldn't hear each other's conversations for the space was so vast. Someone plucked a lonely banjo and its haunting notes travelled through the cool night air to settle around them like a melancholy blanket.

Joseph sat down and pulled his tribal rug around himself.

'Daddy also says you like to keep watch on our claim.'

'We don't want anyone else to steal our conker if it tiptoes up from the earth overnight.'

'No.' She laughed and was surprised to hear footsteps and then a cough. It was her father.

'Oh, this dust. It will kill me,' he said, hacking loudly into their comfortable quiet.

Clementine didn't know a world without the cloud of dust that hung over the Big Hole and she preferred the nights because she didn't have to look at it; it seemed to settle and allow her to instead see the night sky, depthless and limitless in its vast blackness.

'You left me,' James bleated, slumping beside her.

She giggled. 'You were snoring, Daddy. Ooh, look!' Clementine nudged Joseph and pointed.

'What should I see?'

'A falling star. Daddy, you said we must always make a wish when we see one.' She didn't see the Zulu wince as she grabbed her friend's large hand with its grazed, still-bleeding knuckles, and she took her father's hand too, placing both in her lap.

'What shall we wish for, darlin'?'

'That tomorrow we find the big diamond.'

She screwed up her eyelids with exaggerated tightness, squeezing their hands as hard as she could. 'Wish it with me.'

She was pleased they obliged, opening their eyes finally.

'Clem, look how bright Venus is.'

She pointed for the benefit of Joseph. 'That's called a bright planet.'

'Let's continue your astronomy education, Clem,' her father said. 'Do you know the brightest star in the sky?'

'Northern or southern hemisphere?' she asked, wrapping her tongue around that last difficult word.

Her father chuckled. 'Don't be cocky.'

'The North Star?' she tried, looking unsure.

'Good effort, Clem, but no. The brightest star is called Sirius. We can see him from anywhere in the world because he sparkles so clearly. There he is. He has the nickname "the Dog Star".'

'Why, Daddy?'

'His constellation – do you remember us talking about a constellation?' She nodded. 'In Latin the constellation that Sirius belongs to is called Canis Major, or the Greater Dog. If we link the main stars, you can quite easily pick out the shape of a dog. And from here in Africa we can see him arcing across the sky directly overhead, but if we were in England, then he'd be in a more southern direction.' James traced with an outstretched finger. 'From south-east to south-west from your mother's home of Woodingdene Estate.' He nodded as if in private thought. 'He's easy to find, but in case you need help, look for Orion's Belt – you remember that, don't you?'

'Yes. Mrs Carruthers said I was talking a lot of rubbish when I explained it to the class.'

'Mrs Carruthers needs her big backside slapped for talking to you like that.'

Clem dissolved into giggles.

He continued. 'Find those three stars of Orion's Belt and draw an imaginary line through them and keep going and they will lead you to Sirius . . . always chasing Orion.'

She listened to her father sigh.

'I know this is hard to believe but Sirius burns brighter than our sun, Clem, and although I haven't seen it, I have spoken to astronomers who tell me that its radial arms —' he pointed again — 'you see those pointed rays that spike from the main glow?' As he leaned close she smelled the whisky but it wasn't the sour tang of a drunk tonight, as she'd dreaded. Instead his breath had a honey-sweet quality that spoke of the Scottish ancestry he'd whispered about at night when she had cried for her mother. Here, right now, was the father she loved: affectionate and full of interest. She was still holding the hand of the Zulu, too. He was the counterbalance: strong, wise, always sober, always looking out for her. Clementine missed her mother but she never wanted to be separated from the two men in her life – if these were her parents, they were more than enough. She returned her attention.

'Well, apparently those radial arms, they twinkle in a rainbow of marvellous colours. He really is a special star, that one.'

'Then we should call our conker Sirius when we find it,' she said.

'Actually, that's a great name for a diamond, if we ever find one. Here's to tomorrow's digging, then.'

'Coming to bed, Clem?'

'I'll bring her, Mr James,' Joseph assured him.

James yawned and kissed his daughter's greasy hair, then he hauled himself to his feet, nodded goodnight and shuffled away.

Joseph gestured towards the sky. 'The star your father speaks of. We call this inDosa. The star that pulls the night across the sky and draws the dawn,' he said and she saw the gleam of his teeth.

She repeated it and his smile widened. 'You make a good Zulu.'

Joseph squeezed Clem's hand. 'We have to try harder, Miss Clementine.'

'What do you mean?'

The Zulu lifted one of his large shoulders. 'For your father. His shadow is darkening.'

'He wasn't drunk.'

'That is why I feel . . .' He reached for the right word. 'Uncomfortable,' he settled upon, although he frowned uncertainly. 'Mr James was sad tonight. I don't trust this. This is when sickness comes.'

'So what do we do?'

'You must stay close. Keep him smiling.'

'I'll try.'

The Zulu stood without breaking their link, bending so he did not lose hold of her hand. 'Your daddy didn't tell you that inDosa has a star that follows him. Ask him about it. You are that little star that must follow, but one day you will become Sirius and you will shine brightly.'

'But who will follow me?'

'I shall. Always.'

'But what if you die first?'

He chuckled low and deep, his teeth gleaming in the minimal light. 'Then my spirit shall follow you.'

'Tell me about what to do when you die so that I can take care of you properly.'

Again, he laughed, this time openly. 'I am nowhere near my time, Miss Clementine.'

'I don't want anyone to burn you, Joseph.'

'We bury our dead, Miss Clementine, often wrapped in the skin of the animal we kill, as blood must be shed.'

'Why?'

'It's a sacrifice to the gods so that no misfortune comes to the family or to the dead person as they make their way to join their ancestors. It's about giving the dead what we call light feet for their spirit's journey ahead, so they don't get lost or trapped between here and the afterlife.'

'I wonder if your one shoe will make your journey too heavy. Should I take it off your foot?'

He laughed delightedly. 'If you wish.'

'Then you can move easily on your bare foot like a good Zulu and follow me on tiptoe forever, never making a sound.'

He nodded.

'But, Joseph . . .'

'Yes, Miss Clementine?'

'Please don't die.'

'I promise.'

She clung to him suddenly and he lifted her into the cradle of his arms as he stood to his full height and pointed. 'And I will always be watching you and proud of you, wherever you are.'

2

March 1872

Reggie Grant stared at the pages, trying to convince himself that what he had now read three times couldn't be true. The battered envelope had been placed among the other letters to the right of his water glass; its jewel-coloured stamps had dragged his attention away from the morning headlines simply by the fact they were from Africa. His spirits lifted. At last! It had been far too long since he'd heard from her.

He barely looked at the front of the letter. Its underside was smudged with reddish grime, and it had clearly travelled an arduous journey via Her Majesty's Post to reach him. He did not even bother searching for the letter opener, as the envelope's flap unglued itself at the barest pressure of his fingernail at its edge.

Yet before he could read the two pages, he was distracted by the arrival of the newly appointed Robert Milton. Now essentially in charge of running the household staff, he was also available to help Reggie with anything else, from his wardrobe to driving him down to London if need be. *A jack-of-all-trades*, Reggie thought to himself, with only a hint of disgust that he'd arrived on the scene too late to enjoy the full life of the landed gentry with a queue of servants for various duties.

Still, it was a far cry from the damp London flat whose weariness had been hidden beneath overwrought colour and the Second Empire-longing of his French mother; they'd been able to overlook its drab address thanks to his father's promise of good things to come. Nevertheless, Spitalfields was where he had been raised by a mother who shared her favours for the right price. Even in his youth, when she still cut a superb hourglass figure in her bustle and silks, he had known that her breathy French accent and generous manner made her one of the most irresistible prostitutes in London. After the slums of Paris, where they'd started out, the Spitalfields flat – courtesy of Henry Grant, who wanted his 'mistress', as he termed her, on call whenever he wished – was a mansion.

And so Woodingdene Estate, a genuine sprawling country manor that seemed to promise money on tap, might as well have been Buckingham Palace to Reggie.

'What can I get for you, sir?' Milton cut across his thoughts; he'd settled into his new role with ease and gave Reggie confidence that he could head up this family and make his own mark on the world, despite the large footsteps he followed.

'Is Mrs Grant taking breakfast?'

'I gather she's had a tray sent up,' Milton said.

'Is she unwell?'

'That's not my understanding.'

Adroitly said, Reggie thought. Milton would do well, but he would have a long path ahead of him yet to convince Lilian Grant that the family's former butler could not remain. Reggie had graciously fashioned it as retirement. Although he was generous, Bellamy and others had resented the arrival of the 'bastard son' into their lives. The situation had become untenable as far as Reggie was concerned and he had taken a broom to the staff who lived in the past, in which his father's word had been household law. He grieved for his father and regularly wished it had been the viper-tongued

Lilian who had died, but they were now unhappily cloistered together at Woodingdene. He knew it was up to him to make the concessions that made life together bearable, despite how much she loathed him.

'That I have a different mother is not my fault,' Reggie had argued with her not so long ago. 'But I am still Henry Grant's son. You need me now.'

'We got along just fine without you.'

'Did you? Is that why my father went in search of comfort elsewhere, then?'

He had watched the verbal blow land and he'd observed the pain of it glancing across her features: the tightening of her lips and the brief closing of the eyelids until it passed.

'With whom he whored is not my concern.'

'Yes, but I'm the result and he gave me his name. And on his deathbed he gave me instructions. About you, about Louisa and Clementine. Lilian, this is an old argument. You've been at my throat for the entire time that my sister —'

'Half-sister,' she remarked with an acid tone.

He deliberately smiled to show she couldn't hurt him.

'Lilian,' he began again, 'I know you love Louisa. I know you dote on Clementine. I hope you understand that despite our differences I feel the same way about them. They are all we both have. So, love them. Don't fill your heart with any more loathing for me. I gave my father a promise about the three women of this family, and I intend to keep it.'

'Until you find a woman of your own – you're nearly thirty. Then the pecking order will change sharply.'

Oh, a new tack. This fresh argument was revealing. 'You have absolutely nothing to fear there. Nothing whatsoever,' he impressed upon her, hoping she would catch his hidden meaning but not the true one.

He recalled how Lilian Grant had fixed him with her stare, cold as a glacier. He'd refused to look away from it and let its iciness scorch him as she turned over his carefully disguised remark. He'd absorbed the burn and gathered that she'd finally understood. 'I see,' she'd remarked with a single raised eyebrow.

Relief had drained through him. Let her think he was one who preferred the affections of men, he told himself. As galling as that might be, it was preferable to the horror that might unfold if she, or indeed anyone else, knew the truth of his condition.

His mind moved away from the syphilis and back to Lilian Grant. There was no doubting her beauty in her youth; men must have fallen over themselves to win her favour. While faded now that she was well into her sixties, she ate modestly to remain trim, walked daily, forced her posture to be military-straight at all times and kept her mind sharp by devouring the newspaper. He found himself helplessly impressed when he compared her to his slovenly mother, who by this time of day was still recovering from the previous night's debauchery.

'Then I hope you can be discreet,' she'd warned, breaking into his thoughts.

They'd never spoken of that topic again but his had been the right words at just the right time to appease her fears. While their relationship hadn't become closer, they'd reached an understanding – albeit an uneasy one – that Reggie was here to stay at Woodingdene and that her best interests would be protected.

The butler cleared his throat.

'So, can I blame you, Milton, for her lack of interest?' he said lightly, returning his attention to the letter. He wasn't sure yet whether the new butler had a sense of humour.

'I think you can, sir. Mrs Grant is finding it hard to adjust to my presence, I suspect.'

It seemed his most senior staff member was trained in the

understatement. 'Thank you, Milton. Just some porridge and cream this morning.'

'Very good, sir. Would you like me to pour?' the man asked, nodding towards the silver pot not far from where the morning post sat. He reminded Reggie of a donkey: grey-toned and a sad- dish expression within a long face – he'd find what amused him yet.

'No, I can do it.'

Milton departed to leave Reggie alone in the enormous space they called the breakfast room. Reggie poured his tea and, ignoring the tongs for the gleaming, wafer-thin lemon slices that Lilian would have preferred, selected instead the small milk jug and splashed some of its contents into the strong brew. He took a first hot sip of the rich Assam and turned his sights to the folded letter, anticipating a long, humorous missive from his sister.

Half-sister, he clarified in Lilian Grant's voice. He sighed. If he was honest, they had been nastier to each other when his father was alive, perhaps both jostling for his attention and hating the other receiving it. Since his death more than a year ago a new and awk- ward existence, which felt like a truce, had helped them to survive, if just for Louisa's sake. Louisa was the named heir to Woodingdene, not him. Lilian could not run the estate, nor did she wish to, and she had admitted to him that she knew he would do so in their shared best interests. It was the one and only concession he had received from her.

When he opened the letter, sipping his tea again with pleasure, he was surprised to see that it was not from Louisa. He frowned, looked again at the envelope's front and felt a dip of disappoint- ment that it lacked all the loops and beautiful curves of his sister's hand. Instead it was near enough to printing, in the brief and stac- cato style of her engineer husband.

He put down his cup, the saucer protesting with a tinkling complaint at his pressure of disgust. He sighed audibly, wondering now about his porridge taking so long and the day's tasks ahead. He really wasn't interested in anything James Knight had to say; if Knight was writing, then he had likely run out of money. Glancing absently over the pages, he saw that the handwriting began neatly enough but rapidly degenerated over the course of the two brief sheets; he could almost imagine that the man writing it had suffered a seizure of sorts.

It couldn't be true. But it also couldn't be a jest. James was explaining that Louisa had died. Surely he'd misread that? Dead? No! Suddenly, swallowing was no longer silent and effortless but became a dry trial, and he became aware of his breath, could hear it like a loud rasp in the cavernous room – he had to inflate his lungs deliberately, unsure he could rely on his unconscious mind to keep breathing. A firm thump behind his ear was his pulse pounding as shock sprinted through his body. He felt instantly light-headed. Reggie glanced at the date at the top of the letter and let out a soft groan. His sister had not just recently died but was long dead, it seemed, buried in the miserable depths of the African desert where her body would desiccate and disappear.

He read it twice more. It was obvious the man was broken but he couldn't give a flying fig about Knight and his emotions.

Louisa's husband was the sole reason she was dead.

Milton arrived with a fixed smile. 'Your porridge and cream, sir . . .'

Milton stopped his approach at the sound of crockery upending as Reggie stood suddenly. In flinging his napkin and banging the table, he had spilled his tea.

'Mr Grant? Are you —'

'Milton, please summon Mrs Grant. Convey it is urgent. I will be in my father's study.'

They sat opposite each other across the twin pedestal desk. Their enemy status had been reforged into something new through a far keener grief than had marked Henry's passing. Reggie stared at the bright walnut grain, honeyed in parts and embellished on every surface with neo-Gothic decoration. He laid his hands against the warm, tooled-leather writing surface of the desk and drew a low breath. As with all of his father's furnishings it was highly decorated and Reggie found it strangely comforting, as though he was finally experiencing an embrace from a father who had felt duty rather than affection towards the bastard son.

He could appreciate only now that Henry Grant was outstanding simply because of his unique, eclectic, and mostly flamboyant style, which flew in the face of that of his peers. Over this last year at Woodingdene he had come to appreciate that his father had clearly never been afraid of what others thought. His bank account had swelled his ego and that ego had given him untold confidence in his aesthetics. Giving Reggie his surname had perhaps been the ultimate show of arrogance. The house and its surrounds were the physical display of Henry's taste, passion, art and furniture collecting, and indeed his forward thinking. The only person who had known his father well enough to tell Reggie more about him was sitting opposite, and he needed to try harder with her . . . especially now.

Reggie waited, contemplating the view through the picture windows across the verdant valley that Woodingdene claimed as its own. Its beauty never failed to both inspire and somehow terrify him. Today shafts of sunlight made it look as though the angels had punched holes in the cloud to shine their pillars of golden glory only onto this place. He tried to persuade himself that the heavenly light was Louisa trying to reach him, comfort him. But Louisa was lying 6-feet deep in African soil and she was already six months lost.

And it wasn't despair he was feeling; it was rage.

He'd not looked up at Lilian's gasp as the letter paper rustled, or at the sound of her subsequent tears. She wouldn't want him to see her so vulnerable and he felt amazed by his new generosity towards her.

Her tears were brief; she was so different to his mother, who would have raged for hours. She would have needed to demonstrate all her sorrow in a passionate display of hysterical emotion that would have ended with a swoon and a need for smelling salts. A headache, bed, alcohol, drunken kisses to his face amid the liquor fumes – that's how she'd been when she'd learned of Henry's death. It hadn't taken long, however, for her to find a wealthy new lover who could keep her as she preferred: fully entertained and with regular gifts of perfume, chocolates, silks and private parties.

He watched her polar opposite swallowing, forcing the emotion back like staring down a pack of wolves. He didn't like her, but her strength and countenance could be relied upon.

Lilian's few heartfelt tears had left a faint but telltale trace of their passage down her powdered cheeks. He stole a glance to watch her features rearrange themselves to form a new expression of pinched but controlled despair. There would be no more tears, he suspected. He wouldn't waste them on the dead either. So that left two hollow, angry people who suddenly found themselves on the same side and with a decision to be made.

He helped her. 'Lilian, I think we both need some time to digest and come to terms with the contents of that letter. I'm wondering, would you join me for supper tonight and perhaps we might talk then, after some time to gather our thoughts?'

'That's a wise suggestion, Reggie. Yes, I shall see you this evening.'

'Very good. I'm deeply sorry that we are facing this heartache but . . .' What was he trying to say? Just say it! 'No mother should outlive her child. Losing Henry took enough from you, Lilian, and I am genuinely saddened for your loss – for our loss.'

Again, that intense stare took his measure; he could see she really was not yet ready to trust him but she was getting closer. She nodded. 'Keep it simple this evening for I have no appetite.'

She left, her gait stiff from a hip problem, but she carried herself as straight as if she walked with a broomstick hidden beneath her clothes. He thought of the few lighter colours she'd begun to introduce as she emerged from her role as a grieving widow: a dove-grey blouse and even, as of today, a hint of lavender over the darker skirts. These prettier colours would now be returned to the wardrobe and she would be back in the grieving blacks of the past year.

'I'll have a fire lit in the small drawing room – perhaps we can take a simple supper there,' he offered to her back.

She paused at the door. 'No servants. Dismiss them for the evening. I don't want people around me.'

He understood. Everyone grieved in their own way.

3

Lilian's hair had been redone, swept up into a bun almost on the top of her head but still leaning towards the back, with a black lace trim; he couldn't fault her grip on fashion. How she achieved that volume Reggie couldn't fathom. Women's secrets intrigued him but he couldn't permit himself to act upon his interests.

'May I offer you a sherry, Lilian?'

'Thank you.' As she took a seat on the sofa opposite the fire, he watched her carefully position the bustle that hung beneath her waist and heard the thick black silk of her overskirt rustle against the many layers of petticoats that the frame supported. He couldn't imagine wearing all that paraphernalia and was glad his only discomfort was the stiff, high, wing-tipped collar that poked the flesh beneath his jawline. He straightened his white tie as he reached for the heavy decanter.

Lilian was bathed in a shaft of warm light from the vast circular lampshade that hung above the sofa, which trailed filigree flowers and glimmering tassels. It made her look all the more fragile.

'Have you told the staff?'

'Not yet,' he answered in a careful tone, unsure of what she would want. 'I thought tomorrow, after we've had a chance to compose ourselves.'

That seemed to satisfy her, as her shoulders relaxed. 'I'm glad Henry is not alive to share this pain. He was not a violent man but he was a vengeful one. I think he would have done violence to James Knight over this.'

'I wish I'd known my father better, but he kept himself deliberately distant from me.'

'When did he learn about you?'

He held out an upturned triangle of crystal on a short stem containing a rich Spanish sherry, sweet and luscious. She took it and their fingers touched. He felt a strange thrill at this new turn in their relationship. 'I think he knew from the outset. I have gathered that my mother was desperately unhappy to be pregnant.'

'Ruined her figure?'

'Curtailed her lifestyle, too.'

She nodded. 'How do you cope, knowing your mother was a prostitute?'

Reggie let out a low breath. 'She would describe herself as an escort, a mistress. I didn't have to suffer it much. I was sent away to boarding school and —'

'On our account, no doubt.'

'My father insisted. I spent much of my childhood being raised by an institution – my only joys at age fourteen were my regular visits to Woodingdene, trying to know him, loving Louisa, wishing I could impress you. He had me trained in accounting. He said I might as well earn my keep and learn some of the family business.'

'Did he, indeed?'

'I chose none of this. I was born into the situation and I've tried not to overstep – the only reason I'm here now is because my father demanded it before he died.'

'I know,' she admitted wearily.

'You have nothing to fear from me, or my mother – nothing to envy her for.'

'Other than that she won my husband's interest away from his wife, his home . . . and she gave him the son I never could?'

There it was, he thought. The pillars of her pain. This was certainly proving to be a day of surprises. 'And yet I am here and not with her. She lost everything. Could it be viewed that you gained something?' The audacious remark was out before he could censor himself. His high collar felt like it might choke him.

What he didn't expect was laughter. 'When you put it like that, I suppose you're right. So, I win, is that what you're saying?'

'I'm here to look after Henry's interests. I swear to you, Lilian, my mother will not see another penny of his money. If she needs help, it will come from my own investments.'

'Can I trust the word of a Grant, though?'

'This one, yes.'

She sighed, sounding exhausted. 'All right, Reggie. Let's try, shall we? We can both trust each other on one matter for sure.'

'Our love for Louisa,' he said.

'Yes. While I wondered about it in the early days, I had to accept that you both acted as close as a pair of siblings could be. Her love for you was genuine.'

'As mine for her is . . . was . . . no, still is.'

'I must trust that as much as my own instincts now, because I have to say that Henry gave no indication of any fondness towards you.'

She knew just how to hurt. 'Yes, it was confusing during childhood. He provided for me but he wanted nothing to do with me. Sent me away. Never visited. Never responded to my letters. I think it was only because Louisa accidentally discovered my existence that my name was ever mentioned aloud.'

'I remember the day. We had the most fearful row. I left for the London house but Louisa refused to join me, which felt like a double betrayal. She was intrigued because she no longer had to be the only child of the Grants. If your father had been less loud about his wealth and achievements, it might have been easier on her.'

He let out a small chuckle. 'The day we met she came to my school in Sussex and said it was high time I shouldered some of the burden of being a child of Henry Grant.'

Lilian smiled. 'She was so good to everyone, wasn't she? Nothing like Henry or me.'

'The best of you both, I suspect.' He reached for his whisky glass on the mantelpiece. 'Is it wrong to drink to Louisa?'

'Not at all.'

'Then a toast to the most beautiful daughter a woman could love, and to the sister I worshipped.'

She lifted her glass to him and sipped, her expression hard to fathom. He wondered if she murmured *half-sister* to herself, then dismissed the thought.

'I know she hasn't been around us for the past year and a half but I'm feeling her loss physically,' he admitted. 'I've had Mrs Archer make up a soup but frankly I don't think I can.' He glanced over at the china tureen sitting atop a small candlelit burner to keep it warmed, its ladle sitting idle beneath the lid.

Lilian shook her head. 'I cannot either.'

Reggie moved back to stand near the marble fireplace, which might have been considered grand in another home but at Woodingdene was positively plain.

'Louisa told me you'd collected these for her,' he said, admiring the row of exquisitely fine porcelain vases on the mantelpiece, painted in delicate blue.

'We did. We found them on our grand trip to the Orient.' She shook her head at the memory, a bare smile lifting the corners of her lips. 'He never tired of collecting whatever captured his fascination, and while some have unkindly accused my husband of lacking taste, I would suggest he wasn't so much vulgar as unconventional.'

'I gather he lived his life that way.'

'He did. And I'm sorry I was only able to give him one child to share his vision.'

'Her love for you both was vast.'

'Not enough to hear our best advice,' she said.

Reggie moved quietly to sit in one of the creaky leather armchairs.

'Even you were against the marriage to James,' she continued. 'In this her family was united.'

He felt a trill of pleasure at Lilian describing him as family. 'I hated him then, and now I have good reason to hate him twice as much.'

'I wish he were dead and Louisa on her way home to us.' There was no apology in her tone.

Reggie had to agree. 'He will never amount to anything. I suspect he's lost his way as an engineer now, too – others will have overtaken him. He had his head in the clouds. He is not a bad person but his recklessness was always going to be his undoing.'

'Not *his* undoing, however!' she snapped, spilling a drop of sherry on the silk of her dress. If she noticed, she didn't react. 'Ours! I don't care if he's grieving. I hope he never recovers from his grief. He's left me childless; he's left that beautiful little girl motherless and all because he's a selfish, careless nobody with no sense of responsibility or duty to anyone but himself.' She began to cough, losing breath, and Reggie leapt to his feet to fetch a small glass of water.

'Here, Lilian, drink this. Please calm yourself.'

She took the glass with a trembling hand, greedily drinking all of its contents. 'Thank you,' she choked out. 'Forgive me. I promised myself I would not show my upset.'

'No one who matters is watching.'

She paused, considering his words. Finally, she looked up, and the orange warmth of the fire seemed to make her glow with a halo. 'Except you do matter now, Reggie. Much as it galls me to admit this, you're my ally – the only person I feel I can count on.'

He had to run the words through his mind again, not quite believing he had heard her correctly. 'That must be hard to admit.'

'More than you can possibly imagine, but we are now at a terrifying juncture and I need you, Reggie.'

He blinked. How astonishing. Was that pleading in her tone?

'I realise this is all rather surprising,' she continued, 'but there's something you should know. I wasn't going to tell anyone until . . . well, it doesn't matter. My hand has been forced.'

He wished he'd brought his whisky from the mantelpiece and could sip it now. 'What is it?' He took the risk of seating himself beside her, close enough to smell her violet toilet water.

'I'm dying, Reggie.' Lilian let the words hang between them for a couple of heartbeats. 'I've known for a while. I never did tell Henry – there never seemed to be the right moment. My physician has assured me it's inoperable, nor would I wish to go through the necessary surgical procedure. I have an aggressive cancer – any invasive treatment might only hold off the inevitable for a year, perhaps two.'

'I see,' he said, finding it hard to believe how disconcerting the news was. He'd wished her dead only hours before but now felt a profound rage that she was going to oblige him just as they'd built this important bridge. 'How long do you have?'

'Who knows? A few months, perhaps.'

'Oh, Lilian.'

Unlikely though it seemed, she placed a hand on his. He glanced down, startled, trying not to show it, and stared at the pale claw. 'Don't pity me, Reggie. I've made my peace with it, and with

Henry gone and now today's news I have to admit it all feels suddenly easier to let go. There's not much to live for.'

'But . . .' He waved his free hand pointlessly.

'This?' She chuckled. 'Woodingdene was always Henry's folly. I enjoyed his money, Reggie, I won't lie, but living so far north, close to Scotland?' Lilian gave a soft snort. 'I've got the south in my soul – I was born just outside London. I do miss the city and the theatre. I enjoy restaurants and a social life, not this rural existence. But it was bearable because we were a family and because I had Henry.'

'Move to London,' he suggested. 'I'll help you.'

'If I weren't dying, perhaps I would. But it suddenly feels like a lot of bother for a few months. I'm already feeling fatigued and it's going to get worse, and I have good help here.'

'I'm sorry' was all he could manage to say.

'I was thinking this afternoon that the news of Louisa takes away all those decisions I was facing. Suddenly there's only one that matters now and the rest can just take their natural course.'

'Can I help you with the one that matters?'

'It's why I am eating humble pie before you now – why I am prepared to hand over to you all responsibility for Woodingdene and my husband's affairs as of tonight. It's why I am seated here taking sherry and to all intents behaving towards you as though we were mother and son. It's why I need you, Reggie. I need a single favour from you and then I can die.'

This was a little dramatic for his comfort but he couldn't escape the intensity of her gaze or how hard she was squeezing his hand.

'Whatever you need,' he offered, hoping he wouldn't live to regret her dying wish.

'Thank you.' She actually smiled at him. 'Do this for me, Reggie, and you'll have full control of the Grant empire.'

She knew how irresistible that sounded and every inch of his body responded to its seduction.

'What do you want me to do?'

'I want you to sail for Africa immediately and, if you can, bring home the body of my daughter, to bury her alongside her father. If you can't, there's something more important. I want you to bring home Clementine.'

His gaze narrowed. 'Can we not send for —?'

'No,' she snapped. 'This must be done in person. I entrust this duty and responsibility to you as head of the family.'

Head of the family. What a ring that had to it. 'All right,' he replied, his thoughts ranging ahead to all that her request entailed. 'Exhuming Louisa and bringing her home are not impossible. There will be questions and —'

'You can fix it! Make arrangements now.'

He nodded, and blew out a low breath. 'But bringing Clementine home? That's not at all straightforward, Lilian. I would be removing her from her father and presumably he will not consent to that.'

She surprised him with a second smile but it was a sly one. 'I really don't care how you gain his permission, Reggie, or even if you do not.' There was a sinister note in there but he had no time to focus on it. 'Besides, you don't know what he wishes for her. I read the letter too. James is deep in his own grief – his handwriting gives us a bleaker clue to his state of mind. Is a drunk a good role model for a child? Is a father down a diamond mine any use either? He talks about some black man looking out for Clementine. A black! "A Zulu warrior", he writes, as though that should impress us and not terrify the living breath out of us!'

'I couldn't agree more.'

'Then go and get my granddaughter and bring her home! I want Clementine in England, leading the life she was born to.'

He swallowed.

'You owe them this.'

'But what if he fights me on Clementine?'

'What if he does?'

He stared at Lilian, his mouth slightly open in shock. Reggie extricated himself from her grip and moved to the fireplace. He desperately wanted to take a swig of the whisky but that might appear weak. He swung around and glared at her as he continued. 'I expect in all truth that he will say no. That he will not let his child go easily.'

She waited, as though she'd asked another question. With the blaze of the fire making her pale eyes sparkle, he could swear she was lit by an internal passion he couldn't touch. It could be the cancer; it could be the devil himself making her back him into this corner. He wanted to please her. He wanted to be head of the household. Reginald Grant, son of Henry Reginald Grant, wanted to take over his father's empire with the full permission and support of his father's widow and no longer be that bastard son society spoke about behind their hands.

'What do you want me to say?' he uttered.

'I want you to tell me that no matter what stands in your way, Reggie, you will bring me Clementine before I die.'

Now he did reach for the glass. He took a slow sip, even paused to let the heavily peated fumes of the Islay liquor rise on his palate with their charcoal hint. It slipped down to his belly with a gentle burn of comfort and calm. He licked his lips and returned a steady gaze to the devil.

'I will bring Clementine home.'

'At any cost?'

'No matter what it takes,' he replied, surprised by the fervour in his tone.

Lilian rewarded him with a sighing smile, warmer than the fire to his back; it made him feel as though he had just been compensated for years of being frozen out. Reggie could swear a shiver of satisfaction wove slowly through him, its silk-like thread attaching him firmly into the family tapestry.

'Then I shall drink to you, Reggie Grant, whom I now consider my family, and I shall put all of my faith in you for as long as I have to live. Do not let me down. To you!'

He raised his glass, caught up in the surprise of how today's grief had delivered to him such a prize. Bittersweet but uplifting.

'To our family,' he said and swallowed the contents of the glass, this time tasting iodine from the seaweed that contributed to the flavour of the famous whisky. And for the briefest of moments – a single heartbeat – he felt as lonely in his promise to Lilian as the Hebridean island from which the single malt hailed.

4

May 1872

Joseph took something from his pocket. 'For you, Miss Clementine.'

She opened her mouth in surprise as her friend handed her a triangular lump of grey stone. It landed in her palm with a satisfying weight. Its edges were defined but not sharp, and hairlike ivory strands seamed through what she knew the miners called 'blue ground'. But what kept her silent and her mouth still forming an *o* of pleasure was the cuboid, glassy substance protruding from its middle. Clementine was practised enough now to know that if she walked out into the sunlight, the lump she held would give off a blue-ish hue and its passenger would glimmer a truth that couldn't be hidden. If they left it in the open, the earth clinging to that glimmering guest would turn a crumbly yellow. She was looking at a diamond about the size of her thumb tip.

'Found today?' She looked up, her eyes shining and wide.

Joseph One-Shoe nodded. 'Your father is very excited. Our first find in two moons. If there's this one, there's more.' He put his finger to his generous lips. 'Do not speak of it to anyone.'

She didn't need to be told. From the earliest age Clementine had understood about the secrecy that surrounded 'finds'. Her father and Joseph would not want any of the other diggers to get so much as a whiff of this diamond.

'How much?'

He gave a slight shrug. 'Maybe three carrots.'

She giggled. 'Not ca-rrots. Ca-rats, Joseph.'

He grinned and she realised he was teasing her.

'Your father tells me they will sparkle just like the stars when they are properly polished. Let's free our new one.' She watched Joseph reach for a nearby hammer, never far away in the practical hovel she and her father called home, and leaned in as he easily knocked away the stone that clutched the diamond. She'd been fascinated to learn how the diamonds reached the surface where they dug, and had listened to her father explaining it to Joseph one night. They'd had a very good morning, finding half-a-dozen small, half-carat rough diamonds that they sold the same afternoon to the brokers who had set up their gaudy tents around the Big Hole. Their roughs had sold for a tidy sum that had afforded them rent, food, fresh clothes, at last, and new tools for bigger and better finds. They had certainly felt rich that day. Her father had wandered down the main street before going to the pub and had paid a visit to Blacklaws to buy new boots for Joseph One-Shoe and Clementine. She had proudly pulled on her sturdy new footwear, wincing at the stiffness of the leather but entirely in love with them. They were a deep red, darker than the cheap wine her father sometimes brought home and more colourful than the boots Sarah Carruthers wore to school and boasted were polished each day by their Malay servant. Joseph's were shiny black.

'You can see your face in them, Joseph,' her father had remarked as he'd handed them to his friend with a smile.

'I don't think so,' he'd laughed.

'Oh, come on, Joseph. Wear them,' Clementine had scolded.

'I do not wish to scuff them. Besides, then you would have to call me Joseph Two-Shoes.' As she opened her mouth to protest, he had grinned that smile of his – like lightning it came, brightening their world just as suddenly as those electric sketches lit the sky. 'I will wear at least one of them soon enough.'

'Not one at a time, surely?' her father had sighed.

'They will last twice as long,' Joseph had replied, and neither of the Knights could fault that logic.

Clem watched him now as he returned to the tiny wood stove where he was cooking them a meal.

It included meat – some antelope, a rare treat for the trio, who lived predominantly on smaller, meaner meats and mostly yam and maize. They also had cassava, but only if Joseph prepared it.

'Never cook this yourself,' he'd warned James when they'd first found themselves alone with a little girl to raise. 'It has a poison and can harm if it is not . . .' He had struggled to find the word.

'Prepared?' James had offered.

'Not cooked as it must be,' Joseph had settled on. 'It is dangerous – can kill. It also makes a bitter drink that makes people . . .' He'd pretended to stagger to demonstrate the word he couldn't find.

James had later discovered from others that there were high levels of cyanide in the plant, which had to be cooked out.

Over their midday meal Clementine was still handling the new diamond and learned about the blue ground that diamonds were found within.

'What is this stone around the diamond?' Joseph asked over their shared dish of spiced beans and rice. He'd pointed at the remains of some rock from their day's find.

James looked over. 'The geologists now call it kimberlite. It's volcanic matter surging from the earth's mantle. I guess you don't know what the mantle is?'

Joseph shook his head with a frown; so did Clementine.

'Hmm, how can I put this simply? It's where the liquid fire of the earth bubbles away. Have you heard of volcanoes?'

'Yes, Mr James. Miss Clementine has showed me pictures.'

'Ah, good. So, think of the kimberlite like a very small version of a volcano – almost an upside-down one, where its mouth on the earth is wider than where it begins thousands of miles below the surface.' He drew the shape in the air with a finger. 'It's like an underground funnel, and as the magma – which is molten rock like a thick liquid – rushes to the surface, it drags with it the diamonds, which have crystallised under vast pressure and high temperatures over millions of years.'

Clementine had watched her father turn wistful.

'Diamonds are amazing. They allow us to glimpse the remotest depths of our planet, perhaps the beginning of our planet, bringing its precious secrets to the surface.'

'Like fallen stars, Daddy,' she'd remarked through a mouthful of rice.

'Indeed. A perfect metaphor, Clem.'

'What's a metaphor?'

'It's a way of describing something by comparing it to something else.'

'Like what?'

'Like comparing you to a hungry piglet.'

Her laughter, as explosive as the kimberlite funnel, meant rice had catapulted from her mouth and amused both her favourite men.

Such moments of helpless entertainment with her father were becoming rarer. They used to be part of her daily nourishment, but now it was noticeable how little time he spent playing with her. It was not that she was too old for the type of chatter and games they had enjoyed when her mother was alive. She was a bit taller, that's all, as she mentioned to Joseph indignantly. She still wanted her father to play cards with the scruffy pack of Happy Families they'd purchased at Alderslade's. She'd had to teach Joseph One-Shoe how to play hopscotch because her father was no longer interested in bouncing across the numbers they used to draw in the dirt with a stick, throwing pebbles of kimberlite to play. He no longer made up tall tales about her beloved ragdoll, and his bedtime stories were a pleasure of the past; now she and Joseph would read aloud together from her few books. It was good practice for Joseph but she missed her father's presence – he would embellish the stories or even act them out for her, putting on different voices and making her laugh. Now his favourite place was the Digger's Rest, one of the many pubs that had sprung up in the now burgeoning town, no longer just 'New Rush', but referred to as Kimberley. His life consisted of digging all day, drinking most evenings and lurching home to drift into unhappy sleep. The last few days had been the worst; he'd eaten sparsely and had already left for a pint before he'd go back to the claim.

Her father's attention to her was as brittle now as the blueish earth that had fractured and turned yellow to crumble and leave the rough diamond. It was surprisingly heavy and cold to the touch.

Clementine held the diamond up to the light to watch it refract, sending a rainbow fire slanting one way and then the next. Her father had assured her that when these stones were properly cut and polished, they could dazzle with colour so beautiful that you'd never tire of looking at them. 'Maybe three carats – you're right, Joseph,' she said, not really knowing but enjoying sounding knowledgeable about its weight. 'Looks excellent quality,' she remarked, again in all innocence, now holding it up to her eye and squinting as though wearing a loupe like an old professional. 'Maybe I'll be a diamond sorter one day.'

'Why not dream up beautiful jewellery that uses these stones? How many do we have now, Miss Clementine?'

'This one makes twenty-four. Daddy says when we have twice this much we will be nearly rich.'

He nodded appreciatively, understanding that Clementine had no concept of what 'rich' meant. 'All we need is one big one, and maybe your father will stop.'

'If he stops, I'll have to go home.'

He looked at her with the tenderness she loved. 'If he stops, he might have a chance to be well again, and you can start to live like a proper young lady. That's more important. Let us bury this one with the rest of our stash.'

———————

Down in the hole, James Knight toiled feverishly. Joseph One-Shoe had just arrived, saying little, but James could see only accusation in the slightly lowered gaze of his friend. He knew he should have been spending time with his daughter; he hadn't seen her for days, leaving the caring to Joseph. The women's gazes of dismay and recrimination he received when he walked into town, thirsty for his night of beer drinking, told him no one approved of his leaving the young African warrior to raise a white girl. Joseph One-Shoe was popular, no doubt, but there was an invisible line and James was sure he'd forced his friend to not only cross it but to leave it far in his dusty wake. He knew Joseph was cautious; the helplessly modest man worked at not drawing any attention to himself. Yet here James was, callously forcing his friend to be mother, father and friend to his little girl. There were times when he believed Clem loved Joseph more than she loved him, and how could he blame her?

'Careful, Knight, you'll dig through to Australia if you keep going like that!' quipped one of the Irish diggers from a nearby claim.

'Jealous, Paddy?'

'Maybe I will be when you yell "Eureka!"'

The town of New Rush only existed because of this massive hole. He now stood nearly 40 feet deep in a smaller hole with walls that he and Joseph had dug. He straightened up briefly to look around, taking the chance to wipe the sweat from his face, as wet as if he'd stood in the rain for too long. Except rain was rare here, and dust had coated that sweat to leave only the palest part of his features revealed: the whites of his eyes; the laughter lines around them, no longer as obvious as they once were; his teeth. His arms were caked with it, his clothes filthy; Louisa would be ashamed of him. He was ashamed of himself.

It looked like the archaeological digs he'd seen in newspapers, in places like the Levant, searching for tombs filled with treasure and the mummified remains of Egyptians. Except these excavations were not calculated or strategic – they were frenzied. Men had run when the cry went up about the find. Joseph One-Shoe had outrun everyone, of course, and had been among the first to buy a claim, which had already been marked out by the time James and Clementine finally arrived. Joseph had been faced with two broken people who had said little more than a few words between them over the following week. Louisa's death had delayed them by several days, and emerging into the 'New Rush', as it was known, had held no excitement for them.

James didn't like to recall that time, had tried to build walls around what he knew was the darkest moment of his life. Now he deliberately shifted his thoughts away from Louisa's burial and the grief. He had to get his child away from Africa; it was the silent promise he had made over Louisa's corpse, and he hoped she might somehow know that he would return her daughter to her family in England.

Their dig was well advanced, now that they'd left the scuffles and fights behind when the claims were first made.

These months gone every man tried to dig faster than the next. Digs collapsed, toppling into their neighbour's claim. More dust would explode into the air, filling lungs and dirtying skin. Fights would erupt and the violence could be brutal if the collapse buried a diamond find or, worse, revealed a new one. Collapsed walls that revealed diamonds could result in fatal disputes, as men fought over blurred boundaries. Joseph One-Shoe had chosen their claim well and it was large enough that James could give them a solid set of walls: thick enough that the neighbouring claims were not under threat from their dig and vice versa.

The Big Hole had widened, deepened. James estimated that it would take a man a full thirty minutes to walk its circumference, perhaps longer. It could even double if this chaos continued, as the men dug even further hoping to strike a new funnel. Since it was no longer possible to travel easily between claims, they were now accessed by a series of crisscrossing ropes and pullies: from above it looked like a game of cat's cradle being played by a lunatic. There was no order, no plan; the miners all depended on one another's cooperation, and that potential was tested daily.

The wires were strung across up to a quarter of a mile in places and could haul buckets of loosened earth up from the lowest depths of the crater, through a complex pulley system up to the edge of the cliff it had formed, to be sifted and sorted. James had to accept that from a crude engineering point of view, Plato's observation that 'necessity is the mother of invention' rang true.

He paused to pull off the red kerchief and wipe his face yet again. The muscles in his thighs pleaded with him to stop and his spine cracked a complaint.

'You go up, Mr James,' Joseph suggested. 'I'll take over digging.'

'No, I'm fine.'

'I don't think so. You need water, you need a little rest. You do the sifting. I'm feeling fresh and —' he rubbed his fingertips in an attempt to make James smile — 'I think I feel some magic after this morning's find.'

James did dredge up a grin. Clementine had been discussing magic with Joseph, whose culture had its own notions of what could happen in worlds beyond the one they lived in. 'All right, you dig. There's nothing in what I've dug today. Don't even bother with it.'

'I've left a pail of water for you. Miss Clementine has sent some bread and cheese.'

When had his seven-year-old begun worrying about what he ate? James waved his friend's concern away and tucked his shirt back into the loose waistband of his trousers. His clothes hung on his hollow frame as emptily as if his shoulders were a washing line.

'You must eat,' Joseph implored him. His large soulful eyes now regarded him with disappointment.

'I'm doing my best for her, you know,' James murmured, failing to keep the self-pity out of his voice.

Joseph One-Shoe heard it. James could see in the way he lowered his gaze that he was trying to hide some measure of disgust. 'She spends too much time alone.'

James took a short, angry breath to shoot back a response but Joseph was quicker. 'I'm not enough. I'm not her father.'

'You act like one.'

Now the Zulu lifted those dark eyes and James saw anger to match his, although Joseph's voice remained even. 'Someone has to take care of her. You are not present enough.'

'I am digging!'

'You will lose her.'

He shrugged, not meaning to be careless, yet his words betrayed him. 'I've already lost her mother.'

Tongue held, Joseph simply nodded. After a moment's pause he said, 'That's why Miss Clementine needs you. It won't matter how many diamonds you find if you lose the love of your child.'

Joseph was right. He was letting her down with his absent attitude. Worse, he knew that Clementine would be a rich young woman in her own right when she came into her fortune at thirty. He swallowed his frustration that she was already a wealthy little girl. Her mother had left her everything that she owned, and this was on top of the trust set up in her name. Whatever he could earn would never be money that Clementine needed.

He sighed out his angry breath. 'All right, Joseph. I will try harder.'

Joseph's smile always felt like a balm when it came and it soothed James now.

He took his time clambering to the surface, kerchief tied around his nose and mouth to keep out the dust. Up here there was so much more noise. Within the walls of his small pit, the noise was his: the sound of his pick hitting the earth to loosen the ground, his coughing, his heavy breathing and groans. The voices of other diggers reached him but he was so lost in his misery, he barely registered them. Out of his pit, the noise of hundreds of men in their endeavour was deafening, making him realise with a new sense of unhappiness that he was part of something huge and almost angry in its atmosphere. Expressions were pinched, mouths grim, words gruff, activity hostile, violent even, as men toiled to get to Africa's buried treasure before someone else did. No joy whatsoever. And he'd once derived so much pleasure from his work as an engineer, no project more joyful than the bridge he had designed and crafted for his beloved Louisa.

He bent to cough out the dust along with that memory. It did him no good to let her wander back into his mind. He already felt like he was dying. Maybe that was the answer . . . then they could be reunited. He moved on, lifting himself to the surface. It used to be so easy; now it took him fifteen minutes to haul himself high enough and then pick his way to the edge, having to take long detours around walls that were still erect and strong enough to carry a man's weight. Soon they'd need some sort of lift apparatus, perhaps. He'd noticed that a lot of the black workers were already being lowered down in large wooden tubs moving like aerialists on tripwires in a circus. His engineer's mind kicked into gear: an automated lift was surely the future if the Big Hole kept yielding its treasures. Maybe he should design a better haulage system – there might be money in it.

Money. It dominated his thoughts. When would the Big Hole yield real treasure for him, the sort of treasure that could change his life and give Clem the one she deserved?

———————

Joseph took off his shirt in preparation for a long afternoon's toil. He had taken to wearing a hat to keep the sun off his head. The sunlight was so sharp it made his eyes water helplessly and gave him a constant squint. He rolled up his trousers above the rise of his one boot. If not for his single bare foot, he could believe he was becoming a white man in spirit. He spoke their language fluently, could read a few simple words of it too, and he knew that gave him power over his compatriots. Fighting the white man was useless. Knowing his tongue, understanding how his mind worked, made him a different sort of warrior. A clever one who wasn't about brawn and bravery but about intelligence and diplomacy. As he reached for his pick and shovel, setting his bare foot back to anchor himself, he thought about the intriguing question Clementine had asked him as they shared a bowl of porridge earlier that day.

'What is your future, Joseph?'

It was not only a daunting question – for her to even think to ask it was unnerving, but he had answered with honesty.

'Not all of the Africans who come here get treated well or have friends as I have.' He'd let that sink in. 'I think if they too spoke some English, then their lives could be better. They would find it easier to live alongside the white folk.'

'So . . . what will you do?'

The idea had been nibbling at him for a few months now. It had found no real purchase until this moment, as an uninhibited child had regarded him with studious interest.

He had said it aloud. 'I think I'd find a way to teach my people how to speak English, how to do some simple sums and even how to read: signs, forms, that headline in the newspaper.'

She had put down her porridge spoon and clapped. 'Oh, I would love to teach with you.'

It was typical of Clementine to approve; her expression had been filled with nothing but encouragement and pure pleasure that he had purpose.

Joseph squinted through the glare of the day and saw James raise a thumb in the far distance; he was ready for Joseph to send up the first bucket. Joseph gave the same gesture back, liking how well it conveyed a universal message in silence, across distance, amid noise and crowds, transcending cultural differences.

He turned back to his dig and cast a thought to the stars that James and Clementine pondered so often. *Bring us fortune today*, he directed at Sirius, the brightest of them all, and he swung his pick into the crumbly yellow ground, letting his instrument join all the others in the song of the diamond diggings.

James had eaten the food that his daughter had packed for him. He wasn't hungry but guilt was gnawing at his empty belly that she was having to take care of him in this way. He was glad it was a school day and she would be distracted by her letters and sums, although her precocious way made her advanced beyond her peers. She scared James at times with how she greedily devoured new information and she was always hungry to learn. He disliked her teacher, Mrs Carruthers, as much as Clem did, and was not always successful in disguising the disdain he felt in front of his daughter. She seemed to think it was her duty – her right, even – to teach Clementine how to be a little girl. She had no teaching qualifications but had taken on the role with zeal to bring order to the children of what had once been a camp but was now growing up into a town. She was like one of those interfering evangelists. He'd allow grudging respect that someone was looking out for the youngsters, but did it have to be Elmae Carruthers? The bossy, pinch-faced prune of a woman gave the distinct impression that she loathed anyone finding pleasure in skipping, running, laughing aloud, making up stories, talking to a ragdoll – or, indeed, befriending a black man. A lot of the bigoted folks around here – the so-called Christians – found that relationship somehow appalling. The women were worse than the men, he realised; the men approved of Joseph's prowess in the boxing ring and respected how hard he worked. Frankly, Joseph One-Shoe was hard to dislike – he barely spoke to others, barely raised his gaze, intent on not giving offence.

'Morning, Knight. Is today the day, do you think?'

James threw down the final bit of crust he'd been chewing and looked up to see the smug grin of Maximilian Granger. He was one of Fleetwood Rawstorne's now famous party, who had picked up the first diamond at Colesberg Kopje, then an unremarkable hillock.

The hillock had long disappeared, becoming the ever-widening gash in the ground now known as the Big Hole. The town of New Rush, he reflected, had been born because an old Bantu manservant of Rawstorne's had found that first diamond gleaming in the clear moonlight. He regarded Maxie, still wearing the distinctive red woolly hat each man in Rawstorne's group had worn the previous winter so they could be easily picked out among the diggers.

'Maybe you'll dig up something decent, my friend, and get that little girl of yours into better accommodations. Summer this year will cook you in that tin shack.'

He nodded, not trusting himself to speak, but Maxie was right. He could hardly deny the logic, although in this moment he wished he possessed Joseph's powerful right hook. He frowned, wondering why Joseph was taking so long to send up the first bucket.

'Well, I'd better get to it, Granger, if I'm going to find my fortune today.'

'Luck to you, Knight. You and your Zulu need it.'

He let the man move on before shielding his gaze to search for Joseph. He picked him out easily enough, but what was Joseph doing crouched in their claim and not working? The lines of concern deepened on his forehead as he squinted to see better. Joseph looked up, stared back at his friend, kept his gaze steady, earnest.

What now? James thought, exasperated not just with this moment but with life – with the death it brought and the guilt that ate him from the inside out, with his raging desire for a nip of liquor so early in the day and the relentless heat that felt like his jailer and torturer. And now Joseph One-Shoe had decided to go into some sort of trance! They might as well go dig their own graves now. He gave an exaggerated shrug across the distance that separated them.

Joseph shook his head once.

No, he *was* focused, James realised. *In that case, what's wrong?* He stood to show his friend he needed an assurance – an answer of sorts.

Joseph raised a single finger with caution and beckoned. He looked terrified.

5

James blinked and began to move. He wouldn't run – no, that would draw attention, and he had already worked out that Joseph One-Shoe needed no scrutiny from others. Instead he grabbed a bucket and one of the old sieves from their days at the river diggings, which he tucked under his arm in a deliberately careless manner. James set his hat to a jaunty angle, somehow dredged up a whistle and forced his stride to be purposeful but distracted. He kept surreptitiously glancing across to Joseph, who was yet to shift position. James wondered if a wall was caving in, or perhaps Joseph had hit the 'blue' ground where diamonds probably lay but would be impossible to retrieve with only a man's strength and a pick. It was only from the degraded and weathered blueish ground that they could dig into and make any impression upon it. Was their claim proving to be suddenly useless?

James walked nimbly; if he and Joseph acted quickly, maybe they could prevent whatever disaster had struck from doing too much damage. He was close now and Joseph had sensed his arrival, turning to encourage him. Joseph's lips, even from this distance, had lost their usual rosiness and had instead adopted a greyish pallor, looking dry and cracked.

Don't hurry, he urged himself. *Don't draw attention.*

'G'day, Knight,' an Australian called up from his pit. It wasn't nearly as deep as James and Joseph's but there were three of them working it; they would deepen that claim quickly. He couldn't imagine how far this man had come to seek his fortune but his back was bent to his toil, and James had never seen the Antipodean fellows anywhere but rotating in their dig or drinking beer at the pub. The three broad-shouldered men, two Australians and one New Zealander, were hard to dislike despite their brashness and lack of manners, which had many of the diggers' women looking like they had sucked on lemons whenever the men moved through the town, often inebriated.

'Morning, Mr Thompson.'

'Argh, call me Tommo, or it sounds like you're talking to my old man.' Tommo lit up. 'You look like you're in a hurry, mate?'

'My turn to take over,' he replied.

'See you for an ale tonight, then?'

'Will do, Tommo.'

He strode on. He was only a few feet away now and saw that Joseph had sat back against the wall of their dig. He was sipping from a flask, but none of the fear had left his expression.

Is he ill? James wondered suddenly. That would be just as devastating as if their wall had collapsed, and yet as he rounded the final claims that separated him from their own, the walls appeared to be intact. He let out a breath he didn't know he'd been holding.

James had constructed a small ladder to easily get in and out of their dig, but now he used only two of its rungs, leaping down the final four, no longer able to contain his anxiety. He approached Joseph, whose expression had not changed.

'Joseph?' he whispered.

'Mr James. I think we need to look at the wall over here.'

So, it was the wall! James's relief that the problem could be fixed was at war with the fresh concern at what this might cost them. Acid rose – it was a new visitor in his life. An ulcer, perhaps? Joseph turned his back on him, crouching in the corner of the furthest point of their claim. James already knew no one was working in the dig that backed onto that corner – they were probably switching shifts – and he'd noticed when he'd clambered onto the ladder that the other dig abutting theirs had only one man working on the far side. The digger had been bent over and busy at his toil. Good.

James joined Joseph, crouching, frowning. 'What should I be seeing?' he remarked, looking at the intact wall.

Joseph put a finger to his lips. If it was possible, the terror in his face seemed to have deepened. His eyes now looked a depthless charcoal. Joseph used his silence and a frightened gaze to drag James's attention down to where his large fist was closed. It looked primed and ready to deliver an upper cut that could knock out just about any opponent. But now that fist moved, and James watched the ridges of the Zulu's knuckles become defined as he straightened out his thick fingers. Everything else about the moment seemed to slow. His lungs felt like tight balloons of anticipation as he watched Joseph turn his hand around and open it like a starfish. There in Joseph's palm sat a chunk of blue ground, and poking out from that rock was the biggest rough diamond that James had seen – perhaps the biggest that anyone had encountered in this diamond rush. It perched on its unstable surface with great poise, demanding to be admired like a goddess.

James knew that diamonds in the rough were at their dullest, and still this massive conker glinted with glorious arrogance.

He trembled. Suddenly everything that had dimmed became too loud, too bright, too raw. His scalp felt as though it were tightening around his skull and his breath came out in a ragged expulsion that could easily have escalated to tears, such was the surge of relief that rode through his body. It was willpower alone that kept his eyes dry.

James knew he was mirroring Joseph's anxiety. His legs felt unsteady, collapsing slightly. He instinctively pushed out a hand to steady himself against the dirt wall. A new raft of terrifying problems began to line up before them. The threat of violence and theft loomed. He closed Joseph's fingers back into a fist.

But Joseph shook his head and plonked the cool, heavy piece of carbon into James's palm, clearly wanting no further part in the terrifying find.

James couldn't argue with him now. The diamond had to be concealed. He pulled off his kerchief and wrapped the stone as quickly as he could with trembling fingers that didn't want to help him. He was swallowing the fear, forcing it back, trying to replace it with words.

'We will not talk about this here,' he ground out.

Joseph nodded and reached for the pail at his knees that James hadn't noticed previously. He looked inside and was astonished to see a small galaxy of shimmering stars lying on a bed of crumbled basalt. He stopped counting at thirty diamonds, all of them tiny minions to their queen, which was now in his pocket.

'Cover them with more earth. No one must see,' he murmured, in such shock he sounded calm yet was frozen.

Together they forced their limbs to work, scrabbling with small spades to throw blueish dirt over the winking stones until they were no longer visible.

James sat back against the wall, feeling safe only once the stones were hidden. Joseph had not yet relinquished his terror.

'What now?' the Zulu asked.

After expelling a slow breath, James felt the first kick of uncontrolled delight in his belly. He knew it would soon feel like a donkey kick and they needed to get away from this place before the yells of elation became too much for him to contain. *This was it!* This was his eureka moment. This was the find he had dreamed about when he'd gabbled his excited excuse to Louisa at the Cape Town dock.

He wanted to shake a fist at the heavens for taking his wife before he could prove to her his worth – that his instincts had not been wrong. Those instincts had cost Louisa her life, but he could at least make it up to their child. All the hardship, all the heartbreak could be put behind them now that he could afford the life he wanted for them on his own terms, through his success instead of handouts.

James stood because he couldn't bear to whimper in the dirt a moment longer. His legs shook but from excitement now; no longer would he hang his head. Brokers would go wild for what he and Joseph had found. In truth, the diamond world would become frenzied at the sight of this stone. He couldn't accurately calculate in uncut carats – maybe over three hundred. He had to get control of his breathing, which he was sure was now audible. Worse, he could convince himself that the Australians, though several claims over, could hear his heart pounding against his ribs.

He certainly could.

6

May 1872

Reggie Grant longed for the simplest of pleasures, especially that of a long soak.

On the relentless ox-wagon journey to this place they called Kimberley, he had little more than a damp flannel as his only means of toileting. Relieving himself behind trees, eating communally for safety as much as company, and sleeping rough with the constant fear of carnivorous and nocturnal animals on the prowl all combined to make him jumpy – hostile, even. He was assured by one of the drivers that he should count his luck that they hadn't encountered flooded rivers.

'Then you'd have something to complain about,' he said while they sat around a small fire one evening. It was mild so no one was especially cold but the same driver had insisted they all gather close. 'Light your own if you wish,' he suggested. 'Lions don't like the flames but they have developed a taste for human flesh.'

The women in his immediate wagon party gasped, but he swallowed his fear and the revulsion that he was here and so far from home.

He'd agreed to this expedition for altogether different reasons to Lilian Grant's. Her health had worsened since his hurried departure from England and a telegram he'd received aboard the ship had informed him that she was now so fragile her life was in the balance. His trip had taken on such a sense of urgency that much as he'd have liked to linger in Cape Town to enjoy its surprising beauty, he'd had to keep moving north. No point in disappointing her now.

While he'd waited the two days for the coach that would connect him with his ox wagon, he'd spent a splendid couple of days in Cape Town, even hiking partway up the dramatic Table Mountain. He had been treated to a sighting of what locals called the Tablecloth. His guide had explained that this meteorological phenomenon occurred when south-easterly winds blew up the mountain's slope to meet the much colder air at altitude. The ensuing mist formed clouds to billow over the sharply flattened top of the mountain, and Reggie could see how it created the marvellous impression of a fresh white tablecloth being flung over the flat expanse. The clouds were believed to be a smoking contest between the devil and a legendary pirate – a man called Van Hunks.

Reggie wished he could have further explored this dramatic city, overshadowed by its curiously shaped mountain, but he was on a mission. A woman he wanted to impress was dying while a woman he loved had died; he didn't want to lose his rage or the impetus that had brought him this far. A little girl needed saving and he was her only hope for a life of gentility – he was sure of it. And the truth he couldn't share with anyone was that he needed Clementine more perhaps than she could ever need him.

The journey by ox wagon had so far taken forty days. He hadn't known what to expect, having never travelled further than London. The voyage to Africa had been an adventure of its own and he would be lying if he didn't admit that life on the ship had been splendidly lazy and indulgent. Two amorous women had tried in vain to win his attention. Their pretty, tinkling laughs and flirtatious behaviour had been fun, along with the pleasure of being trapped on board with other men for whom the best part of the day was taking leave after dinner to smoke cigars or pipes. It had felt exciting and dangerous at once to be presumed wealthy; this judgement was made simply by the company he kept, and did it matter that the wealth was not his? He'd been tasked with being its caretaker, and that meant responsibility, duty, status. It may not be his money but without him this last year since his father's death and his move to Woodingdene, he wondered if it would still belong to Clementine or have been lost to poor investments that he was working so hard to counter.

Talking to Lilian he'd realised she had not been aware of her husband's precarious financial position while he was alive. A recent meeting with his father's solicitor had been numbing, but Reggie's sharp mind had grasped the chilling situation quickly. They met at his father's legal firm at Gray's Inn. Mr Pottage, the family's solicitor, was a portly gentleman who still favoured extravagant side whiskers and a luxuriant moustache, with a clean-shaven chin that gave him a weighty air of self-importance. Reggie thought about the moustache comb his sister had given him as an early birthday present before she went to Africa to die. He had it in his pocket this moment, a stylish tortoiseshell comb no more than two inches long that folded into an exquisitely wrought, solid-silver case. She'd engraved his name on one side. It was perfect, just like Louisa, and he used it daily. He imagined Mr Pottage could benefit from some grooming tools for his whiskers, which were grey, fluffy and unruly. That lack of pride in his grooming gave Reggie an insight into the conceit of the man's profession.

Pottage sat behind his polished desk, surrounded by sweeps of bookcases filled with legal books, and he clearly enjoyed reading his paperwork to the rhythm of a large grandfather clock that sombrely ticked away the hours for which he would charge outrageously. The room smelled of beeswax polish, hair pomade and boiled eggs. Reggie noticed the detritus of eggshells that had been missed when the staff had cleared away the man's luncheon tray.

'I see you admiring the timepiece,' Pottage remarked.

He hadn't been admiring anything; he'd simply looked away with a trill of panic that somehow all this trouble was angling his way. 'Yes, indeed, a most splendid clock, Mr Pottage. Returning to the matter at hand – actual bankruptcy, do you mean?'

Pottage sighed dramatically, pausing like a hammy actor in a play, giving his audience a chance to feel the moment of tension. 'Foreclosure.'

Reggie blinked with suppressed anger. 'Good heavens!' he said, suppressing the vulgar curse that leapt about in his throat. 'Why am I only hearing about this now?'

Mr Pottage had regarded him with bemusement. 'Because until now your role was to ensure Woodingdene's smooth running, not manage its accounts. That was tasked to this law firm and your father's accountants.'

He hid his indignation at the man's disdain with an even tone. Mr Pottage's arrogance was making his skin prickle.

'And, it's no longer a matter of management, dear boy. Financial decisions must now be made, so your input is necessary.'

Reggie read between the lines. It was obvious to him that they had realised they might need a scapegoat, so the time was right to bring in the inexperienced illegitimate son they despised.

'And Lilian has no inkling?'

The solicitor looked offended. 'We don't trouble Mrs Grant with money matters, Reggie,' he said, sounding almost weary that he should have to answer such a question. 'Your father put us in charge until such time as family involvement was needed; I would like to spare Mrs Grant the ugly truth. And so, you are her daughter's proxy, shall we say.' He smiled benignly at his own clever words. Woodingdene was facing threat – more likely, Reggie thought, the Grant empire was under siege.

'How long do we have?' he replied, no longer choosing to be diplomatic about the news of potential bankruptcy. Reggie couldn't recall offering up his first name either. Why wasn't he Mr Grant, as his father had been? Clearly his father had been speaking about him in such an offhand way that he was known as Reggie in this office.

Pottage continued in a bored voice. 'Your father made some poor investments against the best advice; his worst was to continue ploughing his cash into the Millwall Iron Works.'

Reggie, not trusting himself to speak, gave a slight shrug to encourage the solicitor to elaborate.

'Listed on the London Stock Exchange, the company had a stellar beginning, with names like Brunel attached to it, at a time when shipbuilding and railways were expanding so fast it was staggering. Millwall Iron and Shipbuilding, as it was known, then suffered troubles with failed ship launches. It changed hands, flourished again for several years but began to fail once more. I counselled your father against this company —'

'Why?' Reggie interjected.

The solicitor merely shook his head. 'I always felt its success was transient.'

'There are notes to this effect?'

His unkempt eyebrows flicked up with irritation. 'No, dear boy. This is the sort of private conversation that a solicitor has with his most important client. Your father had a stockbroker, of course, but big investments required a lot of legal involvement, which is why I was privy to most of his money matters.' Pottage tapped a meaty forefinger in time to his words. He was affecting a conversation like a tutor's with a student.

Reggie ignored the scolding and let him continue; he would choose his moment to remind Pottage of his actual status.

'Despite my advice, he was determined to speculate on its success, particularly when it began making armour plates for Russia in the middle of the last decade. Your father was fond of Russia.'

'Go on.'

Pottage gave a nervous tug of his bushy whiskers and explained in a weary tone. 'There was a serious accident ten years ago involving its famous fly wheel, believed to be the largest in Britain. I don't know if that's true but it was certainly spectacular: nearly 40 feet in diameter and weighing around 110 tonnes. It killed a lad who had been raking over the furnace – mangled him, in fact. It was spinning fast and came unhinged to burst away from its tethers, essentially exploding. Bits of metal were hurled in all directions, injuring several other workers.'

Reggie hated the solicitor in that moment. He was sure neither the lad's horrible death nor the plight of the families of the injured had registered as anything more than a passing sparkle of gossip and inconvenience to his city colleagues.

'This blight on the company was exacerbated by the Panic of 1866 in the financial sector, and companies like Millwall, already on the brink, simply collapsed. Your father was not the only one who lost out, but he was the largest stakeholder.' He looked up at Reggie with a sharp gaze. 'Of course, this was one of several poor investments. Your father was an avid collector of the unusual and often paid a small fortune for eclectic items that in the short term offered no investment value. Let's not forget the money pouring in to Woodingdene Estate and its follies.'

'Follies? Mr Pottage, one could hardly consider Woodingdene anything but an asset,' he bristled. 'Is your home electrified through the power of water, sir?'

The man's fleshy chins wobbled.

'I suspect you – like most – rely on gas. But my father's far-reaching plans mean that in just the next few years all the lakes around Woodingdene will produce clean hydro-electricity to light the entire property. No smell, no potential explosions, no ventilation issues or threat of suffocation, no lack of pressure. I shall see to it that his dream is realised.'

The man didn't take a backward step, not even to concede he might have spoken out of turn. 'Well, who would want it, Reggie? Potential electrification aside, you'd need a buyer with an equally, er . . . shall we say, diverse view and similar passion to purchase it.'

'It's not for sale.' Reggie hadn't meant to say this aloud – not yet, anyway. But now it was out and he was committed.

'That's the family's decision, but a property can only be valued either by the land it sits on, or what a buyer would be prepared to pay for the whole. I have to admit I'm not convinced that any gentleman of means would find the house as . . . well, intriguing as your father did when he built it.'

He was not going to argue its aesthetic value with a man who lived in a lost decade. 'So, land value is what you're saying.'

Pottage grimaced. 'You're not selling, so this part of our conversation is purely academic, but let's talk it through anyway, shall we?'

Reggie was pleased to see the man looked at least vaguely embarrassed in that moment.

'The bank would try to sell it, presumably, if the worst occurred, but you would need to be realistic that it would be unlikely to sell as a whole property. Instead it would be broken up and the bank would sell off divided portions and then other people of means could build their glamorous homes among the grounds, which I would be the first to admit are nothing short of spectacular. The house? Well, dear boy, its quality is tempered by its . . . well, its *uniqueness*, shall we say?'

Reggie hated that Pottage spoke as if they were some sort of partnership. The 'we' was beginning to annoy him.

The solicitor continued. 'Furthermore, without wishing to labour the obvious, it's in the north, and it would require a man of money to want to invest far from London. He would need a lot of spare cash as well as a liberal view – not an easy sell.' He took a breath, pleased he'd got that all out of his thoughts, and reached for a cup of tea that was no longer there. 'The point I'm making is that your father invested on whims, on emotion, and I'll grant that much of the time – certainly in his earlier days – he got it right, but his mistakes, which seemed to outnumber his successful decisions as he grew older, are now having a dire impact. You will no doubt wish to take this up with your father's bankers, but from our perspective as your legal counsel, Reggie, the financial situation is beyond precarious. You're going to need to sell off as much as possible, as well as find a serious injection of cash. The best asset to liquidate at this time *is* Woodingdene – purely for its land value.'

'What's the time limit on this?'

'There is no time, dear boy. The limit is reached and the situation is urgent.' He began to land a pointed forefinger once again on the leather of his desk in time with his words. 'Cash is required now before the dominoes begin to fall.'

'Cash,' Reggie repeated, trying not to sound incredulous but failing.

The older man nodded slowly, eyes closing, as if looking for patience while communicating with a dullard.

Reggie waited, forcing the solicitor to focus on him again.

'Perhaps five thousand pounds might give you a couple of years of breathing space so you can find the buyer, but we would also need to dismantle large portions of his portfolio.'

'Mr Pottage, I wonder where you imagine I might suddenly

find that sort of immediate cash.' He offered up a tight, inquiring smile.

The solicitor looked momentarily vacant. He frowned and gave Reggie what sounded like an entirely honest appraisal.

'I thought I'd made that clear. Woodingdene will need to have its financing scrutinised. No doubt you would need to sell off some of its land in the short term to give you funds to cover your immediate and ongoing debt. You would certainly need – and I mean within weeks – to pare back your father's portfolio of stocks and shares. He has so much artwork spread around the houses – most of that should be put up for auction. Do you still need the London house?'

'The London house remains, sir,' he said firmly. 'However, I will certainly take a long, hard look at the family's art collection.'

'You need to be liquid, Reggie. I gave your father identical advice not long before he died.'

'And he didn't listen?'

'He invested in more ships,' the older man said, leaning forward with exasperation. 'You'd think he might have learned something from Millwall Iron, or even the great storm of 1859. More than one hundred and thirty ships were lost, along with eight hundred lives. Your father had investments in at least three of those ships and he recouped nothing. One of them was the *Royal Charter*, a clipper carrying his share of the gold that had been prospected in a place in the Antipodes called New South Wales. A strange name that I can't quite remember. I want to say Lemon but it's not that – it is a fruit, though. Oh, that's right. Orange.'

'Orange?'

The older man nodded. 'Apparently it's a gold rush town. The gold find was considered "notable" and your father put up the money for a team of Cornish miners to sail to Australia in March of 1851. They found plenty of gold, but all those men went down with the ship and so did their bullion.'

'And so did we, it seems,' Reggie said, breathing out with disgust.

'I'm afraid so. Bad luck, yes, but your father was also putting up valuable cash on various speculative investments. He had his hands in so many projects – I have to say, it's never a wise proposition to spread oneself so thin.'

Reggie didn't appreciate this rebuke and looked away while pretending to cough. He excused himself not long after, claiming he needed to head back to Northumberland to make some hard decisions.

Learning the depth of debt, none of it his but all of it now his sole responsibility, made Reggie even more desperate, but in a new way. Mr Pottage managed to make him feel like a conspirator in the fall of the empire. 'Your father would not wish Lilian to learn of this situation,' he counselled as they shook hands in farewell.

That meeting in Pottage's office felt like a lifetime ago, yet it had been barely eight weeks.

They'd made it through the challenging, often tense and dramatic Mitchell's Pass of the Western Cape and were now officially in the Little Karoo Desert. It had required their oxen to haul them up a dangerous ascent of over 600 feet before dropping into the town of Ceres. The pass itself was astonishing, hacked out of the mountains a quarter of a century before by a talented engineer who'd eloped with the fifteen-year-old daughter of a French colonel, Reggie was amused to learn. As far as Reggie was concerned, it was little more than an animal track they rode upon. The only human sound that punctuated the silence was the yell of the drivers as they cracked their whips to urge their beasts to pull harder.

For the most part, Reggie found himself bored by the Karoo: flat, parched bushland with a sparse population of acacia, their long white thorns speaking silently of the region's inhospitable ways. The sense of danger was enhanced by wind, dust and the fact that sanitation was a luxury to be yearned for, along with the unsettling threat of lions and cheetahs. He did hope that the sheer size of the herds of springbok that moved in a relentless migration around these parts kept those carnivorous cats sated. He would be glad not to see any of these famed hunters firsthand, although he'd heard several hair-raising stories from the wagon drivers and was glad to note that each rode with a shotgun at his knee.

Here he sat, quietly removed from the four wagons and their parties, each staying within close range of the small circle of fires. He suspected the oxen would alert them to predators, given they were hobbled beasts and more likely to sense danger than sleepy men with rifles. Reggie assured himself that so long as he remained wary and stayed within sight of the fires, he should be safe from marauding carnivores. Away from the conversations of his fellow travellers and seated near the tethered oxen, he had a chance to think.

He pretended to write in a diary using candlelight, so the others wouldn't think him odd for keeping his own company. He silently conversed with the ox closest to where he sat, mostly to hear the thoughts that had been kept tightly enclosed within his mind.

'You see, Ox, in sharing the secret of my father's debts, Mr Pottage has tumbled a new sense of duty onto my shoulders. Selling off, as he blithely puts it, takes care . . . it needs a strategy. I wouldn't want to give anyone in London the impression that the Grant empire is crumbling – that would bring out the predators, and genuine investors would be scared off. I have to be cunning in a way my father never was. I have to set about saving Woodingdene for Clementine without the rest of the world knowing we are sinking.' He sighed as he got his thoughts more clearly into perspective. 'I am now the person charged with hauling us to the stormy sea's surface so that we can take a breath and look to clambering to safety. I have come to the conclusion, Ox, that the security of the shore can only be reached if I can have access to the trust fund of Clementine.'

There. He'd finally allowed the idea to be exposed. As weeks of churning thoughts coalesced into one, it felt like he was sinking into a bath of soothing warm water.

Clementine's trust fund had been set up by her grandfather and massively boosted by the death of her mother and the imminent death of her grandmother. It meant the little girl was presently worth a true fortune.

He murmured on. 'I just need to have access for a short while so I can save her fortune and save her heritage. I am doing this for her.' It felt comforting to outline his plan to another being. 'She is a child, after all. She needs so little right now. But her livelihood is what I must protect; I've promised Lilian I will safeguard her granddaughter's future and all that my father set up. If I can do this, then I know I will make my father proud and Lilian can go to her death with some regard for me. Above all, I will have done something important in the memory of my sister. I will look after her child as if she were my own.'

A woman strolled over to him, and he halted his conversation with his bovine companion.

The newcomer was the only spinster in the wagon party. Much to Reggie's despair, she and her father had been allocated to his wagon, and as Reggie had dreaded, she was taking a keen interest in his welfare. They were forty days into a tedious and challenging forty-two-day journey and the message of his indifference was not getting through to her.

'Ah, Miss Hampton, how kind of you,' he said, pushing away his vexation and politely accepting the tin mug Anne had brought to him. Good manners that had been drummed – sometimes beaten – into him at boarding school.

'You looked so engrossed in your writing, Mr Grant, but I didn't want you to miss out on the coffee we have made. It's a lovely brew.'

'That's most generous, thank you,' he said, knowing that his smile was dangerously inviting but sure that behaving churlishly would be short-sighted. Her father, Percy, was a wealthy landowner in southern England. He had been in Cape Town for many months acquiring land and was now travelling up to Kimberley with his daughter to see whether property there might deliver rich takings down the track. He was even talking about buying some diamond claims. Reggie had learned from his father that it never hurt to extend one's business network, and so he and Percy had taken to sharing brandy and a cigar each evening, just the two of them, quietly discussing business.

Reggie couldn't be sure that he would never need Percy Hampton's contacts or influence. It wouldn't be wise to burn the connection so he kept his charm flowing with the man's daughter. This balancing act took a nerveless approach: he could offend by simply refusing tonight's mug or later her more intense advances. Anne Hampton was clearly on the hunt for a husband and had decided that he was sound material. Somehow he had to try to keep her appeased yet not lead her on too far.

'Shall I sit awhile with you, Mr Grant? I would hate for you to feel lonely.'

He wished she would observe the etiquette that she was not chaperoned and should not be joining him. However, it seemed the usual rules did not apply when travelling by ox wagon. 'By all means,' he said, sounding far more gracious aloud. 'Although I should assure you that I am a man who finds peace in his own company. To be truthful, I was just thinking of turning in for the night.' He felt awkward that he couldn't stand politely to help her, given he was sitting on the ground and balancing a mug. 'There's a convenient boulder,' he said, pointing, glad it was sufficiently removed that she wouldn't crowd him but not so far away as to make the suggestion rude. 'Could that act as a seat for you?'

'Perfect,' she gushed, moving over to arrange herself. She straightened her many skirts and he had to admire how composed and neat she looked, sitting so straight-backed on a stone in the middle of an African desert. She'd removed the bustle for the journey but he was sure that once they reached the town of Kimberley, she would be straight back into full formal attire.

'It's extraordinary how you ladies manage to keep so clean and pretty despite the dust, the heat, the inconvenience of this terrible journey.' Reggie deliberately kept it general, not singling her out for admiration.

'Not enjoying it, Mr Grant?'

'Can anyone?' he asked. 'I feel like we're on an expedition to build a new world at times.'

They smiled and both took a moment to peer through the night towards the piled-up familiar shapes of furniture, household goods, timber, machinery and corrugated sheeting that the oxen hauled north across the vast desert to build new towns. One of their party's wagons was lugging a portable steam engine to provide power at the Big Hole.

'I am of the opinion, Mr Grant, that the desert is to these transport riders what the sea is to sailors.'

'Born wanderers, you think?'

'Searching for something, perhaps?' She sounded wistful and he suspected she was referring to herself.

'Believing they may find it in the dark heart of Africa?' He disguised his sarcasm with a light tone and a grin.

Predictably, she laughed. 'I must sound like a silly romantic to you.'

Reggie swallowed his coffee and gave a sigh as though ready-ing to bring his evening to a close. 'I see no harm in adopting that view on life, Miss Hampton. There are more than enough of us cynics.' He changed the subject. 'Have you noticed, Miss Hampton, that all the oxen have individual characters?' That should throw her right off the scent.

She looked at him aghast in the moonlight. 'Are you making fun of me, Mr Grant?'

'Not at all,' he assured her. 'I have noted that each has a unique personality, and the skill of the transport men is to know how that ox behaves: some lead, others follow and some are more prone to skittishness.'

'And this beast here?' she inquired with a smile, playing along.

He deliberately answered her with care and gravity. 'They call this fellow Themba. It means "trusted". Knowing where to place them in the line is vital to a successful journey, I've discovered, and much care and training goes into putting together a team of oxen with the right handler.'

'I had no idea,' she remarked, sounding impressed.

'I didn't either until I spent some time with the drivers.'

'Where is Themba placed?' she asked, her smile widening.

'Ah, well, Themba is at the front. He is patient and can be trusted not to panic, not to lead the less reliable animals astray and not to tire first. He also knows how to lower his head when yoked and put his greatest force in pulling forward. I dare not bore you, Miss Hampton, with the science of the bull's head and the angle when it is relaxing in a field untethered as compared to that angle when it is urged to pull a great weight. It is believed the greatest strength passes through the root of its horns.' Was he really having this conversation, he paused to wonder, and privately con-gratulated himself on his brilliance at being somehow engaging and empty at once.

'So Themba is the lead ox?' She had been paying attention, it seemed.

'Indeed, and my favourite. It seems we've been fortunate – I've heard unsettling tales of broken wheels having to be repaired, and about the trauma of having to right a capsized wagon with a big load and a trapped ox. How does one keep that ox calm; how to care for it?'

She shook her head in wide-eyed fascination.

It was true, he'd learned plenty about these teams. 'I was talking to one of our drivers, Henry, who told me that the most feared obstacles are the foot-high tree stumps. That's one of the jobs of the young African lads who run out ahead of us.'

'I've been wondering,' she said.

He nodded. 'Jan must spot the stumps and alert the driver. Hitting a stump can drop the wagon in a dead shock that more often than not results in a violent swerve, which produces panic in the animals and, most chillingly, can result in the main wagon pole being snapped. That can mean many days of delay, frustration and the rationing of water and so on.'

'Good heavens, Mr Grant. I do hope we cover the next days without incident.'

'Fear not, Miss Hampton. It's only two days, I'm delighted to say,' he said, meaning it.

Anne Hampton didn't respond to his assurances, instead tilting her chin as a signal for him to look up to the heavens. 'Until I came to Africa the night sky held no interest for me,' she remarked. That wistful tone, which he thought he'd sent packing, was creeping into her voice again. 'But will you look at that velvet ceiling of twinkling wonder?' she breathed, sounding awed.

It was certainly a bright moonlit evening, and looking at the elegant shape of her neck as she craned to admire the starlight, he felt an uncharacteristic disappointment that he didn't feel any attraction to this woman – or indeed any woman – in the way she would want to be admired. She had so much to offer: beauty, fine manners, a good family name – and an increasingly wealthy one at that. Anne Hampton would not have to worry about her future. Reggie believed her only worry to be securing a good husband, who perhaps would marry her for love first and foremost and give her a happy life.

He toyed with it for a heartbeat. Could he? No. It would be a lifetime of misery for both of them. Her feeling cheated in every possible manner and running to Daddy. His problem could not be revealed.

Poor Anne, searching for a husband. He felt sure there would be many suitors who would marry her for cynical reasons. No doubt this was why the old man kept his eligible daughter so close. Sadly, he now realised, they were both sizing him up, and those quiet fireside chats with old man Hampton were assessing his potential as a husband without any genuine interest in their conversation. Well, he needed to find a gentle way to extricate himself from the increasingly sticky web she was weaving.

'Do you know much about the stars, Mr Grant?' she remarked.

'No. I'm the antithesis of a romantic, Miss Hampton.' He dropped his voice to a sad murmur. 'I am the archetypal realist.'

'You make that sound like an unenviable quality, Mr Grant,' she commented, not moving her eyes from the inky sea of the southern skies. 'As though the trait is villainous.'

'Oh, I wouldn't want you to think that, Miss Hampton. Let's agree instead that life has taught me to be an all-round pragmatist.' And with that he feigned a yawn, shaking his head in apology. 'Do forgive me, Miss Hampton.'

'I do wish you would call me Anne.'

'Again, my apologies, Anne,' he said with a slight bow of his head, 'for such weariness.'

'Well, you walked beside the wagons all day, Mr Grant. That probably accounts for it.'

So, she was watching his every move, it seemed. He wanted to admit that walking the journey avoided the mind-numbingly boring conversation within the wagon. 'At home, I fence and ride most days. I feel obliged to keep up my exercise regime.'

'It's why you cut a fine figure, sir.' She laughed.

He tipped the coffee mug in her direction. 'Thank you again for the kindness. Can I walk you back to the fireside?' He assisted her to her feet, pausing while she fussed to right her skirts which were already well smoothed.

'Thank you.' Although it was not offered, she took his arm and caught him unawares. *Good grief*. Now he was trapped, for to do anything other than smile politely and walk arm in arm with her to the fire would fall into the realm of the very churlishness he had been avoiding. Anne Hampton was making sure that everyone else in their party was aware of their conviviality, giving them all a grand view of them walking back to the large bonfire where later the men would sleep, while the women retired to tented accommodation.

Is she staking her claim? he wondered. *Dismantle her hopes now*, urged a voice in his mind.

He slowed their approach. 'I never did share why I've come to Africa, have I, Miss Hampton?'

'No, Mr Grant. You are indeed rather mysterious about your journey.'

He gave a mirthless gust of laughter. 'Hardly mysterious, but I'll admit I'm a private person. I've kept it to myself because it's for sad reasons that I journey to the interior.' He briefly explained about Clementine's situation.

She stopped walking now, turning towards him, the others forgotten momentarily. 'You mean you're taking on your sister's child?'

'Indeed. That is precisely what I mean.' He hadn't mentioned that Clementine was the daughter of his half-sister, or that she had a living father. 'My role now is to be the very best guardian to Clementine that I can be; I'm driven to protect her, provide for her, raise her, educate and love her so she can grow up with affection and all the care and comfort that her mother would hope for her to have. My sister did not wish to live in Africa; it is up to me now to give her daughter the life that Louisa had planned for her.'

'How very gallant of you, Mr Grant.'

Reggie gently extricated himself but continued to guide her the last remaining steps so she barely felt their link was broken. 'Yes, though I'm not sure the special person in my life is ready for a child in hers,' he said, making his final and more brutal effort to angle sweet Anne Hampton off his trail.

The lie caught her unawares. She paused. 'Oh! Forgive me, Mr Grant. I hadn't realised there was a Mrs Gr—'

'There isn't. But there is someone I care about deeply. And I am yet to explain my decision to bring Clementine home with me. You see, when I left, I believed my mission was simply to return her to England, but I've arrived at the conclusion that her father's family are not the right people to raise Clementine. The Grants are her rightful guardians and we have the means and, more to the point, the desire to give this child the upbringing she deserves.'

Anne Hampton looked crestfallen but she raised her chin. 'I am filled with admiration for your mission, Mr Grant, and look forward to hearing that little Clementine is safely in your care.'

She held up her hand and he duly placed a light peck upon her skin, confident that her hopes for him as a serious contender for marriage had been dashed.

'Sleep well, Miss Hampton,' he said. 'See you in the morning.'

He let go of her hand and, after turning to nod at the others who were surreptitiously watching them, he took his leave to unfurl his bed-roll and sleep beneath one of the unhitched wagons with a sense of relief.

7

KIMBERLEY, CAPE COLONY

May 1872

Two men and a little girl stared at the small pile of crumbled rock on a table fashioned from old shipping crates. The table was propped up against one of the walls of the hut they called home, one leg sitting on a wad of newspapers because it wobbled badly.

James Knight sat on a rickety chair he'd bought off a travelling tinker, his daughter sitting on his lap, while their closest friend, Joseph One-Shoe, sat on his haunches. He had adopted this position since he was old enough to walk around alone, and the Knights had been assured it was no discomfort to him, or insult, to be without a timber chair.

The crudely fashioned door of their corrugated-iron hut was closed. The slit of morning light that squeezed around its poorly aligned edges felt all the brighter because they'd so deliberately shut out the rest of the world. They knew this privacy wouldn't last and so here they sat, rigid with tension, preparing to make their most important collective decision. Behind them on a bench were the remains of a breakfast they'd shared; normally they'd clear up immediately but that meant going outside to draw water.

Instead, scraps of porridge slowly hardened onto tin bowls and three quarter-drunk mugs of tea turned filmy as the washing-up was ignored.

A stirring of the dust on the table by a sudden gust of wind outside gave extra focus to what they all gazed upon.

Even in its rough form it had its own fire within.

'It's a monster. There's no other word for it,' James said, none of the previous day's awe lost from his voice.

Neither adult had looked at their find since the moment they'd discovered it. Now it was revealed in their private space. Around it, in varying levels of quality, shimmered other diamonds, tiny in comparison.

'It's the conker, Daddy,' Clementine murmured, more thrilled that her father seemed sober and himself today for the first time in what felt like an age.

'Yes, it is, darlin'. What do you think, Joseph?'

The Zulu didn't answer immediately, giving it his full attention. Finally, he spoke. 'It frightens me,' he admitted.

Clementine gave him a smile. 'Whatever for?'

'It's dangerous, Miss Clementine.'

She looked up at her father and noticed that all the skin of his face was shrunken and fell into the hollows around his eyes and at his cheeks. She'd seen a skeleton in a picture book and it was horrible but she had begun to think her daddy looked like that skeleton. She could feel the bones of his legs through his trousers and the angles of his body meant it was no longer comfy to cuddle up close to him. Today he had no fever, though.

'Because bad men may steal it?' The little girl looked between both her favourite people now. 'Because they may hurt us?'

James sighed and nodded. 'You catch on fast, Clem, and you're not to worry. No one but the three people in this room —' he touched her chest, then his own, and squeezed Joseph's shoulder for effect — 'even know about these diamonds. Not a soul other than us knows about the conker.'

She gave him a smile to let him know she understood. 'We now have eighty-four diamonds plus the monster, Daddy. That's a lot, isn't it?' She stared again at the scattering of smaller diamonds; most looked like two pyramids glued together.

'It's a haul, Clem,' he agreed. She noticed how her father looked sideways at Joseph. 'Tell me your thoughts?'

'The big one is yours,' Joseph replied, not having to ponder.

'You found it!'

'You paid for the claim.'

'Which we agreed to share.' James smacked the side of his hand against his palm. 'Fifty-fifty, Joseph.'

'How do you cut the monster in half, Daddy?'

Joseph found a grin. 'She understands better than us, Mr James.' Her father hugged her. 'We can't, Clem. Only a diamond cutter can work out how to saw through a diamond.'

She considered this. 'Sell it to those men in the tents and then we can share the money they pay us.'

James glanced at Joseph and back at his child. 'We can't do that, Clem. This rough diamond is too big. It . . . it's frightening, just as Joseph says. It can make other desperate men do silly things. To be honest, darlin', I'm not sure anyone in the broker tents could afford this diamond. And besides —' he kissed her cheek — 'if anyone here gets wind that we have something big to sell, everyone will know about it within the day. It puts everyone at risk, even the broker.'

'They'll all be scared of Joseph and his right hook,' she said, punching the air. Both men indulged her with a laugh and then fell quiet again looking at each other. 'So what will we do?' she asked, frowning.

It was Joseph who replied. 'Your father will take this very big diamond and none of us will speak of it to anyone.' He picked it up and let the light shine through it. Even in the rough it spoke to them of the brilliance that sat beneath its surface.

'It's going to be worth tens of thousands, Clem,' her father murmured. 'That's our future there.'

'What about Joseph's future?' Her tone was worried.

'Mine is here,' Joseph assured her. 'A handful of these, Miss Clementine, and I will be safe and well set.'

James gestured at them. 'Take them all.'

'I don't need so many, Mr James.'

'Even so.'

'I don't even need half. What will become of a black African man with that many diamonds in a pouch around his neck, Mr James?' Again Clementine looked between them, searching for the answer because the question was too subtle for her to grasp its full meaning. 'I shall take six, plus Miss Clementine's age.'

'But that's only . . . thirteen,' she said.

'Clem, I don't know if I'm more frightened of the men out there discovering our diamond or your clever brain.'

'You don't have to be frightened of me, Daddy. I love you and so does my brain.'

His skull-like face creased into a crooked grin, and in that expression she saw the father who had gone missing – a face without sadness, only pleasure.

'Darlin', there's something else I have to tell you . . . Er, no, stay, Joseph,' he said as the Zulu took this as his cue to leave. 'I may need you.'

As young as she was, Clementine sensed that Joseph already knew what her father was going to say.

'Well, now that we have our conker, it's time for me to get you home.'

'To England, you mean?'

He nodded.

'Why?'

'Because that's where you belong.'

'Do you belong there?' Did he think she didn't notice him steal a glance at Joseph?

He sighed. 'I don't know where I belong any more, Clem. I think I've let everyone down, especially your mother.'

'If we go to England, it means we have to leave her alone.'

'I will take care of her grave, Miss Clementine,' Joseph said. 'I will change her flowers for you and I will sweep away the dust.'

'Will you say a prayer for her?'

'If you teach me one, I shall. And I shall ask the spirits of my people to watch over her and keep her soul safe.'

She looked back at her father. 'Do we have to go?'

He nodded. 'You need to learn the role of a proper young lady, Clem.' When she opened her mouth to deny this was her wish, he hushed her, putting a finger to his lips. 'This is what your mother would want. She'd want you to wear pretty frocks, eat proper food, not run as wild as I've let you.' He touched one of her curls. 'She'd want your hair washed and brushed shiny with silk ribbons in it. She'd want you to attend a proper school and go to dances and social gatherings befitting a high-born young woman.'

'I'm not ready for that!' she reminded him.

Both men smiled. 'I know, my darlin', but you're growing so fast.'

'Why can't we all go?' She looked over at Joseph One-Shoe, knowing the answer before it came.

'Joseph belongs here as much as we belong in England, Clem.'

Dark, knowing eyes regarded her with an unwavering gaze. If he felt as teary as she did, he wasn't showing it – or rather, he was being strong for her. That's what adults did. They forced themselves not to cry. Her eyes watered but she wanted to be as strong as Joseph.

'When do we have to go?'

'As soon as I can get our transport arranged,' her father said. 'I think the next party of wagons leaves in a few days. We need to get this diamond out of the country, Clem. Do you understand?'

She nodded, dropping her gaze, feeling impossibly sad and wondering how she would ever feel happy again. She didn't know how she would say goodbye to Joseph One-Shoe, sensing somehow that it would be harder than saying farewell to her dead mother. 'We need to name it.'

'What, darlin'?'

'The conker needs a name.'

'It does,' James said, brightening, looking like a man who had been released from a noose. Joseph, however, still looked grave and she understood in that moment that while her father's life looked as though it was going to get better, for she and Joseph their lives were about to change dramatically. Joseph had already explained to her that he couldn't return to his tribe, which meant he was trapped here in the diamond fields, and now his close friends – his family, really – were going to desert him. And for her? She couldn't remember another life. The Big Hole was her home. Joseph was her family.

'What will you name it, Clem?'

She didn't have to think on it; they already had. 'Sirius, of course.'

Her father sighed with pleasure. 'Yes, of course. The Sirius Diamond. Perfect. The brightest star in the sky, and the brightest star in the earth. Excellent choice, Clem. Now,' he said, shifting so she slipped off his lap to her feet and he stood up to stretch. 'I'm going to make some inquiries about an ox wagon, and I might stop off at the pub. Let's eat something special tonight, Joseph. We should celebrate.'

'Yes, Mr James, we should.' He glanced with hooded eyes at Clementine before turning away.

James didn't return to the hut for dinner, despite a feast being cooked by Joseph. On tonight's menu was chicken, with a spicy gravy that Joseph said his mother cooked on rare occasions and was the family favourite.

He told her its name in Zulu, making it sound easy to say, but when she tried she stumbled. 'We also call this running chicken,' he added.

'Why?'

'Because in my village the chickens are allowed to wander everywhere and when my mother chose to kill one for our special meal, she had to chase it. Some clever chicken could keep her running for some time.'

Clem laughed in spite of how moody she'd felt today. 'I'm sorry Daddy didn't turn up for this. It's delicious, Joseph.'

He nodded. 'Your father is celebrating his own way.'

'Nothing about today feels like we should be celebrating. Only Daddy thinks today deserves a feast.'

'You must forgive him, Miss Clem. I think he is as sad as us but he has reached this decision because it's best for you.'

'Well, I don't want to go!'

'I know. But he is looking ahead to when you are older. You cannot see it now but to return to the world you were born into is important.'

'Then why don't you go home to your tribe, Joseph?' She didn't mean to upset him but she was feeling suddenly angry by the decisions of the adults. They didn't suit her and no one seemed to care how she was feeling – not even Joseph, apparently. And even as she let that thought into her mind, she knew it was unfair to think of him this way. Her father was selfish, perhaps – she'd heard her mother murmur that word about him a few times – but Joseph was never selfish. He did everything for others.

'I think they would treat me badly, Miss Clementine.'

She thought he might have stopped short of suggesting they might kill him but that's what she understood from his tone and his serious expression.

Now she felt terrible. 'Shall we go and look at the stars?'

———————

Under the African night she huddled beneath Joseph's blanket. Clementine wished she could share it with him and sit next to his large, warm, muscled body but he would never agree to that and she knew it was because he didn't want to draw the ire of interfering people like Miss Carruthers. So she sat as close as was permissible – companionable without being intimate.

'I see Sirius,' he said, his long arm reaching heavenward to point a finger almost directly overhead.

She tipped her chin back. 'Sparkling so bright.' She traced with a finger. 'Look, Joseph. You can follow a whole line of stars from the northern horizon down to the southern horizon. There's Orion.'

'He is standing on his hands,' Joseph remarked and won a laugh from her.

'I didn't choose Sirius because it is the brightest star in the sky.'

'No?'

'Do you remember when Daddy said its nickname is the Dog Star?'

He nodded his head; she could just see the movement against the dark shadows.

'Well, Sirius is the Big Dog.' She poked him. 'That's you. You're the big dog – you found the conker.'

'And if I guess correctly, you are the little dog?'

She smiled into the night, glad he understood. 'Mummy said she had a dog when she was little and it was her most faithful friend. I want to be your most faithful friend in the whole world.'

'You already are, Miss Clementine.'

'Good. That means we are the two dogs. Sirius and his little friend, Canis Minor. Shall we call him Little Dog?'

'Your memory is as bright as Sirius itself,' Joseph said in awe. 'Do you forget anything?'

She shrugged. 'Mrs Carruthers always says I'm too smart for my own good but I don't think she means that to make me feel happy. She speaks it with an angry face.'

'Soon you won't have to worry about Mrs Carruthers.'

'I don't want to live without you, Joseph.'

'You won't have to, Miss Clementine.'

She watched him place a hand over his heart.

'You will be in here with me every day of my life and I will be with you always.'

'It's not the same,' she bleated.

'It's better,' he said, surprising her with a grin, but again she sensed this was one of those brave adult smiles. 'You'll always be following and I will always be looking over my shoulder and watching, knowing you're not far away in my heart or my mind.'

Her father returned to their hut in the early hours but didn't make it through the door. He collapsed like an old concertina, wheezing with sighing laughter, drunk to the point of unconsciousness as he met the ground. As far as any onlookers were concerned, James Knight was celebrating the sale of a few good-sized roughs that he and the Zulu had unearthed in recent weeks. He'd been seen at the striped brokers' tents, with their bunting and loud signs to lure the diggers to their counters. If anyone had focused on Knight among the other diggers on the hunt for the best sale, they'd have seen him peddle half-a-dozen quality roughs, each with the classic octahedral shape.

Joseph had agreed with the six that James chose; he knew that they needed top-quality roughs to carry off the story of the Knights' departure from their prospecting life. They didn't want anyone to suspect they'd had a good find and were running away. The six roughs would fetch a top price and provide the cover they needed.

'I'll take most of the cash but I'll leave you with all the diamonds you want,' James told Joseph.

'I've told you what I want. To be found with anything more is inviting trouble. I can change those roughs into money when I have to . . . as you know, Mr James, my needs are few,' Joseph had explained.

'Will you dig on?'

The Zulu hadn't hesitated. 'No.'

James had waited for elaboration but none came. 'Then sell the claim. You keep the proceeds, and don't say you don't want them. I won't have time to wait for money to exchange hands. I'll put it in motion if you wish, but I want you to reap the benefits as I am taking away our big prize.'

'No, you are taking away my family, Mr James – worth far more.' Before James could splutter any apologies, Joseph had continued. 'I will not make it difficult. I will help you to get Miss Clementine onto the wagon and on your way to Cape Town.'

'She will fight it.'

He had simply nodded. 'I will hide Sirius and its companions, minus the ones I shall keep, in her toy.'

'In Gillie? That's inspired.'

'Just make sure she keeps her toy close.'

And now he watched him many hours later, showing the results of the sale. Tonight, as much as it galled Joseph to see his closest friend in such a desperate way night after night, he could forgive him this occasion.

The carousing and laughter plus the drunken state, which most of the regular pubgoers believed was normal now for the widowed Scot, played fully into their plan.

But it was only his child on her cot on the other side of the door and the Zulu who finally unfolded from the shadows at the edge of the Big Hole who knew James Knight was not celebrating his gains but still mourning all that he'd lost. As much as Joseph One-Shoe wanted to believe that his friend would stop his self-destructive behaviour when he left Africa, his wisdom told him James Knight was on a slippery descent of grief into a pit of guilt that he might never clamber out from.

In the distance he could hear the tack piano playing in one of the bars. Joseph loved the mellow, rolling sound that a piano could make when played by someone skilled with the instrument; its almost sorrowful call into the night made him forgive James's inebriation tonight. He could be excused because he had convinced himself there was something to celebrate. But Joseph wondered about tomorrow. What would the next day bring?

8

Reggie let out a long sigh as he pressed a clean towel against his face and flicked water from his dripping hair, fresh from a shampoo. He loved the sensation of being clean again. It had been two months since his last soak in a tub and now, here at the Kimberley Club, a gentleman's paradise within a desert of hovels and choking dust, he had rediscovered one of life's simple pleasures: a hot bath.

The irritating sound of a shrieking whistle leaked into his suite. Reggie padded across the rug to the mahogany dresser, where his pocket watch sat. It was midday and he'd been warned that the whistle was sounded at noon to call the diggers at the Big Hole from their pits or sorting canopies to wherever they would have their midday meal.

He'd made a cursory visit yesterday, cadging a lift from a wagon that was taking supplies to the Big Hole. He'd seen firsthand that at the sound of the shrill whistle the men would swarm up from the astonishingly large gash in the earth like an army of hungry ants, disgorged on a signal to hunt for food. He'd passed these monstrous ant towers during his journey, and if he squinted a little, he could convince himself that the famed Big Hole looked like a small-scaled medieval city of ant buildings. The architecture within it comprised towers of rock and dirt, the taller towers backing onto the busiest of the diggers who dug faster, deeper. He wondered in that moment which claim belonged to his brother-in-law.

Most of the diggers ate around the main pit, forever glancing back to their own claims. The rest – perhaps the more trusting, or those who simply knew they were on a hard-luck streak – strode back to the hideous hodgepodge of iron huts, tents and shanties that girdled the region, where presumably wives and families awaited.

'They have one hour each day,' the driver explained, noting Reggie's gaze. 'Although in the full heat of the summer, they have a three-hour break from noon and work later into the evening.'

Reggie nodded without interest. He wasn't the slightest bit invested in these people's lives. He'd decided they may well consider themselves pioneers, adventurers and excitement-seekers, but to him they looked like nothing more than poverty-stricken peasants living rudimentary lives of survival. They looked dirty and bedraggled, and most of them appeared filled with despair. He couldn't imagine his beautiful, immaculately presented sister living hand-to-mouth like these unfortunates.

In truth his body had become a cauldron of rage since he'd read Knight's letter and it still simmered like the proverbial witch's brew. He'd scanned the men as they spilled over the top of the remarkable wound dug into the land with bare hands and simple tools, hoping to glimpse James Knight. When the only men left still dragging themselves over the lip were black, he lost what tiny amount of attentiveness he'd had.

'I'll walk back,' he said, hiding his vexation, but not wishing to spend another moment in the heat and dust. Camp dogs ran around the beggared men and flies landed on every available inch of flesh. He couldn't believe how their skin didn't flinch. He saw tinkers hawking a range of wares, from cigarettes to iron pots, while women sold fresh goods – eggs, bread, a few bruised apples. He smelled old coffee above the stink of latrines, which were surely no more than shallow holes in the ground. In the distance he could see an old ox being led to a slaughter post. Soon blood and offal would be adding their own particular stench to the already overwhelming aroma of filth.

He was not going to hang around a moment longer to witness this cheek-by-jowl existence, humanity at its most base. *No doubt someone is making a lot of money somewhere*, he thought, *but it's not these poor sods.*

When he emerged the following morning and stepped across the chequered floor of the main reception of the Kimberley Club to have breakfast on the verandah, it didn't take him too long to find where most of the diamond riches were funnelled. This gentleman's haven clearly welcomed only the privileged and the wealthy, and Reggie's good luck was that his father's club in London had visiting rights. Leaning on the Grant name, he'd been warmly welcomed and given a splendid suite on the ground floor at the back of the property, where it was peaceful and shaded.

This collection of rooms gave the wealthy a private place to meet in convivial surrounds. Along the hushed corridors photographs of solemn men watched over the passers-by moving up the grand staircase – polished twice daily, he noted, by the black servants – towards the snooker hall or the library. The walls were also adorned with the heads of wild animals; their benign, glassy-eyed expressions suggested death was pleasant, and not at the hands of a man with a rifle. Reggie deduced the beasts had been proudly shot and donated by big-game hunters who'd enjoyed the hospitality of the club.

That only one chairman's name graced the gold-lettered board showed just how new this establishment was. If Reggie was honest, he was surprised that such a place already existed in what was essentially a shantytown.

On the verandah, he reposed beneath slow-turning fans powered by electricity, which most of England still dreamed of. He ate like a royal – and was waited on like one too, by a host of servants in starched uniforms ready to jump at his every whim. They kept their eyes lowered when they addressed him. He could well understand how men of means could get used to this lifestyle, provided they were kept well away from the filth and flies of the diamond fields.

He said as much to a gentleman who gave him a polite good morning as Reggie passed by to reach his table.

'You watch how this place develops. By next year it will be given a proper name. Perhaps you've walked through what looks like a motley group of huts acting as stores?'

Reggie nodded.

'The plans are big. They'll be bricks and mortar by Christmas next, mark my words.' The man extended a hand. 'John Plume.'

Reggie shook it. 'Reginald Grant.'

'Of the Northumberland Grants?'

He was surprised his father's name stretched this far. 'That's the one.'

'You're his son?'

He nodded.

'I was sorry to hear of his passing. He was a bit of a visionary, your old man.'

'Many wouldn't describe him quite so generously.'

'I've been to your family home in London – mind-boggling, I'll admit, but nonetheless intriguing – like a journey around the world.'

Reggie gave a small laugh. He agreed with Mr Plume's observation; he'd only seen the London house once himself, although he wasn't going to admit to that. 'I hope to spend a lot more time there on my return from Africa,' he replied, suitably vague. The idea of a home in London and another in the north was seductive, to say the least. 'I've been in the north for most of the past year,' he said.

'How is your mother?'

He gave a tight smile. Was it worth telling the truth to this stranger? He opted for diplomacy, neither dishonest nor entirely truthful. 'Mrs Grant has been unwell recently, but she is looking forward to my return and no doubt to the English summer.' When in doubt, always talk about the weather, he'd learned.

'Oh, yes, indeed. It's been a grumpy old winter back home, hasn't it? How long are you here for, old chap?'

'Not long.'

'Here for some diamond prospecting, no doubt?'

'I'm certainly here to stake a claim but I'll be gone as soon as I can,' he said, enjoying hiding behind his cleverly chosen words.

The man sighed. 'The heat can send a man mad, they say, and now I believe it.'

'To me the daunting aspect is the sheer expanse of nothingness surrounding us.'

'It's not all bad. Just the idea that you might dig out a diamond the size of a huge pebble is enough to keep most men sane.'

'That big, eh?'

'My word. The Eureka diamond is why we're all here. It set the world on fire. It was displayed at the Great Exhibition in Paris. I don't think most of us here could imagine its worth, although I'm told it's currently in the possession of the governor of the Cape. The next big find could be a single shovelful of dirt away . . . that's how the men who own the claims think, anyway.'

'Are you one of them, Mr Plume?'

'I'm one of a conglomerate. We hold several claims. We've done very well with smaller diamonds.'

'Still searching for the big one?'

'Oh, yes. Always hoping to unearth that one-hundred-carat egg to set off a bidding frenzy in Europe or America.' He grinned.

'Indeed. Speaking of eggs, I'm starving,' Reggie said, catching the eye of a servant, who hurried over. 'I'll have scrambled eggs and some toast with a pot of coffee.'

'At once, sir,' drawled the man, as he probably did a few dozen times per day.

'See you tomorrow, perhaps, Mr Plume?' Reggie continued, turning back to his companion.

'Hope your claim-staking goes well, Grant.'

It seemed that his secret of the Grant empire's failing health was holding tight. How good it would be to find a haul of diamonds or even a single massive diamond to drag his family firm out of the mire! It was a pleasant thought he played with over breakfast to keep his mind occupied as he chewed mechanically and read the paper, predictably called *The Diamond News*.

The weekly newspaper seemed to be doing very well, from what he could see. Advertisers were busy: a place called the Ice House was offering chilled drinks and refreshments; a group called Christy Minstrels was making its debut at Parker's Music Hall; a man called Joel Myers at the Iron Store was offering to take any form of payment for the full range of tools that farmers and diamond diggers could possibly need. Forty merino sheep were missing, although the report didn't mention the word 'stolen'; meanwhile, a reward of one pound was being offered for a pocket watch that the owner had no issue with claiming had been stolen from Klipdrift. He shook his head with mild awe. Reading the advertisements was nothing short of entertaining, and he passed most of the morning over an expansive breakfast and several pots of coffee.

He finally flapped his newspaper closed, deciding it was time to fulfil his promise to Lilian Grant and find her granddaughter.

He had no proper plan in place, beyond passage on a ship for two adults and a child in just under two months. His hope was to time himself so well that he could board the same ship that had brought him to the Cape and was presently wending its way to and from that great landmass they called Australia. He needed approximately forty-five days to be back in Cape Town, ready for the voyage. Back in his room he looked at himself in the mirror to check he was ready.

'That means you have four days, Reggie,' he told his reflection as he combed his moustache, thinking about whether he should go clean-shaven for his return to England. He stared at the mirror's image. He would look handsome enough without his moustache and he'd also look younger; his intention had been to appear older in order to be taken more seriously. Now he wanted with all of his heart to see every ounce of Louisa that might run through his family blood. That might be a subtle yet powerful Grant family message to pass on to Knight. 'We want our child back,' he murmured to the reflection. *We need her* is what he didn't utter aloud.

Four days to find and convince James Knight that he should come back to Britain; that the remaining Grants would make him welcome, provide for him and his child until he got on his feet. Reggie was already imagining finding Knight an irresistible engineering role in a company far from Northumberland. He even entertained the idea of setting up Knight in his own firm, but whichever way he could lead the man, he needed Clementine to be left behind in the care of her grandmother. The more he could dislocate Knight from his daughter, the more he could draw the child into the bosom of the Grant family until the little girl would refuse to be separated from the only woman left in the world who loved her and could provide everything she needed.

It worked in his mind. James Knight and his pride were the only obstacle.

'So don't lose your calm, Reggie,' he told his reflection. 'Be persuasive. Use all your cunning skills of coercion. Bring them home.' He nodded at his neat image, newly laundered and pressed. He looked convincingly like a man relaxed in his wealth. No one needed to know otherwise, especially not Knight.

'Let's go find them,' he said to his other self.

———

It felt like he'd spent the last few hours chasing after shadows. James and Clementine were here but Reggie kept missing them at every place he was sent to – including a saloon that smelled of stale whisky, vomit and beer swill. Surely James wouldn't have brought his child here?

'He called in for a nip about an hour ago. He'll be back at the fields now. The whistle's gone for the end of the luncheon hour.'

It reminded Reggie he should be hungry too. 'Will he be back later, do you think?'

The man wiping glasses behind the makeshift counter grinned. 'Well, Jimmy loves his liquor but probably not here. He likes to go to the one over there of an evening.' He pointed with his chin. 'Although as I understood, he and his sweet little girl were going over to Bordinckx and Fallek.'

Reggie repeated the name. 'Should I know it?'

'Only if you've got roughs for sale, mister.'

'And where is this shop?'

'They have an office in Main Street, right here. But he bought his little girl a lemonade for the journey – so he said. I'm guessing they are going over to Du Toit's Pan.'

'Dewtoytzpen?' he said, sounding out what he'd heard with a confounded frown.

The man repeated it slowly. 'You'll need to hitch a ride, mister – unless you plan to walk through the scrub in those fancy shoes?'

He ignored the jibe. 'Where do I find Mr Bordinckx or Mr Fallek?'

Now the fellow openly laughed. 'I have no idea if you'll find them, but Jimmy Knight was headed for Martin's Hotel.'

'Why would he journey there, if there is a merchant of the same firm right here?'

'Most likely because he doesn't want to show his rivals that he's had a good find. That's usually why diggers head out to peddle their roughs in private.'

'I see.' He felt a prick of pleasure. So James was finding diamonds. This was a good omen, but it meant the conversation could go one of two ways. Either James would be open to returning home with full pockets, perhaps even relieved to have someone bully him into leaving – or the find could make him more determined to seek the fortune all these men obviously believed they could achieve.

'Then you stay, James,' he murmured under his breath as he lifted a hand in farewell to the bartender. *And we'll look out for Clementine.*

As he turned back onto the dusty path they called Main Street, he decided it was pointless to go hurtling off to another pioneer town. He'd found Knight's claim after searching and weaving his way through the mass of filthy people busy at their toil, but all he could see when he squinted through the dust was an African working the pit. James had hired his own slave, presumably, to give him more time to . . . what? To spend with his child? To drink? He'd asked around, begun building a picture of Knight, and he didn't like what he was hearing. And worse, many people kept referring to a Zulu called Joseph One-Shoe. What sort of name was that? Why did an African feature so strongly in Clementine's life?

'Lock up your supply of whatever whisky, mister,' one wit remarked. He won a big laugh from the other men standing around taking a break from digging, who were watching their women shake through pans, looking for the elusive glint. Most of the women looked too weary to join in the amusement, although one did catch up with him as he departed.

'Mr Grant?'

He turned, irritated that she'd touched his jacket. He glanced at her hands: rough and calloused, although she'd obviously rinsed and wiped them dry on her apron.

'What is it?' He couldn't hide the testy tone. It was hot and he was parched, in every sense of the word.

'Are you family to James Knight?'

Reggie wouldn't say she possessed a cultivated manner, but she was English and clearly educated. He blinked. 'I am his brother-in-law.'

'Oh, you're Louisa's kin. I'm so sorry for your loss. She is missed.'

His lips firmed to a line.

'I'm glad you're here,' she said, sounding suddenly superior. She lifted her chin and tucked back a lock of hair that had escaped her makeshift linen bonnet. Educated but fallen on harder times, no doubt. 'You need to see to it that Louisa's child gets proper care and attend to her education. She's running wild, that girl.'

Well, well. She had the audacity to berate *him*, the very person who had come to help Clementine, to make sure she was raised with care and gentility. 'And who are you, please?'

'I'm Mrs Carruthers. I run the schoolhouse.'

He looked her up and down with a puzzled expression.

'School is three days a week just at the moment,' she offered defensively. 'I help my brothers in the fields when there's no class hours – but even if it were a school day, I doubt Clementine Knight would appear. That child plays truant most days. She's extremely wilful, and do you know, sir, I have a suspicion that your niece considers herself too clever for school.' She leaned in with an extra baffled frown. 'Can you imagine such a thing?'

Schoolteachers had plenty to answer for, in Reggie's cold opinion; she was not speaking to the converted. 'How old are you, Mrs Carruthers? You look very young yourself, if you'll pardon my observation.' He smiled generously but already disliked the woman, with her unsolicited advice and her quarrelsome approach.

'I'm twenty-two, sir. I may be shaking through dirt to find diamonds for my brothers but I had little choice being brought here. My husband was a missionary, and he died soon after our arrival. We had hopes of starting our own mission for these poor unfortunate natives, but I can no longer rely on that dream. I find myself living with my family until we can all return home. All these men hope to make it big.' She sounded disdainful. 'Nevertheless, I have an education and I plan to at least help the children of the diamond fields to perhaps have the opportunity to choose a different path to their parents.'

Haughty little harridan! 'I'm sure all the parents here appreciate the keen interest you take in their children's welfare.' He took pleasure in watching her eyes narrow as she assessed whether this was praise or sarcasm. 'I will ask you not to worry yourself over our Clementine, however. When she left England she was brighter than most twice her age, and I suspect her lack of attendance is because she is bored by the tedium of what you teach, Mrs Carruthers. You have no cause to fret over her education. Clementine will be receiving private tutoring of a far higher quality in the coming months, which will allow her wit and intelligence to expand to their fullest capacity. Good day to you.' He lifted his hat and strode away before the shocked woman could gather her thoughts sufficiently to respond.

He smiled inwardly. No Grant should ever be trifled with – not even a seven-year-old. He did a circuit of the Big Hole, surprised at how long it took him to walk it. By the time he had reached the road that led back into the town, if you could call it that, he noted that the Knight claim was empty. The black worker had left. Reggie, hot and sweaty now, wended his way back towards the rows of shanty huts where he'd been told the Knights lived. It had been such an appalling discovery that he'd avoided walking this way sooner, but now he felt he had no choice.

Names were daubed onto doorways and he found the Knight hovel soon enough. The entrance was open, and he didn't have to peer very far into the gloom. It was a tiny space, hardly bigger than the boot room at Woodingdene. There was no sign of Clementine, so presumably father and daughter were still at that place he could no longer remember how to pronounce.

He was startled by the emergence of a man. This must be the Zulu warrior he had heard about. At least he wore shirt and trews, although they were as rough as anything the other diggers wore. One foot, he noticed, wore a boot; the other was unshod. How peculiar – but now he understood the man's name.

'Good morning, sir,' the Zulu said in perfect English.

That took him aback. 'Er . . . I'm looking for James Knight but I gather he's —' he wanted to say 'out of town' but this was hardly *in town* — 'not here.'

'He has travelled to Du Toit's Pan today, sir, to get supplies.'

Stupid unpronounceable name. 'And when will he return?'

'In time for dinner,' the man said. 'I am Joseph One-Shoe.'

Reggie flashed a contrived smile. It was gone as soon as it arrived. 'So I gather,' he said, glancing down at the man's large feet.

'Miss Clementine named me,' he added.

'I see. Well, let Mr Knight know that his wife's brother is here.' He didn't think the Zulu would understand 'brother-in-law'. 'And that I wish to see him.'

'Yes, sir.'

'I'm at the Kimberley Club.'

The man nodded.

'Do you know where that is, boy?'

The black man's expression did not change; Reggie found his calm vaguely irritating. 'He does, sir.'

'Well, I shall expect to see him this evening.'

'I will tell him, sir.'

'Right. Get back to your duties, then,' he said, waving a dismissive hand. Reggie found the man's dark stare unsettling: it seemed to look deeper into his being than he found comfortable. The Zulu dipped his head in a polite nod and disappeared back into the hovel.

Reggie tugged uncomfortably at his starched collar before turning towards the street that would lead him back to the oasis of the club. He needed to think through his approach to Knight and that was best not done on an empty belly. There was roast chicken on the luncheon menu, he'd noticed, and suddenly he was ravenous.

9

Clementine looked between her two men, sensing a tension that hadn't been there moments earlier when they had arrived back from Du Toit's Pan with a happy air and fresh groceries following the sale of some diamonds.

'Go through it again,' James demanded.

She didn't know why her father needed this – even she could repeat what Joseph had clearly explained once they were both seated and he had ladled out the bean soup he'd had simmering on their tiny wood stove. He'd even warmed some of yesterday's loaf, which he'd cooked in embers the Zulu way. She noted that Joseph didn't so much as blink at her father's bidding; she wished she could learn his patience. He repeated their visitor's words.

'He said to let you know that your wife's brother is here. He is staying at the Kimberley Club and he plans to see you there this evening.'

Clementine thought her father looked suddenly ill, which was sad because they had enjoyed such a happy day. He'd bought her a new dress because he said she deserved to look pretty like her mother; they'd bought Joseph a new shirt because the only one he had was tattered beyond repair. And they'd each had a glass bowl of ice-cream that to Clementine tasted like every birthday she could remember put together. Her father had tipped back his chin and laughed at that, his mouth filled with the creamy strawberry and vanilla treat. She had chosen chocolate as well as a scoop of the pale green mint flavour. As if that wasn't enough, he father had called in to the new establishment by the pastry cook and confectioner Mr Thomas, which had newly opened in Du Toit's Pan.

They had chosen a box of decorated treats, including some rolled wafers enclosing a nutty paste and dipped in chocolate, and a tiny cake each that Clementine was sure she could consume in a single swallow but she would be sure to nibble on to make it last. Hers was so pretty, with dainty sugared flowers that Clementine wanted to learn how to make. The slices of treacle tart they'd bought would keep until tomorrow. As a final treat, she'd been allowed to choose one product in the grocer's store to take back to Joseph and she'd chosen a tin of Lyle's Golden Syrup. The deep ooze that shone glossy amber when she pulled a teaspoon of it out of the tin had entranced her. They'd brought a tin of it with them when they'd come to Africa and they still used that tin now for their coppers; her father shook it each afternoon before he went to the pub.

The distinctive green tin with its odd image of a dead lion and bees swarming around it now sat untouched on the table. All the fun of their trip and the goodies they'd brought home had evaporated at the news that a man had come to visit her father.

'Is he important to us?' she asked in all innocence, while sipping her soup, trying to join the conversation.

'He is your uncle,' her father said in a tight voice. He'd sat back from the table as though he no longer had an appetite.

'Drink your soup, Daddy. Joseph made it for us.' That sounded like something her mother would say. She'd learned from her mother how to encourage him.

'I'm angry now.'

She could see that. 'Why?' she asked, even-toned.

'Because, Clem, this man is here to make trouble for us.'

'If he's my uncle, then he's family. Shouldn't we be pleased to see him?'

'He's here for something. He's hardly visiting.'

Joseph shifted on his haunches. Clem knew it was his way of speaking without speaking.

'What?' her father demanded.

She watched their friend lift a shoulder slightly in a shrug. 'He might be here to visit his sister's grave, Mr James.'

'Mark my words, Joseph, he's here to cause us pain of some sort. I won't go to his rich man's club, I tell you.'

Clementine saw her father stand suddenly; it was an insult to Joseph's meal.

'I'm going to the pub.' He dug in his trouser pocket and pulled out a fistful of money.

Clementine gasped.

'Here,' he said, flinging it onto the table. Notes fluttered around like leaves, some falling to the floor.

No one moved for a moment. Then her father grabbed a small pile of notes. 'The rest is yours, Joseph, and you can keep some aside for food.'

'That is too much, Mr James,' Joseph said, shaking his head with disappointment.

'It's yours, I say. Put it away, hide it, spend it, I don't care. You work harder than I do on any day and you've earned it. We got a very good return on our roughs and we've got plenty more to sell.'

'Daddy, why is he here, do you think?'

'I don't know. He probably wants us to come back to England.'

'Isn't that what you want?'

'I won't be pushed around by the Grants. They've tried that before. They like to own and control. I won't have it. I'm a proud man, Clem, and your mother loved me just how I was. Whatever he wants, whatever he's selling, I don't want it. We'll go back to England, but it will be on my terms, darlin', and not because your wealthy uncle clicks his fingers. We are going to be as rich as him. I'll show them!'

He left Clementine and Joseph in a shared astonishment at his hostility, their soup cooling before them.

'Eat up,' Joseph said, when the echo of the slamming tin door had faded.

Clementine frowned. 'Joseph, I can't follow what Daddy is saying. He wants to go home, yet he's worried this man has come to ask us to come home.'

'I think grown-ups do not always think as clearly as children do, Miss Clementine.'

'Why is Daddy so angry?'

Joseph gave her one of his big shrugs. 'Your father is angry in here, Miss Clementine,' he said, placing a large hand over his heart. 'He cannot forgive that your mother died and he was not able to save her.'

'Who can't he forgive?'

'Himself.'

Reggie whiled away the hours waiting for James Knight to present himself by finding his way to the local cemetery. The man in charge looked up a book and then asked Reggie to follow him. The man was respectful and polite but asked no questions. Perhaps the flowers that Reggie had ordered through the Kimberley Club's contacts spoke enough about why he was here and hunting down the grave of a woman called Louisa Knight.

'Her husband and their little girl visit most Sundays,' he remarked to Reggie as they walked along the indistinct pathway.

Reggie presumed this was the man's attempt at conversation to prevent an otherwise awkward silence.

'I am probably her only other family who will ever visit,' he remarked. 'Can I leave some money behind so I can rely on her grave being kept tidied and tended to each week with fresh flowers?'

'You can, sir, but the family is careful to take care of the grave.'

'Nevertheless, please make the arrangements and forward all necessary documentation to me at the Kimberley Club as soon as you can. I am only here for a few days.'

'Very good, sir.' The man paused, then pointed. 'Mrs Knight sleeps here, Mr Grant.'

Reggie turned and looked to where the man gestured. He hadn't expected to feel such a surge of sharp-edged emotion, and while he was able to blink away the tears that threatened, his throat closed instantly, like a knot around a rubber balloon, trapping air inside. His lungs felt tight. *Sleeping.* What a generous way of describing his sister, who had left him so full of life and its promises, lying beneath several feet of earth and crawling creatures.

After the man had departed, Reggie bent to lift out the dead wildflowers and put his bouquet of carnations and roses into the earthen jar. He touched the stone, glad to see Knight had at least done that much, although he'd failed to mention her loving family left behind in England. All that was carved into the stone was that she left behind her beloved James and cherished daughter, Clementine. Perhaps that was all the text his money could stretch to, but still he couldn't find any forgiveness for Knight.

'You are so missed, Louisa. Life has not been the same since you passed. I know you live on in Clementine, and I've come to fetch her home, Louisa. It's what your mother wants, it's what

I want . . . I will make sure she is raised as you would wish for the child of a gentlewoman. She will want for nothing, I promise.' He paused, taking a breath. 'Give me a sign that this is your desire,' he pleaded. Reggie believed in omens and he fancied himself a good reader of portents. He waited. Was the breeze stirring the grasses beyond the cemetery a message from the grave? He doubted it. He wasn't quite so gullible. But as a single petal from one creamy rose fell to land on the grave, to Reggie it was as though Louisa had invisibly reached up from the depths with a ghostly finger to tap the flower and give him the permission he sought.

'Thank you,' he said fervently. 'I will not leave Africa without her, no matter what it costs or takes from me. Rest peacefully now, my darling.'

Reggie touched his hand to his lips and then placed those kissed fingers on the cool granite of the headstone once again. 'Clementine will be in my care by tomorrow.' It was an audacious graveside promise. Even Reggie was surprised by what had slipped out. It was as though his words were riding a wave that was all emotion: fierce and white-capped, he'd ride it all the way home.

James Knight had not doffed his cap to the Kimberley Club. He knew its members were not the sort of men who clambered into pits and dug for a living. No, these were the men who used their existing wealth to generate more, and in this town that meant acquiring other people's claims. There were educated men, like Mr Cecil Rhodes, and there were the rougher sort, like Barney Barnato, but they all made their extravagant fortunes selling diamonds to merchants in Europe. Was Reggie Grant now planning to become one of them, he wondered? Copying him! Living off the fat of the Grant empire wasn't enough for the jumped-up half-brother. Now he had to come and lord it over his sister's widower – rub that viciously rough salt into a gaping wound that simply wouldn't close.

James swallowed the dregs of his fourth pint and signalled to the barman for another chaser of whisky. They no longer gave him that perplexed look – the one that said, *Haven't you had enough, Knight?* No, now they just poured so he could wallow deep in his sorrows.

'Wouldn't take much to blow you over these days, Jimmy,' the barman observed. 'You look like a walking skeleton, man. Get some food into you before you keel over and die.'

James raised a dismissive hand and gave a sound of disgust. 'I'm just fine, Mac. My life's about to take a turn upwards,' he slurred, voice getting louder.

Men nearby laughed with expressions that said they'd heard it all before – from others and from him.

James turned towards them, half standing, half falling off his barstool. 'You got something to say, you fellows?'

They waved his question away but he wasn't about to be ignored. 'You know nothing! But in the next few weeks you'll know all about James Douglas Knight.'

'Oh, yes? Why's that, then?' someone asked.

'You'll see,' he slurred, staggering. 'I'll make the newspaper.'

'Is that right?' the barman said with a grin. 'Go on, Jimmy, get yourself home. I'm not serving you any more. You've got a little girl to look after.'

'Don't you fucking tell me my business, Mac.'

Mac looked surprised to hear James swear. He glanced over at a burly guy by the door, who was paid to keep the peace. While James Knight didn't look as though he had enough strength in him to swing a punch, he sounded as though he was working up to picking a fight. The minder strode over and manhandled James outside to the street, his stubby finger in James's face a sufficient threat.

'Don't come back tonight, Jimmy. Get yourself cleaned up and sober, and eat something, for Pete's sake.'

James responded with a stream of curses that won laughter from passers-by. The local minister unfortunately happened to be on the other side of the street and clearly felt obliged to check on one of his congregation.

'Mr Knight?'

'Minister,' James said, obviously believing himself to be entirely in control and able to hold his head up straight.

'Shall I accompany you home?'

'I'm perfectly well,' he ground out.

'You don't look well, Mr Knight?'

'See you on Sunday, Minister,' he said, lurching away.

'But it is Sunday,' the church man called to James's back. 'I didn't see you this morning.'

James was past caring about manners, about appearances, about what people thought of him.

'We're leaving tomorrow!' he growled at the heavens, shaking a knobbled fist that looked more like a clenched claw.

His awareness was dulled and he didn't see the tall, dark-suited figure angling towards him until Reggie Grant's sneering face was close enough for him to discern.

'Don't you dare ignore me, Knight.'

'Get your hands off me,' James slurred, pushing at the fingers that clutched his bunched shirtfront.

Reggie let him go, but even through the liquor James felt the bastard son's furious expression momentarily pinning him as effectively as if he'd closed a hand around his throat. James knew he was no longer that strong, wiry man who'd brought a young wife and child to the diamond fields. And the strength that his hard work as a digger had given him had evaporated when he'd turned to the bottle. Only in this heartbeat, as he witnessed his brother-in-law's hatred and disgust, did he understood that all the hard work of recent times had been shouldered by Joseph. He had become an overseer, happy to give orders, unaware of how comfortable he'd clearly grown at watching another man do the strenuous toil, and utterly at ease in his mind that they should share the spoils. He'd obviously convinced himself that he was being fair by ensuring Joseph got his share, but it was not the right share. It was relatively tiny, and though Joseph might deny that he wanted more, James had become a useless burden.

As if Reggie could hear this internal conversation, he joined it. 'All you've ever done is take, James. And before you fuss and remind me you've not taken a penny from us, I'm not referring to money – not yet, anyway. But you took away something far more precious to the Grants: our women. Clementine is our heir. And by bringing my sister and niece to this hell, you took away their lives. At least in Australia my sister might have lived the life of a gentlewoman, but look what you did to her. You surely killed Louisa with your desperate and useless bid to make a name for yourself.'

James wasn't going to hear it. He shoved Reggie aside, and he knew the man only toppled away because he was taken by surprise. If Louisa's brother had been ready for James, he'd hardly have shifted the tall man more than a step or two. Why weren't there others around to help him? The wretched minister was not here when James really did need him. The street was empty and veiled in darkness, save the thin luminosity that spilled from the candlelight through the hut windows but could not reach them.

He passed a group of African men seated around a small fire. They were singing a song in a language he didn't know. It didn't sound uplifting; it was a song of sorrow and matched his mood. He stumbled, lurched, wove his hideously drunken path past them. Not one even glanced up to notice him.

James looked back. The action made him dizzy and nauseous. But he could see the shape of Reggie following. Reggie was not so tall that people might comment but he appeared overwhelming to James in this state of mind and body. Reggie wasn't even hurrying.

So now James tried to hasten. In his mind, he was sure he was running. He didn't want to head for home and Clementine – he wanted her nowhere near this uncle of hers until he could sober himself up and face Reggie feeling more in control. Instead he veered towards the Big Hole itself. Reggie wouldn't know his way around but James felt confident, even in his hazy thoughts, that he could outmanoeuvre his brother-in-law in and around the pits. He could walk those narrow ways like a tightrope, while Reggie would find the maze too hard to navigate.

He risked the nausea and glanced over his shoulder again. Reggie hadn't gained on him, but he didn't look at all bothered by the distance between them. He was advancing at a slow, steady pace that was perhaps meant to intimidate. James yelled back something unintelligible, although to him he was cursing the Grant family in perfectly understandable English. He tripped and fell over but somehow hauled himself back to his feet, pausing briefly to empty his belly. He vaguely imagined the contents spattering onto his boots, and it was a vision of Louisa looking disappointed that flashed through his mind. The vague sense of dampness at one knee, suggesting he'd broken the skin and was now bleeding, spurred him on. He staggered and was befuddled to see that there was no one at the Big Hole. He pulled at his pocket watch but couldn't see the hands for the dark. How long had he been drinking?

He swung around and Reggie was just twenty strides away, maybe. James took off – or so he thought. He loped in the opposite direction to the most densely crowded maze of structures. He had arrived into the darkest, most deserted area. And then he couldn't go any further. James bent double and groaned up the rest of the liquid that had been sloshing around in his stomach. The whisky came back up; it hurt as if a cauldron of acid had spilled out of him. He was sure he wept, tears mixing with spittle as he gagged and cried long after his belly felt empty. The noxious smell enveloped him and for a while he lay staring at the black dome of the sky, its moon and stars hidden tonight beneath clouds. Much-needed rain was coming.

He came fractionally back to his senses and wondered if Reggie had been a ghost – a trick of his imagination. He looked around and felt his painful insides twist harder when he saw that Reggie had found some crude bench on which to make himself comfortable while James was being sick.

James watched him light a cigarette and fling the spent match aside; it fluttered like a firefly to the ground. He hauled himself up with another groan, regretting his decision to come to the Big Hole. 'Why are you even here, Reggie?'

'Good question, James. The right one, too, because it cuts straight to the point. As you know, my father died.'

'So what?' He could see this surprised and perhaps wounded Reggie. When had he become this nasty person? He didn't like himself any more but he also detested this man, so it mattered less, he supposed.

'So what? Well, I'm now in charge of the family firm.'

'Why should I care, Reggie?'

'Because I am now the sole custodian of the business and those who depend upon it.' When James said nothing to this he continued. 'Lilian is dying.'

'Good.'

'I didn't know you to be cruel or quite so ill-mannered.'

'And I didn't know you to have a single feeling for Lilian Grant. She hates you – or at least she didn't mince her words in public about the bastard son of her husband.'

'And yet, in spite of that, Lilian and I have recently found common ground.'

'Is that so?'

'It is. The common ground, James – figuratively speaking – is right here in Africa.'

His gaze narrowed, both with the headache that was coming on and his confusion at Reggie's words. 'Don't tell me you're planning to make a diamond claim?' He could hear the loathing but also despair in his tone.

'Oh, I may well do that. I find this whole set-up intriguing. Hire some Africans, like that burly fellow of yours, and perhaps I can find myself some of these gems that the world lusts after.' He took a long drag on his cigarette and James watched the glow from the tip light up Reggie's face. He saw a keen resemblance to Louisa that hurt his soul – and then it was gone, as Reggie pulled the cigarette from his lips and blew the smoke in his direction. 'No – as I said, it was figurative. The common bond that glues Lilian and me together is, funnily enough, family. I think she has come to accept that Grant blood runs freely in my veins, and I've come to realise – too late, I'm ashamed to admit – that Lilian is a formidable woman whose only desire is to keep her family strong and close.'

James gave a jeering laugh. 'So she's left with you?'

Reggie did not react as James had hoped. Instead he shook his head as if genuinely considering the question. 'I don't qualify as family entirely, and neither do you . . . entirely. But Clementine does. She is heiress to a mighty fortune, as you may have guessed.'

'Do I look like I even care about her fortune, Reggie?'

'Care? The word is irrelevant. Addicts don't care about anyone or anything except whatever it is they're addicted to. Frankly, you're acting like a man who would drink that fortune and piss it down the drain, James.'

'So why are you here? To save Clementine her fortune?'

'Whatever I set out to achieve, I realise I'm now here to save a man's life.'

James half closed his eyes, baffled, trying to work out what Reggie wasn't saying. 'I don't understand' was all he managed to reply.

'You're a drunk.' He held up a hand. 'No, please don't argue with this. I have asked around and I know that you are battling demons but you're using the wrong weapon, James. The bottle won't save you, it will kill you – but I suspect you are feverish; I saw it in your glassy eyes earlier. You are sickening.'

Fever. So that's what had been chasing him since yesterday; it hadn't occurred to him that he was becoming ill. It had been such a happy day with Clem today, too, and he'd pushed aside the nag of the headache, the slight tremble, the chills when everyone else was in shirtsleeves puffing at the heat. He had no time for fever. 'That may be. But very shortly I'll be using my own fortune to drink with. Meanwhile, you'll always be beholden to the woman you hate, and trying to live up to your sister's memory.' James didn't know he was capable of such cruel words, but Reggie had made it clear years back that he wanted as little as possible to do with the man who was stealing his sister.

'Listen to me now, James. It's time to come home. Clementine cannot grow up here, wild, like a poverty-stricken urchin, being raised by an alcoholic and a black. Come on, man! If you won't think of yourself, think of Louisa and what she would want for her only and most precious child.'

'I think of nothing *but* Louisa,' he slurred, spittle dribbling angrily to the ground. 'I *am* bringing Clem back.'

That seemed to shake Reggie. 'Back to Northumberland?'

He laughed without mirth. 'I'm not that stupid. Back to Scotland, probably. As much as it galls you, her surname is Knight. And when I get back I will have enough money to support us without needing to touch the fortune you jealously guard. She can have it when she turns thirty. Until then she's my responsibility and my child to take where I please.'

'Now, listen to me. I want to help.'

James hauled himself to his unsteady feet. 'Help whom? Yourself? Why else would you come unannounced if you didn't have a plan, Reggie? I seem to recall you were always someone with a plan – a plan for Louisa, a plan for us when we got married, a plan for all of us to go into business – do you remember that?'

'I do. It was a sound idea.'

'Yes, but it was all about you. Her money, your great investment idea. At least I tried to set up a life based on my own abilities.'

'And you call this a life, do you, James? Digging around in the desert of Africa, living in a tin hovel, barely able to feed yourselves. Your daughter scruffing around like a gypsy rat, waiting for her drunkard of a father to bother to return. And if he doesn't, never mind, there's a thick-skulled Zulu who'll take care of her needs.'

'He's a warrior – don't you dare insult him. He is important to us and he does take care of her . . . of us, actually.'

'James, are we talking about the same person? He's a barbarian who walks around barefooted – no doubt if you gave him half a chance he'd prefer to be naked and flinging a spear at us.'

James advanced faster than either of them thought possible and stabbed at Reggie's chest. 'At you, maybe.'

'Take your hands off me.'

'No one asked you here. Go back to your lazy life in England. We're going to be fine.'

'You're going to be dead soon, more like, and then what?'

'I'm going to be rich soon, you bastard.'

'Oh, yes? With what, you disappointing porridge-toad?'

The insult was so base, so full of prejudice, that James felt a need to strike back, and he had one ace up his sleeve. *Two, actually,* he thought with a heartbeat of smugness, if he counted Clementine. And so James wielded them as weapons. The secret he'd insisted to Clem and Joseph must be kept between the three of them at all costs was now given to the one person he never thought he'd share so much as a convivial nip of whisky with, let alone his most important confidence. To his credit, Reggie remained silent while James did his utmost to smirk his way through his news.

'You're lying,' Reggie finally said, after an uncomfortably long hesitation.

'Believe me or don't. Why should I care? All you need to know is that Clem's future with me is secure. I've booked our transport to Cape Town and tickets are already reserved on a ship back to London.' James grinned lazily, although it wasn't all bravado; the fever was beginning to loosen his mind and make his skin feel clammy. His clothes, baggy though they were, were suddenly slimy around him.

'Show me again how big this diamond is?' Reggie demanded.

James laughed, and could hear that he sounded like a hyena. 'Shhh! The Big Hole has ears.' That amused him further, and his laughter had a manic quality.

He came briefly to his senses as two fists gripped around his shirtfront. 'Tell me about this diamond,' Reggie demanded in a low growl, so close to James's face that on his breath James could smell the fish that Reggie had eaten for dinner.

James pushed away and staggered backwards, aware that he was dangerously close to the lip of the Big Hole. He pointed at Reggie. 'Oh, interested now, eh?' He lurched back once again towards his scowling brother-in-law, no longer able to tell if the Big Hole was to his rear or in front of him. He shook his head, feeling suddenly useless, as the euphoria of the day fell away. The thought of Louisa and the memory of losing her sat on his shoulder; he felt like the ancient Greek figure of Atlas holding up the sky, lest it all fall down and kill the world. Yet his world was already dead. All he could do now was live long enough to see Clementine home, safe, provided for. 'It's worth tens of thousands . . . maybe even scores of thousands – just that one diamond alone. Clem and I can live off it for the rest of our lives.' He wasn't going to mention that he felt his own days were few. 'It's hundreds of carats, Reggie. You probably have no idea what that signifies. But let me assure you, I can tell even as a rough it's damn near perfect. They call that a clearwater stone – I'll put my life on it, it's one.'

'Clearwater? What are you raving about, Knight?'

James, helplessly gripped now by the fever, leapt around Reggie, grinning madly. He knew he must look like a court jester. 'Clearwater. Paragon. Perfect, Reggie. Something you aren't, but your half-sister was. Not a single flaw did she have.' Then he groaned. 'Other than to marry me, perhaps.' He waggled a finger as though he was pleased with himself for making that last remark before Reggie could. 'And when that stone is cut and polished, I daresay they'll write songs about it. I have no doubt in my mind it will be shown at one of the huge international exhibitions. We are talking a once-in-a-lifetime find – and by that I mean . . .' He stooped to cough, threatened to vomit and then changed his mind, holding his chest as he belched. He didn't think Reggie could look upon him with any deeper contempt than he did in that moment. James found his train of thought again, surprised that he could. 'Every single digger here could smash away for a lifetime in this enormous pit and between us we might be lucky to ever find something as remarkable as this stone that Joseph One-Shoe revealed yesterday. Yes, Reggie, the black man. The Zulu warrior who you dismiss as a barbarian. Technically, the stone is his, as is half the claim. He dug it out of the pit. But he gave it to Clementine and me.'

Reggie, trapped in the wonder of the tale, looked stunned. 'Why?'

'Because he possesses something that you've perhaps never experienced in your whole pitiful life. He knows that we love him. And in return he loves us. He has no use for a stone of its size or quality because he knows that men like you jump to conclusions and he would never be permitted to benefit from his find. He wants Clem to enjoy its proceeds, as do I. And that's why we're going home, Reggie. I'm going to sell it, make my fortune, and Clem and I are going to grow old and fat and happy without worrying about Africa or the Grant family or her mother's death ever again.' He was raving. Even he knew it. 'So even if I do die soon, Reggie, it won't be in vain. I will have achieved my aim to make my fortune, and not a penny of Grant money required. Clementine Knight will be a double heiress.'

He did vomit now, bending double and weeping with pain at the burn of the alcohol as still more of it made its vicious way up to scorch his throat on its journey out.

10

Reggie was in shock. As his much-loathed brother-in-law brought up impossible amounts of foul-smelling liquid to splatter near the edge of the Big Hole, his thoughts were already reaching to an even quicker way to alleviate the burden of debt on the Grant family. Perhaps James could be persuaded.

'I came to fetch you both. Let me do that – get you both home safely.'

'We don't need your escort,' James groaned, his throat raw. 'I really do not know why you came all this way. Go away. Leave us alone, Reggie . . . for good.'

'I cannot do that, James. Clementine's grandmother is dying, and she may hate you for the rest of her life if she discovers you prevented her seeing one of the last two living members of her Grant family. Where is your heart? More to the point, where is this diamond you boast of?' He said the last in a tone just above a whisper.

'Safe with the others,' he murmured.

'Others?'

James smiled secretively. 'Plenty of small ones. Her ragdoll won't be able to take another stone now that Sirius is sewn in. Clever Joseph One-Shoe. No one would think to look in a child's toy.'

Her ragdoll? They'd put the diamonds inside Clementine's toy? That had been a gift from the Ghillie. Lilian had thought it frightening and vulgar for a little girl but Louisa had adored its permanent grin and mad hair.

James was still slurring. 'Time for us to go back to my bonny Oban. And you, Reggie, can go back to your father's wife and see what little handouts she'll give you so you can keep pretending you're a man of means and not reliant on an old woman's spare change and a dead half-sister's goodwill.'

It was more than Reggie could stomach. Even now he nursed that old sore: his belief that for all his years he'd been sneered at, even by the very man who'd sired him. He loathed himself for feeling pathetic but he could hear that small voice crying, *I am the innocent – I didn't ask to be born*. He was still doing what Henry wanted; his demands reached from beyond the grave, forcing Reggie to use his agile, street-smart mind to protect the Grants and their assets. Clementine was an asset in myriad ways, not least because of the powerful, strategic marriage he could negotiate for her in years to come. But in the meantime, there was her ongoing trust fund to manage, plus Woodingdene and all of its assets, some of which could be sold for cash. And now – he felt like he was mentally rubbing his hands with anticipation – now there was a cache of diamonds, with one in particular that could solve all the family's liquidity issues in a single transaction. Reggie was dizzied by the potential.

He advanced on the swaying James. 'You have no right to talk to me like that. I came here in good faith to offer you and my niece a home, a chance to set up a fresh life and to give Clementine all that she is entitled to.'

'Reggie,' James slurred, breathing hard. 'In the time I knew you well, you did nothing that wasn't calculated in your own best interests. I've never understood Louisa's devotion to you.'

The damaging remark surprised Reggie in its viciousness as it fizzed and frothed in his mind. James wasn't finished either – he added a final dose of venom.

'There is no love lost between you and me. So stop pretending you care about us and know that I see through you, Reggie. You're up to something and you obviously have a need from us but I can't imagine what unless you plan to steal my little girl from me for some reason. Her name is Knight, not Grant, no matter how hard you wish it to be otherwise. She is simply distant kin through marriage. And by the by, she is not Louisa – you could never make Clementine love you blindly, no matter how hard you want her to. My daughter is far more discerning than her mother.'

James suddenly poked a finger into his chest as the final insult hit. Both hurt. The drunkard didn't know when to stop; didn't realise that he was poking a sleeping wolf when he began again, punctuating his slurring words with another jab to Reggie's sternum.

'You are not worthy of Clementine.'

Enough! Reggie's rage was old, constantly bruised, forever painful, rising out of a wound that refused to heal.

'No, James. It's you who are not worthy of her, or Louisa, or the family name you scorn.' He shoved the lurching, sickening Scotsman to make his point, about to tell him that he would report James to every authority, and even if he had to bribe the man in charge he would use a legal precedent to extract Clementine from her wayward, useless drunk of a father.

Except James was no longer there.

In a flailing cartwheel of limbs, James toppled backwards into the pit of the Big Hole.

11

Reggie stared, open-mouthed, at the space where James had been standing and hurling his abuse just a heartbeat earlier. Now it was empty. He had not made a sound as the pit swallowed him, while the void left by his body was devoured by the dark.

Reggie rushed to the edge and peered into the gloom: he could see nothing. He struggled for his pockets and found a box of matches and lit one. For a brief moment he looked upon the twisted figure of James Knight below. The match burned out as the darkness closed over like the final curtain at the theatre. Horrified and petrified at once, Reggie stared into the vacant blackness it left behind. And then he was on his feet, looking around wildly – there was no one that he could see. To his knowledge, no one had seen them up here talking, let alone arguing. Was that a groan? What should he do?

Go! the voice inside him urged. *Get away from here, now!*

He forced himself not to run. Instead he backtracked, going the longest way around the pit, picking his way with incredible care, with the single intention of being seen coming from the opposite side from where James had fallen. Fallen, yes. That already sounded so much easier to accept.

And as he neared the main street, he dusted down his clothes, straightened himself. He remembered the loose cigarette in his pocket. It would soothe him as much as help him to achieve a casual air as he loped back towards the Kimberley Club, giving the appearance of a man who had been out for a night's stroll after dinner. He smoked slowly, blowing out his fear with each exhalation. The obstacle was out of the way. He could be gone in days with Clementine and that diamond. He wasn't ready to smile yet but the tightness in his chest was loosening and he was sure a brandy would slow his pulse. By tomorrow morning it would all seem easier to stomach.

He had a whole night to get his story right, calm himself and have a plan for tomorrow morning when James was found and they would have no choice but to place Clementine in the care of one of the last remaining members of her blood family.

A day ago Joseph One-Shoe might have claimed he'd experienced the worst shock of his life. Before he'd unearthed Sirius, it was the early death of a distant cousin in a hunting accident that had scarred the young Zenzele. The shock and grief from watching his cousin die from the wound were lasting; the business of being a man, providing for the village, suddenly felt real and dangerous, and he felt he had lost his innocence that day. Sirius had brought a dawning of a different kind. Watching the fall of James Knight, however, trumped them both. The relative who had come with his sneering expression and oily words had just stolen something more precious than any diamond from the Zulu.

He had gone looking for his friend but had melted into the shadows after seeing him being accosted by the visitor, as he had no right to interfere with family business. And so he had watched and followed. He could hear their angry exchange. Understood that this man from England had come to offer them passage back there, to give them a home and particularly to help give Clementine a proper life. With this, Joseph agreed. Allowing her mother's family to help raise her made sense to a man who came from a tribe where everyone looked out for the youngsters. The men obviously disliked each other but James, drunk again, was being obstinate and deliberately perverse.

And then it unfolded so quickly that Joseph had to replay in his mind what he'd witnessed. James had struck the first blow, and despite warning had continued to poke and prod at the Englishman, baiting him. Watching from nearby, his skin already his best defence, Joseph had been shrouded by the dark; even when the man looked up wildly, terrified, he would never have been able to pick out Joseph. He'd scanned for anyone lurking, found no one and believed himself alone.

Joseph grasped it was not intentional murder but James had cried out. Had the man not heard it?

Now crouched over the only man he loved, he accepted that James was dead. He had expelled his final breath in Joseph's arms. By lighting a match from the box the visitor had cast aside in his panic, he could see the pallor of death. He wasn't sure how to feel; Joseph could only touch the numbing sense of loss right now, for him and especially for Clementine. As he cradled his friend's head, sweeping back the lock of thick, dark hair that had fallen across his handsome face, Joseph was already resigned to the futility of raising the alarm that the newcomer had killed James Knight.

Nevertheless, the uncle had released the most important person in this whole sorry story from the future she would have had if she had remained under the care of her father. He would put Miss Clementine's life ahead of her dead parents. Now she had a chance of freedom and a far brighter future, if he could protect the lie that he could already tell was in the making.

With tears tracing a guilty path down his cheeks, Joseph One-Shoe hefted his dead friend over one shoulder. He couldn't bring to mind whose claim this was but it was particularly deep, so the fall had been long. Mercifully, there was a ladder, and with James's lifeless fingers drumming against the back of his thighs, Joseph One-Shoe made the ascent with the heaviest of hearts that his silence was going to help one family member get away with the death of another.

Reggie slowed and shortened his stride, so by the time he arrived at the township he was almost strolling. He hoped only he knew how contrived his casual air was. Reaching into his pockets, he remembered he'd smoked his last cigarette and suddenly yearned for some calming tobacco.

James was dead. The man who had stood in the way of his bringing little Clementine home to the bosom of her family was gone. Reggie now had a very real chance of wiping all the family's debt in a single transaction. The idea sparkled like the diamond that he hoped would be the saviour of the Grant family and its empire.

While he couldn't produce the jolly whistle that he wished he might achieve for its effect, he managed to arrive at the grand entrance of the Kimberley Club, its multicoloured leadlight double doors opening to him like a lover's safe embrace.

'Good evening, Mr Grant.'

He was impressed that the servants already knew his name. 'Nice night,' he replied in a jaunty tone. 'I walked right around the town – it's quite a busy place of an evening.'

'Certainly is, sir. Best to avoid the Big Hole at night, sir. Too many dangers.'

'Oh, I wouldn't dream of it . . . er, Godfrey, is it?'

'Godfrey, yes, sir. Will you be taking a nightcap, sir?'

'I'm a fraction weary. Maybe someone could send some brandy to my suite – enough for a couple of nips? I might do some reading.' He was amazed at how normal he sounded, given he'd just effectively killed a man.

'Of course, sir. I'll have that sent to your suite at once. Enjoy your evening.'

He tucked some money into Godfrey's palm – far more than perhaps was wise, but it never hurt to insure against a loose tongue.

'Sleep soundly, sir,' Godfrey said, pocketing the money.

Sleep itself felt unachievable right now. He crossed the black and white chequered tiles with a pounding heart and the churning thought that a police whistle would go up any moment and a burly hand would grasp his shoulder.

Neither occurred. He heard no disturbance in the quiet streets other than the happy sound of crickets chirruping. Reggie sipped his cognac – a bounteous half-decanter of some of France's finest had been delivered, on Godfrey's instruction, no doubt – as he repeatedly replayed the scene in his mind.

It was an accident. He hadn't set out to hurt James. James had pushed him too far, sneered too often, insulted him too much.

Nevertheless, you are heartlessly going to take his child and steal his diamonds, a voice argued.

And he had nothing to assert that could dispute both of those facts.

———

Amazing himself with his nerveless calm, the next morning Reggie indulged in another splendidly cooked breakfast beneath the cool verandah of the Kimberley Club. He'd sent his suit for cleaning and his shoes for polishing, and was dressed in paler linen so he could present the image of a man taking a break from his business dealings.

He had his gaze firmly fixed on a novel called *Twenty Thousand Leagues Under the Sea*, about the improbable sighting of a sea monster. He preferred the pace of the adventure story to the more plodding drama of the Dickens novel he had also brought along.

'What are you nose-deep in there, Grant?' It was the gentleman staying across from his suite. They'd passed a polite time of day but he hadn't thought the man knew his name.

Glad to be interrupted and to test out just how normally he could behave, he dredged up the perfect grin and showed him the book's cover.

The newcomer nodded appreciatively. 'I do like good illustrations,' he remarked, taking the book and flipping through a few of the leaves.

'I had to order it from Paris.'

'Good story?'

'Just starting, really.' He tried to be sure his voice was steady, confident now that people would be looking for him. 'You're very welcome to read it while we're here.' He wanted to give a strong impression that he was in no tearing rush.

His neighbour nodded. 'I might. Thank you.' He lifted his pale hat and moved on.

They would come soon. James would have been discovered soon after dawn; Reggie had been told most of the diggers got going at first light to avoid the worst of the day's heat. It was Reggie's contention that James was already on a slab in the local morgue, if there was one. He returned to his book.

'Morning, Grant.'

He looked up, trying his best to appear as though he'd been interrupted. 'Ah, hello again.' It was the fellow from the previous day. 'I was just thinking it was time I headed out.'

'Breakfast already done? Good grief, man. Couldn't you sleep?'

'Not really. Today I'm meeting family I haven't seen for a couple of years. Very much looking forward to it – to seeing my niece, in particular.'

'Your family are diggers?'

'My sister died out here. I've come to visit her husband and their child.' He gave a sad gust of a sigh. 'Actually, I'm hoping to persuade them to come home with me.'

'Has he had much luck, this brother-in-law of yours?'

Reggie shook his head. 'No. Fallen on hard times, as I understand it. Another reason I'm out from England. Extend the family hand of generosity, bring them home, put a new roof over their heads, that sort of thing.'

'Most magnanimous,' the passer-by remarked.

Reggie effected an embarrassed shrug. 'The Grant family way.'

The man grinned. 'I hope your day goes splendidly, then. I gather there's been a bit of a ruckus up at the Big Hole.'

'Oh, yes?' He held his breath.

'Something about a body.'

'Heavens! Who?'

'Er, coffee and scrambled eggs,' the man said to a passing waiter, and then waved his morning paper towards Reggie. 'All I heard was it was a drunken digger, found by one of the Africans. No doubt it will all come out over the course of the day. Nothing new about that, though, is there? Will barely cause a ripple, I'm sure.'

'I suppose,' Reggie remarked, feeling his hopes rise. 'Well, I had better start my day. See you this evening, perhaps, Plume?'

'Maybe not. I'm off to Barkly West today to look at some of the alluvial diggings. Might continue on from there.'

'Then I'll say farewell. I hope to be on my way tomorrow with my brother-in-law and niece in tow.'

'That soon?'

'Oh, yes. I'm sure our conversation will be brief. James will either agree or not. I can't fight him.'

Plume shook his hand. 'You're a good man, Grant. We must meet again in England. I should be back in a few months.'

'See you at my club.' He felt his spirits soar as he uttered those words. Now he sounded like a real gentleman. 'Come and have dinner some time at the Travellers Club on the Mall.'

Plume looked impressed. 'Excellent. Travel safely, Grant. I just saw Fry in the reception. Be careful of that one. Heart of a heathen.'

Reggie had no idea what his companion was talking about but let him depart without further query. Feeling calmed that he'd laid two paths with reliable men should he require an alibi, he turned to gather up his book, notepad and fountain pen, only to hear someone clearing their throat.

The club manager regarded him with a darting gaze. 'Mr Grant.' He seemed embarrassed, and hurried along a hovering waiter so they could be alone.

'Yes?' He hoped his frown looked innocent and suitably puzzled.

'Er, Mr Grant, sir. This is slightly awkward but Detective Fry is in the foyer.'

'Detective?'

'He's our senior policeman here,' the manager said.

'To see me?' He sounded appropriately confounded.

'I'm afraid so, sir. A word of warning, sir. Detective Fry and justice do not necessarily walk the same path.' He touched his nose gently in the universal sign language of keeping something private.

'Did he say what this is about?' Reggie asked, picking up his things.

'Best let him explain.'

'Right . . . well.' He gave a flustered sigh. 'Lead the way.'

They walked in frigid silence to the foyer, where a man in a dark uniform was waiting. He stood a head taller than Reggie, who prided himself on his height. The detective's luxuriant moustache twitched as he saw them approach.

'Mr Reginald Grant?' He didn't wait for confirmation. 'I'm Detective Fry. My apologies for interrupting you.' He didn't look at all apologetic, Reggie noted.

'Er, shall we go in here?' the hotel manager offered, quickly ushering both men into the deserted billiards room. 'It's more private.' He closed the swinging double doors and stood to one side.

The room felt vast around him but Reggie avoided looking at the taxidermied heads that hung upon the walls. Their dead eyes nevertheless seemed to stare directly at him, accusingly. They were like a jury, ready to pronounce the murderer guilty.

'What's this about, Fry?' He was glad to hear his own tone of indignation and irritation. It was pitch-perfect.

'It's not pleasant news, sir.' The words were formal; the tone felt unsympathetic.

Reggie looked into a face deeply scarred by smallpox and a throat that wobbled like a turkey's gobbler. 'Is it my stepmother, Mrs Grant?' He sounded appropriately broken. 'I . . . I was hoping to get back . . .'

'This is a local matter.' He sounded heartless now. 'I'm aggrieved to tell you that your brother-in-law, Mr James Knight, was unfortunately found dead this morning at the Big Hole.'

It was real.

Amazingly, it was as though he was comprehending this fact for the first time and it didn't require much acting. Reggie stared at the policeman. He shifted his gaze to the hotel manager, who dipped his eyes out of respect.

'That can't be right,' he choked out.

'It is, sir. One of the diggers found his body and alerted us. Although, as you're the closest adult next of kin, I would be obliged if you would formally identify his body.'

'But I was supposed to meet him today!' His words squeezed out as if he were in pain. 'He and Clementine were coming home with me. It's why I'm here, man!'

'Brandy, please,' Fry snapped at the manager, who moved immediately. 'Mr Knight was not well, sir. I gather he had never fully recovered from the death of his wife, and the barman at one of the locals has confirmed he was well into his cups by the time he left the saloon.' He cleared his throat and his turkey neck waggled. 'Actually, Mr Grant, he was abusive, behaving badly. We believe he was very deeply intoxicated and wandered up to the Big Hole and . . .'

'And what?'

The brandy arrived in a balloon glass on a silver tray.

'Drink it, sir,' the policeman urged.

Reggie obliged. It helped. He must have blanched. His hand even shook when he reached for the glass.

'Your niece is of prime concern.'

'She comes home with me. I'm all she's got. I shall take full responsibility for Clementine.'

The detective's face relaxed and Reggie realised it was Clementine the authorities had been anxious about, and that he had just presented their most-hoped-for solution. And there he'd been believing he might have a fight on his hands but he could now sense the relief like a fourth person in the room, sighing – just short of applauding.

'That's good to know, Mr Grant.'

'Where is Clementine now? Does she know?'

'She has been told. I don't know if you're aware of this but I am assured that she is very close to a Zulu they call Joseph One-Shoe.' He shrugged. 'I've seen them. They lived like family, that trio. I have asked One-Shoe to bring Clementine to the police station.'

'Good. Is that where we're going now?'

'My driver's waiting.'

Reggie didn't finish the brandy, replacing the glass on the tray and thanking the club manager with a nod. 'Lead the way, Detective Fry.'

It didn't take him long to recognise James. He was laid out on a table in what could only be described as a makeshift morgue. It was connected to the police station, which he realised comprised little more than some cobbled-together corrugated iron. He worked hard not to show his bafflement at the surroundings and schooled his features to appear grave. He even managed to tremble as the sheet was pulled back to reveal the slackened features of the brother-in-law he loathed. He turned away from the shrunken version of the man whose looks he'd once envied with a feigned sigh of sad disgust.

'Yes, that's James Knight,' he said. He was glad the body showed no evident signs of a struggle; there was no wound that he could see.

'Thank you, Mr Grant.' Detective Fry nodded and returned the sheet across the corpse's face.

'He didn't suffer, did he?'

'He must have fallen and hit the rocks at the bottom. Our doctor said it would likely have been instant or very quick. Mr Knight was profoundly intoxicated, so it would not be wrong to assume the poor wretch knew nothing about it.'

Reggie nodded with relief, his expression sombre, composed. 'This is most distressing, as there is a child involved.' He needed to move to the pertinent matter swiftly.

'Do you need some time with . . .?' Fry nodded at the corpse.

'No. But thank you. What happens next?' he asked wearily. 'For Clementine, I mean. She is my most important responsibility, now that she's officially an orphan.'

'Yes, yes. Quite true. In fact, she may already be here.'

Reggie gave a pained but barely perceptible shrug as though feeling helpless at such a state of affairs.

'If you'd like to follow me, Mr Grant.' Detective Fry held the door open for Reggie. 'Er, about the burial?'

'Whatever arrangements can be made, I'd be grateful. I'll organise payment to your funeral parlour. You do have one, I presume?'

'All can be arranged, sir.'

'Fine. Bill the Kimberley Club and I'll leave instructions for payment.'

The detective stopped walking. 'You're not staying?'

'No, no. It's far too upsetting. My father died, and my sister not long after. Now James. I must head straight back to England as Clementine's grandmother is gravely ill. Besides, I don't believe Clementine would benefit from seeing her remaining parent buried atop the other, do you?'

The man looked as though he couldn't care any less, so Reggie pressed the point; he wanted to get away from this town as fast as life would permit. 'Lilian Grant is barely clinging to life,' he said, not in the slightest embarrassed by the lie. 'Her dying wish is to see her only grandchild once more, and this is the reason I've made the journey to Africa. I had hoped to persuade James to bring Clementine back to England. We had visions of seeing our family again, giving them a beautiful home of their own and a way of life most would envy.'

The policeman nodded. 'He knew this?'

'I got here too late. I arrived yesterday and missed him and the child by minutes, I gather. They'd gone to some town to get groceries, sell diamonds, I'm not sure . . .' He gave a shrug, pleased that his alibi had so much truth to sit upon. 'I think James would have said yes, given how low his life had stooped.' They started to walk again, slowly. 'And with that in mind, I don't want to waste any time. James is dead, but I can make Lilian Grant's final wish come true by letting her hold her beloved granddaughter once more. The next party leaves here tomorrow, I gather?'

The man nodded. 'Sounds about right.'

'Then I should like to be on that wagon, as I have three berths booked on a ship to London in forty-five days.'

'We just need to see documents that you are who you say you are, sir.' The detective held up a hand. 'Purely a formality. Clementine couldn't be in better hands than her own family.'

'Thank you, Detective Fry. I appreciate your understanding. What about the Zulu who is so protective?'

Fry looked back at him as if he'd just spoken in a language he didn't understand. 'The black?'

Reggie nodded.

'Don't you worry about him. He'll be on his way soon enough, back to his tribe. He'll be in his leopard skin before tomorrow's out, you mark my words.'

12

They stood in what Detective Fry called his office; to Reggie it seemed merely a partitioned-off area of a large hut. Nevertheless, Fry had the semblance of order – a desk and a filing cabinet – although Reggie still held the notion that the man was more like the gun-slinging sheriffs in the vast west of America than the police constables of northern England that Reggie was familiar with. Reggie sensed that the man was not entirely lawful himself, and he had plans to test his hunch. For now, though, he had to face the awkward first meeting with Clementine and separating her from all she knew.

I can make you forget this sorry episode, little Clementine, he promised silently as he waited in the airless room for her arrival. Mercifully it was a mild enough morning; he didn't want to imagine how hot this space might be by midday. He could already smell Fry's perspiration, and the odour suggested to Reggie that the detective likely hadn't bathed in days. Although he too was beginning to feel claustrophobic and moist, he was glad that he could only smell the comforting perfume of his toilet water wafting with the freshness of his laundered cotton shirt. He wanted – needed – Clementine to like him.

Fry cleared his throat and Reggie turned to see the enormous Joseph One-Shoe being escorted in by one of Fry's men. Clinging to the warrior's thigh was a little girl. Despite her waif-like build, urchin clothes and red-rimmed eyes, she could not hide her mother's beauty. It seemed to Reggie that Louisa was not gone but had, in fact, escaped death by inhabiting her daughter. Louisa was in the room, alive and watching him. Those huge eyes! He recalled how he'd once compared them to massive glass marbles that looked too large for Louisa's sockets. He could swear they were her eyes regarding him with an impaling stare of silvery indigo, full of inquiry rather than shyness. It gave Clementine that other-worldly quality her mother had possessed. Reggie felt his heartbeat become erratic for a moment or two, enough to audibly catch his breath.

'All right, sir?' asked Fry.

The bulk of Clementine's companion dominated the room. He stood massive, powerful, compliant. Reggie noted how tightly his niece held onto him. The man's hands, like the paws of a bear, encircled her angular shoulders. She was a tiny ragamuffin in the clutches of a monster. But he was clearly her monster: silent, watchful, her loyal sentry, Reggie decided. These two would not be easily parted.

He stepped forward. Even the wide Cupid's bow of her mouth belonged to Louisa. He saw only Grant in her, and with this recognition Reggie felt as though a special permission was being granted to him by Fate. With no Knight obvious in this child, it was right that he should take her back to the home where she was born, as her mother had been before her, to the sole surviving female Grant.

'Good morning, Clementine,' he said as gently as he could, and crouched so she didn't have to look up and feel overwhelmed.

'Good morning, sir.' Oh, she even lisped slightly like Louisa had as a child. His heart had found its rhythm but now it pounded. He hoped she couldn't sense his tension.

'Do you remember me? I'm your Uncle Reginald. You're most welcome to call me Uncle Reggie.'

'And do you like me?'

It was disconcerting how composed she appeared. '"Like" is not the word that touches how I feel about you, Clementine. When you were in England I loved you as if you were my own daughter, and I was deeply saddened when you and your mother had to leave.'

'Did you love my mother?'

'Yes. I did. My sister was the person I loved most in the world, so perhaps we have that to share?'

'I wish I had a brother who felt like that about me.'

He grinned. 'Well, now you have an uncle, and he wants to take you home to meet your grandmother. She is very ill, Clementine.' He blinked. 'And her one wish is to see her beautiful granddaughter once more because we miss you and wish that you could see where your mother grew up into the happy person she was.'

'My mummy was never happy here,' Clementine said, sounding like someone ten times her age.

'I know, darling. She wrote to me and told me this. But she loved you and your father more than she worried about her worries, and so she did her best.'

'You can leave,' Fry said offhandedly to the Zulu, waving his dismissal.

Reggie wanted to hit the man. He was tiptoeing his way across the hardest of territories and had just begun to feel like he was getting through to his niece, finding common ground, and this oaf had exploded the tender moment.

'No!' Clementine looked suddenly terrified. She swung away to cling to her companion.

Reggie stood with a sigh. The man they called Joseph One-Shoe looked embarrassed but not humbled. 'May I keep Miss Clementine company, Detective Fry, sir, until your business is concluded?'

'Good grief, he speaks like an Englishman,' Reggie said in jest.

'Mr Knight and your niece have taught me well, sir,' the Zulu replied, clearly taking no umbrage at the remark.

It was a mistake. He'd underestimated Clementine's minder. He could see the furrows of bafflement forming on his niece's forehead. She should not be underestimated either, he decided; her age belied her intelligence. He realised he must display no offence that he was being addressed by a slave in such a conversational tone. The man stood with squared shoulders and a look in his eye that spoke of recrimination. He was irritatingly self-possessed in the presence of his superiors, and it was Reggie who was the first to look away. It struck him then with a feeling akin to a cold hand being placed on his neck that Joseph One-Shoe knew.

I didn't push him, his whole body screamed into the anxious silence. *He tripped, fell.*

Joseph's expression was implacable.

You can't know anything! Reggie's breathing shortened and turned shallow. He stepped back to gather his composure, his gaze not leaving the minder.

He was sure the African replied: *I was there. I saw everything, heard everything, understood everything.*

He had no intention of having a conversation with a slave in front of anyone, and he certainly was not going to panic. Instead, he returned his attention to his niece, who despite her alarm was skewering him with her mother's gaze. It was appalling how guilty it made him feel.

'Clementine, my darling, Mr One-Shoe may remain, but I have something important to tell you.' He had wanted to say *discuss* but this was not a situation to be negotiated. One way or another, he was leaving with his niece on that ox wagon tomorrow morning.

'My daddy said you were here to cause trouble, and now he's dead.'

He sucked in a breath. 'Clementine, no. That's not true. I wanted to bring you both to England. Here, look.' He withdrew the ship's documents along with the identifying paperwork he'd shown Fry. He pointed. 'That's three berths on the ship to England. Trouble was never my intention. It was always about bringing our family together.' He could feel the dark gaze of Joseph One-Shoe upon him, daring him to meet his stare. He did not. He kept it firmly on the child – the prize.

'I think he wanted to die,' she replied, shocking Fry as much as Reggie with the remark.

'He was sad, appallingly drunk and extremely angry last night, Clementine,' the policeman concurred.

'Because he knew Uncle Reggie had come?'

Reggie couldn't let Fry speak for him. 'He didn't meet me at the club as I'd hoped so we could have a chat between gentlemen.' He had to shift the topic. 'I want to tell you why I'm here.' No one interrupted as he carefully chose his words and navigated his way with stealth, a gentle tone and a kindly smile to tiptoe once again into her trust. He told her everything, even about the long journey and his wish to see his sister's grave.

At last he shrugged. 'I so wanted to bring you and your father home, Clementine. May I take you back to your grandmother? Would you like to come back to where you were born, see the home that is yours? All of your toys are there. All of your mother's toys, like her doll's house and her rocking horse, await you.'

'Is there anything that belongs to my daddy at Woodingdene?'

She remembered its name. He was impressed, and the fear began to recede as he knew he was likely saying all the right things. 'Indeed, there is. There's a beautiful bridge over a small brook that he designed and built in your mother's honour, but perhaps the most interesting is his telescope.'

Now he'd definitely hit the right note. What did a little girl know about a telescope? And yet she responded with widening eyes and a smile.

'He told me about how he used to look at the stars through it.'

'It's a splendid piece of equipment, and I'll be honest, I know nothing about astronomy – barely the names of the stars.'

This made her smile and he felt his spirits soar.

'I know lots. I can teach you.'

'Will you? That would be splendid, and we'll have so much time on our long journey home on a ship.'

'Joseph One-Shoe may not like travelling on a ship.'

And here it was. They were at the delicate juncture he had anticipated. Reggie sighed and straightened up again, finally meeting the African's calm stare and seeing all too clearly the fire of accusation blazing behind it.

'Clementine, Detective Fry is going to take you to get some lemonade.' He turned and the policeman scowled. 'Joseph and I need to talk, but we will only be a couple of minutes. Go on now,' he said, and was relieved that her friend gave her an encouraging push towards the door.

Detective Fry, though unhappy with the task, seemed glad to extricate himself. Reggie watched his niece glance up at Joseph One-Shoe as she let the policeman escort her out the door.

Reggie returned his attention to the African, who watched him assuredly, his body still.

'Mr One-Shoe, I am taking my niece home. She cannot remain here.'

'Yes, sir.'

That surprised him but he pushed on. 'She is obviously attached to you in ways I do not understand but it makes no difference – you understand this too?'

'Yes, sir.'

'So, it would be easier on her heart, I suspect, if you could encourage her to return to England without fighting it. I will drag her screaming if I have to but I would prefer not to.'

'I understand, sir.'

'And what else do you understand, Mr One-Shoe?'

Joseph One-Shoe blinked slowly, as if giving himself that heartbeat to consider.

'And before you answer that, be very aware of how difficult I can make your life.' Reggie remained matter-of-fact, wanting to make clear that his position was not negotiable. 'You cannot change the outcome, Mr One-Shoe. James Knight is dead, as is my sister, and my niece is an orphan. That's a fact. No one will permit her to remain with you – *no one*, no matter what you allege.' He fixed him with a cool stare and leaned on reason. 'Her remaining family is wealthy, we love her, and we want to give her a proper home and upbringing in the manner to which she was born. Surely you want only the best for her, and the best situation is for her to return to England and leave behind all the sorrows of Africa.' He waited and the diamond digger said nothing, also waiting. 'Tell me you want what is best for Clementine, Joseph.'

'I do.'

'A man of few words, eh? How about I pay you?'

'For my silence?'

Reggie bristled. 'To allow her to go without a fuss.'

'I have my own money.'

'You're very confident, aren't you?'

'I don't know what that means, sir.'

Now Reggie's jaw ground silently. 'I mean, you seem sure of yourself.'

'For an African, do you mean, sir?' He was politely inquiring.

'For a black savage, yes.'

Joseph One-Shoe nodded thoughtfully. 'I am Zulu. We are warriors who must trust in our . . .' He tapped his belly.

'Instincts?'

'I do not know this word, but if it means to trust in our own feelings and knowledge from within, then yes.'

'And what do those feelings tell you?'

'I do not discuss my feelings with strangers, sir. They are mine.'

'Wretched man!' Reggie growled. 'Don't be slippery with me.'

Joseph looked back at him with an unchanged benign expression but said no more.

'So, will you let her go without a fuss?'

'Yes, sir.'

'Why?'

'It's *for the best*, sir, as you English say.'

'And —'

'I will say no more about her father's death. It does not help her. Her life should be spent in her true home and she should be raised in a better way than she has been.'

'Bravo, Mr One-Shoe,' he breathed, his chest swelling. He wanted to clap. 'I'm pleased you're putting Clementine first.'

'Always, sir.'

'Then you will help me convince her to leave?'

The man finally dropped his head and nodded.

Reggie needed him to know that none of what was occurring was spiteful. 'Joseph?'

He looked up.

'I can tell you this – I loved her mother with all my heart. That is no lie. And when Louisa left us, taking Clementine, it felt like the sunshine had left our lives. Now, I don't claim to know my niece very well any more, but when she was an infant I did, and I love her. I promise you she will want for nothing. She will never feel unloved or frightened. I will take care of her until the day I die, by which time I hope she will be happily married, with a family and a very good life of her own.'

Joseph let out a slow sigh that was visible but not audible. Reggie could feel anguish in it, as though it was painful for One-Shoe to make this decision. 'I will help her to leave, sir.' Without another word the huge African turned and left the policeman's office, and it was only as the door closed that Reggie realised he didn't know what the African knew, or even what he may or may not have seen.

Reggie allowed Clementine to go back with Joseph for a final fare-well while he returned to the club to settle his account and organise his departure with the child.

'I will need this message delivered to the home of Mr James Knight, please. It is not sealed so whomever you send can confer its contents verbally. While the African man speaks good English, I doubt he can read.'

'Actually, Mr Grant, Joseph One-Shoe reads fluently,' the manager replied.

Reggie swallowed his scorn. 'How is that possible?'

He shrugged. 'The Knight family obviously made it their business to educate him.'

'Right, well, so as not to antagonise an already delicate situation, I am keen that the club organise for Mr One-Shoe to deliver my niece to me before noon. We leave at two o'clock. Is that possible for you to organise?'

'It is. It shall be done. And, er . . . Mr Grant, about the funeral for James Knight.'

'I will make arrangements for the provision of his burial along-side my sister, his wife. I will leave instructions for his headstone, and I would appreciate it if a photograph could be taken so that Clementine has a memento of her parents' graves.'

'Oh, we have the latest photography process, sir. Mr Field has imported a lenticular stereoscope and I believe the *cartes-de-visite* craze has reached as far as New Rush.'

Reggie shook his head. 'I don't need all that equipment. She is very little right now and I imagine not much is making sense. However, in time I would like to give her a single photograph – a daguerreotype would be ideal. I want the clearest detail, so she understands that she was an orphan and her family needed to make this decision to take her back to England. Please make sure its glass cover is well fixed and I'll pay for it to be sealed in leather.'

'I understand, Mr Grant. She is fortunate that you are here at this awkward time and in a position to provide for her immediately.'

'It is certainly serendipitous,' Reggie replied. 'Although,' he added, his confidence rising, 'Fate does work in strange ways, don't you think?' The two men stood to shake hands. 'Oh, one more thing – could you ensure that Clementine packs with her some of her favourite things, especially that ragdoll she holds dear, I gather? I think it's vital I try to keep as much comfort and familiarity around her as possible. I will leave money for anything we cannot take with us on the wagon to be sent on later.'

'Very good, sir. Consider it done. And we shall look forward to your return to the Kimberley Club.'

Reggie smiled and hoped the man did not see his insincerity. He had no intention, not a smattering of desire, to visit this forsaken land again, the fine club notwithstanding.

They parted company, and now all Reggie had to do was pack up his few belongings and keep his patience in check. Everything was set. All he could focus on now was the arrival of Clementine . . . carrying her favourite toy.

13

Joseph One-Shoe had suggested Clementine not say goodbye to any of the folk she had come to regard as extended family. 'It will only upset you further,' he had counselled, regarding her eyes, red and burning from too many tears.

A man from the Kimberley Club had recently arrived bearing an unsealed envelope and confirming that he would not leave without Mr Grant's niece. Joseph had told Clementine the man might as well be from the police, or from the royal court of Her Majesty Queen Victoria in England, given the power the wealthy men of the Kimberley Club wielded. The man had offered to read the letter, but Joseph had asserted that he would prefer not to have it read aloud.

Clementine stared upwards, watching Joseph's eyes moving slowly but steadily as he absorbed the contents. She was certain he made his careful way through it twice and assumed he wanted to be sure he understood it fully. As he read his gaze became leaden. Clementine could see in the slope of his shoulders and the way he bent down to her – something he didn't often do – that it was all bad news.

'Do I really have to leave you?' she said, unable to wait for the patient man to find the words that would land mostly kindly upon her.

'Your uncle loves you, Miss Clementine. He wants you to see your mother's mother before she is lost to you.' He blinked, perhaps realising he was being oblique.

Everyone she loved seemed to die anyway. 'But you'll be alone.'

'I promise I shall be strong, Miss Clementine,' he said, and she saw in his crooked smile that he was a true Zulu warrior because he was being brave when he wasn't feeling it.

'I won't know how to live in England. I only know how to live here with you and Daddy.'

'You will learn. I learned the white man's way. You will learn the gentleman's way . . . not that your father wasn't a gentleman, Miss Clementine.'

'It's all right, Joseph. I know my daddy let us down, but we loved him.'

'We did.'

'And the angels took him to be with Mummy because she's lonely.'

She watched his large, expressive lips curl slightly as though trapped in an awkward thought. 'Yes. They are together.'

'But we are being pulled apart.' She couldn't keep the tears from falling any longer. Her courage failed and she was disappointed to let him down.

'Miss Clementine. We are never apart.' He risked holding her close and the man from the club shuffled, either embarrassed or dismayed by the show of affection. She clung tighter, then it occurred to her that maybe Joseph One-Shoe might be punished for his tenderness, so she forced herself to let go.

Joseph's gaze held hers and he looked proud of her. 'Good girl, Miss Clementine. Find your strength. It's always there. It will never fail you if you know where to look.'

She wasn't sure what that meant but it sounded brave and she wanted to be strong for him. She sniffed. 'When will I see you again?'

He pointed upwards. 'Look to the night sky and I'll be there right behind you. I have changed my mind. You are now Sirius. I am your faithful friend and I will follow you always as Little Dog.'

Glistening tears spilled again. 'When I grow up, I'm going to come back and I will find you.'

He risked hugging her again. 'And I will wait to be found, Miss Clementine.' Close to her ear he whispered, 'Your uncle loves you and I believe it, but he doesn't always tell the truth. Never forget that.'

She stared into his face and saw a river of sadness. They held a silence and to her it felt like they'd made a secret pact.

'She is to bring some of her favourite things,' the man reminded Joseph, sounding bored by the emotional scene.

'I can read,' Joseph One-Shoe replied.

'Don't get testy with me, One-Shoe. You forget your place.'

Clementine scowled. 'I'll get my things. You can wait outside, Mr Whoever-You-Are.'

The man grinned and it wasn't pleasant. 'No, I was told to wait with you. Hurry up, little girl.'

She was in her new dress. Joseph tied a ribbon at the bottom of each plait before he handed her the only bonnet she possessed and never liked to wear. He gave her a soft glare. 'You will look very pretty in this.'

'I don't like pretty.'

'You will,' he said. He closed the carpet bag that easily held all her worldly goods.

'Where's Gillie?'

'Here. Keep him very safe.' He fixed her with a gaze that wasn't his soft, affectionate one. This was filled with intensity, as though passing her a message. 'Very safe.' He glanced back at the waiting man watching them. 'She's ready.'

'Let's go.'

'I want Joseph One-Shoe to come as well.'

'There's no point. He is not permitted on the club premises.'

'I'll follow. I will leave when she is delivered to her uncle.'

'Suit yourselves.'

They left as a strange trio. Clementine felt no obligation to walk alongside the gruff servant sent to fetch her. She defied him by staying at Joseph's side. The man didn't seem to care, so long as they were all moving towards the Kimberley Club, a place she had never seen and didn't care about. Joseph carried her bag and she understood that she was not permitted to place her small hand in Joseph's large one, even though she wanted to more than anything. So she clutched her ragdoll tight, finding his strange weightiness a comfort.

The diggers were all at the Big Hole but many of the wives stepped out of their tin shacks and tented hovels to wish the little girl well. Infants clutched their mothers' petticoats and the women wiped hands on aprons, or shielded the sun from their eyes as they gave encouraging words and soft farewells.

'Godspeed, Clem.'

'Blow a kiss to England for me, Clemmie.'

'You're going to break some hearts, child.'

The voices followed her and she gave a few waves to the women. Some of the younger children skipped alongside her for a way before peeling back at the sound of their mothers' calls.

'Joseph —'

He didn't let her express whatever fresh fear was coming. 'Be strong, Miss Clementine. Not far now.'

She said no more but she could sense Joseph's pride that she'd found a stoic silence and purposefully followed their escort.

The double-storey building reared up in front of them. She looked at the sweeping arches of the colonnade that formed the verandah, and through an open pair of wide, stained-glass double doors; inside she could see the vast polished handrail of a staircase.

At the gate, sentries wearing the Kimberley Club's special uniform guarded the comings and goings of its members.

'No further, Zulu,' the man said, and they all paused. 'Come on, little girl. Mr Grant is inside waiting for you.'

'Can you fetch him, please? I wish to say something to Joseph. It's private.' And now she did defy him by wrapping her arm around Joseph's leg.

Their escort let out an audible gust of vexation. 'Do not move from here, Joseph One-Shoe.'

Joseph said nothing but glanced at Clementine. They watched the man whisper something to one of the sentries, who nodded, and then he disappeared through the gates and headed deep into the heart of the club itself.

She could see men on the verandah, seated in cane chairs reading newspapers, sipping from cups or having quiet conversations. No one bothered to look up.

'Joseph, will my daddy be buried . . . near Mummy?'

He nodded. 'I promise, Miss Clementine, although your uncle might have already made arrangements.'

'I should be there to watch him being buried, shouldn't I?'

'I think you should remember your father as he was when he used to make you laugh and tell you things about the world beyond Africa. I don't think you need to remember him at his grave. He wouldn't like it any more than you.'

'I'm coming back, Joseph.'

'I know.'

'Don't forget me.'

'Never.' He touched his heart. 'You are here forever, and inside Gillie is a very special part of Africa. It belongs to you now.'

She thought she understood what he was saying; he was giving her a message without actually speaking the words.

She jumped and he caught her and she wept into his shoulder. It was unseemly but even Joseph didn't seem to care. Now the men on the verandah were taking notice of them. There was an angry rustle of newspapers and baffled, inquiring voices.

It was Uncle Reggie's voice that broke their spell. 'Ah, now, come along, Clementine. Let's behave well, shall we?'

She slid down Joseph's body as he carefully lowered her back to the ground. Uncle Reggie was beaming, although she sensed his discomfort when he glanced back over his shoulder at the club members, now all watching them.

'Let's not make a scene, eh?' He nodded at Joseph and smiled wider for her. 'There's a good fellow.'

Joseph let go of Clementine and the world she knew was rent from her. There was no physical sensation and yet she felt a searing pain – worse than losing her parents. They'd both left her. But Joseph One-Shoe was here and he was being forcibly wrenched from her, out of duty but mostly because his skin was black and hers was white.

He'd been the best parent a child could want. Why couldn't anyone see that?

'Joseph . . .' She sounded panicked.

He bent and whispered close to her ear. 'I want you to be me today, Miss Clementine. Be a warrior. I know it lives in you. You are brave in the face of all danger. Be fearless, Miss Clementine. Be Zulu!' He whispered something in his language that she couldn't understand but the words melted around her like the soft blanket of comfort they shared when they watched the stars.

When he pulled away, he nodded once. 'Goodbye, Miss Clementine. Remember what I warned you about.'

She was weeping but those were simply tears of emotion; she

was not dissolving or losing her ability to function or think straight. Today, she was Zulu.

'Goodbye, Joseph One-Shoe. I love you.'

He lifted something from his pocket and she saw that it was a tiny beaded panel. She knew what this was – had touched it and spoken with him about it before. He had threaded the minuscule beads himself into a panel just a few inches wide. She had counted the familiar Zulu bead colours, knew there were five, but it was the bright blue of the African sky that dominated the pattern of diamonds. The blue diamond was outlined with beads the colour of blood and outlined once more with beads the colour of Joseph's skin. The geometric diamonds that linked, tip to tip, sat against beads the colour of her skin. It was she and Joseph One-Shoe beaded together in one of the Zulu love charms he'd told her the men made for the women they felt a deep connection to. He pressed it into her hand. As he backed away from her, Joseph One-Shoe spoke in silent Zulu and she lip-read him saying *I love you* – words he had taught her in his language.

'Clementine, let me take your bag,' her uncle said in a kindly voice. 'Oh, it's not very heavy, is it? I think we need to get you some things when we reach Cape Town. Come on now, darling, we have to leave shortly.'

One last look at the man she loved most in the world and Clementine Knight turned bravely away and followed the other man she knew she had to learn to love. Through the gates she moved, listening to the clang of the metal closing behind her, keeping Joseph and his kind out; keeping Clementine and her kind in.

She turned but he'd gone and she knew it was for the best.

'That beading is very pretty,' Uncle Reggie said. 'Is that something important?'

'Yes,' she said, taking on Joseph's manner.

'Well, you hang on to that and keep it close because I can see that it means a lot to you.' He smiled at her. She tried to find a smile of her own, and hoped it worked. 'Here,' he continued gently. 'Let me take your ragdoll for you. I'll keep that very safe for you while we sort out our departure. I'll give it back a bit later, all right?'

Clem hesitated. She wanted Gillie close, wanted to keep him safe like Joseph had told her, but it didn't really matter. Her parents were dead. She was being forced apart from Joseph. She was being taken to England. Nothing mattered any more. She wanted to cry, but Joseph had asked her to behave like a Zulu warrior. For him, she would be strong. She handed over Gillie.

'Good girl. We are going to make a very special and wonderful life together, you and I, Clem. May I call you Clem?'

Uncle Reggie clutched her ragdoll tightly as though it was as important to him as it was to her. She curled the beaded panel in her fist; this Zulu love letter had now become more important than Gillie. This truly was Joseph One-Shoe travelling with her, and Clementine vowed to herself that she would never let it out of her possession . . . not as long as she lived.

Part Two

14

October 1894

The skirt of Clementine Grant's sailor-inspired ensemble swooshed half an inch from the floorboards. She preferred a tailor to make her walking-out suits. Her seamstress would have used thick bands of white to achieve a fashionable look; her tailor had agreed to apply a thin outline of white along the belt and on the edging of the sailor collar to break up the dark fabric. It looked like a grown-up version of a school uniform. Given that she was about to meet children, she felt it might be less intimidating, plus the navy kept the look restrained. She wore no jewellery, no showy hat, and her soft boots made the barest of sounds against the floorboards.

Her presentation was a contrast to the ostentatious purple velvet and silk affair that she was following down the corridor. Clementine wondered if her host deliberately dressed like a matriarch, her taffeta crunching and complaining at every step. She'd learned that Mrs Collins was a new volunteer, and recently married to one of Britain's industrialists, who was twice her age and lavished her with everything . . . except intelligence, Clementine decided. If he had, then Mrs Collins would have researched her guest and discovered that Clementine Grant was a regular and generous financial contributor as well as a frequent visitor to the orphanage through which they were presently strolling. She would already know of Clem's plans for the north.

They were traversing the hall of a female orphan asylum in the neighbourhood called Saffron Hill, in the borough of Camden. The old mansion had been converted to house five dormitories, which accommodated fifty girls ranging from infancy to fourteen-year-olds. Several rooms had been fitted out as communal bathrooms and lavatories. A large kitchen, parlour and a washhouse had been created within the original house, with private rooms for the women who took care of the large family that was being raised here. Outside there was a yard for the children to play in, as well as a stable. Understandably, the dining hall was perhaps the busiest space of all, and this was where Clementine was headed.

'I'm a little surprised at your interest in the blackamoor children, Miss Grant,' her companion said over her shoulder, her chin only just visible over voluminous leg-of-mutton sleeves.

'Really? Why do you say that?' Clementine couldn't help baiting the woman. They'd only met ten minutes earlier and she was already struggling to hide her disdain.

'Oh, I know they need help, and they're really so very lucky that the home even takes them in,' came the haughty reply, 'but it's best the boys stick to being shoeblacks and the girls become the lower sort of domestic servant.' She tinkled a laugh. 'At least it wouldn't show if they worked the coal scuttle.' Clem had to close her eyes for a calming heartbeat to stop herself shoving Mrs Collins and with any luck toppling her ghastly hat, made in the fashion of a gentleman's top hat, except in revolting purple. 'I have it on good authority that their brains are underdeveloped, and they tend to remain dull-witted and placid.' Mrs Collins had made the fatal error of assuming she was talking to a like-minded woman. 'You know, like tethered oxen.'

Clementine bristled but kept her tone mild. She knew all about oxen: intelligent creatures trained relentlessly to do the white man's bidding. 'According to whom?'

'Pardon me?' said the mutton sleeve; the pinched face was now lost to its capacious folds.

Clementine increased her speed to come alongside Mrs Collins. Yes, she was going to enjoy this. 'I'm intrigued to know which authority gave you such a notion. I mean, if we're talking about the children when they arrive here, their quiet manner could be attributed to anything from normal shyness or melancholy at losing their parents, to malnutrition or illness. It is hardly a measure of their intelligence, surely?'

'No, I'm quite certain my husband read somewhere that a scientist said the negro brain is smaller, incapable of the same learning as we are,' her companion said, as though a vague rumour were more than sufficient evidence. Over the click-clack of Mrs Collins's heeled boots, Clementine began to think of all things purple to which she could compare Mrs Collins as an insult. Drawing on her fine memory and relentless thirst for knowledge and enrichment, she felt a ripple of pleasure to remember a specimen of an underwater snail she'd seen in London's natural history museum that emitted a purple stain when frightened. There was a sea slug that wore purple, and a purple frog from India that was also known as a 'pig nose'. *Perfect.* She would think of Mrs Collins as 'Pig Nose' from now on.

'Let's be frank,' the woman continued. 'Respectable Victorians want nothing to do with these darkies invading our shores. Really, why can't they just stay where they were born? I mean, I've heard they can make docile servants, but really – can we truly trust these blackies in our homes?'

'Well, to answer your first query, I think it's because we didn't stay where we were born, Mrs Collins. We enslaved a lot of their parents to work for us and many of the African children here have worthy parents who fought for England as soldiers, and —'

'Oh, even so, Miss Grant, social inequality cannot be avoided. It's all part of our empire's structure . . .'

Clementine stopped listening; she felt a strong urge to raise her parasol and bring it down on the woman's head. Instead, she thought of Joseph One-Shoe; he had taught her how to employ the benign smile to hide her emotion and take control of it. 'Only show emotion when you love someone. Hate is better to hide. It makes you power-ful when you realise you are stronger than the lion within.'

She leaned on his teachings now, quietening the roar of her lion. 'Do you know any people from Africa or the Caribbean personally?' Her voice sounded mild – interested, even.

Mrs Collins stopped walking as though she were just about to step in a mess left by someone's pet dog. 'Good heavens, no!' she said. 'I see the coloured orphans here, of course, although I haven't spoken to any. And an acquaintance of mine has a mulatto maid, who waits on me rather well, I must admit, but no, no, I'm afraid it wouldn't be seemly in my situation to associate with adult black-amoors. Surely you don't?'

'I would – I do,' Clementine took delight in replying. 'I have,' she added. 'I used to live with an African man when I was small. He was Zulu. I considered him a father. I loved him, Mrs Collins – I still do love him with all my heart and I think of him each day.' Her walking companion looked scandalised and dismayed at once. 'And . . . I'm not sure, have you heard that I'm negotiating the adop-tion of an African child from this orphanage?' That wasn't strictly true, but it was not so far from the truth that she felt any remorse.

'Whatever for?' Mrs Collins uttered, having found her voice.

Now she did laugh. 'To give her a home – why else? To give her a life . . . a future.'

'But you're not married, Miss Grant.'

That was the remark that Clementine felt gave her final permission to burn all potential links with this ghastly woman. 'Mrs Collins, I do not need a husband to validate my position or my decisions – not now, not ever. And any man I agreed to marry would welcome the arrival of a child in need into his life. I wouldn't allow myself to be involved with a man romantically if he did not at least have sympathy for my views, and I hope he would share them when it came to the welfare of young people in need – no matter their colour.'

Mrs Collins looked at her blankly as they stood outside the dining hall. Clementine could hear the soft voices of children and the clink of cutlery against crockery, but she wasn't so sure Mrs Collins could. Her next remark nearly made Clementine laugh out loud.

'Er, will you be coming to the fireworks display, Miss Grant?' she asked, as though Clementine had not said anything.

Nothing had changed in two decades, it seemed: an African man would continue to be considered as a handy, perhaps even appreciated, servant but should not get above his station. Her only satisfaction was knowing that she and her parents had treated Joseph One-Shoe as not only a fellow miner but their family.

'Fireworks?' she replied.

'Oh, you must. All the patrons will be in attendance on Guy Fawkes Night. The children are busy making guys to burn on a bonfire that I swear you'll be able to see from Primrose Hill. Oh, it's going to be splendid fun. Mr Collins and I shall certainly be there.' She reeled off a list of names of other seriously wealthy people and their contributions. Clearly, this event was more about the pomp and ego of the patrons than pleasure for the children. It was a chance to show off their wealth and broadcast their philanthropy. 'And, of course, Mr Collins is funding the fireworks,' she added, trying her hardest to sound modest but failing.

'Most generous. Mrs Collins, you've been kind in escorting me, but I should admit this is not my first visit and I rather like lingering and talking to the children.'

'To the children?' she repeated, aghast. 'But I thought I'd introduce you to the dining hall team.'

'I've met them previously. I don't have a lot of time in London this visit but I do want to see some of the children. I didn't wish to sound churlish and decline your generous offer to walk with me, but the truth is I am a regular visitor.'

'But why? I mean, why do you want to spend time with the children and not the people who make this generous place function?'

'Because I enjoy them, Mrs Collins. I am planning to set up a similar orphanage in the north and I want to find out exactly what the children need, what they want, what they aspire to.'

'Miss Grant, it's my understanding that the children here are already destined for service. We shouldn't fill their heads with aspirations.'

Clementine smiled in a way that she knew would make Joseph proud, and gave a small shrug. 'That's how this orphanage operates, and it does a very good job of training its girls and sending them into domestic service. But I want to work on education as much as training, perhaps find out which little girls want to be artists or writers; I want to find out if they have a talent for sewing and might like to become seamstresses in charge of their own businesses, or run their own guesthouses because they're good at management.' She took private delight in seeing Mrs Collins's complexion blanche. 'I shall be helping boys as well – those who dream of being builders, merchants, businessmen.'

Mrs Collins looked faint. 'Turn them into us, you mean?'

'To give them opportunity. A chance to fulfil their potential, to make the most of their inherent talent. I want to see how we can give children hope. Anyway, forgive me for carrying on. Thank you again – I'm glad we met,' she said, holding out a polite gloved hand. 'I shall definitely attend the fireworks and admire your family's display.'

That seemed to brighten her companion. 'The pleasure's mine, Miss Grant.'

Clementine was glad they parted on a smile but she was convinced Mrs Collins would be talking to all those in her network about the opinionated visitor from the north with her strange ideas. Clementine didn't think she could care any less and continued her way through to the dining hall. It wasn't noon so the dinner bell was yet to be sounded but girls were busy setting tables, and she spotted several familiar faces.

The orphans were kitted out in their strict uniform of black tunics with white aprons and white cotton bonnets to keep their hair tidy. It made her smile to see her favourite, who risked a shy wave and then giggled with her best friend. They were a striking pair. Nel, with skin like the polished Whitby jet Her Majesty favoured, and her companion, Amy, with the palest of freckled skin. They both possessed shocks of hair: one the colour of boot polish, the other like a ripe carrot.

'Morning, Miss Grant,' they chorused, and the other women and girls in the room turned and curtsied.

'Good morning, everyone.' She smiled. 'Don't let me interrupt you.'

One of the supervising adults walked down the rows of tables to meet her, beaming across a rosy-cheeked moon of a face that spoke only of generosity.

'I was passing,' Clementine fibbed. 'Hope you don't mind me calling in, Sally.'

'You are always welcome, Miss Grant. How are your plans going in Northumberland?'

'I think I might have found some premises. I won't lie – I'm excited.'

'Would you like to meet with any of the girls?'

'I would love to chat to Nel and Amy, and perhaps Dolly, if she's around?'

'She's helping out the back but, please, would you like to sit in the small garden – it's not raining – and I'll send the girls out? Dinner's in about twenty minutes.'

'Thank you. Er, Sally?' She reached into her leather holdall. 'I've brought some Yorkshire toffee for the girls. Will you see that they all get one or two, please?' She knew Sally would make sure the girls got their fair share, which is why she had not left it at the reception. 'I also want to reward the children helping me but without making the others feel left out. I've got a very tiny gift for the three girls, if that's all right?'

'How kind. Of course. Doesn't hurt to feel special now and then.'

They shared a knowing smile and then Clementine wandered out into the yard.

Suddenly small hands were gripping hers and she found herself flanked by Nel and Amy, both talking rapidly and excitedly. Neither of them wore coats; she suspected they didn't own more than a shawl to keep out the wintry cold. If they felt the chilly nip of October, it didn't show, but she still felt guilty for wearing gloves.

'Slow down, girls. Come and sit with me. I have a gift for you.'

With happy squeals they made themselves comfortable on a bench beneath a gnarled apple tree. She removed two tiny parcels from her bag and Amy began to weep upon being handed one.

Nel didn't shed a tear; instead she laughed a deep sound of pure delight to be given something precious of her own, and Clementine was reminded of Joseph One-Shoe's chuckle. She had already spoken to the orphanage's hierarchy about taking Nel back to Northumberland as soon as they would release her into Clem's care. But as she'd watched her with Amy over recent visits, it was fast becoming clear the girls were inseparable, and to take Nel from Amy might cause unhappiness for two children who'd already had enough sorrow in their lives.

'You don't have to open them now. They're little ribbons. A beautiful green one to go with your eyes, Amy, and Nel, I picked red to perfectly set off your gorgeous skin and hair. I can show you how to tie it into your curly hair.'

They both threw their arms around her without encouragement, hugging so hard she had to untangle herself from them. Clementine felt a pang of fresh guilt that she had thought a ribbon to be of little consequence – after all, she'd had ribbons aplenty since she'd arrived in England, in an array of colours to match an equally daunting array of outfits.

'Am I coming to the new home yet, Miss Grant?' Nel asked, her soulful eyes searching Clementine's.

'As soon as you turn ten.'

Amy's tears threatened again.

'Amy, please don't cry. You will be coming with us, I promise.' Clementine nodded encouragement, then lifted a finger. 'No more tears. This is surely happy news?'

Amy couldn't stop the well, and Clementine watched the little girl reach out to take Nel's hand. She was struck by the arms across her lap, the black skin bright and strong against the pale, and she was again reminded of Joseph and how her tiny hand would sit in his large fist. This was a sign, wasn't it? She had to return to Africa. Lay to rest those thoughts about him that refused to be quiet.

She smiled at her resolve and then at her two young charges. 'I thought I could make you joint prefects. I could use your help.'

Amy's eyes, the colour of faded grass, lit. 'Thank you for letting us stay together! I think I'd die if I didn't have Nel to sleep next to.'

'I wouldn't dare pull you apart,' Clementine admitted. 'All right, go on with you now. You have chores. What is the month?'

'October,' they chorused.

'All right, then. And when is your birthday, Nel?'

'I do not know, Miss Grant. Miss Jackson decided I shall be ten in May.'

'And I'll be ten in April,' Amy hastened to add.

'Excellent. As soon as you're both ten you will be allowed to come back with me. Next time I visit we'll talk about our uniforms. Maybe they don't have to be this colour . . . dark green, perhaps?'

She laughed at their excited cheers.

Another girl, mature and graceful in her movements, arrived. 'You wished to see me, Miss Grant?'

'Off you go, lovely girls,' she said, giving Nel and Amy a final hug. 'I'll see you soon. My, Dolly . . . you've grown since I last saw you.'

The worried expression relaxed slightly. 'Miss Jackson had to order a new uniform for me. She said it would have to see me through.'

'When do you leave?' She patted the bench and Dolly sat down gently beside her. She struck Clementine as a watchful gazelle, big-eyed and elegant. Dolly was from the Caribbean. She spoke with a lilt that had a musical quality.

'Early next year, Miss Grant. I am being sent to work as a maid for a family in Wales.'

'How do you feel about that?'

'I am grateful. I am nearing fourteen and I have had nearly eight years here. It is time to give up my place to another girl who needs help.'

It sounded rote, as though Dolly had heard the sentiment over and again from the adults around her. It hurt Clem's heart. She'd always liked this youngster – something about her stillness and peace as much as her generous manner.

'If you could do anything, Dolly, with your life, what would it be?' The girl, on the cusp of womanhood, was tall and willowy. Her features had a haunted quality, her eyes seeming to look beyond the world she walked in. Those dark eyes cast themselves downwards to stare into her lap. 'No one's here but us, Dolly,' Clementine pressed her. 'You can tell me.'

'I would be a nurse . . . or a nun.'

'A nun? Well, I certainly wasn't expecting that. Nursing, though, that's superb.' Clementine paused to think on this. 'What if I said I might intervene and see if we can't find a way of getting you some training in that field?' It wasn't entirely responsible for her to be offering this, but she was committed now. Dolly's gaze lifted to meet hers. It was filled with fresh hope.

'Why do you do this for us?' And before Clem could answer, she added: 'There are white children here but you have always been so especially kind to me, and I know Nel considers you her very special friend.'

'My closest friend was African. A Zulu warrior. My father worked in the mines and I lived there as a very little girl.'

'Was?'

'He . . .' She'd never said it aloud to anyone. Dolly waited, her forehead creasing in a frown. 'Well, he died.' There, it was out of her now, and yet it felt wrong. She'd learned within a year of arriving back in England that he had passed away but little comfort had been offered.

Clem could remember that day very well – Uncle Reggie reading the morning paper, her scraping butter across newly toasted bread. He'd suddenly folded down one corner of his page to glance at her.

'Clem, darling?'

'Yes, Uncle Reg? Are you going to read me something interesting from today's news?'

'Not today, Clem. But I wanted to tell you something important.'

She had waited, anticipating that he was about to tell her they were off on a big journey, or he was going to London and might not be able to take her, or what might she think of having a pony for her next birthday.

'You know you were asking me recently about that Joseph Black-Shoe fellow in Africa?'

'I ask you all the time, Uncle. And his name is Joseph One-Shoe.'

'Well, darling, I do have some news that arrived in a letter last week, but it's not very happy, I'm afraid. You see, there was a mishap.'

Mishap. She didn't know this word, so she waited for more.

'Apparently he ate something poisonous. It's something called casseeva —'

'Cassava,' she corrected, trying to absorb what this revelation meant.

'Oh, well, I don't know. I'm told the Africans like it but that it's dangerous. It made him very unwell and he didn't survive.'

'No, Uncle Reggie, that can't —'

'Now, darling, don't go upsetting yourself. It's not as though you have seen him in a long time, or ever would have.' He stared down around the corner of the newspaper. 'Africa is much too far away for a little girl and I certainly have no intention of returning, so please, for me, accept this unfortunate news and let it go.' He sighed at her crumpling expression. 'Tears are fine, Clem, if you must,' he said, reaching into his pocket to retrieve a large handkerchief. 'Here you are. Why don't you take your toast up to the nursery and I'll have Jane send up some cocoa. You'd like that, wouldn't you?'

'You said cocoa was only for night-time.'

'Did I? Well, I make the rules so that means I can break them for my favourite girl in the whole world, doesn't it? Off you go, darling. If Nanny complains, tell her I said it was all right for you to take food up. Walk carefully up the stairs, darling, that's the way,' he said as she walked obediently, tentatively, towards the breakfast room door. 'And, Clem?'

In her sorrow and disbelief she turned back to him.

'There's a new aquatic circus in London – that means water, darling. Loads of fun. And look!' He withdrew something from an inside pocket of his jacket. 'We have tickets! Not front row or we'll get wet, but only a few rows back – the best seats in the house. Get packed, we're going tomorrow.'

And that was that. Joseph One-Shoe was dead – what a shame, but how about we cheer up at the circus?

She'd thought of that moment so many times since but forgave herself because she had been so young. Her only anchor was Uncle Reggie, but she'd never forgotten Joseph. And she had never fully accepted that he'd died, because if anyone knew how to prepare cassava and be wary of its toxic properties, it was Joseph. There must have been some mistake.

Over that miserable cup of cocoa in the nursery that day, Clementine Grant had decided not to speak of Joseph One-Shoe again to anyone but her inner self. He was her secret – and her secret self at eight had decided that one day, when she was old enough and had saved enough, she wouldn't rely on anyone else to take her to Africa. She would take herself and she would either find Joseph, or his grave, and prove once and for all what had really happened.

That promise had burned in her heart since she was a child. And Clem had convinced herself that if she never uttered a word about his death, then it wasn't true. The childish notion had stuck and she'd clung to it – until this moment, when a direct question from a dark-eyed youngster forced her to speak a truth she had never accepted.

'He died while you were with him?'

She shook her head sadly. 'No. Apparently his death occurred not long after my family brought me back here.'

'You don't believe he is dead, Miss Grant?'

She shook her head. 'I don't know what I believe, other than that I feel in my soul that I would have sensed something if he had died. I can't shake the sense that a mistake has been made, and news came to us of the wrong man.' She gave a soft sigh. 'I've promised myself that one day I will make the journey to find his grave, if one exists. Until now, the time has not been right.'

'Is now the right time?'

'It is, Dolly. I'm old enough, stubborn enough, determined enough, and I have the means to do so.'

It was uplifting to hear Dolly laugh. 'And what shall you do if you find that grave?'

Clem shrugged. 'I really don't know. Weep, no doubt, as I have kept a little flame burning in my heart that he is still alive. The man is Zulu and he needs a proper Zulu farewell. If I can find a grave, then I can do that much for him, because he did so much for me.'

Dolly smiled. 'He will know you have done this for him.'

'I think he will. He made me a promise that he would always follow me.'

Dolly grasped the poignancy of the moment and let a small silence hang. Clementine cleared her throat of its tightness, feeling briefly elated that she had made this decision; it felt real. People would try to talk her out of it but nothing and no one could now. Her fortune would be hers in a few months as they turned the corner on the new year; she would be thirty in January. No more elders making decisions for her. To be finally and wholly in control of her own fortune felt important. And this decision was part of that, because no other adult could wield any power over her.

'Back to you, Dolly. Now, you may need to do a couple of years of service with the Welsh family, but I believe we can negotiate it so that by sixteen you can begin your nurse's training. How does that sound?'

Dolly blinked in disbelief. 'You can do this?'

'I can,' she replied confidently, her mind already considering which arms would need to be twisted; she gave herself a mental nudge to set aside some money for Dolly's care and training. Dolly would be wasted in service but she'd need support throughout her nursing education.

'Oh, Miss Grant, is that a promise? I will work very, very hard with my family to please them.'

Clementine crossed her heart. 'I promise. And I shall arrange it before I leave for Cape Town.' She picked up her final parcel. 'I thought you might like this – it's a couple of ribbons to enjoy wearing on your days off once you start work.'

Dolly held the tiny paper-wrapped parcel next to her heart. 'I hope I deserve this.'

Clementine felt her emotions soar for this delightful child. 'You deserve it and so much more, but especially your education. You are going to make a fine nurse one day, Dolly, and you'll make us all proud. Patients will be lucky it's you who takes care of them.' She hugged the slim girl, loving the warmth of her silken skin against hers.

'Dolly is not my real name,' the girl said.

Clementine pulled back to look at her closely. 'I . . . I didn't know that. What is your name?'

'I was baptised as Sarah.'

'Sarah,' she breathed. 'It suits you. Why Dolly?'

'The family that my mother was in service to before she died used to jest that I looked like a little golliwog.'

Clementine blinked with guilt on behalf of that family.

'Golly turned to Dolly and . . . well, no one bothered with Sarah any more.'

'That changes from today. I shall insist. It may take a while for people to get used to it, but when you go to Wales you will be known only as Sarah. And one day you will be Nurse Sarah.' This made the girl smile and Clementine felt her spirits flutter with hope and ambition for this sweet young woman. 'Don't miss your meal. I'll see you in a few weeks and maybe I'll have some news for you then.'

Dolly must have thanked her a dozen times before she finally let go. Clementine's heart felt full.

As she pondered the lives of the three youngsters, she became aware of Sally watching her. Clementine stood, smiling.

'You can't save them all, Miss Grant.' It was said kindly.

She grinned. 'Oh, but I can try.'

15

Will Axford sat in the Grand Divan at Simpson's in the Strand and took a slow breath of pleasure. It was a relief to escape the shoppers with their bags and boxes, the day-trippers with their wide-eyed wonder, the startled horses, the lurching carriages and the general noise, dirt and dust of Piccadilly and the adjoining busy Regent Street. But even with all this activity, he still preferred the anonymity of the West End to the ever-present scrutiny at the Royal Exchange in the City's financial district, where he conducted his business.

A copy of *The Adventures of Sherlock Holmes* was not far from his reach and he hoped he might be able to finish the story he was enjoying before his guest arrived.

'You look like a parched man finding the proverbial oasis, son,' said a passing patron, a glowing cigar hanging from his lip.

Will stood, feeling Sherlock Holmes slip from his thoughts. He recognised the man as an old acquaintance of his father. 'Good afternoon, Mr Barden. Did I give that impression?' He sounded innocent but knew the old codger was spot-on.

'I thought you young bucks liked to hang around the City – close to the action.'

He nodded with a smile. 'It's the action I'm trying to escape, actually, sir. Most of my peers feed off it, but I like to head into the West End, well away from the bedlam that Lloyd's of London seems to elicit.'

'At least we don't still have the royal wedding to contend with. All that bunting and constant cleaning of the streets and roadblocks and crowds.'

Will thought Piccadilly felt much like that now, but he still preferred its more innocent unbridled commercialism to the cunning, hard-nosed business world that he was part of.

'I gather she is tough from those who've met her.' Barden said. 'I also hear she's witty and worldly but also cold.'

'They might be reading strength as chilliness. I admire her.'

Barden looked back at him, incredulous. 'Have you heard there's now a ladies-only golf tournament at Royal Lytham?' he remarked.

Will's face creased in a smile. 'Ladies will enter Oxford for the first time later this month, sir.'

The old man gave a *tsk*-ing sound. 'Whatever is the world coming to?'

'Finding its balance, I suspect, sir.'

'You mean you support all this suffrage nonsense?' Unruly eyebrows, streaked with grey, crawled together like friendly caterpillars.

He gave a slight shrug. 'It's inevitable . . . and, I think, wise.'

'Good grief, man! Does your father know?' Barden sounded genuinely worried for Will, who laughed.

'So long as I keep making sound decisions about insurance, I think he's relatively happy with me.'

'Going well?'

'Yes, sir. More business than we can handle.'

'Very good to hear, son. I guess you'll be funding ships regularly to the Australian colony now?'

Will frowned.

'Gold in some wretched place I can't pronounce.'

'Ah, Kalgoorlie. Yes, indeed. That's all underway, sir. Several ships have left with miners, and we'll be insuring them on their return, too – hopefully with gold in their cargo holds.'

'Excellent, excellent. Well, I'll leave you to it. I can recommend the mock turtle soup and the baked cod.'

Will opted not to tell his companion that he detested both. 'I'll bear that in mind, Mr Barden, sir.'

'Call me Geoffrey. Toot-toot, William.' He wandered away, a billow of sweet-smelling cigar smoke trailing behind him.

So much for anonymity, Will thought. He wasn't looking forward to today's luncheon. Mock turtle soup aside, it could turn into an awkward conversation with a man he wanted to like but had long ago found to be a manipulative sort, plus his financial situation could be flaky. According to his father, who regularly remarked on it, Will was showing an uncanny intuition for sensing potential bad debt.

'Welcome back, Mr Axford,' the sommelier cooed, arriving at his table. 'May I fetch you something to drink while you wait for your guest?' He offered the wine list.

Will nodded. 'Something light, refreshing?'

'How about a flute of Crémant de Bourgogne, sir? It is predominantly pinot noir but you'll find it fresh and fruity.'

'Very good.' Will checked his fob watch. He still had nearly fifteen minutes of quiet time and hoped he might make it through without further interruption.

He had his back to the arched entrance of the Grand Divan, which got its name from its modest beginnings as a cigar-smoking room. Today the establishment was better known as the preeminent venue for British chess players, who half a century prior had reclined on sofas to play while messengers in top hats were sent to despatch news of their latest moves. Today the Grand Divan served as one of the nation's top restaurants: roasts were a specialty, no matter what old man Barden claimed.

Will was sitting in the position that Charles Dickens had favoured before him. Should he mention that to his guest? He was from new money – plenty of it, too – and impressed by that sort of snippet.

'Am I late, Will?' A voice disturbed his faraway thoughts.

He looked up, surprised. 'No, Mr Grant, not at all. I was early.'

'As I've mentioned before, please call me Reggie. You make me feel like my father otherwise, and those are boots I can't possibly fill.' Reginald Grant smiled with that infectious grin of his. Seeing Grant look so jaunty, Will was reminded that Reggie had survived his first brush with insolvency. He wondered whether the rumour of a second could be correct.

'Reggie it is. How was the trip down?'

Grant lifted a hand with casual carelessness. 'I'm at the London house for a few days. You should come over. I'm having Henry Irving and some others for dinner tomorrow.'

Will smiled. He was impressed, and no doubt was meant to be. Irving was the darling of London's theatre scene.

'A delightful, exquisitely beautiful new starlet called Minnie Ashley may be joining us, along with sundry other stage folk.'

The waiter arrived to save Will an answer, and he allowed his guest to fuss over the choice of wine and then scan the menu. Will quickly settled for a simple roast chicken, preferring the house specialty. He kept the talk over luncheon small and unimportant, politely inquiring after the niece he knew Reggie Grant to be proud of.

'Oh, she's the most precious of all the wonderful things that surround me.'

'Truly?'

'I've told you the story of finding her in Africa, haven't I?'

'Yes, an astonishing tale.'

'What a time it was.' He shook his head in awed memory.

'Sounds rather heroic,' Will remarked, only half facetiously.

Reggie brushed aside what he clearly took to be a compliment with a shake of his head and the final mouthful of his baked cod. 'Our time there was so limited. I knew her grandmother was dying and she did just that a month after we returned. At least they got to know each other again, although of course it was another great loss to the child. She's resilient, though. Grown up to be a fine, fiercely intelligent woman. She seems to know something about everything, I swear it.'

'How old is Clementine now?'

Grant frowned. 'She will be thirty next birthday.'

An eyebrow rose of its own accord and Will wished he hadn't shown his thought quite so expressively.

'I know, I know what you're thinking, Will. Still a spinster, but I have not been able to bring myself to marry her off simply to heed social norms.'

It wasn't what Will was thinking. He had been wondering at the youngster growing up with Uncle Reggie as her main influence.

Reggie spoke on, oblivious. 'I think you're right. My father's ability to stand apart from the conservatism of his time – and even our era, which is still so constrained by social conformity – runs thick in my blood too. As for Clementine, she's nothing short of brutally independent, and she can be because she is astoundingly wealthy in her own right. She doesn't have to make a marriage for security. My girl will marry only for love, and in this she and I are in wholesome agreement. I want whomever she falls for to worship her, as I have for years now.'

Will found himself smiling nonetheless, enjoying the middle-aged client's display of tenderness. He'd not seen that in Reggie before. He now found himself more interested by talk of the young woman.

'How does she fill her days?'

'Not sewing or running a household, I can assure you,' Reggie bleated, as if he'd run out of patience. 'She chairs two committees for charities in which she has a profound interest and investment. She is patron of a small London orphanage but is also busy founding one of her own up in the north using her own funds. That's what is so admirable. She doesn't wait for others to do anything. Most would hold fundraisers and lobby the wealthy but Clementine has set her own course. And, if that isn't enough, she has a keen interest in jewellery. I swear she'd like to design some. I know she's angling towards it, maybe doing some study overseas.'

That surprised him. 'How fascinating.'

Reggie swirled the contents of his wineglass; there was only one quarter left and he was on his third. 'Mmm, I suppose. It comes from her days in Africa.'

'You said she was a little girl when you collected her.'

'Yes, seven. But she'd spent almost all of her life running around the diamond fields. If the Jews of Hatton Garden would only let her in, my niece would learn to sort diamonds quicker than any of their sons, I swear it.'

'She does sound intriguing.'

Reggie dug in his pocket for a silver case, withdrew a slim cigar and offered one to Will. 'Do you mind?'

Will shook his head. 'I won't, though, thank you.'

'Here,' Reggie said, slipping out a small photograph that was tucked into the case. 'Here she is. This was taken a few months ago in the gardens at Woodingdene.' He handed Will the photograph.

Will regarded the close-up of a clear-skinned young woman whose striking features sat symmetrically upon a round face. Her eyes appeared larger than most, and while he couldn't tell their colour from the sepia image, they seemed to look directly at him . . . into him. Her gaze was not intense so much as wistful, and only the vague hint of a smile caught at the edges of the wide bow of her lips. It was as if the photographer had caught her in an amusing but private thought. The wind was obviously tugging at her bun, one slim arm reaching behind to clutch at it, while straggly wisps of what could be blonde or reddish hair were dangling carelessly around her chin, giving her a wanton look of being newly stirred from her bed. The notion provoked a rush of embarrassment and Will found himself recovering with a light cough. He reached for a glass of water.

Reggie waved away his cigar smoke. 'Sorry, old chap.'

Will shook his head. 'It's fine.'

'She's a gem, isn't she?' Reggie nodded towards the small photograph, which Will now handed back.

'Very lovely. She must be in high demand at society events.'

Reggie emitted a soft snort. 'Clementine can be contrary about these things. Sociable when she chooses to be and a most capable and charming hostess. And other times, she is quite a loner.'

'Her terms?' Will smiled.

'Exactly. Capricious but addictive, you could say. I think she's received maybe a dozen proposals of marriage over the years but not one has been even close to being successful.'

'Well, she's obviously looking for someone specific.'

'I don't think she's looking at all, Will, that's the problem. Well, not a problem, actually. I feel blessed that she's still with me. I'm in no hurry for her to marry, but at the same time I know she must.'

'You sound very close.'

Reggie took a long, slow drag on his cigar and took his time to exhale the smoke casually before answering. 'Inseparable since she arrived back in England. I remember how she hurt herself on the ship's journey. She wasn't a good sailor and was feeling nauseous. There wasn't much I could do for her then, especially as I must have seemed like a stranger. I recall she stumbled, hit her head. A bruise came up on her forehead and one of those beautiful eyes of hers turned black for a week. She became vague for the seven days during which she sickened and felt frightened. I was her constant and she learned not to feel scared of me – it was during that voyage we found first companionship, then friendship and finally a kinship. That has, over the years, developed into a love that I am sure is as deep as any father and daughter might feel. I would die for her.'

Will felt moved by the passion in Reggie's words. It was a helpful glimpse of the man he'd not previously thought had this sort of depth.

'I'll look forward to meeting her some time.'

'You should visit us up north. Come and see Woodingdene Estate – far more fun than a dinner with actors!'

Will laughed. 'Maybe I shall. For now, though, Reggie, let's talk about this latest venture of yours. It's certainly audacious. Risk insurance, you say? I understand risk, of course, but tell me what you understand.' He signalled to the waiter to bring coffee.

'Well, now, Will. Lloyd's is looking beyond the marine insurance it has been so deeply invested in, and I would imagine that finding new and creative ideas is at the forefront of the minds of canny underwriters, particularly the new breed like you.'

'My father would not touch anything but marine.'

Reggie shook his cigar fingers at Will. 'But you would, Will. I know it. And you must, if you're to survive and flourish into the new century. Anyway, to the entrepreneur of today's Britain, what we see ahead right now is progress and prosperity.' He swept a hand, trailing cigar smoke. 'We own an empire!'

Will nodded, letting Reggie speak as coffee was quietly poured and the waiter withdrew. 'Corsets are loosening, the old chophouses now fashion themselves as fine dining establishments, coffee houses turn into restaurants, and people spend, spend, spend in their new mood for luxury and ostentation.' Reggie laughed. 'I know all about it because my father led this charge well before his time.'

Will agreed; it was true that the wealthy in these good times were looking to spend on all manner of new forms of entertainment and consumer goods.

'Music halls and theatres shot up at the beginning of this decade like daffodils in spring, Will. Glamorous new hotels, clubs and other establishments that take guests – well, there is going to be risk, whether it's a failed theatrical presentation or a fire. The owners, the promoters, the participants, they all need insurance. You simply have to extend your thought. If a ship needs insurance for safe passage with lives and cargo to protect along with the vessel itself, why wouldn't the Savoy Theatre need to insure its premises, its patrons, its productions, its people?'

Will's gaze narrowed. Reggie was certainly talking to his sensibilities, especially his modern approach to today's commercial insurance. Despite his conservative upbringing, he wanted to be at the forefront – to take his firm into the new century strong and as a market leader.

'Do you know, Will, I can see a time —' he lifted a shoulder as though unsure — 'not yet, I grant you, but some time not too far away, when insurance will stretch to underwriting the star tenor's voice, the eyesight of an artist, the hearing of a composer – not that it bothered Beethoven – the legs of a ballerina —'

Will began to laugh, stopping Reggie mid-flow. 'I hope I'm alive to witness that,' he said, sipping his coffee, genuinely amused.

'Oh, you may jest, but mark my words.'

'I don't doubt you, Reggie. I know you've a sharp mind for business opportunity and I suspect you've inherited your father's talent for anticipating tastes and fashions before the rest of us. The point is, however, that you are likely well ahead of your time.'

'I'll take that compliment, Will Axford,' Reggie said, beaming. 'And for now I content myself with suggesting to you that we work with theatrical companies. They need insurance against potential disasters, from starlets breaking an ankle to fire closing not just a show but the theatre itself.'

'I don't disagree. Certainly, it is a concept I'm prepared to seriously consider.'

'Is that a diplomatic way of saying no, Will, because you're not prepared to risk offending your father? Rather odd for a member of the new generation to be resistant to change.'

'I just need to do some research and canvassing of my own.'

'Well, don't take too long. I plan to put money into some big shows this year.'

The coffee was drunk. It was time to get back to the City and the frenzy of Lloyd's.

'Come to dinner with the theatre folk. We can start seeding the idea over champagne and happy conversation.'

'Reggie, we should talk about how you will fund your part in it.'

'Is my line of credit in question?'

Here we go, Will thought, *softly, softly*. 'No, it's not that. My father is a cautious man, as you well know. And the moment I broach the subject of insurance beyond ships, he's going to shut down. His memory is long, Reggie. He will immediately remind me of your insolvency.'

'Of two decades ago?' Reggie sounded incredulous.

Will sighed. 'Your insolvency was not a secret.'

'It was not *my* insolvency. I had to take the reins after my father died. Keep in mind my sister had just died too. My stepmother was dying and I had a tiny niece orphaned in the African

198

desert that I journeyed to rescue. Despite all that family drama I still resolved the debt I inherited.'

'I'm sorry I have to ask.'

'I can't imagine why this is important now.'

'Because my father has the memory of an elephant. And any business I propose that links you to our firm will inevitably trigger the conversation about Millwall Iron Works.'

'Heavens! Even I've forgotten that disaster – and I didn't make the deal. My father did!'

Will waited.

Reggie began speaking slowly, as though forcing his breathing to remain calm. 'While in Africa, I funded some diamond diggings. It was a long shot but I was hearing about nothing but success at the Big Hole.' He pressed his cigar hard into the ashtray on the table. The motion was an angry one. 'When I arrived, a new seam in the diamond funnel had just been discovered. Men were nearly hysterical at their claims. My own brother-in-law was one of them, working himself to death.'

'I had no idea about this.'

'No, well, why should you? I met a skeletal, feverish drunk when I travelled out there to visit my sister's grave. James Knight died a few days after I arrived.'

'Clementine was lucky to have you there.'

'Yes, I feel it was Fate pushing us together. To this day I don't know what she lived on. It looked to me like fresh air and laughter. Anyway.' He waved a dismissive hand. 'Someone who had exhausted his funds sold me his claim for a song. And I guess I just brought luck with me because two days after I took over the claim, the man I'd employed to dig for me unearthed a splendid cache of roughs. I brought them back, sold a few and restored balance to the books.' He shrugged, lifting his hands to emphasise he had nothing more to say on the topic. 'That's it.'

Will didn't feel entirely satisfied but before he could prod further, his companion leaned in and fixed him with a stare.

'You really must meet Clementine, Will. She has had a very solid idea that I think you could help her with . . . and benefit from. I told her I'd introduce you.'

Ah, so that's what the photo and the tender history lesson were all about. Will kept his expression neutral. 'I'm listening.'

'I mentioned her interest in jewellery but she has a specific and perhaps predictable leaning towards diamonds. Clementine has been preparing to approach various parties about an idea to reduce risk in the diamond industry. I think your professional expertise would be wisely accepted – and there's money to be made, Will.'

He blinked. 'You wish me to have a business meeting with your 29-year-old niece?'

Reggie exploded into laughter. 'Watch out, Will. That starched collar is creating a visible red mark. People like Clementine will shake off their petticoats and probably run the bloody country.'

Will looked around to see who might be listening. He turned back to see Reggie grinning. The man spoke in a softer voice. 'Meet her.'

'Humour her?'

'Heavens, no! Have you not listened? This is a modern woman with modern ideas. I promised her I knew someone her age who might be willing to listen to her proposal.'

'Is it going to upset my father?'

'Most definitely,' Reggie replied with glee. 'And it's about time you cast off your own blinkers, Will. Her Majesty won't live forever, and the heir apparent is a man for the age. He'll bring innovations when he wears the crown.'

It felt like advice to ruminate on. Reggie's ideas were like a powerful current through him, lighting up his mind so he could see a clearer path. And it wasn't marine insurance – it was finding new avenues for risk cover. Only in the last few days he had been pondering the potential for insurance against burglary. A spate of violent break-ins in London had prompted residents to call for police to be armed with proper weapons; a corps of vigilantes had even been proposed. Will's thoughts, however, had roamed to insurance against the risk of theft. It was so audacious he hadn't yet dared mention it to his father, but listening to Reggie's smirking criticism he felt freshly motivated to act on his idea. If he didn't, someone else would. The wretched Rupert Perkins was always sniffing around in the underwriting room, hoping to eavesdrop on unsuspecting merchants and perhaps pick up ideas he could cash in on.

'All right, Reggie. I shall meet with your niece.'

'Excellent decision. Come up to Woodingdene. How is your weekend after next?'

Will smiled. 'I am free, as far as I know.'

'Take the train. It's a marvellous journey – I'll send the coach to pick you up on Saturday. You'll get in around noon. Lunch on the lawns if the weather's kind. Should be splendid.'

How could he refuse now? 'Fine.'

'Leave this with me. I'll settle up,' Reggie said, waving him on. 'You must need to get back to the office.'

Will stood and the waiter was at his side to pull away his chair. Out of habit Will began dusting himself down of any crumbs. 'I do, but —'

Reggie gave a tutting sound. 'See you in the north, Will. Bring warm clothes and stout shoes.' He held out a hand, its nails neatly trimmed and buffed.

Will shook it. 'Thank you for lunch.'

'The least I could do, dear boy.' He turned to the waiter. 'Please tell the chef the cod was beautifully cooked, but just on the lemon sauce . . .'

Will departed, moving through the large dining room. The crystals of the chandeliers threw their light upwards so the whole space was bathed in a muted sunshine glow of wellbeing and calm. Its wall sconces and softly burnished timber walls created a warm, cosy atmosphere that could trick the luncheon patrons into losing their sense of time.

So why didn't he feel that way as he left Reggie Grant and his assurances in the restaurant?

'Slice of stilton, sir, before you leave?'

Reggie couldn't stomach another morsel. Throughout the luncheon his belly had been churning and he had felt nauseous throughout. Will Axford was a sharp young operator but a careful one. The prod about Millwall had been particularly painful, cutting deep to where Reggie's fears lived. Nevertheless, his performance had been solid gold . . . diamond, even. He allowed himself a smile and turned it on the deferential servant awaiting his instruction. 'I won't, but thank you. Big meal coming up this evening with friends.'

'Right you are, sir. Should I put this on the account?'

'If you would.'

The waiter shuffled off in his polished shoes and Reggie was reminded that the man with the ever-helpful demeanour could so easily have been him. His life must be one of forced cheer, laughing at jokes he didn't find funny, hoping for that big tip, and probably getting by on little sleep and lean pickings while the hotel's customers ate like kings.

His thoughts shifted and he privately congratulated himself on how adroitly he'd redirected young Axford from arguing for financial stability to considering new forms of insurance. It was a double coup, drawing Will into the web he was cleverly spinning. Now all he had to do was ensure the two young people became such excellent companions they couldn't imagine life without each other, and then he would have Will Axford in his back pocket. The man was hardly going to feel inclined to ruin his father-in-law.

Regarding the more urgent matter of his almost certain insolvency within the year, he would need to act swiftly. At least he'd not had to confront that with Will – and if Axford didn't know, then the greater financial community had not sniffed the rot . . . not yet.

It seemed he'd inherited more than just his father's predilection for speculating. He'd also absorbed the old man's audacious taste for investing at the highest possible point of risk. This approach could mean either great rewards or crippling losses. His father had enjoyed years of reward but Reggie, it seemed, was less adept. He had the will and the passion but not the skill to know what might win or what might fail. He put it down to the era he had been born into. It had all been so much easier for his father.

He refused to accept that his investments were rash to the point of being suicidal. And then there was the gambling. It was astonishing how that 'distraction', as he liked to think of it, had trapped him in its grip. It had all seemed such fun – simple entertainment, even. But now his gentleman bookmaker was calling in the debt and the less gentlemanly men he played cards with were making rumbling threats. His liabilities were mounting up around him.

If Will Axford even caught a whiff of the true extent of his debts, he would not only close all lines of credit but would no doubt bring hell down on Reggie and all his business dealings. Will was that sort of man: the kind with a conscience and a moral fire within.

Reggie thought about what potentially lay ahead if he was found out. It frightened him. Would she remember? She rarely spoke about Africa these days; in truth she'd barely spoken about it since she first set eyes on Woodingdene and fell under her grandmother's spell for those few bright weeks. And then, her heart broken once again, it was into the arms of her uncle, who had soothed her and made promises. He had worked hard over the years to push Africa from her mind, removing all reminders, burying her early childhood with each new summer bringing new frocks, picnics, friends' birthday parties and distance. It was that last he was most interested in.

By the time she'd been presented at court, Clementine had taken her mother's surname – although he preferred to think of it as his, because he thought of her as his daughter, anyway – and her only link to the desert was her love of diamonds.

He'd had one of the roughs cut and polished for every birthday, so by the time she turned twenty-one she had sufficient diamonds in the bank to make a magnificent bracelet. Reggie couldn't fathom his luck that Clementine, who had proven herself to be relentlessly sharp and forever curious, had never asked about the provenance of those diamonds. She had simply believed him when he said that her father's diamonds had been lost in the drama following his death.

Even so, this fortunate situation sat like an anxious shadow in the background of his life. Clementine's questions about Africa had given way to melancholia at losing both parents and being wrenched away from the life she knew. He had kept her life busy, engaged, so filled with affection and activities that a young child could hardly fail to enjoy it, and soon enough the questions had stopped, the memories had faded and Africa was simply her past.

But the truth was he'd never fully relinquished the fear that one day Clementine might decide to remember the diamonds in the ragdoll.

16

November 1894

Will Axford watched Reggie wince as he leaned on the walking stick.

'Clem, perhaps you wouldn't mind showing Will around the grounds?'

'Of course,' she said, turning that dreamy-eyed gaze upon Will. He had not been wrong when he looked at that photograph a fortnight ago. 'Mr Axford?' She gestured towards the charming stone path that led down through the various levels of the surrounding garden.

Will was not one to lose his head over anyone or anything, but since his gaze had first lighted on Clementine Grant he'd felt a powerful attraction he had been fighting for the past hour since coffee and sandwiches had been served in one of the many drawing rooms of Woodingdene.

'We call this the Vase Room,' Clementine had said, relaxed and immediately easy in his company. He'd noticed her hand did not shake as she poured him his coffee and she had not lowered her gaze when offering him some of the delicacies she admitted she had helped to prepare. She was not in the slightest intimidated by his presence.

'Your sandwiches are most delicious, thank you. And the staff don't feel awkward about you being downstairs?'

She immediately made him feel stuffy by letting out a soft laugh. 'I don't run that old-fashioned sort of household, Mr Axford. Besides, I've been a general nuisance in the kitchens since I was seven. I'm like a much-loved old saucepan down there.'

Hardly a saucepan! Clementine Grant looked unlike any of the beauties he'd been associated with previously, and she looked ten years younger than her age. There was something unusually confident about her. Her eyes, which were larger than he'd first assumed, were a rare shade of green-grey, reminding him of a valley mist he'd been driven through on his approach to Woodingdene. Within minutes of being in her company he knew that her looks, though mesmerising, were irrelevant. More importantly, he felt he was in the presence of a woman the like of whom he had never encountered before.

It was not that he considered himself especially handsome – though he was ribbed by old friends and colleagues that it was only because of his looks that he'd got anywhere. And it was not that he believed himself to be such a catch, despite plenty of women waiting for the elusive card announcing that Mr William Axford had come to call. It was simply that he was a target for many families looking to make the ideal marriage: he was young, healthy, possessed good teeth and had his features all in the right place. His surname snapped many to attention, his financial status part of the strong appeal to parents, and his connections and status were impeccable. He was the ideal husband for the ambitious woman being married off.

'You're very independent, aren't you?' he'd said, accidentally letting his thoughts become audible.

Even Reggie had laughed. 'Now you see what I've been raising all these years. Clementine is my rock, aren't you, darling?'

Will had watched Reggie's niece lean down and kiss the top of her uncle's head.

'We're inseparable,' she confirmed. She looked back at Will. 'Because he doesn't suffocate me.' It felt like a warning, but as quick as it had come she changed the subject. 'As I mentioned, we call this the Vase Room, Mr Axford, although perhaps you've guessed that?' she said, a smile reaching those unusually coloured eyes. He was startled by the feeling that his heart had decided to pause ever so briefly and then, as if realising it had missed its rhythm, it gave a powerful thump against his ribcage.

'Er . . . yes, I think I had made that leap,' he replied, feeling oddly warm as he looked around at the collection of vases on a high shelf that travelled the circumference of the room.

'My grandmother liked the colour green, apparently,' Clementine continued, the understatement making him smile. The vases were of various hues, although Will noted that none matched the colour of Clementine's eyes.

Her voice dragged his thoughts back to the present and the courtyard where they had paused. 'Would you care to join me in a tour, Mr Axford?' Reggie had already limped out of sight.

'Only if you promise to call me Will,' he replied.

She gave a gesture that was a cross between a curtsey and a bow and he could tell she liked the laugh it provoked from him.

'It's down this way, Will.'

He'd fallen in step with her, moving in front to carefully pick his way down over the moss-covered slabs.

'All of these misshapen stones are from the property. My grandfather selected them all and laid them himself.'

'That's impressive.'

'I have no recollection of him, which is a pity.'

He paused. 'Look at all of this, Clementine – one can tell your grandfather had a unique approach to life.'

She stood higher than him on the steps and half sighed, half smiled. 'Yes, I like that he was so unafraid to be himself at a time when everyone else conformed so tightly to social expectations.'

'Not just in his time. I think we still do.'

'You might,' she quipped.

'Too much of your grandfather in you?'

'Perhaps. My mother certainly didn't conform.'

To Will's eye it looked like the moss was winning the battle on the stepping stones. He offered his arm.

She pushed gently past him, politely ignoring the assistance. 'This bit's tricky and very slippery. Let me lead.'

All he knew about Louisa Grant was that she had been a delicate beauty who ran away to Africa with a penniless engineer . . . or so the story went. He wasn't as interested as the gossipmongers who fed on this sort of information. 'When did your uncle hurt his leg?'

'A few days ago. He was coming down here to cut some roses for my room. He slipped, twisted his knee awkwardly. I'm hoping he won't be using the walking stick for too long.'

———————

Reggie cast aside the walking stick with disgust as soon as he rounded the corner out of sight, tucking it under his arm and losing the limp in an instant. What a nuisance this ruse was! He'd dreamed up the cunning way to fling Clementine together with Will in the hope that nature would take its course. Reggie had become convinced the young pair were equal in mind and that both would recognise the fact after a single day together. He had extremely high hopes that his trick might influence the forming of a relationship.

He hurried to the bay window in the dining room and looked down over the stepping stones. Reggie watched Clementine push politely past Will to lead the way. *Typical! Ah, well, it's early days*, he reassured himself.

Time for a chat with Jane, the cook, to see how the various dishes for their meal were coming along. He thought the picnic-style luncheon was especially inspired. And surely a walk around the heavenly grounds of Woodingdene would push the pair into the right frame of mind for love?

Love. He genuinely wanted Clementine to know romantic love, something he'd denied himself since contracting syphilis. He blamed his mother, as he did for most of his failings. She'd urged him to lose his virginity.

'No man wants to still have that heavy burden. Get rid of it,' she'd encouraged him, waving her hand as though it were a mere trifle.

The early-developed fourteen-year-old had found it confronting to have his virginity dismissed as a weight to be rid of . . . but then his mother had never been one for subtlety. In fact, it was she who had organised for him to give up his 'treasure', as she began calling it to taunt him, arranging for one of her friends to take care of the riddance.

Soon enough, a middle-aged woman with a trim body and voluptuous breasts had terrified him one weekend visit to his mother's new London home – courtesy of Henry Grant – by entering his room with nothing more than a translucent gown and an equally clear intention.

'Don't worry, your mother has paid for this. Let me guide you into manhood,' she whispered in a smoky voice he found irresistible.

Nancy was the name of his gift, and Nancy had given him her own gift known as Ricord's chancre – a single lesion that appeared on his most private of parts one month to the day after his fifteenth birthday. It was neither painful nor large and it disappeared a few weeks later, leaving as its only trace a tiny silvery scar. In his naivety he was too embarrassed to mention it to anyone, and when it left him he felt only relief and release.

It was during his summer school break that Reggie noticed a rash on his hands and feet. The discolouration was light, not painful, and was gone by the time he headed back to school. Once again, he did not mention it to his mother because she had decided to remain in France, so he lived alone with his anxiety until the strange sores and discolouration on his palms and soles had passed.

It was only because of a chance meeting with Nancy's closest friend, who called at the London apartment to let his mother know that Nancy had passed away, that he learned she'd died from complications of what they called the 'French disease'.

'Warn your mother,' the friend advised.

'Why?'

'In case any of her clients have had relations with Nancy.'

'Why?' he repeated, his throat tightening as though his body knew before his mind would accept it.

'Because they've also likely caught the great pox! If they've got the sore or the rash, they'll need to take the mercury very quickly.'

That was his curse. Seventeen by now and diseased. And he vowed that day that he would never lie down with anyone again. He would not do to another what had been done to him.

Reggie Grant sighed at the window and realised he hadn't taken his calomel today. Reggie preferred to use the brand name rather than call the drug mercurous chloride. It sounded somehow more elegant to his ailment, latent though it was now. How long it would remain so, he couldn't know. But for the time being no one knew anything of his permanent companion. It had prevented any meaningful relationships, and he was ever careful around Clementine, concerned despite his thorough research that she might somehow contract the disease from a simple goodnight kiss, or a sneeze or a cough. He had been assured by one of the most respected physicians in the country that this was of no concern. The disease was his alone, it seemed, to live with and to die with when it decided to take him. For now, he would swallow his pills and rub on his mercury lotions and ensure that when the madness found him, Clementine would remember him as the man she loved as much as, if not more than, her own father.

He glanced down once more to see Clementine loosely clasp Will Axford's offered elbow. He knew where she was headed and nodded to himself: it was probably the most romantic of all Woodingdene's many landscaped and incredibly beautiful gardens. It was a place where love had once developed between her parents and hopefully would again.

17

Clementine led Will onto to the footbridge that spanned the small but fast-flowing stream cutting through the valley overlooked by Woodingdene.

'My father finished building this just before we left England.'

She watched him place his large hands on the wire rail. 'It's so elegant,' he declared. He shook his head, clearly impressed. 'It's like spun sugar it's so light.'

This pleased her inordinately, although she couldn't explain why it meant so much coming from her guest. 'Thank you. Memories of my father come in fleeting spurts but what I know of this bridge I have learned from others.'

'Tell me about it.'

'Oh, I don't want to bore you, Will.'

'No chance of that. I like listening to you speak.'

She wasn't ready for such directness but in truth she liked it. Clementine gave him a smile that was neither shy nor flirtatious but she left him in no doubt that she was enjoying his company. 'Beneath us runs this brook, which is known as a burn in this part of the world. Most people think the bridge is iron, but it's made of steel. I think it may have been the first of its kind in the country. I like to think so, anyway.' She grinned. 'In his time it was all about iron lacework and the like. Using steel means it's lighter and that's how he was able to get this almost fairylike construction, as though it just sits in the air, as you beautifully noted. My father claimed that the airy structure and the delicate parapets symbolised my mother.' She pointed and he leaned in to follow her line of sight. 'If you look over there, you will see initials cleverly picked out in the metal.' She waited for him to make it out.

'I see *L* and I see *J*.'

She nodded, satisfied. 'You only properly see it when it's pointed out, otherwise it appears as a pretty piece of decoration.'

'I see a *C* too, if I'm not mistaken. Is that for you?'

Clementine smiled. 'I had just been born. Everyone was so happy, my grandmother said. The whole family was in love with each other because of my arrival.' Her tone sounded ironic.

'Because the Grant family had an heir?'

'Another one, anyway,' she said in reply. 'Everyone hated my father, you see. He didn't fit their idea of who Louisa Grant should marry. But I admire my parents hugely for not bowing to the pressure. I gather the feelings of goodwill at the time of my birth were simply about the next generation. It thrilled my grandfather, or so the story goes, and so he didn't mind paying for the bridge, which was good news given that my father was about to ask my mother to leave England with him. You know the rest, I imagine – defiant, proud, dashing . . . both of them.'

'James Knight sounds like a dreamer.'

'Yes, I think you're right. I believe he was deeply romantic. Apart from the initials, he made sure the main span of the footbridge was 64 feet.'

'Should that mean something to me?'

She shook her head, amused. 'No, only to two people. Eighteen sixty-four was the year my father came to Northumberland. He met my mother when he knocked on the door of Woodingdene seeking work.' She continued, moving her hand beneath the railing. 'Three main spandrels – one for him, one for my mother, one for me. He personally planted pale pink rose bushes to cover the half-height brick piers so whenever my mother crossed her footbridge, she would not only enjoy the fragrance of roses through spring and summer, but the bridge would look like it sat on nothing but air and festoons of beautiful flowers.'

'Heavens! How does any man follow that?'

She laughed aloud. 'I know. It's just so sad he died a penniless, pitiful man. He deserved better, I'm sure.'

'You don't remember him well?'

'I have solid flashes of memory. I remember his voice, especially with that delicious Scottish brogue of his. I know we used to talk about the stars and I recall a silly rhyme he made up; I can still picture riding his shoulders and the scenery I watched from that vantage. I know what he smelled like as he shaved, after a day of work, after a night of drinking,' she said more solemnly. 'I know I loved him and he loved me – that feeling can't be dismissed.' She shook her head, frowning. 'It was so long ago. Shall we go on to the temperate ferneries?'

'By all means, but tell me more about Africa.'

She led him off the footbridge and he followed in a wake of a perfume. He was used to women smelling of roses, violets, musk and ambergris – predictable fragrances for wealthy women. But Clementine, perhaps the wealthiest woman under thirty he knew, trailed a fragrance that spoke of warm spice and wood with just a hint of lemon.

He had to mention it. 'I think your perfume smells of Africa,' he said, feeling ridiculous the moment it was out.

'Have you been to Africa, Will?' she asked over her shoulder.

'No, I . . . I mean, it's how I think it would smell.' Her uncle had warned him and here he was acting like a fool in her presence.

'I actually remember the smell clearly. My world in Africa started smelling of linen dried nearly crisp in the sun, of earth as old as time being dug over and its dust crawling into every corner of my life, of my mother who . . . her perfume was . . . oh my gosh, I've just had a flash in my mind of what the bottle looked like.' She drew a bell shape in the air. 'And it looked like raindrops were clinging to its clear glass. A green label, as I recall . . .' She sounded excited.

'Go on,' he urged.

She closed her eyes and seemed to inhale, silently, and he knew in that moment he could watch her like this all day long . . . every day.

'She smelled of orange, lemon and lime . . . and something herbal. Rosemary, perhaps? Those early childhood memories come in unpredictable flashes like this. The, er . . . ferneries are this way.'

He was pleased when she easily took his elbow and they walked companionably. 'What else do you recall?'

'Well, the smells changed after my mother's death. All that comes strongly to me from then is sweat, whisky, beer, cigarettes, dirty laundry, stews and the smell of leather boxing gloves.'

He gave her a perplexed look and she laughed.

'I can smell the hot tin of the iron walls that made up the shanty we lived in. We lived alongside another man . . . although he tended to live outside the shanty. Only one foot was clad in a boot. The other was bare. And his skin was black.'

Will stopped walking, shocked. 'An African?'

She nodded. 'Shiny, like the engine of a new locomotive.' They faced one another and she gave him a smile that seemed to enter him and warm him. 'His name is . . . was . . . Zenzele. But we called him Joseph One-Shoe. Everyone in New Rush knew him by that name. Oh, Will, I loved Joseph as much as I loved my father. By the end . . .' She stopped and shook her head.

He encouraged her to finish.

'I was going to say that by the time Daddy died, Joseph was my father, to all intents. He took care of all my needs; he told me about life as a Zulu warrior – the woman he loved, the village he'd left, about the skies, their gods and healers – and I taught him how to do sums, his ABC, some writing. He was my best friend in the world.'

There was that whimsical expression of hers, and Will's throat felt so tight that he had to keep his breathing shallow. He wanted to kiss her. What a stupid, boyish, unprofessional thought. 'Er . . . you speak about Joseph One-Shoe in the past tense?'

'Because he's dead, sadly, or so I learned. I don't cry any more – I gave all my tears for my parents and Joseph.'

'I don't know what to say,' he admitted.

'Sorry, I didn't mean to make you feel awkward. No one can hurt me any more, is what I meant . . . Here we are,' she said, waving a proud hand. 'My grandfather collected these specimens.'

———————

He let her show him around the massive boulders where common and exotic ferns grew, spreading their fronds as if in invitation.

'We have so many flower specimens that we're in touch with Kew Gardens. My grandfather's rare heathers are protected now,' she remarked at his sigh of pleasure.

'I saw them. The carriage ride from the station felt like I was arriving at one of the great parks of London.'

'They called my grandfather a magician. When it comes to the house at Woodingdene Estate, I think he built his dream castle. I know people have criticised him for his eclectic taste, but the purists be damned. You can't look at Woodingdene and not be filled with helpless pleasure, can you?'

They stepped back to regard the splendid mansion atop the hill.

'No, Clementine. I must say the view from here pleases my soul.'

She looked up from where she stood, at his shoulder – no taller – and understood that his stare had been focused entirely on her.

'Er . . . my grandmother once told me that he wanted everything about Woodingdene to defy what people expect. He created two lakes that look as though they've always been in this valley. He even created a glen with a brook that teems with fish. He demanded that at every turn a beautiful picture was framed for the onlooker.'

'Amazing,' Will murmured. 'You must never lose this, then,' he said, before he could stop himself.

Clementine blinked long lashes that he could swear were tipped with gold. 'Lose it?' Her expression was all query. 'Why might I lose it?'

He shook his head, unable to find the right excuse. 'Just a figure of speech.'

'It's more than that, Will. I'm an orphan and my family's collective spirit seems to run in Woodingdene's streams, play in its grounds, rest in its valley. I love my ancestors, and here at Woodingdene it's as if they have their arms around me and nothing frightens me. I need to preserve Woodingdene and its land for posterity – for my children, for more Grants to come.'

'Have you plans to marry?' he asked in an arch tone, to keep their conversation light.

'I do, of course I do.' She laughed. 'But I have to find him first.'

Clementine began walking and again he followed her, finding himself in a glass-roofed colonnade, surrounded by fragrant flowers.

'I sit here most days in spring and summer,' she said. She arranged her flint-coloured velvet skirt, which had bold silver embroidery around the hem. A pale shawl sat like a soft fairy cloud around her narrow shoulders.

'It's such a place of peace and I get to look out over all of this,' she added, sweeping a slender arm.

'What a splendid secret spot,' he agreed. 'Maybe it's here you will contemplate which of your many suitors to marry,' he added, helplessly returning to a topic he couldn't leave alone.

She sighed. 'Uncle Reggie has been loose-lipped, hasn't he?'

He gave a shrug of apology. 'I promise he didn't dwell on it. He simply said you were not in a rush to marry.'

'I'm not. But I would rush to marry someone I loved.'

'You're clever with words, Clementine. You should teach.'

'I used to, in Africa.'

He held up a hand. 'I know. You were highly intelligent?'

'Not *were*, Will.' He saw a glint of wickedness in her smiling eyes. 'I'm teasing you. You're too easy, you know.'

It was true. In her company he felt inadequate – a bumbling, hesitant version of himself. 'That's because you're not what I was expecting.'

'The truth is I am spoilt,' she said. 'I know that's what you anticipated and why wouldn't you? My uncle has indulged me.'

A breeze blew up over the rise and Will watched, his throat catching once again, as it stirred her hair and then, as he'd hoped, managed to snag a lock of it free to tumble around her chin, just as he'd seen in the photograph.

'I just make sure I don't show how indulged and privileged I am.' She looked vaguely troubled. 'Somewhere in the recesses of my mind is that urchin girl who never had ruffles or ribbons or excesses. My uncle has tried to coax the tomboy out of me but it lives within. I would be lying if I said I didn't like pretty gowns, but I don't need —'

'I hear you,' he said gently. 'And I admire you all the more.'

She paused, and regarded him with a clear, penetrating gaze. 'Thank you. I'm sorry to go on . . . I've just never had anyone to talk to about these thoughts, or my past.'

'I'll listen whenever you want. I'd also like to learn about the orphanage you're founding.'

'Why, are you interested in becoming a patron?'

The gauntlet was flung in front of him; he could hardly not pick it up. 'We donate to various charities. Why not yours? As a new venture it needs plenty of early investment.'

'It's not a business, Will.'

'But it needs to behave like one so that it does not grind along, forever with a desperate hand held out hoping for charity.'

Clementine blinked as she considered his advice.

'What I mean is let me help you approach your fundraising in a targeted manner.'

She grinned. 'I thought you were a busy city underwriter.'

'I am, but we make our money by avoiding problems. Let me at least lend my expertise.'

'Will, I am not too proud to accept your donations as much as your expertise, but I would have thought the London charities had their hands in your pockets constantly. Why a northern-based orphanage whose founder has no track record?'

He gave half the truth. 'Because I'm impressed by your endeav-our, your energy for philanthropy, and I'm inspired by your drive. I admit, Clementine, I am used to meeting women of your age and position who aren't as selfless. Their heads are filled with parties and outings, fashion and status.'

'How do you know mine isn't?' Her smile told him she was teasing now.

'I don't, but given you've not muttered important names or social events since the minute we met, I think I'm a reasonable judge. Your uncle tells me you have a different proposition that is all business and no charity.'

Clementine met his gaze fiercely, as if taking his measure afresh. 'All right.' She turned away to look out over the patchwork fields. Black-faced sheep in a nearby field munched contentedly, glancing now and then in their direction. 'I happen to know that in Hatton Garden, dealers are walking around with thousands of pounds' worth of diamonds stashed in their pockets as they move between merchants and jewellery houses.'

'Good grief!'

Clementine nodded. 'It's a small neighbourhood, so it's not as though you would leap into a hackney cab. It's faster to move around the narrow streets on foot. But if I know this, then so do others, and that makes the dealers vulnerable.'

This fitted perfectly with his plan to offer insurance against theft. He could barely believe what he was hearing. She took his silence to be encouragement. 'I read in the newspaper recently that there has been a spate of break-ins in London and that burglars are getting bolder, using violence.'

He felt a momentary astonishment that she would be reading the newspapers – but of course Clementine Grant would read the London news. 'This is true. The wealthy are being targeted.'

She gave an expression of soft despair. 'It is surely just a matter of time before those thieves go for even easier targets who are on the move, out and about. They don't even have to hatch a plan of how to break into the property, or spend time hunting for valuables.'

He frowned, distracted, as he ran a hand through his hair. 'Just threaten a lone individual,' he murmured.

'Exactly. A smart criminal knows the man will be carrying a stash of valuables if he times it right.'

Will nodded, understanding. 'Don't tackle them when their pockets are empty,' he said.

'That's it. Time it for when the diamond merchants move around "in the wild", you could say, without protection. You can steal valuable roughs or, if you're lucky, polished diamonds, and get away fast, disappearing into Holborn and greater Camden before the police could give chase. They're easy to carry, even easier to hide. And they can be liquidated fast enough through Amsterdam or Antwerp.'

He shook his head at her. 'That's most insightful.'

'I'm glad you approve – because I plan to use my funds to set up a new business offering insurance policies to protect the dealers in Hatton Garden against theft, both within their premises and while their representatives are transporting their product around the neighbourhood. I would like Lloyd's to consider a partnership.'

He gave a gusting sound of surprise. 'You're so direct.'

'I can't waste time with ambiguity or opaqueness, Will. I'm a woman!' She laughed at both her own remark and his alarm. 'Not used to a woman making business proposals?'

'Not used to a woman making any proposal,' he said. 'I'd like to help you make your plan happen, Clementine.'

She gave him the full heat of her smile. 'Excellent. I feel strongly about the diamond industry – for obvious reasons – and if I can't join it because it is a men's club for now, I can work on the fringes and perhaps pave the way for women of the future. Shall we?' Clementine stood up and began to walk back towards the house.

'I do support women's suffrage,' he added, catching up with her in two long strides.

She chuckled. 'Good for you, Will Axford.'

They began to stroll uphill along the winding path. He heard her give a small sigh. 'What was that sigh for?'

'I miss summer's butterflies, don't you?'

Will smiled. 'I'm very fond of butterflies.'

Maybe this is the moment, Will thought, and didn't give himself time to back away. 'I hope this doesn't sound impertinent.'

She cut him a wry glance.

'It's just that I have never seen diamonds as roughs. I wonder, do you still have some?'

'Diamonds?'

'Yes. Rough diamonds – from the ones your uncle brought back from Africa.'

'He didn't bring any, to my knowledge.'

'Oh . . . forgive me.' He looked thrown off course. 'I was of the understanding that he used the diamonds he'd excavated to help fund some of his, er, projects back then.'

Now she smiled in soft bewilderment. 'Will, to my understanding, Uncle Reggie came to Africa to pay his respects at my mother's graveside. As I remember it, he arrived one hot afternoon, the next day he came looking for us, and by the following evening my father was killed in an accident. By that fourth afternoon he was back on an ox wagon to Cape Town with me in tow.'

It was Will's turn to frown. 'So your father was looking after you at the time?' This did not match up with Reggie's account.

'Of course. Granted, he left most of the caring to Joseph One-Shoe but I never felt abandoned or unloved. I had two wonderful fathers. Uncle Reggie told my grandmother he found Joseph detestable but I think it's because he hated that a black man was caring for me.'

They were standing below the large, flattish boulders that formed the steps up to the main courtyard of the house.

'Can I tell you a secret, Will?'

'I'd be offended now if you didn't.'

She skewered him with her gaze. 'I'm planning to go to Africa. I have to find Joseph.'

'But you told me he was dead.'

'My uncle told me he was dead.'

'You don't believe him?' He could almost wish she would say yes and stop him wondering at his own doubts.

'I didn't say that,' she said softly, looking away. 'I just need to lay it to rest for myself. I saw my mother's grave. I never saw my father's but Joseph told me that my father had died in his arms. I have no doubt about either of my parents. But Joseph . . . Joseph and I were connected in ways that are hard to explain, so I am not prepared to trust hearsay. My uncle can't recall now who told him of Joseph's death, nor does he know where he's buried or even *if* he's buried.'

'Would he have not returned to his people after you left?'

'I doubt it. He admitted he no longer belonged with his tribe and if my uncle was told of his death then someone at New Rush had to pass that information on. That said, I am not yet ready to believe he's gone. However, if Joseph is dead, then I want to find that grave and perform some of the rituals that will allow his soul to move on. Zulus have much spiritual belief and he deserves this from his family . . . I am his family.'

Will swallowed. He didn't think he could be more impressed by a woman if she tried. 'Does your uncle know your plans?'

She shook her head. 'He would wage a campaign against it; find all sorts of ways to dissuade and divert me. He's very good at it, although it took me a long time to work that out. Every time I talk of Africa he expertly distracts me, but I cannot be pushed off this pathway. I'm an adult now and the moment my fortune is fully realised, I shall make the journey to the Cape Colony and that town that was New Rush and is now Kimberley.'

Clementine gathered her skirt and many petticoats. 'We made a pact, don't forget,' she warned gently.

'Our secret, I promise.'

'Thank you. All right. Now, Mr Axford, this is the hard bit – conserve your strength and don't talk,' she threw over her shoulder.

Even so, he thought about it as she mounted the steps, listening to his own breath turning slightly ragged as they ascended.

At the top he watched her gripping her tight waist and bending over. 'It never gets easier,' she said between breaths.

'You made that look effortless,' he replied, dragging in a deep lungful of air. 'You don't realise how fast you are. I think you might have killed me.' She burst into genuine laughter at this. He held his heart. 'Actually, I think I need a doctor,' he said in a voice meant to amuse.

And amuse it did, all the way into the garden room, where Uncle Reggie had organised their luncheon.

'Well, listen to you two. How marvellous to have laughter echoing around these walls. I do love to see my beautiful Clementine entertained.'

'She deliberately brought me the hard way,' Will jested.

'Up those wretched stones, eh?'

'Uncle Reggie, how are you feeling?'

'Knee is fine. I won't test it, though. Let's sit.'

'I hope cold chicken and new potatoes with greens are agreeable to you, Will?' Clementine said.

'We keep it simple here,' Reggie murmured.

She cut him an admonishing glance. 'If my uncle had his way for meals, we should have to roll down the hill and we'd never make it across the footbridge.'

Will gusted a laugh. 'I'm all for small portions and lighter meals, to be honest, sir.'

'Oh, she keeps me like a stick; insists it will help me to live long.'

'Trust your niece. I do.'

'Is that right?' Reggie said, pouring himself a glass of wine. He offered but Clem and Will declined, choosing water freshened with a sprig of mint. 'Milton is off on some private errands today – hope you don't mind us keeping this informal.'

'Much prefer it, sir.'

'Excellent. Well, to your health, Will, and welcome to Wood-ingdene.'

Clementine echoed the toast.

'This is delicious,' Will admitted after his first sip. 'I've never tasted such a thing.'

'She's full of these weird and wonderful ideas.'

Clem shrugged. 'I don't know who taught me how to flavour water with herbs to make it interesting. Probably Joseph One-Shoe.'

'Well, it certainly was not your mother, I can assure you. Louisa loved champagne, my darling. And your father, well, he was a whisky man. As much as he could possibly get . . . Anyhow, cheers,' Reggie said, lifting his glass. 'To you bright young things.'

18

'Uncle Reg?'

'Yes, my darling?'

'We didn't bring any diamonds home from Africa with us, did we?'

Will was startled to see Reggie choke on what he was swallowing. His host reached for his wineglass and drained what was left, coughing and digging in his pocket for a handkerchief.

Clementine was on her feet, tapping his back and looking anxious.

'I'm all right, my dearest, sorry,' he said in between gasps. 'I must apologise. Fancy draining that superb wine like that.' He gave a tutting sound. 'I'll just ring for some more.'

Will narrowed his eyes as Reggie limped over to pull on the cord that would alert the downstairs staff. Was Reggie deliberately distracting them?

As Reggie resumed his seat, wincing at the pain in his leg, Will returned them to the topic. 'Actually, that was my fault. I mentioned to Clementine about the diamonds you discovered at the Big Hole.'

Reggie held his gaze and Will noted that something in it was amiss. Possibly irritation, or was that fear? 'I'm not mistaken, am I?'

'No, you're correct, Will. I funded a dig over a day and one night based on a tip-off I got at the Kimberley Club. The guests were mostly claim owners or merchants, some of them jewellers or brokers. The collective knowledge of that one type of gem was vast. And they were happy to share it with me. I took a chance, hired some men on one particular chap's recommendation.' Will thought that Reggie frowned expertly as he reached back to remember the man's name. 'Can't recall the wretched fellow's name. Bellows? Bellamy, perhaps? My men got lucky – there had recently been a solid find in a neighbouring dig, but it was first timer's luck that my dig produced immediately. I simply put up money for someone who had run out of it. We split up the roughs we found – I got a reasonable haul because I'd funded the dig and bought food and beer for the men.'

'You've never mentioned that, Uncle Reg.'

'You were so little. Why would I, darling? Ah, Jane, could we get some more wine, please?'

Will decided Jane's arrival could not have been timed more exquisitely.

'Maybe we should talk about those days,' Clementine offered, her tone light. Will cheered inwardly.

'Any time, darling, but it was such an unpleasant period. I don't like to recall it myself, let alone burden you with those memories.'

'They belong to me, though,' she said. 'I would love to discuss all that you remember from that time, especially about the day we left. It's a blur to me.'

'Eat up, you two,' Reggie said, and Will could see he'd had time to gather his wits.

Clementine offered Will some sliced chicken and he nodded his thanks.

'I don't like reminding you of it because it upsets you.'

'I'm not upset, Uncle Reggie. I'm interested.' She put the platter down. 'Tell me again.'

Will paid close attention, taking in every nuance of Reg's explanation as they began eating. Reggie spoke in a breezy tone.

He finally shrugged. 'And it was your father's servant who encouraged me to take you back as soon as possible.'

'Not servant, Uncle, as you well know. He was our friend and my father's digging partner,' Clem admonished him.

Will leapt in. 'So he spoke English to you?' He felt Reggie's gaze land on him heavily. Clearly Reggie did not need Will becoming interested. Why? What was he worried about?

'He had good English. My niece had taught him well.'

'So you were alone with him?'

Reggie shook his head, baffled. 'Yes. This sounds like an interrogation, young Will.'

'Do forgive me. I'm just amazed that a native could speak so well and that they'd risk him alone with you.' He glanced Clem's way as a means of asking her to trust him.

He watched Reggie's shoulders relax. 'Oh, I wasn't scared of him. The man was fairly terrified of me, though – of all the police and the questions. I think he was glad to see the back of us, darling, to tell you the truth. I paid him handsomely.'

'I don't believe that for a moment, Uncle Reg. You know how much Joseph loved me.'

'Only because you tell me, but you are remembering the thoughts of a little girl. It's not as though you had much to rely on at the time – a drunk father and a Zulu savage.'

'He was *not* —'

'Forgive me, Clem. But you must understand my position – on arrival I found my niece, the only heir to a great fortune, living like an urchin and being cared for by a huge Zulu.'

Will watched Clem frown and nod, doing her best to put herself in her uncle's shoes. 'But you didn't know him as I do.'

'Did, darling. He's dead now.'

Will thought the remark harsh, but Clementine didn't react strongly to Reggie's bluntness.

'At the time I wanted to see him well looked after, of course, because he had certainly done his best by you, plus he had lost his income.'

'So where is he now?' Clementine asked. 'I mean, his grave?'

'How should I know? His spirit is surely running around the jungle in a loincloth, I suppose – hunting lions and dancing with witch doctors.'

'He was living alongside my mother from the moment we met so he was hardly savage,' she said with appeal towards her uncle.

Reggie wasn't letting up, though. 'Ah yes, alongside your mother, who lived in a *tent*, d'you mean, darling?' His tone was on the wrong side of caustic. 'Savage by Woodingdene standards, I'd suggest.'

'My mother chose her life, Uncle Reggie. And to be fair, as I understand it, she thought she was travelling to live in an Australian city among society. It's not fair for any us to lay blame.'

'Oh, Clem.' He reached for her hand and closed his around it. 'No blame. Just poor decisions. Your parents could have had a fine life here and they'd both still be alive if they'd listened to us all. You'd have both of them in your life – that's all I mean.'

Will could see that Reggie had likely spent years soothing Clementine like this. With a soft tone and a kindly manner, generous and affectionate, always looking out for her and her needs.

'I know, Uncle. I just need to learn more. Perhaps I should return to Africa some time?' It was said casually, as though testing the notion, with a small glance Will's way.

'What?' The silverware made a rude sound on the china.

Tut, tut, Will thought. Reggie was forgetting himself.

'I mean, darling. Don't be ridiculous.'

'I aim not to be.'

'Africa – certainly that hellhole they now called Kimberley – is no place for women. Your mother's plight and her terrible end so young should tell you that. Please consider your safety and my health, Clementine. I think I would die of worry if you pursued such a journey.'

Clever, Will thought, not enjoying his private suspicions.

'On a different topic,' she said, 'our guest approves of my business proposition.'

Reggie turned and Will saw a fixed smile. It was hard to know in this moment whether Reggie was delighted at the news or wished him dead for witnessing what had just unfolded. Perhaps the latter, as he surely hadn't anticipated Will's presence stirring a pot that had mostly been left untouched for two decades.

'Well, well, young Axford, that is excellent news. I told you she would surprise you, didn't I?'

'You did, sir. Clementine's idea is as inspired as it is relevant. I had no idea about Hatton Garden's needs – but of course it makes perfect sense now. I will gladly help her.'

'Thank you, Will,' she said, and her smile threatened to bring a warmth to his cheeks he hadn't felt since he was a youth.

He was glad to see Reggie pick up his cutlery again and recommence eating. Will sipped his water and glanced at Clementine over the rim of his glass. He liked the fresh, cool scent of mint wafting from it, but he liked more the smile Clementine Grant directed at him. There was nothing shy about it; nothing unmistakable in the message that spoke of friendship and perhaps more. *Romance?* he wondered. He hoped so.

Will swallowed his minted water. 'Clementine, did you know that in Greek mythology, mint is known as the herb of hospitality?'

Now she grinned mischievously. 'Did you know that, Uncle Reggie?'

He shook his head. 'I didn't.'

Clementine looked back at Will. 'Well, as we're on Greek mythology, there was a beautiful water nymph called Minthe who was besotted with Hades and offered herself to him, but Persephone, enraged with jealousy, turned the beautiful nymph into the herb we're enjoying in our drink.'

'I heard a different version,' Will responded, 'but poor Minthe still ended up trodden underfoot.'

'I suppose the moral is not to seduce another woman's gentleman.'

'Indeed, but if there's no other female interest, why not make your intention known? Romance can be an ordeal – certainly a confusing labyrinth for most men.'

A deeper, smokier laugh erupted from Clementine.

Again, Reggie stood up to pull the cord that summoned staff from the bowels of the grand house.

'Come to London,' Will murmured to Clementine, barely above a whisper. 'Please? I know people connected to Kimberley. I can begin some enquiries.'

Reggie sat down again with a sigh, but not before Will caught a nod from his niece. It was like a candle's wick catching alight and a strong flame erupting: a juvenile thrill moved through him that they were conspirators.

'Er, that was delicious, thank you both so much,' he said, to cover his delight.

Reggie no longer looked at him with intent. 'Come on, I thought I'd show you around. People take electricity for granted but my father was a pioneer of hydro-electricity. You'll love the pump station.'

Will dabbed his mouth with a napkin and obediently stood. His new confidante threw him a glance of sympathy.

'You two go on. I'll have coffee set up. What time is your train, Will?'

'Just after four o'clock,' he replied, wishing she would accompany them because he suspected Reggie was going to have a stern word. 'I planned to be on my way by three, if that's no burden?' He looked between them.

'Uncle Reg, leave time for us to get Will back to the railway station. I'll make sure the carriage is ready.'

'Thank you,' he said, following her limping uncle out of the room.

———

They'd toured the house and were now inspecting the hydraulic lift. Reggie sounded in awe of it, even though he lived here.

'The servants appreciate it more than any of us, frankly, because it means they can carry coal easily to all of the upstairs rooms.'

'Of course. I hadn't even considered that. I was thinking more of the ease for you and Clementine.'

'My father used it but my niece and I do not. However, Clementine is always looking out for the staff. It was her idea to let them use the lift and save their backs. And not just for coal, mind – washbasins, hot water, heavy trays to and from bedrooms.'

'And to save time, no doubt.'

'Well, there's eight of them on permanent staff so Clementine is all about keeping them happy.'

'I'm betting no one wants to leave your employ, Reggie.' He'd dropped the polite 'sir' since they'd left the dining room, but he was still careful to show respect.

'None at all in recent years. Clementine has ensured that the youngest, especially, are taught their reading, writing and arithmetic. She teaches many of them herself, determined that these young women will grow up with skills that can help them later.'

'She's rather amazing, your niece,' Will admitted, instantly wishing he hadn't shown his feelings so obviously.

'She's about loyalty, Will. So am I.' He didn't hide the barb in his tone. 'The gamekeeper here has been with this family for a quarter of a century, and the head gardener has a decade more service on him. We demand loyalty by looking after those who look after us.'

Will sighed. 'Reggie, I can't guarantee that our firm can —'

'No, but you can guarantee not to turn my niece against me, Will.'

'What do you mean?' He knew, of course, but needed time to formulate a response.

'She's sensing that you might be a confidant.'

'She admitted to me that she would like to return to Africa.'

'Don't put notions into her head that could turn around and bite her. She's so vulnerable on the topic of Africa, Will. Just don't prod it. Only pain awaits her. I know, because I was there.'

It sounded a reasonable enough request, but Will couldn't ignore Clementine's secret. How could he not help her?

'I won't raise it again,' he assured Reggie, hoping that she would raise it herself and so not make a liar of him.

'Very good, Will, thank you.' Reggie's tone changed, instantly relaxed. 'So, what do you think of Woodingdene, then? Worth fighting for, eh?'

'Oh, it is,' he agreed. 'I understand your passion.'

'So, you'll . . .'

Will smiled. 'I'll talk to my father about your idea. I recommend you put together a written proposal – if he won't consider it, I will.'

Reggie looked delighted.

'I would be lying if I didn't admit the idea to insure against fire and the closure of theatrical productions makes excellent business sense.'

'I'm thrilled.'

'But Reggie, if I'm to defy my father and become involved on the strength of my own funds, it will require a commitment from you. A financial commitment.'

Reggie's delighted expression fell.

'I'm in the business of risk but it's not feasible without some security. You will need to come up with fifty per cent.'

'Fifty . . .' Reggie muttered.

'I have to insist. Then we really will be partners, our commitment will be fair, and both of us as eager to protect it.'

'I don't know where you expect me to come up with that sort of money, Will.'

Will shrugged, and while he didn't say the words he essentially reflected the query back on Reggie. He tried to soften its effect. 'I will insist on the same for Clementine, if we go ahead with her plans. For something this innovative, I think we all must protect ourselves from exposure.' He tapped Reggie gently at the top of his arm. 'Think about it. I'll look forward to your proposal in writing.' He slipped out his pocket watch. 'We'd better not keep your niece waiting.'

Clementine had organised for coffee to be set up on the garden terrace.

'It's a bit cool, I'll admit, but I've brought out rugs. It's just too beautiful a day for us to ignore.'

'Quite right,' Reggie said, sounding cheered, although Will suspected it was for the benefit of his niece.

'Enjoy your tour?' she asked, pouring steaming coffee from a swan-necked silver pot with an ivory handle. It was ornamented with a brightly crested crane on its side. Will recognised the work of London silversmiths Garrard.

She saw him admiring it. 'This was my mother's gift from my

grandparents on her sixteenth birthday. It's an odd present for a young woman but I gather my mother fell in love with the bird engraving. My grandmother was always one for practicality. She'd have preferred to give her this instead of jewels.'

'Of course, my father didn't agree,' Reggie chimed in. 'He lavished my sister with a breathtaking pearl necklace – part of a Byzantine collection from an eleventh-century harem in old Constantinople. Apparently, it was made for the murad's second-favourite wife.'

Clementine chuckled. 'You should hear about the pearl item he gave his favourite before it was stolen – it was extraordinary. They say it was to be worn naked, and there was a massive jewel that pointed to . . . well, let's just say it pointed south.' She grinned. 'The story goes that the chief eunuch stole that magnificent piece and sold it off. No one seems to know to whom or even where in the world it has ended, but oh, the young nubile odalisque who wore that in the harem would —'

'Now, now, Clem. Keep that for tea with the ladies.'

Will enjoyed the wicked glint in her eye. 'Your uncle was telling me about how well you look after the servants. The hydraulic lift obviously makes life much easier for them.'

'Will, have you ever lifted a full basket of ironed linens?'

'I can't say that I have,' he replied, taking an exquisite porcelain coffee cup and saucer.

'Probably heavier than me without all my clothes on.'

Reggie chuckled at Will's cough of embarrassment.

'Yes, well, I can only imagine.'

'Do you mean you can imagine the laundry, or me without clothes on?' she queried, straight-faced.

'Clem, stop! Don't tease our guest, please. Will, she's been doing this since she was a little girl. Don't go up against her – she's always one step ahead.'

'I shall be very careful,' he admitted and drained his delicious coffee. 'I think I must make tracks.'

They all stood. 'The carriage is ready to take you back to Widdrington station,' Clementine said.

'What a splendid day it's been. Thank you for being such generous hosts.'

'It's been our pleasure,' Reggie said, although Will knew he was leaving each Grant with a separate dilemma.

He bent over Clementine's hand to kiss it. 'Thank you. I hope we shall see each other again.'

'I am sure we shall. In fact, I have to be up in London in a few days. Did I mention that, Uncle Reggie?'

Reggie shook his head.

'I'm going to see Jennifer Hepburn for lunch and Penelope Ireland for dinner and a show. I'm also rather hoping to see the French artists on display at the new Grafton Galleries. Have you heard of it, Will?'

'I have. I saw its first exhibition of paintings and sculptures, and more recently the Society of Portrait Painters held an exhibition there.'

She looked impressed. 'Well, its latest is its first of French decorative art.'

'Sounds deeply boring,' Reggie remarked. 'Please don't ask me to come, Clem.'

'I shan't, Uncle Reggie. I know how you become. Besides, you couldn't possibly go down to London with your knee in such poor shape.' And now Will understood: she'd trapped her uncle in the north with the most innocent-sounding remarks. He could hardly deny her statement after his sighs and limps all day. 'Perhaps you'd like to accompany me, Will? I mean, only if you can spare the time.'

And there it was. Clementine was clearly a match for anyone who aimed to manipulate her.

'I'll make the time for you, seeing as your uncle is not available. I shall be delighted to escort you, but no doubt you'll want a chaperone.'

'Such a bore, but easily fixed.'

'Are you staying at your uncle's house in London?'

'That would be Clementine's house in London, Will,' Reggie reminded him, just a fraction tersely. A nerve had been hit.

'Well, we shall meet again at Holland Park, then. Have you been to the house?' Clementine asked.

He shook his head.

'Then you're in for a treat or a shock, Will, depending on how you lean.' She handed him her card. 'I shall be there on Friday, staying through the weekend.'

He smiled. 'Thank you.'

Jane arrived with Will's hat and coat. 'Sir,' she said, nodding. 'The driver is here, whenever you're ready.'

'Thank you.' Will walked over to shake hands with the head of the household. 'Hope you recover soon, Reggie, and no doubt we shall speak shortly.' He slipped into his coat.

'We shall.'

He turned and gave a small bow. 'Clementine, enchanted. Thank you again for the lovely day. Until the weekend.'

19

Clementine could not regret that she'd taken Uncle Reggie's advice to meet William Axford. There was no doubt he'd had a less progressive upbringing, likely with few of the freedoms she'd enjoyed, yet already she sensed he privately railed against conservatism.

It was easy to fall for his appearance. It wasn't just youth keeping him trim; she suspected he took good care of himself. His clothes, she'd noted, were immaculate, although anyone could achieve the look of a gentleman with the right barber, tailor and address. Being a gentleman came from the inside, her mother had taught her, and Clementine had so far found his directness and also his tender manner charming.

She had expected to have to navigate around conceitedness, and yet she had seen no sign of it getting in the way of his companionable manner. Even his moustache, begging to be waxed, refrained from that ostentation and was instead neatly clipped. His hair was not overly coiffed but neatly parted, although he couldn't hide its lustre or the golden glints that remained from the summer sun. Everything about Will had seemed contained to her, and she sensed he was simply cautious with words and honest with them when he let them free. It was refreshing. Will was a surprise of the most pleasant kind. He was also waiting; the bell at the door had chimed.

She didn't wait for Mrs Johnson to answer the call on her behalf. She wanted to enjoy Will's expression when he first clapped eyes on her grandfather's other folly. She smoothed the front of her forest-green skirt, which she had chosen carefully today, and unlocked the door, surprising Will but also herself at the unexpected pleasure of seeing him again. She'd anticipated enjoyment at his arrival, but not this deep feeling of connection, or the sense of anticipation of being near to him now that she looked upon him once more.

He was broader than she recalled; taller, as well. She'd even convinced herself that his hair was receding, but what a lie!

'I don't much care for standing on ceremony,' she said, responding to the silent question in his expression. 'I was already in the sitting room, and ready.' The explanation was too complex. Goodness, she must be nervous – how unlike her.

He grinned, removed his hat and leaned slightly on the umbrella he carried. 'I think you're just impatient to get on with life.'

'That too,' she admitted. 'Now, are you braced for the onslaught?'

Will looked perplexed. 'For what should I be ready?'

'For this.' She swung open the door and moved aside in invitation.

Will stepped onto the charcoal and ivory mosaic floor of the reception hall and his face blanched, precisely as Clementine had anticipated.

She clapped her hands and grinned. 'Ghastly, isn't it?'

He turned slowly, taking in the astonishing medley of styles crammed into the reception alone: from classical Greek alabaster columns with their capitals picked out as birds, to the intricate

Roman floor. As his mouth opened in bewilderment, his gaze was dragged helplessly towards the brilliance of the glazed tiles gleaming on the walls, a swirling blue Mediterranean sea. First-time visitors often complained of feeling dizzy, which always amused Clementine, who would quip that it was probably seasickness. They never fully got her jest but it mattered not. This magnificent wall of water, as she liked to think of it, was interrupted by dazzling Byzantine panels in the brilliant blues and crimsons of the Ottomans. And still the assault on the senses continued. A staircase, framed by thick mahogany bannisters, swept to the upper level, giving on to an even more astounding Arabic-themed room. As Will's gaze lighted upon the carved wooden latticework, she filled him in.

'Apparently seventeenth-century from Damascus, where it was used to separate the women's quarters. They could look out onto the street or courtyard but not be seen.' She grinned at his silence, adding, 'The Turkish tiles are at least a century older.'

He stammered. 'Er . . . not ghastly,' he said at last. 'Certainly overwhelming.'

She laughed delightedly. 'Will, you're the master of the understatement. I assure you that you cannot offend me, but my grandfather's taste in decorating this house is so confused and outrageous that many shocked visitors come full circle and begin to enjoy it.'

'You'd need a day in this room alone just to take it in.'

'Yes, you're right. Individually, each element is exquisite and historically important to take care of. But he didn't know where to put it all.'

'Or how to curate it,' Will added with a generous smile.

The housekeeper appeared and Clem nodded to her. 'We're ready, thank you.'

She led him into a drawing room. 'All this clutter makes you want to cough, doesn't it? Coffee?'

'Please.'

Mrs Johnson arrived with a pot on a tray and poured.

'You can leave it with me now, Alice. I'll see you all later this afternoon.'

The housekeeper nodded graciously and left.

'I made these,' she said, offering him a sugary-looking delicacy from a plate slick with syrup. 'They're called *koeksisters*.'

'Say it again?'

She repeated it. 'They're a South African treat, but the origins are Dutch. Don't be scared of them, Will. They're a pastry, plaited and deep fried and then plunged into cooled sugar syrup.'

'You cooked these?' he asked, incredulous.

'Is that so odd?'

'In the way of my life, yes. The woman of the household may order the menu but that's as close to the preparation of food as she'd get.'

'I learned to cook when I was a young child.'

'You are definitely one of a kind, Clementine.'

She smiled. 'Well?'

'They look sticky,' he admitted.

'I promise they are delicious, and I think you will offend me if you won't at least bite into one. I made them for you.'

He looked taken aback at how personal that sounded. 'One bite, then.'

'Go on – I dare you to stick to one,' she urged him, watching him attempt to sample the delicacy without getting sugary syrup on his lips. As she'd anticipated, he not only failed but his expression as he chewed told her that her recipe had not let her down.

'My goodness,' he said, his tone filled with admiration. He bit into the pastry again.

'You lose.'

Will swallowed the last sticky morsel, licking syrup from his fingers, and then looked at her with gratitude as she offered a fingerbowl of warm water she'd had the foresight to arrange. She had to look away from his neatly defined mouth, now shiny with syrup, and had the outrageous thought that it would be pleasant to kiss that sugar away.

She blinked, disconcerted by her own silliness. She never thought like this about a man. Clem suspected that Will didn't appreciate his boyish looks. A beard might help to make his appearance less youthful, but she would be sad not to be able to admire the sharp jawline if it was covered by a beard. His nose was firmly angled, and above it his forehead seemed to frown with permanent worry. It relaxed only when he laughed, and so she was determined to see those soulful brown eyes of his reflect laughter; she wanted to ease his concerns, whatever they may be. Those eyes flicked up now and caught her staring.

'What is going through that clever mind?' he asked.

She didn't dare reveal the truth. What she did say surprised her, though. 'I was thinking that going out with some old school-friends feels like the last activity I want to do today.'

'I thought that was a fib to get down to London.'

'No. But I might beg off.'

'But what shall you do instead?'

'Well, I know you thought we might visit the gallery, but if you're free, why don't we spend the day together? Visit the orphanage of which I'm a patron. And then . . .' She shrugged.

'I can make all of today free. After the orphanage, allow me to take you somewhere. May I use your telephone?'

'Of course. I'll get ready while you make your telephone call.'

'Take your time. I'll hail a carriage.'

Clementine spent a few minutes in her bedroom checking herself in one of her grandfather's massive Venetian mirrors. She'd always favoured less outrageous colours than the current fashion.

Some of the crimsons and purples were nothing short of gaudy, and in her opinion best suited to burlesque or music hall outfits. Her skirt was as slim as she dared take it, and far narrower than fashion dictated. The fabric was a simple, light and luxurious wool with no pattern beyond some looping embroidery in the same green. The obligatory bustle was as small as her seamstress would permit without sighing in despair.

'I don't want a shelf on my bottom, Mrs Woodrow,' she'd complained. 'It's the most ridiculous contraption. Exactly as I've drawn, please. No wiring – a pad instead.'

'Well, it will show off your tiny waist, I'll give you that, but Miss Grant, this is almost . . .' The woman swallowed her words.

'Say it,' she encouraged her.

'Well . . . it's almost masculine in its appearance.'

'Which man walks out dressed like this, Mrs Woodrow? With a cinched waist and a jacket flaring over hips accentuated by annoying and unnecessary padding? How about all the layers? Does a gentleman's suit require petticoats? Or is it masculine to you because it doesn't have a garish pattern or colour?'

The seamstress took a breath to object but Clem jumped in first. 'Because I'll be honest, I detest looking like a pair of curtains.'

The seamstress looked back at her, shocked, and then they both laughed. Mrs Woodrow had worked for Clementine long enough to expect her to be contrary.

'You are so difficult, Miss Grant. What am I going to do with you? The young women of this region look to you for inspiration.'

'Good! Then I'll teach them to throw away their stupid bustles, to wear narrow, practical skirts, to get rid of their explosively puffy sleeves, big hats, silly hair pieces —'

'Enough! I'm going to make this up so it fits you like a second skin, but I am going to insist on wide, decorated lapels and – there will be no escaping this, no matter how much you rage at me – you *will* be getting slightly puffed sleeves, or my reputation will suffer.' She wagged a thimble-clad finger as Clementine leapt to object. 'And for beneath it, I will make a frothy, silken blouse that is all woman! It will *not* be practical, or suitable for anything other than looking dazzlingly feminine and showing off your beauty.' She stared Clementine down over her pince-nez spectacles. 'And that blouse is going to be made from the palest of shell pinks.'

'Mandarin collar, no bows,' Clem insisted. 'And positively no train!'

'Just a tiny billow of fabric, then, which will be pleated from here,' she said, twisting Clem around to touch where a bustle would end.

Clem stared at her reflection in the long mirror. She wore only undergarments, made of the softest cotton and decorated with tiny rosebuds and ribbons. She sighed. She was not especially tall and she would hardly call herself willowy, yet she knew her body had attractive proportions. Her waist was not too close to her breasts and that length meant clothes hung well from her frame. Her breasts – in her opinion – were neither alluringly full, as those of so many other girls she knew, but they were not inconsequential. They were pert, at least. Her hips were narrow, and her legs had grown strong and lithe from running up and down the hills and glens of Woodingdene Estate.

'Miss Grant, you must trust me. This will look elegant.'

Clem nodded with resignation.

Now, with Will waiting and dressed to step out, she turned to admire the silhouette; her dressmaker had been correct to make her final suggestions. There was balance and an elegance she couldn't deny. The exceptionally feminine blouse was made from a sheer silk, ruched so that it looked like a cloud; it was superbly crafted, with a thin beading of pearls at the base of the mandarin collar.

'You'll do, Clem,' she said to her reflection.

They met on the steps outside the house.

'Clementine, is it permissible for me to take you on this journey unchaperoned?'

She smiled. 'I have never been known to stick to the rules, Will. Neither did my mother. We're ruined beyond all repair.'

Will aided her into the hackney and waited for her to settle her skirts before he joined her.

'I do sympathise,' he said, as she got comfortable. 'I've never understood women's fashion.' He squeezed onto the remaining bench next to her. 'Do you mind? I detest being driven backwards.'

'I have the same loathing.' She grinned before further adjusting herself on the bench. 'It must have been a man who devised the bustle – surely no woman would dream up such impracticality.'

'At least those ridiculous crinolines have lost their dominance.'

'Ah, now, they had some benefits.'

He looked at her with aghast amusement. 'They had to build special corridors in hotels and public places for two women to pass one another.'

'Nevertheless, they were light and airy. Some women these days look like they're modelling sofa upholstery. All that draping and the tassels and the heavy brocades in rich colours. It's an enormous weight to carry around.'

He laughed. 'Do we blame our queen?'

'We had better not.'

'And yet you make it seem effortless, in your neat ensemble. You look very beautiful.' He glanced away; clearly he had not meant to be so direct.

'Thank you,' she said conversationally, as if he'd just said, *I've brought a spare umbrella – it looks like it might rain.*

As the hackney pulled away to join the traffic, Clementine felt as though she was about to turn a corner – what lay beyond it she couldn't yet see. It was exciting. And that inner voice of hers, which had always been reliable, warned that around the corner awaited Africa and some truths she was yet to touch.

20

'Well, that's left me feeling both hollow and motivated at the same time,' Will admitted, as they settled into another carriage.

'Good. A mix of guilt and inspiration is ideal for easing donations from people. Have you never visited an orphanage before?'

He shook his head and looked embarrassed.

'Don't be ashamed. It's very easy to overlook that forgotten layer of society when you don't have to confront it in your daily routine. I include myself in this. I move in carriages and have lots of clothes; I go to the theatre and meet my friends for tea. I take long baths with hot water and I am never thirsty, never so hungry that I feel faint, never so cold I can't move, or so tired I can barely open my eyes.'

'But at least you're doing something; you're actively helping.'

'I am. It's like a single raindrop, though, onto parched earth. There's always more each of us can do, but even if we all help just one other person who is poorer, less fortunate, we're doing something to demonstrate our humanity.'

'Oh, Clementine, I don't know if we can all live up to that ideal. It's a lovely thought.'

'I know. I don't judge, Will. The only reason I'm so involved is because I saw a woman – I think she had been a domestic – who had a son to an English sailor, and the family had not wanted her and her bastard child. The little boy's hand was so tiny it could barely clasp around the few pennies I pressed into it, and it was at that moment I knew I had to do something meaningful with my time, my energy, my money. We enslaved these people from Africa and irrevocably changed their lives – we use them as soldiers, seamen, servants, but we don't wish to make them citizens.' She shook her head with regret. 'Sometimes I think we treat our animals better. That little boy deserved more from the country that had essentially stolen his life. He kissed my hand and that small hand in mine reminded me of the power I had to change his life. His name is Jacob. He's now twelve and a fine young lad in service at our stables. His mother works at Woodingdene.' She nodded. 'Don't feel bad, feel driven – take action. There's always room for more compassion in the world.'

'You inspire me, Clementine.'

'Thank you. I'll look forward to your cheque,' she said, making him laugh.

'It will come next week. So, beyond your new business project and charitable work, do you have other passions?'

'Plenty,' she admitted. 'Jewellery design is a great interest of mine and when I can create more time for myself, I shall follow that interest. I enjoy art, the old masters and contemporary. I'm interested in improving the yield of wool from Woodingdene's sheep and I share my father's fascination for the planets.'

'The sky? How intriguing.'

'The stars connect me to Africa, especially to Joseph One-Shoe, because he and I spent many a night worrying about my father. We distracted ourselves by staring into the vast sea of black overhead and its glittering life. He taught me about the stars in Zulu and I taught him our names for the astral bodies.'

'I'm beginning to understand how important this man was in your life.'

She gave a gentle sigh. 'Uncle Reggie has looked after my every physical need – he's become the best sort of father – but Joseph gave me a sort of spiritual love. He lives here,' she said, a hand covering her heart. 'Now, enough of all that. Where are we headed?'

'Sorry, we're off to meet my aunt.'

'I see. I guess you really impress the women in your life with that kind of excursion?'

He gusted a laugh. 'I think you'll enjoy an aspect of where she lives.'

'I'm in your hands this afternoon.'

'That sounds splendid,' he admitted.

She covered her thrill with a response delivered dryly. 'This had better be good, Will. We've cancelled the art gallery for this.'

'Better than any old master, I promise.'

'I'll hold you to that. Where is it, by the way?'

'Primrose Hill. I've asked the driver to take us via the Strand to avoid some of the congestion.'

'Now, your turn. Tell me about your work.'

He gave her a potted version of insurance for shipping, during which all the familiar sounds of London seemed to dull and her whole focus was on his voice: gritty, but gentler than those of the men in her life, like a summer shower, light and amused.

'So you're underwriting insurance for the ship itself, its cargo and the lives on board?'

'Correct. It's been the lifeblood of Lloyd's, but the new generation – people like me – well, we're looking for creative ways to apply what we know. Of course, I didn't think the daughter of a diamond miner would be a step ahead of me.'

'My father once accused me of thinking like a man. I was seven.'

'Clementine, you don't seem to act or think like most women of your age.'

They'd entered the Strand, the iron-clad wheels of their carriage joining the metallic throng of all the other carriages in motion along the vast street, and it was more crowded than Will had anticipated. He sighed, and sat forward to watch as a horse shied and people crossing the road cowered, women shrieking. It seemed someone's load had spilled, creating havoc, and the smell of dung was overwhelming. The driver made the best decision to get off the famous street and they wended their way up and through Covent Garden, where the number of costermongers intensified.

As they passed, they could hear snatches of calls for everything from roasted potatoes served in twists of newspaper to the thick ham sandwiches that were so popular with the British worker. And the newly popular meal of fish with potato cut into batons and fried the European way was busy being cooked.

'They smell wonderful, don't they?'

She couldn't deny it. The oily, toasted smell of deep-fried potato made her feel hungry. 'Oh, look at that pitiful child.' It was Clem's turn to point and Will leaned closer. 'What is she selling in that basket of hers?'

'Watercress, I think. There's a hierarchy with all these coster-mongers. Look, see that woman selling flowers from her basket? She was just elbowed out of the way because she got too close to the saveloy stall. They're ruthless, these men. They're paying for their spot, and they need a good take for the day – their families' welfare depends on it. But now, look at this kiosk,' he continued as they hauled to a stop again. 'This is a champion pie maker, apparently.'

'Have you eaten his pies?'

'No. Chances are they contain cats or dogs . . . or both.' He winked.

Clem was aware of how close he leaned. She could smell the sweet lemon scent of his shaving soap. She closed her eyes and she was back in Africa, just for a moment, standing and watching her father shave using the identical soap. She couldn't conjure his face, only his hands. They were large and the fingernails were grubby; her mother must have died by then or he would have taken more care. The flash of the cutthroat razor reflected sunlight slicing its way through a thin gap in the corrugated-iron walls of their shanty. And then the fleeting vision was gone. To cover the suck of her disappointed breath, she spoke quickly into the pause she'd created. 'Tell me about these women to whom you referred earlier.' *What an odd question*, she privately berated herself. *Where did that come from, Clem?*

'What can I say? The women I seem to come into contact with are either vacuous spinsters scheming towards the ideal marriage, or they're raging suffragettes who are just plain scary.'

She laughed aloud. 'Priceless but cruel.'

Will shrugged. 'Much worse are the elder women in these circles, who hover like vultures. They've turned their youngsters into women who think snaring a man with status and wealth is more important than any happiness.' He shook his head. 'All of that said, I don't blame them – they will of course do their utmost to ensure their daughters and grand-daughters make the best unions. But they all but sneer at the notion of love, and especially compatibility. It's not something to which they encourage their girls to aspire. To me, marriage has to be about enjoyable companionship first. If I'm going to spend my life with someone, I want to truly like her. Not just how she looks or how she treats me – I want to like the person she is: how she thinks, her aspirations, how she moves through the world.'

'Gosh, Will, that sounds daunting.'

He pressed his lips together with resignation. 'Hence no marriage, and me moving towards my thirty-second birthday, much to my father's despair. He wants grandchildren – grandsons, to be specific.'

'Girls not good enough, eh?'

'He's old-school, Clementine. And because my mother died soon after my brother was born – and died – he hasn't had anyone to counter his gruff, rather medieval attitude.'

She smiled sadly for him. His upbringing made more sense when he put it into context. She hadn't known he too was motherless or that he'd lost his brother. Maybe that began to explain his often-sad expression.

'Must've been hard growing up with a tough father and no mother.'

'No harder than for you without your parents, Clementine.'

'Yes, but I was loved, Will. Adored. My uncle knows no bounds when it comes to me, and I don't say that with any pride. But I do love him back with all of my heart.' She didn't understand why something akin to pain ghosted across his earnest face. He looked away, trying to dodge her notice, but she saw it nonetheless.

'Now, my Aunt Esme is quite the character. She's my father's sister and the antithesis of him. I think you'll enjoy her.'

They'd moved well and truly out of the city now and were skirting Regent's Park.

'Oh, I see where we are,' she said. 'London Zoo is over there.'

'Correct. And we are but minutes away now from Primrose Hill. The whole region was originally part of one of Henry VIII's famous chases. It was purchased from Eton, actually, about half a century back to extend parkland for the poor of north London, so they could have open air space for recreation.'

'I like that,' she admitted. 'Those of us who have must try harder for those who have not.'

'Spoken like a true humanitarian.'

'I do hope so, or what's the point in being influential?'

They turned into a wide street, its two sides separated by communal gardens in the middle. The tall terraced homes were picked out in pastel colours, as if they had been fashioned from ice-creams.

'Oh, Will, it's beautiful. Surely these inspired the doll's houses that little girls play with.'

He grinned. 'You could be right. My aunt's house is not one of these. Not quite so narrow.'

Aunt Esme's house turned out to be so splendidly large that it could have swallowed three of the terraces they'd been admiring. It sat alone among extensive grounds that backed onto open parkland.

Will's aunt came outside to meet them. Even from inside the carriage, to Clem it looked as though she were wearing a pair of curtains.

'Oh, heavens. After our conversation I realise she really does look as if she's torn down the bedroom drapes and thrown them on!' Will admitted.

Clem burst into astonished laughter. 'Don't be unkind,' she admonished him.

He helped her out of the carriage. 'Thank you, driver.' He'd already paid the man but flipped him a coin as a tip.

'Oh, my darlings!' Esme said, fluttering down the steps like a mother hen rounding up her chicks. 'William,' she said, offering both of her powdered cheeks for kissing. 'Hug me, you wretch. It's been far too long.'

He obediently pulled his cooing aunt close as Clem readied herself for the onslaught.

'And who is this delicious creature, Will?'

'Aunt Esme, I'd like you to meet Clementine Grant.'

'Grant? The Grants of Chester, or the Grants of Northumberland?'

'The latter,' Clem obliged, a little disappointed that his aunt seemed to possess the pretensions she found loathsome.

'My dear girl, how wonderful. Your grandfather was born in an age that wasn't ready for him.'

That surprised Clem. She admonished herself for judging too fast. 'So they say.'

'I should warn you that my aunt rarely forgets anything. She reads the newspaper as you do, and that makes her a formidably well-informed dinner guest.'

'It's why I don't get invited to dinner much any more, my darlings. I think I make the women feel uncomfortable and the men awkward. I just prefer intelligent conversation to banal chitchat. Now, dear Clementine – your name is as sprightly and pretty as you are . . .' Will cut her a brief look of apology but Clem was now intrigued by his aunt. Besides, she made it sound more like an observation than a contrived compliment. 'I was at court when your mother attended her first ball. She was a stunner and I don't think the apple has fallen more than an inch from the tree.'

'You knew my mother?'

'I wish I had, my dear. I observed her, as many did, but she was in a space of her own – if I might put it that way? People could hardly tear their gaze from her.'

Clem followed Will's example and kissed his aunt on both cheeks. 'Thank you for welcoming me to your home on such short notice.'

'Nonsense. The pleasure's mine. I love to have young people around me. Come in, come in.'

She led them through the reception hall directly to an orangery that contained its own water garden; the sound of the water dribbling over a mound of mossy rocks was as soothing as it was attractive.

'Oh my, Aunt Esme – I hope I may call you that?'

Her elder nodded with pleasure.

'This is very beautiful.'

'Thank you. I cannot claim the glory. This is all darling Freddie's vision.'

'Uncle Fred was a keen naturalist,' Will explained. 'He built this space so my aunt could admire the outdoor world, which tends towards inclemency, from the comfort of inside.'

Aunt Esme sighed. 'Freddie loved this outdoor room, but his real prize is somewhere Will shall take you after some refreshment.' She dragged on a bell pull.

'You look like the cat that's licked the cream, Aunt Esme. What are you up to?'

'Oh, you know me, Will. Sit, my dear.'

Clem seated herself in a high-backed cane chair. 'How lovely.'

'My husband was a helpless traveller – like your grandfather. He collected these in India. The harlequin-pattern floor tiles are from Italy, and the pots are from China, the citrus trees from America . . . and on it goes. But you know plenty about all that, I'm sure, Clementine?'

'I am surrounded both in London and in Northumberland by the world,' she said in a breezy tone.

'Oh, I wish Freddie were alive to hear you speak about it all. Ah, here comes our treat. Have you tasted the sponge cake named after our queen?'

'I don't believe so.'

'Our recipe comes from the royal household. My cook used to work at the palace when she was much younger and she had access to this recipe. The jam is blackcurrant, from our garden.'

Clem admired the two-tiered sponge being delivered by a smiling household servant: its top layer sat upon a cloud of whipped cream like a cumulous drifting upon an oozing sky of glistening black jelly. Icing sugar was dusted across its top. 'That looks nothing short of sensational.'

'Tastes even better. Yes, please, Holly, if you'd pour. With lemon or milk, Clementine? It's a fine orange pekoe from Darjeeling.'

'Just lemon. No sugar, thank you.'

'I haven't offered anything savoury because Will has asked me to pack a small picnic for you both.'

'Has he?' Clem replied, accepting her slice of cake from Holly. 'Thank you,' she murmured.

'Yes. He wants to surprise you, so I'll leave it at that.'

The Victoria sponge fulfilled its promise and soon they were all momentarily silenced, chewing on the plump and airy sugary confection which ultimately drew groans of pleasure.

'This is so light and delicious,' Clem admitted.

'We should thank the heavens for the invention of baking powder,' Esme said around another forkful of the cake.

'And thank heavens for our cook, who knows how to use it,' Will replied.

Clementine was soon entirely under Esme's spell. This was a woman after her own heart, who was far more interested in the world around her than her own private world of privilege.

Their conversation roamed from the introduction of numbered plates for cars in France to the aim of liberation of Macedonia from the Ottoman Turks and the world's fair in Chicago, which had been held the previous year to celebrate the four-hundredth anniversary of Christopher Columbus's arrival in the New World. There had been a sideshow and an amusement park, apparently, Esme exclaimed. The discussion moved on to reading and whether Will had read Arthur Conan Doyle's 'The Adventure of the Final Problem'. He assured his aunt that he had. And their discussion came to its close on the topic of a pair of extraordinary Persian rugs known as the Ardabil Carpets.

'Mid-sixteenth century,' Esme said. 'Freddie would have climbed over hot coals to view them. They're in tatters, apparently, but they are likely to sacrifice one for the other so it can be pre-served at the Victoria and Albert Museum.'

'I would definitely wish to see that,' Clementine admitted.

'We shall go together, my dear. I gather they may call upon public funding, as the restoration is going to be exorbitant. It will take years, no doubt.'

'That's a promise,' Clem assured her.

'Well, Aunt Esme, thank you for this spread. I think it's time to take Clementine through.'

'Through to where?' Clem wondered. 'This is all so mysterious.'

'Off you go, you two. Consider yourselves chaperoned. I shall be resting for an hour and then I have a dinner engagement. Bit of a journey by carriage, so I may not be here to see you off, but the picnic will be ready for you.'

Clem glanced at the clock with its sonorous tick and wondered when this picnic would occur and why. It was already late after-noon but Will clearly had a plan.

'Goodbye, my dear. This has been a true pleasure.'

'Thank you. I've enjoyed myself very much,' Clem replied, hugging Aunt Esme and realising that beneath her billowy sleeves and heavy clothes the woman was rather hollow and fragile.

'Aunt Esme, thank you as always,' Will said, hugging his aunt tightly, then offering Clementine his arm. 'Shall we?'

'I can't wait. All this cloak-and-dagger has me intrigued.'

'The honey is on the hallstand for you, Will,' his aunt said in an airy tone as they walked away.

'Honey?' Clem repeated.

'Be patient. You'll find out.'

21

'Uncle Fred called this his "tropical house",' Will said, as they emerged around the corner of the building into the vast side gardens. The honey he carried glimmered like late-afternoon summer light, its colour reminiscent of those dying moments as the slipping sun kisses the world golden and daubs the fields with amber as dusk's shadows start their march.

If Clem had thought Aunt Esme's orangery worth commenting on, this palatial glasshouse stole her breath. She stared at it in wonderment. It was a huge and gloriously decorative construction of metal and glass, yet it looked so spectacularly light that it appeared to hover above the ground. She must have murmured this aloud in her awe because Will was suddenly answering her thought.

'Yes, I gather that was the effect he wanted, and you'll understand when we go inside.'

'The glazing is damp?'

'We're lucky it's a cool day. Come on, I'll let you discover why.'

They stepped inside and Clem gasped at the breathless warmth.

'Tropical garden; be warned. It's humid in here but it's worth it. Maybe you remember this heat from Africa.'

'No,' she said, unbuttoning her jacket, which already felt too clingy; she was unaware of the effect her gesture had on her companion. 'It wasn't a wet heat like this. It was fiercely dry.' She was surprised how she could suddenly feel that ferocity of long ago, like a furnace in her mind. Her jaw fell open with surprise at the sight of a butterfly with a wingspan larger than her hand, dancing through the air.

She gasped again. 'Oh, Will!'

He slid her a grin of genuine pleasure. 'It's my uncle's butterfly house. Before he died he collected every specimen he could from around the world, and faithfully cossetted the cocoons and caterpillars to keep their species going. We have butterflies here from every continent, and my aunt employs a permanent butterfly keeper.'

'Extraordinary,' she breathed in wonder, now noticing dozens more of the winged beauties. 'But you'd lose so much heat through the glass, surely?'

'You're right, but Uncle Fred wanted everyone to gaze at the specimens and learn about the natural world. Some people are scared of flapping wings, so the glass makes it possible for all to enjoy it.'

'Now there's a humanitarian at heart.'

'Come on. Let me show you.'

He led her around the enormous space – as tall as it was wide, with the November day a broody presence above them. It felt as though they were floating in the sky, with so much glass surrounding them.

'I adore this, Will. I feel like I'm in a fairytale cathedral.'

'Excellent. Pleased to find something new for the girl who has everything.'

'You have certainly impressed me.' She breathed out a happy sigh as a butterfly landed on her arm. It was a tawny colour with cream shadings and what looked to be an eye staring back at her.

'That's called the owl butterfly. *Caligo memnon*, I believe.'

'Oh, you dreadful show-off!' she said, falling just a little bit deeper for his helpless charm.

'I learned every species when I was growing up, so I have to show off to someone. Now, watch and see why it's called the owl.' He touched the wing softly and the gentle creature obliged, spreading both wings.

'Oh!' What looked to be an owl's face with serious, staring eyes fixed her with a stern gaze. 'How splendid,' she exclaimed as her winged companion flapped away.

'That one is from Central and South America, but look, here comes another – this one hails from Mexico through to the Peruvian mountains. It's called *Heliconius hecale*, or Hecale longwing.'

A startling orange and black butterfly with brilliant white spots danced past them.

'Beautiful,' she cooed.

They entered the full space of the glasshouse, where palm trees bent their fronds, rhododendrons with glossy leaves provided settling spots, and tropical blooms offered nectar. The air moved with rapturous colour as butterflies from around the world flew in their erratic manner.

Again, it was though Will could read her thoughts. 'They have evolved to fly in this strangely non-linear style as a way to avoid predators. This way, their flight can't be easily predicted.'

'Clever little things,' she said absently, mesmerised by a superb blue butterfly that shimmered around her. 'Let me guess, South American?'

'Bravo!' he said. 'Blue morpho. Ah, now, look at this beauty, called a tailed jay, this time from Asia.'

'I don't think I've ever seen that shade of green before. It's as though it carries its own light beneath its wings.'

Will pointed. 'Over there is a large tree nymph. And that one, sitting in the trumpet of that flower, it's one of my personal favourites – its wings are so elegantly striped but exquisitely bright with those vivid red edges. Meet the scarlet Mormon, from the Philippines.'

'Dazzling,' she said, shaking her head and pointing to a blue, yellow and black butterfly. 'Go on, show off.'

'India leafwing, and there, a red lacewing, also from India.' He turned back to her, looking oddly hesitant. 'I'm so glad this has made you happy, but will you allow me to show you why I brought you here?'

She nodded.

He took her hand and she felt a spark of pleasure at the sensation of his skin against hers. Clem wanted to convince herself it was the humidity making her feel momentarily light-headed, but his sudden exclamation distracted her from pursuing the truth.

'Look,' he whispered, sounding triumphant. 'Here is the *Danaus chrysippus*.'

She knew the butterfly instantly. The sight of it trapped her voice, and the sensuality that had been sparkling through her fled. Now, even though it was suffocatingly warm in the hothouse, she felt chilled. Clem could swear there was a ringing somewhere deep inside, like church bells.

She felt instantly illuminated and free. It was as if a door was yawning open and she was being ushered through it – back to childhood, the butterfly her guide. She could smell Africa; she could taste it on the wind and hear the haunting sounds of the wilderness in her soul. It was spring in Kimberley and butterflies were emerging to paint the air with their bright orange wings. As a child she had always thought that a famed artist must have come up with the elegant design painted on their wings, the orange striking against the black and white tips.

'We call these tigers,' Will offered, unaware of the profound effect of her seeing one again.

'And we called them African queens,' she whispered.

'I've never heard that,' he said with an intrigued smile.

Her voice felt as though it were travelling from far away to speak in the dense humidity of a glasshouse in southern England. 'No, it's a familiar name, used only in the Cape. It was Joseph One-Shoe who taught me that name for them. He knew all the creatures of our region. And while you know them in Latin, he knew them by their tribal names as well as how they were known in English or Afrikaans. Why did he have to die, Will? Why does everyone I love have to die?'

It was Will who spoke first into a silence so taut she could feel the power of its straining tension, desperate to spring back and release them. 'I'm sorry, Clementine.'

She smiled sadly. 'Don't apologise. This is an old hurt. I normally have it under control but just sometimes when the mood catches me off guard, I get sentimental. All this beauty, and to see these African queens again . . .' She shook her head as if unable to finish.

'How old was he?'

'I'm not sure. He may have been thirty or so when we met. What people don't understand, and I only grasped as an adult, was that the diamond diggings were different. The Africans may have been segregated in other parts of Africa, but in New Rush the police force was made up of pretty thuggish men who weren't above breaking the law themselves, and the military had no real reach that far out – it meant we all sort of did our best to get along as one. A lot of the Africans worked shoulder to shoulder with the white men, and many of them were friends. Joseph was quite simply part of my family. I can remember that a lot of the native Africans who worked as diggers had begun to cleave to our ways and thought of themselves as civilised colonials, as opposed to the tribespeople who had not yet fallen under the influence of Europeans. Both white and black would refer to these people from outside our digging community as "blanket kaffirs".' She shook her head. 'Uncle

Reggie never understood the relationship we had with Joseph, but he'd never lived outside his cosseted world in England.'

'And why, how, did Joseph die so young?'

'Some sort of poisoning. I kept nagging Uncle Reggie for information about it, so he made contact with the locals via his London club. They somehow got word back that he'd succumbed to an illness, but I never had any detail. Besides, Joseph knew how to cook cassava.' At his look of query she shrugged, as if to say an explanation of the vegetable wasn't worth pursuing.

'And you trust what you were told?'

'I had to – I was a child. I had no voice.'

'But now you do.'

'Yes. Now I have a voice. I have the means. I have the desire. I'm going to find where he's buried and do the right thing for him; for my parents, too. I must visit their graves.'

'Let me help you.'

'What do you mean?'

'To find him. I have contacts, perhaps even better than your uncle's network. My club can reach out to the Kimberley Club with a simple telegram.'

Clem grinned. 'They have the telephone, too – and the railway, and electricity. It's one of the most modern communities in the world. Apparently being in a desert on a distant continent is no hardship when the land yields a fortune every day for the company that mines it.'

'Then a telephone call might be all it takes to get your hunt started in earnest. May I help you?'

'Will, you hardly know me.'

'I know you, Clementine,' he said, and reached for her.

Unaware of any conscious decision to do so, Clem moved into his arms as butterflies took wing and they held one another.

'Thank you,' she whispered, her cheek against his chest. In the silence she could hear his heartbeat: it was powerfully rhythmic against her ear and Clem felt a new stirring. She moved away from it by stepping back. 'Forgive me.'

'Nothing to forgive. I enjoyed it.'

'And the honey?'

He gave a burst of laughter. 'I forgot about it. Let me show you.'

Will was grateful for the warmth of the glasshouse, which was to all intents staining his cheeks with colour. He was not used to this feeling of wanting to please someone because it mattered so much. 'This doesn't always work, I must tell you,' he qualified as he retrieved the jar.

'Mr Axford, you cannot tease a girl and then disappoint.'

'Never my intention,' he assured her humbly. 'Here goes.' He lifted the large cork stopper and the viscous honey winked at him, all the richer for the dull light around it. He dipped a forefinger in gently and pulled out a glistening whorl of stickiness which he proceeded to daub on his nose, much to Clementine's surprised delight.

'What on earth are you doing?'

'Be patient,' he said, but they didn't have to wait long.

It was one of the passing African tiger butterflies that landed on his nose.

'They taste with their feet,' he whispered.

'Don't lie.'

He made a gesture as though crossing his heart. 'It works better with sugar syrup, I'll be honest. But my uncle used to do this to amuse me. It's fun to keep the tradition alive.'

'Priceless,' she admitted. 'Thank you. I needed that.'

'Come on, do you feel like a walk? I have one more surprise.'

'How can a girl resist?' she said, and he felt as though the butterflies had landed briefly and then taken flight in his heart.

22

The late afternoon was mild for November but by the time they'd ascended Primrose Hill their breath was still steaming out of them like the famous *Puffing Billy* of the north from decades ago.

They stopped to catch their breath, Will clutching a pair of blankets he'd insisted upon carrying.

'We're lucky the place is deserted.'

'Are you worried about a chaperone again, Will?'

He hesitated and then admitted it with a nod. 'It's your reputation I care about.'

'Well, don't. Because I don't really care if the gossipmongers talk. They have no idea that you are honourable and I am impervious to your charm.' She grinned.

'Aunt Esme is sending someone up the hill for appearances' sake.'

She shrugged as if to say, *So be it*.

'Do you see that oak over there on the slope?' Will pointed back to where they'd hiked.

'I do.'

'It was planted nearly one and a half centuries ago, when it was called "Shakespeare's Tree", to mark three hundred years since his birth.'

'Good grief,' she said. 'And it's still flourishing.'

'Just,' he said. 'I'm very fond of it. Uncle Fred would bring me here and tell me that tree held the wisdom of England in its heart.'

'And you thought you could gain some?'

He lifted a shoulder almost shyly.

'I was a child who needed reassurance. It felt like the tree could give it to me when I touched it.'

'Reassurance for what, Will?'

'That my mother's death wasn't my fault; when I was little I believed I should have somehow saved her. Also, that my father's unhappiness wasn't either.'

'Oh, Will. Truly?'

'Fret not. I did work it out for myself. But while my childhood was privileged it was also a little grim, other than when I was here with my aunt and uncle.'

'We both have lots to thank our uncles for.'

He threw her a look that said, *Touché*.

Will had something on his mind – of this she had no doubt. They were circling each other from a polite enough distance but it felt as though their heartstrings were reaching out to each other and deliberately snagging, weaving themselves together tightly.

It felt exciting, yet also easy – as though this coming together had been predetermined somewhere in the stars. The stars. She closed her eyes momentarily and reached out.

'Clem?'

'I'm fine. I keep being reminded of the stars, as if they're important.'

'Ah, good. It's why we're here.'

'I wondered why you'd bring me so late.'

'There's a police constable patrolling. You have nothing to fear.'

She opened her eyes to look at his earnest expression. It was like their own special secret.

'Nor does it occur to me to worry.'

'Come on,' he urged, offering a crooked elbow. 'We have the hilltop to ourselves.'

As they crested the hill and looked back, Clementine let out a sigh of pleasure. 'Will, you've given me another beautiful gift. I've never seen London from this vantage.'

He smiled. 'The best is coming.'

Clem watched him unroll one blanket, liking the way he moved. He was her counterpoint; all sharp angles against her neat curves. His strong jaw angled down from its pronounced hinge beneath his neatly fashioned ear towards his pointed chin. His precise nose was straight, with not so much as a rogue ridge. Even the darker line of his lashes had no gradient, as though they'd required a mere horizontal skim of his maker's pencil. His obedient features barely cast shadows across the planes of his face. Nothing out of place with Will Axford. Tidy in his appearance, his mind, his words and his emotions.

He turned to offer a hand to help her sit down and the smile that moved across his orderly lips made her want to disorder them with a kiss. She hoped he couldn't read her thought because he'd already shown a remarkable tendency to answer a question before it was asked.

'Aunt Esme kindly sent some refreshment. Look.'

Clem could see a man hurrying up the hill with a basket.

'Oh, really?'

He chuckled. 'I think she wants you to feel welcomed.'

'What's on her mind?'

His eyes lowered and he tugged at some grass. 'Keen for you to like me.'

'I do like you, Will. I did from the moment I met you.'

He still didn't raise his gaze. 'I'm usually a bit brusque around women – or so Esme insists. She made me promise I'd be a generous listener to you.'

Clem opened her mouth to speak but he anticipated this and continued. 'Before you leap in and ask if it required some sort of coaching from my aunt, the answer is no. I find you easy to talk to . . . easy to be with – and that's not easy to admit.' He shrugged, smiling in his own defence.

The fellow arrived. 'Mr Axford, sir. I'm Johnny. I was asked to bring this up from the main house and to, er, wait.'

'Yes, thank you.' Will pulled a farthing from his waistcoat pocket and flipped it; the man caught the copper expertly.

'Thanking you, sir.'

'Are you happy to sit on that bench over there?' Will pointed halfway back down the hill.

'I am, sir. I shall have a quiet smoke, if that's all right with you.' They watched him retreat.

'Is that our chaperone?'

'Apparently.'

Soon he was an indistinct huddle on the distant bench, until both of them forgot he was there.

Clem noticed now how quickly dusk had crept across the skyline. The Houses of Parliament and the dome of St Paul's Cathedral were thrown into sombre silhouette as a moody purple began to pull a blanket across the sky.

Will unpacked the basket and they munched on ham sandwiches with a tangy pickle in a companionable silence as Nature put on a colourful show in the heavens.

'Are you cold?'

'A little.'

He unfolded the other blanket and offered to place it around her shoulders. 'May I?'

She nodded and enjoyed feeling his careful attention as he draped the woolly cocoon around her.

'Tuck yourself in.'

'Thank you for this, Will.'

'Oh, Aunt Esme wouldn't —'

'No, I mean for this.' She gestured towards the darkening vista. 'It's beautiful – and earlier, the butterfly house.'

'You don't have to thank me. It is a true pleasure, to be able to share these places with you.'

'Don't tell me you don't bring all your female companions here?'

'I've never brought anyone here, other than Uncle Freddie's favourite bulldog, Nelson. I had to carry him most of the way up the hill.'

She giggled, and felt a fresh eruption of warmth at the thought that this place belonged only to her in Will's mind.

'Well, you've given me two special gifts today, for which I'm grateful.' She liked him so much for not trying to impress her with fancy entertainment or chocolates and bouquets of flowers. 'No doubt you write poetry in your spare time. I think you're a romantic at heart.'

'I hope so, Clem. I think the world needs romantics.'

It was the right answer. She felt herself melt a little closer.

'Aren't you cold as well?'

He turned his hand into a fist and pumped his biceps.

She laughed and opened up her blanket. 'Come on, no one's watching.'

He looked around and she realised his conservatism was showing now. 'I won't offer again,' she warned him.

Will allowed her to enclose him within the blanket. Clem felt sure his aunt had deliberately chosen this one for its generous size. Perhaps she had gone so far as to hope that this particular situation might occur? She was pleased to have the sense of the older woman shoving them together as if pushing them in the back – if that's what was occurring.

She had no time to think on this further because Will was letting cold air into their shared cocoon as he pointed.

'This is why I brought you here.'

She followed his line of sight. 'The North Star?'

He nodded. 'I know how much you love the night sky, so I thought you might enjoy gazing at it from this lookout, away from the light of the city.'

She glanced once more at the horizon, which was surrendering its day into night, but the battle was on. A cauldron of boiling ambers and scarlets were fighting to the death. Meanwhile, a heavy shroud of imperial purple dipped like a crusading army to overwhelm their efforts, blanketing their fire.

Clem returned her attention to where the North Star winked its sparkling eye at them from the velvet of the universe, feeling something of a seismic shift inside herself towards Will. It wasn't just his romantic nature that had softened her gaze and banished her defences. It turned out he possessed qualities she couldn't help but admire – in truth, there was so much to like about him, to fall for. Or was it too late? Had she already fallen? Being needy was not her way, and yet how wonderful it felt to need someone. It was something more than that, though, and this was her most intense surprise: she desired him. Her life since returning to England had been one of adoration and affection, wanting for nothing – until this moment. No one had inflamed her passions but now her heartbeat seemed to be making up its own erratic rhythm. It made her throat ache softly but in a way she hoped might never stop.

He pointed. 'Well, I know that one, the North Star, brightest star of our skies – but tell me about the African sky.'

This remark, which required her to look up and stay focused on that glimmering star of the north, suddenly felt like the edge

of a surgeon's scalpel, cutting through scar tissue to reveal the original wound.

His words transported her with the same breathless, dizzying
speed as the sight of the African queen butterfly had done. Suddenly
Clementine was no longer beneath a blanket atop Primrose Hill in
1894 but sitting beside the Big Hole at New Rush, beneath Joseph
One-Shoe's blanket, flanked by her friend and her father. She could
see them so clearly now, as if she were standing to one side and watching this strange, close trio. Her father was in the motley outfit she
knew so well, a bottle of beer to his lips. Joseph One-Shoe's clothes
were just as ragged; although he blended into the night, the flash of
his eyes and his glorious smile lit his face for her. They were laughing
with the little girl between them. She had unruly hair and wore a
baggy blouse that had belonged to her mother and second-hand
trousers that made her look like a little boy – not that she cared. She
was pointing at Orion's Belt and asking what if it broke – would his
trousers fall too, and would the stars fall out of the sky?

It all returned like an old friend. She didn't need light. She
knew the minutiae of Joseph One-Shoe's face, down to the tiny
depression of his chin, as though he'd been dropped when he was
knocked out of his mould. His expression was always thoughtful;
she had learned that his words were not plentiful, so she'd taught
herself to read his forehead instead. His dark eyes had their own
light, always giving her comfort and wisdom.

Oh, Joseph, she thought with despair, gazing towards the
horizon, where the earth disappeared to the other side of the world
where he was. *Are you following me, as you promised you would?*

Will pulled a small silver flask from the basket and flipped off
the lid. 'Aunt Esme's idea,' he explained, offering her a sip.

She barely hesitated before tipping back her head to swallow
a tiny mouthful of smooth cognac, which made her think of fruit
for the Christmas cake steeping in the kitchen at Woodingdene.

Hints of toffee and warm spices came to mind as she gave a soft groan of pleasure and handed back the flask. She watched his lips pucker to take a sip, and just for a moment it felt like a kiss because he hadn't wiped the mouthpiece.

'The North Star is a name we give to Polaris,' she said. 'It's also commonly known as the Pole Star.' She paused before grinning at him. 'It is not, however, the brightest star in our system.'

She heard him chuckle. 'You're going to correct me, no doubt, although I should warn you, I learned this from an amateur astronomer at his private observatory in Sussex.' He packed away the flask.

'Well, next time you meet you can sound knowledgeable and be accurate. Polaris is a very bright star that you can pick out easily in the northern hemisphere. But now look over there.' She pointed. 'There he is. Do you see handsome Sirius? He is the brightest star you can see from anywhere on earth, but here in England we have to look for him over in the south.'

He stared and then smiled into the closing night. 'You clever thing. And what is the Zulu name for Sirius?'

'InDosa,' she said.

'I promise you that we're going to find his grave.'

Darkness had fallen and she was glad because it meant he couldn't see what those words did to her. She didn't know what to say or how to thank him.

She didn't need to. Will said it for her when he set aside his reservations and leaned in to the cosiness of the blanket they shared and chanced a lingering kiss. Clem didn't fight it. There was no guilt at all; to the contrary, she defiantly fell deeper into his embrace to let Will know she welcomed his touch, his lips, his butterflies, his sunsets, his sincerity.

When it ended, he didn't pull away very far. They could both still taste the cognac they'd shared in the tiny breath of air between them.

'Forgive me.'

'For kissing me?'

'For not asking —'

'You need to live more dangerously, Will,' she breathed, and this time she took control and felt his shocked thrill beneath her as she turned his polite kiss into something far deeper, filled with the underlying message that she didn't make this gesture lightly. He returned her passion, and in the time it takes for a butterfly to flap its glorious wings, Clementine felt herself truly lost to the universe.

She broke the kiss, feeling breathless and dizzy.

He didn't want to let her go. 'Are you all right?'

Clem nodded. 'I am now that I have found you.'

'Clementine,' he whispered, his voice croaky with desire. 'I don't just want to help you. I want to be with you . . . all the time.'

'That's very demanding,' she quipped, but gently.

'Please, Clem —'

'I know,' she whispered. 'I feel the same way.' She didn't have to see in the dark to know that he was smiling with relief.

Just as he was about to kiss her again, a fresh thought erupted like a dazzling diamond catching the sunlight and splitting it into colours like the rays of Sirius. The memory made her breath hitch and she felt a pain like a thorn prick.

'What?' he said, clearly sensing her body becoming tense.

'There's something else about Sirius.'

'Tell me.'

'We named a huge rough diamond after him. Apparently, it was going to make our fortune – it was worth a mint back then. But my father died the next day and I haven't seen it since.'

Will's soft smile fell in the shadows.

23

Will arrived back at his house in Berkeley Square feeling brightly unsettled and dark of mood.

He had listened with increasing dismay as Clementine told him the story of the magnificent stone discovered by Joseph One-Shoe at the Big Hole. She'd explained that they'd named it, and that it had been hidden to be taken home in secret. Most importantly, she'd impressed upon Will, was that as little as she was, she had been sworn to remain silent about their find.

'And you're sure he didn't keep it?' he pressed. 'Your recollection could be hazy.' He heard her take a breath of soft vexation. 'I'm sorry, but —'

'No, I can promise you that Joseph One-Shoe didn't want Sirius. He said no white man would ever be convinced it belonged to him if he tried to sell it. Of course, he did keep some diamonds as my father insisted. They were partners. I haven't thought about this in so long, but the diamonds were hidden in my ragdoll.'

'You are certain about this?'

'Yes. My father used to make me perform the power of my memory like a party trick.'

Will frowned. The air of the dark carriage was filled with a new tension. Clementine was suddenly frustrated by his mistrust of her memory; only an hour earlier he'd been keen to unleash it.

'What do you mean?'

'He'd try to get his drinking companions to bet that I couldn't remember ten items on a tray – coins, stamps, a photo, a letter, a comb, anything they could fit on it. If he was feeling especially confident, he'd raise the stakes and let them place twelve items. I'd be expected to recount each of those items to the last rusted nail or grubby ticket. If I got the list right, my father was assured of an evening's drinking the following night. If not, he would be beggared for the week, as he would have to put money on the bar and buy drinks for all who participated. I'm telling you so you understand that my father was so sure of my keen memory that he was pre-pared to bet his livelihood on it – our livelihood.' Her voice was now tinged with sorrow.

'Did you ever lose?'

She shook her head. 'And before you ask, yes, I'm as certain about the diamonds hidden in my ragdoll as I'm sure that I am sit-ting here next to you now, Will. I just haven't thought about them since leaving Africa.'

'But they weren't still in your ragdoll when you arrived in England, I'm guessing?'

'No. When I asked Uncle Reg about them – when I was a little girl – he said if they existed, then presumably my father removed them before he died. But that's not the impression I was given by Joseph. To be honest, though, everything was so confus-ing around that time. I was in shock and I hit my head on the ship. Uncle Reg says my recollections are hazy and probably wrong. I cannot deny that; I couldn't remember my name for a whole day, and I cannot be sure that my memories aren't just something I believe occurred.'

Will could almost wish Clementine hadn't discussed Sirius. The stone's disappearance played to his worst suspicions; a convenient answer to his questions.

They parted with a cordial kiss to Clem's gloved hand, which lingered perhaps longer than it should have.

She waited at the door, silhouetted by the golden light of the reception hall, and watched him depart.

If only he'd kept going, got into the carriage and tapped on the ceiling for the man to drive on. But he paused, turned and walked back up to the doorway. He watched her smile widen at the thought he might return for one more kiss.

She grinned. 'Can't stay away, Will?'

'Clearly you're an addiction,' he quipped. 'I thought I'd give your neighbours something to chat about over their evening meal.' He kissed her carefully on the cheek and gave a low, delighted sniff. 'I meant to tell you again how delicious you smell.'

'Thank you. I use a perfume that has its origins in the middle centuries. Spiced roses, herbs, berries, even grasses. My mother used this same perfume and Uncle Reggie wanted to keep her alive in my mind. Thank you for today, Will, it was very special.'

'I'm the one who should be grateful, because today brought me you.' He was not used to speaking about his emotions and yet he could no more hold back his honest thoughts with her than stop breathing.

Here was a final chance to depart on a happy, romantic note, but as usual, his sense of honour got in the way.

'Clem, would you mind if I urged you not to say anything about Sirius and his companions? The matter has obviously slept soundly since your childhood – no need to wake it up in everyone's minds.'

Her face suddenly creased into a frown as she tried to guess at what he was not saying to her.

'Despite your careful generalisation, Will, I believe you don't mean *everyone*, but specifically Uncle Reggie. Am I right?'

She was no fool. Her voice was even but her tone was suddenly pointed.

His unruly breath smoked between them in the chill night, and a sense of dread crept up to join it. He'd hesitated for too long. Before he could give her any well-constructed and elegant reassurances, she spoke into the awkward pause. 'You think he stole the diamonds.' The accusation felt like a knife stab.

'Don't you?'

Instantly Will wanted to bite his tongue out. He hadn't meant to say it but out it had flown, followed by a horribly uncomfortable silence.

'Goodnight, Will,' she finally said, closing the door on him.

He stood there feeling faintly ridiculous, staring at the shiny black paint where a heartbeat ago she had stood smiling at him affectionately. He didn't move even when the inside light suddenly blinked out. He imagined the woman he wanted to marry ascending the stairs in the darkest of moods.

He stepped lightly into the carriage and closed the door, not giving in to the temptation to look at an upstairs window. He rapped on the window. 'Drive on. Mayfair, please.'

Now, at home by the warmth of the fire, he stared out across the gardens of Berkeley Square. He sipped his Armagnac, swirling the spirit around the balloon glass. He wasn't sure he necessarily liked it more than cognac, but he took pride in knowing the difference. Right now he needed the higher-alcohol kick of the Armagnac and its ability to instantly warm him.

His mind wandered along with his gaze. It followed the curve of the plane trees cloistered in the Berkeley Square Gardens and he was prompted to consider the proposal to put up iron railings. It would look attractive, no doubt, but he wondered about the cost. He was aware that during the Regency days, Berkeley and Grosvenor squares had battled it out to be the most fashionable. He didn't know which had the upper hand at present, nor did he care nearly as much as his father did. His father lived at Grosvenor Square. Will had inherited the house out of the family holdings as he turned twenty-five and came into his trust. It was his home. He thought no more of it – didn't boast about his address or make mention of it in conversation, as so many others might. The gas lamps were burning gently around the square and the golden glow lit the gardens handsomely; the trees were naked, so he could see all the way through to the statue of the nymph that graced the fountain.

Her pretty female form reminded him of Clementine. He shouldn't expect her to accept his theory simply because he couldn't rid himself of the notion. He would have to prove his point – but how would he achieve that? Where would he get his evidence?

The clues were there. Reggie had been broke in 1872. He'd taken the helm of an empire facing bankruptcy. Fact. In this same year his sister had died and he was sent to retrieve the child, the sole heir to her mother's private funds, her grandmother's private funds and whatever could be salvaged from the extensive and complex Grant businesses. He remembered Clem's comment that her uncle had not touched her inheritance, and yet somehow he had returned from Africa and saved the company so it could continue to trade. Will's father remembered all too well how strange it had been that Reggie produced the required funds so quickly. Whenever Will spoke about doing business with him, his father would reinforce the point that something was bent about Reggie Grant.

And now the Grant empire was in trouble again. Will knew it and so did Reggie, as did some cluey people in financial circles, but apparently Clem was none the wiser.

How had Reggie survived? Where had the cash injection come from on his return from Africa? *It had to be the diamonds from Clem's doll. It simply had to be*, Will thought. And yet Reggie had nonchalantly passed off the cache of diamonds he'd liquidated as a matter of being in the right place in the right moment.

'Balls!' Will said in an uncharacteristically vulgar outburst, as he raised his elegant glass of Armagnac, backlit by the window of his Mayfair mansion. 'I'm not going to let you take her down with you.'

There was still the question of the Sirius diamond: if Will was right, this was still in Reggie's possession. From Clem's description, that stone would create a stir no matter how secretive Reggie might be. People in the know would hear about it.

And if I am right, any time now you'll need another injection of cash. I'm onto you, Reggie.

Will knew what he had to do. It would be painful for Clementine, and he may well lose her respect and certainly her affection in the process, but he didn't think he could lie straight in his bed if he didn't pursue his suspicions.

He checked his watch. It was not yet seven. Hardly late. If he dressed quickly, he could still make it to his club and hunt down his old school chum Billy Maidstone. He'd be able to connect Will with the people he needed to talk to.

Will drained the final sip of Armagnac, the double distilled cognac's flavours of fire and earth echoing Will's mood. He was about to burn down a name, an empire – one that was rotten at its core.

———

Clementine couldn't know where Will's thoughts were ranging but her mind was navigating similar terrain in Holland Park, where she was sipping cocoa and hugging her knees to her chest. She had retired early and was in her bed, leaning against her green velvet headboard shaped like a leaf. Her grandfather had found this intriguing piece in France and fashioned a small suite of rooms around it for his daughter, which his granddaughter now called her own.

It was the most restrained decor in the London house, not because it lacked ornamentation– quite the contrary, as it was a bold design – but due to the fact that it favoured a single main colour. For this, Clem was sure, her grandmother Lilian had been responsible. The walls were exquisitely painted with willowy branches and small leaves, as though her bed sat in the middle of a copse. She could sit in bed and almost feel the swaying of saplings when her window was open to let in a breeze. The pale background paint colour was somewhere between soft sage and tea. She slept in white linen and her nightdress was the softest pure white cotton. Among this calm, her mind fizzed and simmered, not only with disappointment at Will's attack on Uncle Reggie but because of what his remark had stirred up.

She couldn't let it go now that it had been aired. The more she turned it over in her mind, the less she was convinced that her father had moved the diamonds.

Will's suggestion that Uncle Reggie had stolen the diamonds was heinous, but the scenario was not implausible. But had her father told Reggie about Sirius? And if he had, his only chance to move them would have been on the night of his death. But that scenario was impossible. He'd died at the Big Hole. He had not returned and could not have moved the diamonds. That left Joseph or Clementine herself, the two other people who knew about them. She hadn't moved them, and she doubted with every ounce of her conviction that Joseph would have so much as touched them. He hadn't wanted any more than the few he'd agreed to keep. Besides, he had made a point of communicating to her where the diamonds had been hidden when he said goodbye to her. It was a clever ruse – few would think to check the little girl's toy. Her thoughts rambled but came full circle, back to Will's intimation that her Uncle Reggie had not only known about the diamonds but had taken them after her father's death, perhaps while they were en route to England.

It sat trapped in her throat. Could Uncle Reggie have done this and lied to her? Why would he have done that? And if he had, what had happened to the roughs . . . and to Sirius?

Even the cocoa began to taste sour and she set it aside, leaning her chin against her knees, her arms wrapped around her legs. The quilted coverlet billowed around her and the fire in the grate began to lose its pop and crackle, dying back to glowing embers with the odd eruption of a flame. She could request more fuel, but why wake the household? Besides, she didn't feel like talking to anyone while she was still rigid with internal rage.

Why had Will stirred this wasp nest? Now those buzzing thoughts were angry, looking to strike. Clementine turned to face the fireplace and became lost with her wasps until the coals had burned down to little more than ash. Shivering, she ignored the pressure on her bladder and snuggled under the coverlet. She had a plan now. She knew what she had to do.

24

Clementine spent the first part of the morning cajoling her neighbour to play chaperone on her trip into the City, with the promise of a visit to Charbonnel et Walker afterwards. She knew Mrs Chattoway would not be able to resist the exquisite chocolates and bonbons of the Parisian-born confectioner in fashionable Bond Street.

In the meantime, a telephone call meant the gentleman she needed to see would meet her at short notice.

As the carriage slowed, Mrs Chattoway immediately recognised their destination as Izak's, one of the finest jewellers in London.

'Good gracious, Clementine. I had no idea you were bringing me into Hatton Garden. What a surprise. I do believe Charles bought my wedding rings here.'

Clem nodded. 'He's our family jeweller.'

Mrs Chattoway looked intrigued. 'Are you having a ring made? Is Will Axford —?'

'Er, no. I'm just having some of my mother's jewellery remodelled,' she said airily, hating to lie but the fib was necessary to protect everyone involved. As they emerged from the carriage, she added, 'So, perhaps half an hour? Would that be fine for you, Mrs Chattoway?'

'Certainly. Plenty to enjoy around here, my dear. And do call me Elspeth, darling. I shall meet you back here in forty-five minutes. Is that suitable?'

'Thank you. I am already anticipating a violet-scented cream.'

'I can't wait.' She pecked Clementine on the cheek. 'Diamonds, darling – don't hesitate. You can never wear too many.'

Clem chuckled. If only Mrs Chattoway knew.

A gentleman opened the door. A bell sounding overhead announced her arrival, and then door was locked behind her.

'We can't be too careful these days,' he said with a self-conscious shrug, noticing the query in her expression. 'You must be Miss Grant? Mr Izak is expecting you. Please go through.'

Clem saw a smiling couple, clearly about to become engaged – the woman was trying on a ring as the man behind the counter beamed. Another gentleman was frowning at a ring, as if trying to decide whether the lady it was intended for would like it. She heard the assistant murmur softly, 'We do have a marvellous oval emerald if you think the sapphire is too dark. Together with the diamonds it would look exquisite.'

There weren't only rings on offer, of course. Clementine knew Izak's was just as capable of selling a magnificent strand of pearls, a ruby necklace, an opal brooch or a dazzling bracelet of amethyst, as catering to the engagement and wedding market.

The assistant who'd welcomed her was guiding her down a small entrance hall to the back, where some steps led up to what she presumed was the house. She was relieved that this was to be an intimate conversation. A small man with a jolly glint in his wise eyes met them at the top of the stairs, where they widened onto a landing. He was wearing a tailored morning suit with a high collar that was crisply starched, as were his cuffs.

'I'm Sammy Izak. Welcome to my home, Miss Grant.'

She stepped past the deep mahogany door into a panelled drawing room that was painted in a soothing duck-egg blue, with moulded plaster cornices. It spoke of wealth, and at first glance she sensed only restraint. Granted, the decorative shields competed with gilded carvings, and the heavy velvet curtains of navy blue surrounding the elegant windows were tied in place with ostentatious golden ropes, but beyond that there was no crowding of ornaments – the only possessions were books. A fire burned gently within the pale marble fireplace. Coves on either side were loaded with leather-bound books: so many she could smell the soft animal hide. A table beneath one of the windows acted as a desk, and upon it, Clem noted, was a cabinet within which jewellery glinted. Perhaps this was where Mr Izak checked the final pieces in daylight before they were sent downstairs for one more polish. Other plain mahogany doors were closed that led off elsewhere. This was Mr Izak's private domain. It was a large space, presumably covering most of the shop below, with two seating areas. An arrangement of sofas close to the fireplace felt intimate and social. Instead, her host guided her to a different area inhabited by four armchairs clustered around a low table.

She rarely felt nervous, priding herself on her composure in all situations. But not today.

'Miss Grant,' Mr Izak said, offering her a seat. 'It's an honour.'

'The pleasure is mine, together with my gratitude that you have allowed me to meet with you here.'

'Well, I admit to being intrigued.'

She smiled, wondering if he would be feeling quite as cheerful after she finished telling him why they were meeting. Seated, pulling off her gloves, she sighed, looking for the right way to start. 'I feel it will sit between us if I don't apologise for May 1883.'

He grinned, knowing precisely why she had raised the date. 'Nothing to apologise for.'

'I'm not one much for parties and balls now, but I was really rather objectionable on the topic when I was eighteen. These days I am far more reasonable and can be persuaded to attend social gatherings that matter to others. You see, that's what I was missing about Queen Charlotte's Ball – how much it mattered to my uncle to see me make my debut during the London season.'

'I am not a betting man, Miss Grant, but I would happily wager that Mr Grant wouldn't think any less of you because of it.'

'Thank you. Mr Izak —'

'Call me Sammy. I insist.' It felt instantly awkward because the man was three times her age, and though known to be modest, he was one of the legends whispered about in jewellers' circles. 'Please, I do prefer it. Everyone calls me Sammy.'

Clem didn't feel ready to jump right in, so she remained on the solid ground of small talk. 'I believe you made my grandmother's engagement ring.'

'I certainly did. Lilian Hatherby, before she married your grandfather. She was a tough taskmaster – she wanted it just so,' he said, smiling benevolently. 'But you, my dear, are the image of your mother. The likeness is astonishing.'

'You knew her?' This was an unexpected surprise, but of course she hadn't known her mother long enough to learn such history.

'I made the tiara that Louisa Grant wore as a debutante for her Queen Charlotte Ball.'

'Oh, I didn't know that! I'm sorry – my grandmother never mentioned it.'

He waved this away and continued his recollection. 'Your mother needed no adornment, to tell you the truth. She was a great beauty with a spirit to match.' His voice was like runny caramel: sweet and smooth. It relaxed her to be with him.

'Thank you,' Clem said, feeling suddenly emotional to meet a stranger who'd perhaps known her mother better than she had.

'Now, I have brewed some fresh coffee. Please?'

'I do mean it – thank you, Sammy, for meeting me under all this secrecy.'

He poured her coffee into a glass, which she found novel and delightful. 'Your grandfather and I go back. You probably don't know that I introduced your grandparents to each other.' He sipped on his coffee and nodded to himself as if approving of the flavour.

'I did *not* know that,' Clem replied, trying to mask her amazement.

'It was many years ago, when your grandfather's head was a mass of thick, yellow hair. He was such a scallywag. Your beautiful grandmother was never going to resist him or his charm and ambition.'

Clem sipped her coffee and savoured its rich, chocolatey roast. 'My uncle's version of Henry Grant doesn't quite match up to yours.'

Sammy chuckled, almost to himself. 'It isn't always helpful to swell a son's ego. Better to keep him striving for his father's approval – especially such a wealthy father as his. Meanwhile, to his confidants, he was concerned for Reggie's waywardness but privately he was impressed with his son's clever mind.' Now he tapped his nose as if to say her grandfather was wise.

She wished Uncle Reggie knew this, but there was nothing she could do to save the soured relationship he'd had with his father. 'And . . . and your family, Sammy?'

'All well, and expanding. I have eight grandchildren now. They run me ragged but life would be far poorer without them. So, Miss Grant —'

'Fair is fair, Sammy,' she interjected. 'I prefer Clementine.'

He gave a gracious nod. 'Please do tell me how I can help you.'

She couldn't avoid it any longer. Clementine laid out her thoughts methodically. Sammy remained silent throughout, nodding now and then to show he was listening carefully. At last she sat back, feeling somehow grubbily treacherous for having shared her dilemma.

'What you're asking surely risks damaging your relationship with your uncle. Are you prepared for that?'

'I've made my peace with it over a restless night, Sammy. I really cannot tolerate that something that belonged to my father might have been taken from him dishonestly. And if there is nothing to discover, then my uncle will be none the wiser to our conversation.'

'And it wouldn't be easier on your heart to ignore what is little more than suspicion and let life be? You have both already seen your fair share of sorrow.'

She opened her palms helplessly. 'And wonder forevermore if he stole something? I could wish the notion had never been put into my head, but now that it's there it won't leave. It has to be addressed.'

'You will need confirmation that the diamonds were in your toy and not left behind; you will have to prove theft, Clementine,' he said. 'Do you still have connections in Kimberley?'

She shook her head. 'But I know someone who does,' she replied, presuming Will would be happy to oblige.

'All right, good. Now, be assured, I have no intention of making inquiries about Mr Grant – that is not my place – but I can make inquiries in connection with the diamond you mention.'

'I feel I'm betraying him even by saying this but I know he's familiar with Amsterdam; I often wondered why he travelled there. His excuse was that it's a city his mother took him to as a child and he remembers being happy there, but it doesn't take much of a leap to work out why if we believe he stole the diamonds.'

Sammy nodded. 'The smaller ones are less problematic, and if he had the right connections then no questions would be asked and they could be quickly turned into cash. However, if this diamond is as big as you recall, then we're talking about a fortune here. He could not have rid himself of it as easily, if indeed at all.'

'Sammy, I know I was a child when I last saw it but I am not exaggerating when I say it's as large as a golf ball.'

Sammy gave a low whistle. 'There have been some big ones, especially early on when diamonds were first discovered in the Cape, but they're rare now and so they tend to cause quite the commotion. He couldn't have rid himself of it through normal channels, even in Amsterdam – the world of gemstones would have erupted. Nevertheless, let's say he moved through an underworld in Europe and it's gone. I can assure you it would have been turned into a dozen or more pieces by now. It would not be recognisable.'

'It hasn't gone,' she countered confidently. 'The person who put this doubt in my mind is a business associate of my uncle's. I do believe that he may have cause to be anxious about my uncle's financial security. It's not in his best interests – business or personal – to turn me against my uncle, or to stir up problems. In fact, the contrary.'

'So he didn't share his concerns lightly, you mean?'

'Exactly. I think he might hate himself for it, but his conscience wouldn't permit otherwise.'

'I see. And now neither will yours.'

'Not until I clear Uncle Reggie's name. That's what I'm hoping, anyway. I don't want any shadow hanging over him, especially in the circles my friend moves in.'

There was a soft knock at the door and Sammy's assistant stepped in. 'I'm sorry to interrupt, Mr Izak, Miss Grant, but a Mrs Chattoway has arrived.'

They stood and shook hands.

'I shall be in touch, Clementine,' Sammy said with a gracious bow. 'Ben will see you out. I have plenty to think on now, and some telephone calls to make immediately.'

Back downstairs, Clementine set aside the hollow feeling she was experiencing at going behind Uncle Reggie's back and pasted on a smile for her beaming neighbour.

'Oh, my dear – a private consultation with Mr Izak. How did it go?'

'Excellent, thank you. He's thinking on some ideas for me.'

'Marvellous. I have a carriage waiting. Off to Bond Street, then?'

Clementine followed her chaperone to the carriage and let Mrs Chattoway speak on; she was conveying some apparently juicy gossip about the family who lived across the street from them in Holland Park. Clementine didn't know who these people were so she didn't feel guilty about even pretending to listen. It was dull, anyway – something about suspicions to do with legitimacy – but it kept Elspeth entertained and allowed Clem to disappear into her own thoughts as her companion gossiped on. 'And you know I've long suspected that the son looked nothing like the father.'

They were passing through the most populated part of the City. She noted that although ready-to-wear suits were now commonly available from gentlemen's outfitters, it was obvious that the typical man who walked around these well-mannered streets had his own tailor. Dark suits with frockcoats and increasingly narrow trousers were still the norm. She wondered if Will wore a swallow-tail frockcoat for his work; the shape was enjoying a small revival, it seemed.

They look like a murder of crows, Clem thought, glancing around at the moving shapes in black and charcoal. Top hats and walking canes completed the look of busy birds, some with umbrellas in case this November day should turn wet on them. The word *murder* popping into her mind gave her a new and terrifying thought.

Murder? It whispered across her mind and she was horror-struck by its potential.

Surely not. Clem dismissed the thought but could not unthink it, and so it sat at the edge of her consciousness, staring accusingly her way. She deliberately made herself focus on Elspeth's conversation.

'. . . of course, I didn't know that.'

'Pardon me? Sorry, my thoughts wandered.'

'I was saying, dear girl, that I was unaware that the beautiful chocolates that Charbonnel et Walker make are numbered. That's how seriously Mrs Walker takes her chocolate-making.'

'I just love the boxes and the satin ribbons,' Clementine remarked, deliberately vacuous, and it prompted a fresh outpouring of joy and chatter from her friend that helped pass the journey and distract her thoughts.

———————

Clementine sat in her favourite spot in the London house, stretched on a day bed next to the ancient window screen originally from Damascus, which allowed her to look down into the hallway from the first-floor room that had always been called the Arabic Chamber. It was a moody nook with a single lamp for reading, providing a comfy, dark corner in which she could hide from the world. She'd always liked that she could watch the movements of the house – its staff, the comings and goings of visitors, her uncle shifting from his study through to the drawing room – and no one would know she was there. But she wasn't sitting here to follow the ebb and flow of the household. It had only a skeleton staff while she was its only occupant; right now she was eating little and the two staff on duty had realised they should leave her to her quiet.

She had not yet heard back from Sammy Izak. It had been a week since she'd closed the door on Will Axford and his painful words.

A day that she could have held up as the happiest she'd had in a decade had somehow spiralled into the worst. It had left her feeling uncharacteristically angry, but mostly she felt let down.

Like most other women, she dreamed of finding a companion for life with whom she would enjoy making a family and a home, yet she was aware she had a reputation for being contrary and, difficult to get close to. It was deliberate. She and Uncle Reggie often laughed about it – not unkindly, for they were all earnest, well-bred and highly suitable young men who had pursued her, but each was dull in his own stuffy way.

Will Axford was just as conservative, of course. Everything about his life had been founded on privilege, but she had discovered aspects of Will that she found irresistible. He continued to work hard at impressing the father whose affection he craved. In this he was like Uncle Reggie, but without the bitterness. She saw his vulnerability and understood his desire to embrace modern thinking without snubbing all the factors that had given him such an affluent life. Plus, only a true romantic could dream up a visit to the butterfly house and Primrose Hill. He'd taken a chance and left himself open to ridicule, perhaps, for these were not excursions most spinsters would have thought worthy.

Perhaps most revealing of all, Will hadn't tried to impress her with his wealth, his status, his connections, or the power accorded to his family name. Most men who had attempted to romance her had been slightly intimidated by her wealth as well as excited by it. They hadn't been able to see – as Will had from the outset – that she wanted for nothing material. What she wanted was romance, sincerity, and a future based on love and respect.

With Will she'd eaten sandwiches on a cold hill and swigged cognac from a hip flask. They'd huddled under an old picnic

blanket and named the stars. She couldn't imagine an eligible partner who could be more in tune with what might delight her than
him. And then, the kiss. *Kisses*, she reminded herself, feeling a fresh
tug deep within, which demanded more of those and only from
Will. Previous objects of her affection had been far too needy.
It was different with Will – the kisses were shared. It felt like she
imagined love should. He kissed her in a way that said he wanted
nothing more from her but for this kiss to last a lifetime, and for her
faith in him to last beyond that.

And Clem had fallen. She no longer needed to be wary;
this was the man she had hoped would find her one day . . . or
she him.

With Will awaited a grand love of the kind her parents had
shared.

But then . . . such treachery. It hurt more than any pain she
could recall.

He had also enraged her, and the anger transformed the hurt
and turned it into regret. Her temper was still simmering. She
wanted answers. She needed to look him in the eye, fully composed,
and demand his explanation. She had to admire his wisdom for
giving her a few days to find that composure and her perspective.
Then they could at least speak as calm adults.

A week, though. That was bordering on snubbing her. Well,
she would give him this last day, but if he failed to turn up or
impress her with his explanation, she would return to Woodingdene
Estate tomorrow and Will Axford would not be welcome on her
doorstep again.

He tested her resolve. For another two hours she read impatiently for distraction before she heard a knock on the front door,
almost directly below her. The housekeeper duly arrived, stepping
lightly across the tiles, checking a watch she kept hanging from a
fob in the pocket of her dark uniform.

Clementine heard the door click open.

'Good morning, sir?'

'Good morning. Is Miss Grant at home, please?'

She flinched at his kind, slightly gritty voice. Had he heard her private ultimatum?

'It's Mr Axford, isn't it?'

'Er, yes.'

'Do come in, Mr Axford. I shall inquire. You can wait in the vestibule here. May I take your hat and umbrella?'

'Thank you.'

Clem listened to footsteps and then shuffling beneath her. Will came into view, and she helplessly let her gaze take stock of the man she had just been pondering.

His jaw was working. He was either worried or embarrassed, or both. Good. She wanted him on the defensive. The thin sunlight slanting through the arched windows lit him in a golden pool, glinting off his hair and suggesting that this man was kissed by an aura of goodness.

She sighed silently with exasperation at such a ludicrous sentiment. Clem heard Mrs Johnson arriving at the top of the stairs, and as she appeared in the arabesque doorway, Clem put a finger to her lips. Her housekeeper smiled and nodded.

Clem tiptoed to the housekeeper and pulled her into an adjoining room. 'I overheard,' she said.

'As you have since you were seven, Miss Clementine.'

'Terrible habit.'

The housekeeper smiled kindly. 'Are we receiving Mr Axford?'

'We are. I'll meet him on the patio. It's a pleasant enough morning and I could use some air.' What she didn't say was that it meant their conversation could be kept private.

'Very good. Any refreshments?'

'I don't think so. Perhaps I could ring if we need?'

'Of course. I'll show him through.'

'Thank you. I'll just fetch my wrap.'

'Mr Axford?' she said, sounding bright as she emerged onto the stone patio overlooking the lawns and rose gardens. Tall trees that provided shade in summer looked forlorn, with naked branches held up as if pleading to be clothed.

'Don't, Clem.'

'Don't what?'

'Go formal on me.'

She eyed him and realised her brimstone still bubbled yellow and angry within.

'I've received you, Will, which means I'm obviously in a cordial mood and keen to hear what you have to say.'

'You may not like it.'

She felt her hopes sink. 'I see.'

'No, I don't think you do.'

'So you're here to hurt me more?'

'That's not my intention but —'

'But what, Will?' She advanced on him, pulling the knitted shawl even more tightly around her shoulders, not enjoying the pain that stared back at her from those kind eyes. 'What can possibly be achieved by calling my only living relative's credibility into question? Firstly, what business is it of yours anyway, to be on this sort of crusade? And secondly, I decide whom I love – in spite of their faults.'

Ah, that hit home. His head snapped up as though she'd given him one of Joseph One-Shoe's famous roundhouse blows.

'Say what you came here to say, Will. Don't make it a wasted trip.'

'I didn't come to say anything.'

She rounded on him now, her tears mercifully blinked away. 'Well, what are you here for, then?' She scowled. 'It's obviously not to apologise.'

'Not for telling the truth, no. Not for telling you all that I shared the last time we met, or right now telling you that I love you.'

She took a sharp breath. 'You barely know me!'

'I know you, Clementine. I know your pain and sadness. I know your Africa, which perhaps no one else does. I know what you want.'

'Oh, really?' she said. She wished in this heartbeat that he was incapable of such ruthless honesty.

'I think you want the truth.'

She didn't hold back. 'And you'll sacrifice our potential?'

'Yes. If it means you discover the truth.'

'I hate you more for that.' She folded her arms even tighter and turned to stare out across the garden, where the morning frost had melted to leave all of its plants glistening with water. Even the garden was weeping for her.

Will continued from behind her while she seethed. 'I have asked a friend of mine from the club to see if he can find out any details about Joseph One-Shoe after 1873.'

She nodded. 'Well, I am certainly grateful for that.' Clem suddenly felt too angry to tell him about her meeting with Sammy or her need for proof. She needed to become calm. 'Thank you, Will.'

'Is that it?'

She turned to fix him with a glacial stare she imagined even her grandmother would be proud of. 'Yes. I need time to think. You may call on me in three days.'

They were both breathing hard. Steam puffed from their mouths and their breath entwined like ethereal lovers before dissipating into the air.

He gave a small bow, and without another word he departed.

25

It was easier to walk than to be enclosed in a carriage with the awkwardness squeezed between them like an unwelcome passenger. Will had suggested they alight as the traffic became more congested and she couldn't have got out of the hackney and into the open air any quicker.

Her feelings were mixed. She wanted so much to prove Will wrong in his assumptions – for surely that's what his claims were. But then she couldn't ignore her sickening curiosity to learn what Sammy might know. He had sent a courteous message the previous day for them to meet again, and that afternoon Will had duly presented himself as she'd suggested. She had to applaud him for his sincerity; it was a mark of his honourable nature that he was prepared to come back and risk facing more of her chill.

Yesterday, Will had learned of her initial meeting with Sammy. This time she had invited him into her private drawing room, where they sat opposite one another. She hadn't yet offered refreshment and perhaps wouldn't, as she saw his expression darken at her news.

'But I thought —'

He looked confused and she could understand it, but she felt little sympathy. 'Look, Will, I feel disgusted that I am even a party to this. But how did you expect I might feel after your not-so-subtle accusation? It has put a demon in my mind, and the only way to cast it out is to get answers to questions I don't like asking.'

'And you've asked them, it seems.'

'I have, because I now feel obliged to clear his name.'

'Clem, my accusation, as you call it, has simply prompted a line of inquiry that has surely sat in the back of your mind for years.'

'You're wrong.'

'You admit you asked your uncle about the diamonds.'

'I did when I was little. And he gave me his answer, which I accepted.'

'Because you were a child.'

'I guess the point you're missing, Will, is that I don't care about the diamonds.' That wasn't entirely true, but she hoped it would put him off his course.

It didn't. He leaned in further to press his point. 'That may be, Clem. But I suspect you care very much about being lied to. And that's what this is about. I don't care about the diamonds either. But I am not going to associate my good name with that of a thief, who has potentially stolen something extraordinary from his own family – from the very niece he claims to adore.'

'Claims to adore?'

'I'm sorry, that was uncalled for. I know your uncle loves you, but perhaps back then he felt indifferent.'

'You certainly know how to woo a girl, Will, but I can see why you aren't married yet. You have a cruel way about you.'

She watched his jaw work as the barb found its target. She'd hurt him. It wasn't something to feel proud of but she could not let herself be trampled in his crusade to find his truth – the one that would satisfy him but leave ruin in its wake.

'Cruel? And there I was believing I was protecting you.'

'Protecting? Will, don't be so pompous. What you've done is undermine me, made me feel uncertain about the one aspect of my life I have always felt was secure.'

At this he looked immediately ashamed, as though the notion had never occurred to him. She could tell he'd had to swallow a retort; he was vexed because she'd managed to shame him.

'I do now wish I had approached our dilemma more carefully and perhaps with less fervour.' He cleared his throat and shook his head with regret. 'But to undermine you was not and never could be my intention, Clem. I would never want to weaken the person I have come to admire above all others.'

She let the pause lengthen as they both shifted awkwardly.

'Nevertheless,' she finally began with a sigh, 'we find ourselves in this situation now, and today Mr Izak wishes to see me. I'm hoping he has nothing of significance to share, of course, and then that will be that, Will. I shall be satisfied and will not think on the accusation or those diamonds again.'

'May I at least accompany you when you meet with Mr Izak?'

He watched her inhale as she considered this. 'You may. We're both involved now so you might as well hear what he has to say.'

'If I could have my time again, Clem, I would say nothing – I would simply not do business with your family. I must reiterate, though, that your idea is sharply observed and splendidly conceived.'

She nodded. 'Retrospection only helps us learn for the future. It makes no difference to what has transpired. You made a choice and now we must deal with its consequences. Mr Izak is expecting me at eleven. Shall we go?'

'How often have you been here?' Will asked, clearly desperate to puncture the silence, as they reached Hatton Garden.

'A number of times.' *Pathetic answer, Clem*, she admonished herself privately. She tried harder. 'I know that the land it sits on was originally a gift from Elizabeth I to one of her favourites, Sir Christopher Hatton. It became a hotly pursued residential district once his mansion was up and the orchards of the region became his garden. And then lots of merchants moved in.'

He nodded. 'I believe it's been a jewellery quarter since the days of Shakespeare. More to the point, the world has focused on it for diamonds from around the time your family went to Africa in search of them.'

They were passing fine Georgian buildings as they moved deeper into the diamond district she knew much better than she was letting on.

'Do you know why it became such a centre for diamonds, though?' she asked, glad they had something to discuss to keep that awkward passenger from catching up.

He shrugged. 'I thought it was a natural extension of the jewellery trade.'

'No, actually. The king of diamonds was waiting to be crowned at around the time I was brought back from Kimberley. His name is Cecil Rhodes.'

He smiled. 'Of course. Yes, I do know of him. I think my father has met him, but I gather he lives in South Africa.'

'Cape Town,' she said matter-of-factly. 'These days, diamonds from the Cape are controlled by Rhodes's corporation, De Beers – in fact, it virtually controls the diamond market across the world. When my father was digging, Cecil Rhodes was just starting out, but he was smart enough to buy up claims and have other people dig for him. He and a fellow called Barney Barnato were both vying for ownership supremacy of digs. I met Mr Barnato once because he came to New Rush as a boxer and Joseph One-Shoe beat him. Anyway, these two men were in fierce competition but ultimately, Cecil Rhodes acquired Barnato's claims and he merged them to form De Beers Consolidated Mines. Just a year or so ago he invited a group of Jewish firms operating out of Hatton Garden to form a buying group – a purchasing syndicate, I think it was called. And that meant all the De Beers diamonds – and you might as well say all diamonds from the Cape – passed through the Hatton Garden diamond merchants. They in turn became diamond distributors to the world.' She glanced up at him and noted he was looking at her with something akin to awe as they walked.

'Clem, you astound me.'

'I don't know why. This is common knowledge in the right circles.'

'Not among the women I know. This is not the sort of conversation I could have with anyone else but . . . but a colleague from the industry.'

'We have our differences, Will, but it doesn't mean I can't be a colleague – and then you wouldn't have to be astonished by my conversation. You could treat me just the same as any other business partner. Of course, if you don't plan to proceed with the underwriting offer, that's fine, too. I shall press ahead anyway. Look.' She tipped her head in the direction of a man wearing a dark three-piece suit and a bowler hat. 'In that gentleman's inside breast pocket will be a cache of diamonds. No doubting it. He's one of the runners, taking gems to a jeweller who might require some stones to show a customer.'

'How do you know that?' He sounded incredulous.

'I've observed them. Look how neat and tidy he is – you just know he works in an office of sorts and must be presentable to clients. I have learned how to recognise them by their brisk pace and slightly furtive glances. It's just how the diggers used to move when they'd struck a good haul and had their stash hidden on their person. Watch how his gaze is never still – always glancing around to see if he's being followed.' She smiled. 'He's good – he's even whistling. But he is a definite target for the new criminal underclass that is becoming such a blight in London, because if I can recognise him, so could lots of others, who would perhaps spend months spying and learning. They'd probably know all the runners' names and habits, where they drink, who they work for, which routes they like to take. The merchants have to be smarter, have different routes each day, change the men who carry their gems, and above all insure themselves against theft.'

'I couldn't have said it better. You should consult,' he said.

Introductions were made, Will and Sammy connecting the links they had through Jerome Axford, his father; it turned out Sammy had also made some jewellery for Aunt Esme. They sat down and accepted cups and saucers, and thought about declining biscuits until they saw Sammy's expression drop.

'My wife and daughters made these *kipferl* for Hanukkah. They're fresh and delicious – please, do try them.'

It only took a bite. 'Oh, they are truly delightful,' Clem said. 'Almond?'

'Yes, gives them that lovely texture.'

They smiled and drank together and finally, when there was no more small talk to make and no other polite rituals to be observed, Sammy's face grew serious, his brows knitting together.

Clem found herself holding her breath in terrified anticipation, and she was convinced Will felt the same.

'Mr Axford . . . er, sorry, Will – Clementine asked me to find out if any remarkable diamonds were coming onto the market or had come onto it in recent times. I gather you have cast some doubt on Mr Grant and whether diamonds belonging to Clementine had been acquired without her permission.'

Will looked momentarily aghast at Clem, as though she'd walked up and slapped him hard across his handsome face.

'I'm sorry to be so direct,' Sammy continued, 'but this is quite the accusation and I don't wish any of us to be confused about what I have been asked to find out, or indeed where this could lead. I am only the messenger and I do not wish to have any part in making these accusations.'

Clem watched the hinge of Will's jaw working; it was obvious he was wrestling with several responses. He chose one. 'It is only about truth, sir. I did not wish Clementine to go through life living a lie.'

She tipped her head slightly to one side and felt an ache pass through her. They could have been such a brilliant couple, but that notion felt further away now than it had even an hour earlier, when they'd started this awkward journey. 'Oh, Will, truth is so often about perspective. Your truth, my truth, Mr Izak's truth – we could all be talking about the same thing and skew it differently because of how we see it. And just sometimes, Will, the truth you put so much faith in can harm people.'

She didn't think she could have hurt him more if she'd picked up his umbrella and clubbed him with it. However, she wasn't pre-pared to see his expression change from wounded to resolute. Clearly, she'd only made him more stubborn in his pursuit.

'The reality is, Clementine,' he said, ignoring poor Sammy, who had taken a breath to answer, 'this is about honour. I cannot be privy to a lie and simply accept it or profit from it because it's not *my* lie. In this instance, it potentially injures someone I care very much about. This is my decision, so please do not lecture me about how I should behave or feel.'

Now who sounds virtuous? she thought with a flash of

irritation. 'But my uncle and his relationship with me is none of your business, Will!'

'It is if he was complicit in your father's death and then stole his diamonds and his child.'

The room turned hideously still. It was as though a spell had been cast that forbid them to move anything but their gazes. She couldn't even swallow for the horror of what Will had said, and she could see he too was in despair at having let that thought out. It hung like a stench, polluting the space.

'Will?' Sammy appealed.

Will rubbed his face. 'Clementine, I unreservedly apologise.'

'I can't pretend it has not been said.' Her voice was scratchy, her mind racing. It was a shock but not entirely a surprise, given the thought had been dancing on the outskirts of her mind like a gleeful demon. Hers was a vague, perhaps even dismissible suspicion. Will believed it, though. She could see it written in his open face. He would never make a gambling man, certainly not at cards. What did he know that she didn't?

'Clementine, would you prefer to leave this?' Sammy asked. 'I could call you a hackney this moment. I am so sorry.'

She sat up even straighter. 'No, Sammy. Will's made a heinous claim now – he needs to substantiate it, or I might feel inclined to talk to our family solicitor.'

Will looked like he was going to respond but thought better of it and lowered his gaze.

Sammy opened his hands beseechingly. 'My dears, it's clear that all this passion is primarily because you like each other so much. It is always hurtful if a friend seems to be working against us, but sometimes that can be interpreted wrongly. Let me tell you both what I have learned.'

Clem felt her insides clench; she could believe she had stopped breathing or that her heart had paused in that expectant moment.

303

There was physical pain somewhere but she couldn't locate it – her mind had dulled, all other sounds blanketed, awaiting Sammy's words.

'I know nothing about your family's doings, Clementine,' he began, his kind eyes darkening with sorrow. 'But I do know that a remarkable stone in the rough has been quietly touted for private auction. This occurred in October, so about five weeks back. The gentleman offering this diamond said its origin was the Big Hole in Kimberley and that he'd owned it for nearly twenty years. He stipulated firmly that he did not want his name attached to its provenance. He wanted to remain entirely unconnected with it.'

Clementine could swear she heard her throat click as if a padlock had been unlocked on a vault of angst.

'But not its proceeds, presumably?' Will chipped in.

'No. He wanted to know the stone's worth.'

Clem sat mute while they spoke. It couldn't be anyone but Uncle Reggie, could it?

'And its value?' Will continued.

'He was told that if it lived up to its promise, it would likely be turned into one very large, exquisite stone, and then a series of smaller stones that could either be split up and sold separately or form a necklace with the large one as a centrepiece. The price that would likely be put on it is staggering. I dare not repeat it. It runs into many scores of thousands.'

'Did the gentleman in question have a name for this rough?' Clem asked.

Sammy looked back at her, puzzled. 'No mention of that.'

Will leaned in. 'Do we have a description of the seller?'

'No. As far as anyone can tell me, he was simply well-spoken, well-dressed, well-mannered. He was keen to exchange the diamond for money swiftly. This naturally draws suspicion.'

'A name, surely?'

'James Milton is the name he gave.'

Will nodded and repeated it, as if hoping that by doing so he could bring the man into focus.

Clem heard a thin voice of doubt in her mind.

James, your father's name. Milton, our butler's name.

Was she reaching or was the coincidence too obvious? Surely, if it was Uncle Reggie, he would have come up with a less obvious name?

Pressure can do that, the voice cautioned her.

'So there we are, gentlemen. I think I've heard enough,' she said, overly brightly.

'It could be a false name,' Will offered, and awaited her rage.

'Yes, it could,' she said, faking calm. 'But what you still haven't grasped, Will, is that only you seem to care.'

His gaze narrowed in confusion. Creases appeared around the eyes she had hoped to look into for the rest of her life, but she now wanted to run from.

'I don't need that stone or its proceeds,' she reiterated.

'Yes, but he does! And he's always known the day would come when he would sell it for his own profit, you none the wiser and still thinking he's your knight in shining armour. You know this is Reggie touting *your* stone. And in your heart you know he stole your father's diamonds and has been using the proceeds to prop up the family firm, and now he's desperate, down to his last – the one he probably hoped against hope he'd never have to bring out into the open. But that stone will give him untold wealth.'

'So what?' she said, her manner so offhanded that Will raised his hands to his head in dismay. 'I don't care!' she said, enunciating the words as if he struggled to understand English. 'If he did take the diamonds and he did use them to keep our family concern going, then I take my hat off to him. All my father would have done is squandered it. I loved my father with all of my heart but he was a larrikin, Will. He was irresponsible, irrepressible and full of grandiose ideas and dreams that could never be fulfilled. When I was a child he was my hero – but I wonder if my mother felt that way on her deathbed, with him still digging in the river.' She took an anguished breath. She mustn't lose control now. 'My uncle has done nothing but take care of our business and his sister's child. He's the hero.'

She could see that Sammy was feeling awkward. He stood and began pacing near the windows.

'That's just it, though, Clem. I didn't want to tell you this . . .' Will's expression was a mixture of shame and pity.

'Tell me what, Will? How else do you plan to hurt me?'

He stared at her, closing his fists as if that gesture could stop her being so cruel. 'I really do not wish to cause you any pain.'

'Then leave me and my uncle alone. We're happy. We're safe – we're getting on just fine.'

'But you won't be soon,' he said in a tone of resignation. 'The bank is foreclosing on him.'

She felt like a heavy stone had just dropped into her belly. 'Did you set that in motion?'

He half gasped, half laughed. 'I don't have that power, Clem. Your uncle is so far behind with the repayments on his loans, the situation is beyond dire.'

'How do you know this? Actually, don't answer that, I can guess. White's Club and its loose-tongued gentleman's network, no doubt.'

At least he looked ashamed at that. 'The news came to me. I didn't inquire. Someone told someone, and probably told someone else they'd seen me stepping out with you.'

She turned away from him with an angry sigh. 'Then he can have my money. It belongs to the family, anyway.'

'For his gambling debts too, Clem?'

'What gambling debts?' She swung back, her fury setting off a low headache.

'He owes a fortune in debts to unsavoury people. That criminal underclass you spoke of earlier? They won't be polite like the bank. They'll just as soon break his legs as cast him a smile. They want their money and he's got none.'

She'd had enough. 'What do you want me to say, Will?'

'Enough, Will,' Sammy ordered, walking over to put his hands around Clem's shoulders. 'This is not fair. This is an ambush and none of it is Clementine's doing.'

'Sammy, she's wearing blinkers. He's going to ruin her like he did her father!'

'Oh, you dreadful man. I thought I loved you, Will. I couldn't hate someone more than I hate you now.' She launched this at him with all her might, as if she were hurling a spear. It landed true and all the fire of his words blinked out.

He looked beaten, his gaze flicking between then. His shoulders dropped. 'I can't help you if you won't help yourself by just trying to see clearly. Look at the facts, for pity's sake . . . no, for *your* sake. He will take you down with him and I wanted to save you from that. I wanted to make you my wife, give you my name, throw a ring of protection around you so that when Reggie Grant hit the skids as he is poised to do, you would be safe.'

She shook off Sammy and advanced on Will. 'What a hero you are, Will Axford. I feel like you offering to marry me would be granting me some sort of great favour. Well, you can take your thought of marriage and you can —'

Sammy clenched her shoulders again, making a soft tutting sound. 'Please, my dear, do not upset yourself any further.'

But Will, it seemed, was not finished. 'And your father's death?'

Her belly churned with nausea. 'Bring me proof, Will. Prove to me that Uncle Reggie was involved in his death and I will cut him loose.'

'Is that a promise?'

'It's an oath. But get it wrong, Will, and you've made an enemy out of me.'

Sammy made a sound of despair and flicked a hand towards Will. 'Go, Will, now! I want no more harsh words spoken in this room. I will see Miss Grant safely home. Shame on you, boy. Look at her, shaking with upset.'

Will strode to the door. 'Clem, I . . . I'm going to get you that proof.'

She sniffed. 'I shall not pine for the knock at my door because I don't believe there is proof to get.'

He hauled open the door, taking hat and coat from the hook in the landing. He stepped back in, lifting his topper. 'Good morning,' he said, throwing a look of apology Sammy's way. 'Clementine, I hope you will find it within yourself to understand that I do this out of love and respect for you. No other reason. Remember the butterflies, remember the stars. Remember everything, Clem, especially that you were taken away without a chance to see your father buried and ask yourself why.'

After his footsteps had died away and they'd heard the distant bell of the shop jangle, Clem turned towards Sammy's embrace and wept.

'Oh, my dear child. The Axfords are not, how shall we say, known for their emotional outpouring. Will is surely deeply in love with you or I suspect he wouldn't create so much trouble for himself.'

I know, she admitted, but not out loud.

26

November 1894

'My darling girl!' Reggie said, flinging the newspaper aside as Clementine arrived in the Vase Room at Woodingdene. A blast of air that came in behind her made the fire gutter. 'Good grief. Why didn't anyone tell me you were coming in this evening?'

He was on his feet and gathering her into a tight embrace. His affectionate hug felt familiar and comforting. She smelled the cognac he had been sipping and the fragrance of tobacco from his dinner jacket, mixed with the scent of smouldering pine cones in the fire.

He saw her notice them. 'When I miss your presence around here in winter, I turn into a sentimental old fool and do this sort of thing – sit alone and burn pine cones like we have since you were a tot.' He smiled fondly at her. 'Welcome home, Clem.'

'Have you already gathered cones for Christmas?'

'Not at all – those are just a couple I picked up today while walking. No, no, that's a ritual for us,' he said, feigning shock that she'd even ask. 'Now you're home we'll clamber into galoshes tomorrow and drag back a haul to decorate properly. Gosh, is it really December the first tomorrow? It is. Unbelievable. Oh, and look, darling, I had Milton bring these up from the cellar.' He pointed towards the end of the room.

She saw an open chest with all the familiar Christmas decorations they'd gathered over her lifetime in England. Many of them she had made herself, and were especially poignant to Uncle Reg; there were also some exquisite hand-blown glass baubles from Europe – one for each year since she'd arrived.

'Milton was poking about down there looking for something else and I had him bring it all up nice and early for us to sort through. He's also sourced us a tree. It's arriving in, well, twelve days. He says it's enormous, so we might put it in the hall and get a smaller one for us in here. What do you think?'

She grinned and gave him another hug. 'Sounds excellent, so long as all the staff are invited to join us in decorating the tree.'

'Good. I might add that your Christmas bauble for 1894 is being blown now,' he said, kissing her on both cheeks with heartfelt affection.

'And what's the theme for this year, Uncle Reg?' she asked. Every year he had a glorious scene made in glass to sit inside the bauble. Each one was named for her and dated. Her collection was glitteringly impressive. She could remember a time when the bauble was huge in her hands and Uncle Reg had needed to cup her hands in his in order to hold the fragile sphere.

Their history together felt suddenly precious. She had no history with anyone else that stretched back so long or affectionately, which made the business of today feel even more unpleasant.

'Oh, no, you won't get it out of me, but it is a little special.'

Her heart thudded dully. 'It's Africa, isn't it?' Were the fates conspiring?

He looked instantly crestfallen. 'Oh, now, don't ruin it, darling,' he said, none the wiser of her pain. He rallied fast. 'You always were too clever by half. Just hold off and act very surprised when you open your box.'

Her laugh was genuine. She did love him.

'So now come and sit down and get warm. How did you get home?'

'Mr and Mrs Evanston were travelling back on the same train – they offered to bring me home in their carriage.'

'That's kind of them. I don't ever wish to be clingy but it's so quiet here without you nagging or prattling on.' She play-slapped his arm. 'No, I mean it – I've missed you. I know London will always draw you to it but . . .'

'London can enjoy itself without me,' she said, pulling off her gloves and bonnet. 'I'm far happier here.'

'You can't mean that.'

'I do, Uncle. *You* love London, and you presume that because I'm young and single I must surely adore it just as much. I don't. I go there because I have to mix with city people from time to time. But no, give me Woodingdene all the days of my life and I'll be a happy woman.'

His eyes narrowed slightly. 'Has something happened?'

'No, not really.' She sighed. 'I might have some supper.'

He was sensible to leave it at that. 'Do. And if no one's in the kitchen, don't disturb Jane. I'll go down and rustle something up for you.'

She grinned. 'You are so sweet, really.'

'Only for you, mind,' he said. 'Now, warm up. Would you like a sherry or something?'

'Yes, that would be lovely.'

'I've just taken delivery of an unctuous sherry made with Pedro Ximénez grapes from Andalusia. It's so delicious I want to order a barrel of it!'

She grinned, took the small crystal sherry glass and sipped. 'Ooh, that's rich, isn't it?'

'Like liquid plum pudding,' he agreed. 'Now, let's get you something to eat.'

———————

Later, with two table lamps and the fire throwing a glow around the wintry darkness, her belly full of warm soup and bread, Clem sipped her second sherry of the evening. Her uncle had returned to his reading and the gentle crack and spit from the fireplace felt familiar and soothing.

Just the two of them, as it had been for so many years now. He'd never shown interest in another woman, although several had tried to catch his attention. She did not suspect for a moment that he had a preference for his own sex. No, there was something lacking in Uncle Reggie's appetite – either that or he was disciplined with it. If he had relations, then he was discreet; he made sure his world revolved around only her. Her heart ached that she was allowing this most precious of relationships to come under threat. She was only just now untangling her thoughts from this morning's revelations and accusations. Her anger had cooled into despair, like an old grief only her heart remembered: of losing her mother, then her father, and finally being taken from Joseph One-Shoe. She couldn't really touch that pain, but her unconscious mind was recreating it in the face of what might explode between her and Uncle Reggie.

Why couldn't Will grasp that whatever the outcome, there were going to be broken hearts? No one was going to win so long as he pursued this course. As to proof – what was he talking about? Nearly two dozen Christmases had laid their snowy blankets over her father's memory. Both he and her mother were dust in the African desert. The people they'd lived among were presumably long gone, having scattered to the corners of the earth or become dust themselves. They would hardly have let Uncle Reggie leave

Kimberley with her, she reasoned, let alone the Cape, if anyone suspected her father's death had been anything but an accident. Will's claim was heinous; she reassured herself she was right in her contempt for it and for his actions.

She watched her uncle absently twirl his cigar stub. He had an odd habit of making a cigar last all evening. 'Then I smoke less,' he often quipped, but she knew it was about discipline. Perhaps his doctor had suggested he stop smoking; could this be her uncle's form of compromise? *Or maybe he can no longer afford to smoke his huge, expensive Cubans from Havana?* she heard in Will's voice.

No, she reasoned. Uncle Reggie was disciplined about most aspects of life. He followed rituals, traditions, did most regular tasks at the same time each day. He had tried to instil a similarly tidy attitude in her, but Clementine had heard time and again that she'd been given too much rein by her parents – her father, especially – until she'd become untameable.

She thought about her father in his desert grave. Who had buried him? Who had stood and taken their caps off and said a prayer over him? Perhaps Joseph One-Shoe had not even been allowed to take part in the burial; he may have had to watch from afar and cast his Zulu prayers to the heavens. Why hadn't they stayed longer? Now that she finally thought about it, it was unseemly that Uncle Reggie hadn't stood at the graveside and paid his respects – and allowed her to weep for her father, buried with her mother.

It was certainly odd. And it had taken Will's anger to remind her of this fact; something that had no doubt been pushed too deep for her to think about previously. Uncle Reggie always dismissed talk of her parents – he spoke incredibly fondly of her mother, it was true, but he spoke only of his recollections of Louisa as a child or living here at Woodingdene, never of her life as Clementine's mother.

'What are you thinking about so quietly over there?' he asked.

'Nothing much.'

'Oh, come on. Do share.'

She smiled, and then it slipped out before she could stop it. 'I was recalling Africa.'

His gaze slid over to her but quickly returned to his newspaper, as if he didn't want to be caught unawares. 'Oh, yes?' he replied absently.

'Mmm. I've been thinking about some diamonds that my father dug up.'

'Really?'

Did his voice sound choked?

He folded his paper in half to look over the top. 'Something *did* happen in London, didn't it?'

There he was, trying to deflect her as usual. Unfortunately, he'd given her the opening she needed. 'I met Will.'

He nodded. 'Well, I suppose he's a good match for you, Clem,' he said.

'Oh – I, er, didn't mean that.'

'No, but I presume he took you to all the swanky spots, did he, and impressed you? Don't worry, I'm not going to say no. I think he would be an excellent choice for you. So where did you go?'

This was how well Uncle Reg could change the subject or at least skew a conversation away from its original path. She hadn't realised until now how adroit he was at this. He must have been doing this all her life.

'Swankiness was not his intention. I met his Aunt Esme.'

He looked unmoved. 'Should I know her?'

'No, no,' she replied, as if it weren't important. 'Lovely person. We had tea.'

'And?' He frowned.

'And nothing. Her husband was a naturalist – in his lifetime he gathered together many species of butterfly in a wonderful tropical greenhouse.'

Reggie looked at her with a bored expression. 'I hope this is going somewhere, my darling?'

She laughed at his sarcasm, more than used to it. 'I saw an African queen butterfly for the first time since I was seven and it was like the golden key. It unlocked memories.' It was a fib but one she needed.

He smiled pityingly. 'And because of a butterfly you have recalled diamonds?' he said, with only a hint of condescension. 'Given you were around the diamond diggers all your early life, I'm not surprised you have a vivid recollection of diamonds when your memory is jogged.'

'I want to remember that time properly.'

'For heaven's sake, why? Is Will Axford putting ideas into your head?'

'Now why would you say that?'

'Oh, even I don't know why I said that,' he replied in a bright tone, as if to say, *Let's move on from this conversation, shall we?* 'I don't want you getting hung up on this business of your childhood.'

'I'm not. The point is, you can remember yours and I want the same opportunity.'

'Oh, darling girl, my memories are worthless to me. It wasn't a happy childhood.' He frowned at her. 'What's going on, Clem darling? Is everything all right?'

She shook her head.

He folded his newspaper properly and tossed it aside. Carefully knocking the ash from his cigar, he left it to smoke itself out and joined her on the sofa.

'Africa was all about sadness for you. You lost your mother at a tender age and put all your love into a father who drank himself towards an early grave and fell to his death in a drunken state. I never talk about it because I really don't want you to be reminded of it.'

'I'm an adult, though, Uncle Reg. I think it's important we do talk about it.'

He sat back and regarded her. 'What would you like to know?'

This was it. With surgical precision she cut to the heart of her angst about the uncle she wanted to trust but could no longer believe in unassailably.

'Diamonds were hidden in my ragdoll. There was a collection of the best we'd gathered – just before you arrived, as I recall. They were from a special haul unearthed by Joseph One-Shoe.'

'In your ragdoll?' He sounded astonished.

She nodded, watching him carefully. 'You never knew anything about that?'

Now he just looked offended. 'What are you saying to me, Clementine?'

She was politely direct. 'I'm asking if you recall anything about diamonds in my ragdoll.'

'Good heavens, no!'

'Only the three of us knew they were in Gillie and I was sworn to secrecy. I never told anyone about them, I'm sure of that. Joseph One-Shoe would have taken that secret to his grave.'

'But hang on, darling.' His forehead creased into a frown and he looked up towards the row of vases that lined the room. 'The day I came to meet you both, neither of you were at the hovel you called home. The Zulu was there, and it was my understanding that your father had gone to another town to sell some diamonds.'

She frowned too, recalling it now. 'Yes . . . you're right – and we had ice-cream.'

'Well, there you are, then,' Reggie said, as if he'd just solved all the problems in the world.

'Except I stood next to my father and he sold just enough diamonds to cover our passage home. The rest must have remained in Gillie. I carried that doll everywhere. My father insisted I never lose sight of it.'

'Clementine, I don't believe that your father would have entrusted so many diamonds to a seven-year-old child and her toy. I think you'll find he removed them.'

'But when? I had Gillie all of that day and all of that night and all of the next day, when I learned that my father was dead. I carried Gillie in my arms and did not let him go. Daddy died that same night, so he couldn't have removed them.'

'The Zulu —'

'Uncle Reggie, Joseph One-Shoe did not want the diamonds. That's the point. He took some very small ones to convert into cash. The rest, even though they were equal partners, he told my father to keep and take home. We had everything booked for our departure and I was fearing it because it meant leaving Joseph. No, the main haul of diamonds that was going to set up our lives back here in England was in that ragdoll.'

What she didn't add was that the only time the doll had left her arms was when her Uncle Reggie made a specific point of holding Gillie for her. Her belly felt like a cauldron, as nauseating memories pointed to Will Axford's theory being correct.

'Well, Clem, I don't know what to say to you. It was a long time ago. I have no memory of any diamonds in any of your possessions. This Joseph fellow never mentioned them.'

'And did my father, when you spoke with him?'

'I barely spoke to him. The words exchanged were brief and argumentative. He wanted me gone. He was drunk that night, making no sense.'

'Where did you meet him?'

'Pardon?'

'I said, where did you meet him that evening? It wasn't at the hut, because I was there.'

'No, no. I figured he wouldn't be exactly thrilled to see me, so I met him coming out of the pub. I walked with him for a way. He was hostile, of course, didn't want me alongside him, but I needed to discuss your life and care, your grandmother dying, your mother's gravestone – so much I wanted to talk to him about. Most of all, I wanted to extend the hand of friendship and family; I wanted you both to come back and make Woodingdene your permanent home. He wanted nothing to do with me or my proposals. He was verbally abusive, darling, and then he got physical with me, pushing me around.'

'What did you do?'

He shrugged, bemused. 'I left, Clem. What else could I do? I thought I'd let him sleep off his liquor and try again in daylight – hopefully when he was sober. I didn't want him to worry about money or your future – I had it all worked out for the two of you.'

'And then he fell?'

Reggie moved closer and wrapped an arm around his niece. 'Yes. Tragic. A ridiculous waste – I've always said so.'

'You have, Uncle Reg. Thank you for talking about this with me.'

He stroked her hair. 'Clem, I would die for you, darling. I haven't talked about all this before because it's upsetting. Look at you – you look sad now, understandably.' He pulled her close and hugged her. 'Let's do something fun tomorrow – just us.'

She smiled for his benefit and murmured something about how nice that would be, but behind the smile there came a fresh surge of anxiety. He was lying. A fresh memory bloomed of Joseph One-Shoe cautioning her that this man, whom Joseph believed loved her, did not necessarily tell the truth.

Clem could feel only a quaking fear: loving her uncle as she did only made his alleged betrayal so much worse. She thought of all the warmth in her heart for this man. He was the bedrock of her existence, the landscape over which her life had grown, but all the warmth she felt for her Uncle Reggie was suddenly insulated; to release it again she needed the truth, just as Will had demanded. She needed to hunt down the final pieces to this jigsaw.

And with that decision came a terrible choice.

27

December 1894

Two days prior, Will had answered the telephone and been genu-inely surprised to hear Clementine Grant's voice.

'Oh, Will. Er . . .'

He listened to her clear her throat as he corralled his galloping thoughts.

'I'm sorry to interrupt you,' she said.

'Is something wrong?'

'No . . . er, not really, no. Sorry. Let me start again. How are you?'

He blinked in consternation. 'I'm . . . I'm well, thank you – just leaving from Berkeley Square, actually.'

'Oh, my apologies. This can wait,' she said, sounding more embarrassed and in a hurry to get off the line.

'No, Clementine. I was preparing to leave for the office but I'm in no particular hurry,' he lied. 'It's good to hear from you,' he offered, sounding relieved. He hadn't been convinced he might ever hear her pleasantly raspy tones again. 'Are you at Woodingdene?'

'No. I'm returned to London.'

Hurrah! nearly spilled out of his lips in relief. Instead, mar-shalling his thoughts, he nodded. 'So soon?' he said.

'Yes,' she replied, and it came out as a sigh. 'I had no intention of coming back into the City for a long while, but I have some important business that cannot wait.'

'I see.' He couldn't help the disappointment that escaped into his tone and flew down the telephone line like a bird let free from a cage. Did he really think she would say that she had returned just to see him? To make amends? To repair their damaged friendship? *What an idiot*, he said to himself.

Should he tell her what he'd been up to these past days? Should he mention the telegram he was eagerly awaiting? He desperately wanted to share his endeavours, but he didn't want to suffer her ire again. He played it safe. 'So, how might I help?'

'I'd rather not discuss this matter over the telephone.' All the ears eavesdropping at the various telephone exchanges from north to south would have pricked up at that. 'Could we meet somewhere convenient for you, perhaps?'

'Of course,' he said, without hesitation. 'Do you mean today?'

'I do . . . I mean, only if you —'

'I can meet you wherever you wish, Clementine. Do you have a chaperone?'

'My neighbour, Mrs Chattoway. She's a good old stick.'

He understood this was code for Mrs Chattoway being unlikely to interfere. 'And where do you propose we meet?'

'How about Twinings?'

'On the Strand? Yes, easy enough.'

'Mrs Chattoway has said she could easily run into some friends there.'

Maybe there was some hope for them. 'What time would suit you and your chaperone?'

'Shall we say three o'clock?'

'We shall. Until then.' He didn't want to move the receiver from his ear and was glad he didn't.

'Will?'

'Yes?'

'My behaviour the other day was emotional.'

He sighed silently with relief. It wasn't an apology, but it was at least conciliatory. 'You were angry.'

'I still am.'

He frowned. 'I don't wish to argue with you again, Clem. In fact, I feel I need to make amends, yet I am following a similar course to yours.'

'Oh? And what is that?'

'I think one of your most important qualities, Clem, is that you are as straight as a plumb line. No kinks, no bends, no curves around the truth. Straight at it.'

'I like to think I will always be direct and honest, Will.'

'Good. I am the same. And if an apology is due, then it should come from me, for being so determined to get to the truth. That's all I'm doing – and it's not just for your benefit. I am safeguarding myself, my reputation, my family's firm, and my profession.'

This was received with a thick silence. The pause lengthened. At last, she spoke. 'I understand your motives and your desire to be honourable but the repercussions cause me pain. Thank you for agreeing to see me. Good morning, Will.'

Was that it? It was. The line went deader than the void of a moment earlier. He couldn't have offended her again, surely? Why was she permitted to be so blunt, but he somehow let her down if he was equally direct?

Will left for work, sulking in the carriage all the way to the trapezoidal building that sat between Cornhill and Threadneedle streets. He alighted from the hackney at the western end and took a moment to glance up at the pediment. Its frieze depicted the figure of Commerce, its Latin inscription declaring that the Royal Exchange had been founded in the time of Queen Elizabeth and was now presided over by her descendant, Queen Victoria, some three hundred years later.

To protect Lloyd's from tricksters – particularly those he suspected of fraud – was one of his responsibilities as one of the individual brokers that upheld its name and history. He found the grand walls of stone, which hugged the massive courtyard where the insurance brokers traded, reassuring. This was not just about him. It was about his duty and honour as a man of business.

He lifted his chin, tugging at his tight starched collar, and forced himself to accept that his course was the right one. If Clementine Grant felt no need to apologise for her behaviour, then nor should he.

———

Will helped Clementine and her chaperone down from their carriage. They were near Temple Bar, one of the original gateways into the City of London. Their destination, opposite the imposing Royal Courts of Justice, was a narrow doorway flanked by simple white columns: the famous tea company Twinings had sold its wares here for almost three centuries. Above the door was a statue of a British lion, picked out in gold, sitting between figurines of Chinese merchants: a regal-looking emblem for the company that supplied Her Majesty.

The bouquet inside was earthy with toasted notes that made one's mouth water. Clementine noted parcels of tea, coffee and cocoa, all for sale in abundant quantities.

'Did you see the lion?' Will asked, making conversation as they waited to be shown to their table. Both women nodded. 'This shop was called the Golden Lion when tea was first sold here. I gather the artist Hogarth was such a frequent shopper here he accumulated a sizeable debt and paid it off with a portrait of Twining.'

'Gosh, you are knowledgeable, Mr Axford!' Mrs Chattoway beamed, looking around at all the shelves laden with a huge variety of products. The dark wood and soft lantern lighting added to a moody atmosphere that spoke of the exotic places where the tea, coffee and cacao pods grew.

The senior waitress ensured they were comfortably seated and took their orders.

'First or second flush for the Darjeeling, madam?'

Elspeth Chattoway giggled. 'Surprise me, dear. I'm really not that specific, so long as it's Darjeeling.'

Clementine smiled at the waitress. 'First flush, I think, for my companion, and I'll have a pot of your first Assam, please.'

'Make that two pots of Assam,' Will chimed in. 'Ladies, anything to eat? Can I tempt you with a little biscuit, perhaps?'

Both declined, although Clementine assured the waitress she would be purchasing some Earl Grey and Jasmine tea before she departed.

'Now, young man,' their elder said, returning the conversation to something more intimate before their tea arrived. 'Dear Clementine failed to mention that you were William *Axford* until we were introduced. How is your father?'

'He's hale, thank you, Mrs Chattoway. Rather grumpy at times —' he grinned, turning on his charm — 'but still working, still fully engaged with life.'

'Oh, that's wonderful to hear. I haven't seen him in years. He used to be quite the gentleman about town.'

At this Will raised an eyebrow, knowing it would draw the older woman's laughter.

'Yes, indeed. I am sorry for the loss of your mother – you were so young. They were a dashing couple. But after her passing he became the most eligible Londoner, and he broke the heart of many a widow who decided she and he had plenty in common.'

Mrs Chattoway put a hand to the side of her mouth. 'To tell the truth, William, forget the widows – I happen to know many a beautiful young spinster who had designs upon your father.'

He shook his head with genuine surprise; it was a novel thought that his father had any romantic drive. 'He was still in his thirties. I wonder why he never acted upon any of those potential unions? I mean, I was at Rugby – hardly in the way.'

Their tea arrived and they fell silent as it was served.

'And it seems you survived?'

He liked the wicked glint in her sharp-eyed stare. 'I slipped through its halls without too much burden, yes.'

She nodded. 'The good-looking, very wealthy ones always do.'

He didn't agree but kept his thoughts private, glancing towards Clem. She was studying him in that intense, wide-eyed way of hers, as though she were capable of sifting through his most private thoughts. He fought the inclination to swallow, wishing hard he could make things right between them so he could kiss her again, ask her to come to a church and marry him tomorrow. But he had learned that this free-spirited woman would do exactly as she chose, and right now, marrying the man she held responsible for the anger he could see was still simmering seemed unlikely at best.

'Anyway, Will,' Mrs Chattoway continued, 'to answer your query – and I'm surprised you have to wonder – it was because of you that the dashing Jerome Axford never remarried.'

Will stared at Clem's chaperone, impolitely holding a large sip of tea in his mouth. He blinked and then finally remembered to swallow. 'Whatever does that mean?' he finally said, his shock obvious.

Mrs Chattoway tinkled a small laugh. 'Exactly as I say, dear boy. Your father's life revolved around you and you alone. No other woman was going to be permitted to enter your life and have any influence. With the love of his life gone, he was determined to raise you his way.' She nodded as if remembering. 'I recall a conversation your father had with my Henry, bless his soul. He wanted you back in London and in his presence, so that he and his circle would be your influence, as your mother would have wanted you to be brought up. So forward in his thinking.'

At this Will had to take a breath. Were they really talking about the same person?

'I remember how determined he was that you would enjoy a home life, feel the care and security of a parent around you, and that you would grow up in his mould rather than someone else's. You look surprised?' It was an understatement.

He glanced at Clem, whose expression had softened. He wished it hadn't. To have her sympathy now but not to be able to act upon it hurt more. He looked back at her companion. 'I am, Mrs Chattoway. I've always thought I never quite lived up to my father's hopes.' He regretted sharing this secret the moment it escaped him.

But she simply waved a bejewelled hand at him. 'That's typical of Jerome – never one for bestowing compliments. I'll tell you this, though, William. Surround me with the Jeromes of this world. Beware the silver-tongued, who lavish their thoughts and affections for public knowledge, I say.'

He didn't mean to glance at Clem, but he knew she understood his look to be about her uncle – as though Mrs Chattoway had just referred to Reggie Grant. He blinked with exasperation, wondering if he could try any harder to let her see him in a worse light.

'You're very quiet, my dear,' said Mrs Chattoway, squeezing Clem's hand. 'And look, there's Eugenie Collet. She's headed this way. You will excuse me if I just turn and have a little chat, won't you?'

Mrs Chattoway swivelled in her seat to talk to a big-bosomed woman wearing the tightest of S-shaped corsets of a fashion years gone, which made her waist ridiculously tiny and gave her an odd swan-necked shape.

Will looked at Clem. 'A set-up?'

She smiled self-consciously. 'It's very kind of Elspeth. She knew I needed a private word with you.'

'Does she know everything about everyone?'

Clementine chuckled. 'Yes, I believe so.'

He smiled, pleased just to hear that sound of her amusement, but he waited; only Clem could determine what happened next.

They both raised their cups and drank.

'We don't have long, Will. Do you mind if I am brief?'

'Not at all.'

She paused, as if the asking was hard. 'I need your help.'

'Anything,' he murmured softly, filled with fresh hope. 'Name it.'

Clementine explained succinctly, and by the time her chaperone turned back towards them, all which had needed to be discussed by the two young people had been said.

'Thank you,' Clem said to Elspeth.

'Oh, my dears. I haven't forgotten what it is to be young and desperate to be alone with the one person in the world with whom no one will permit you to be alone,' she said, her tone one of kind amusement. Elspeth sipped her tea with a pleasurable groan.

Will hoped Clem wouldn't correct her. He wanted Mrs Chattoway to believe they were in love. Maybe she would help him to repair the damage?

'It was just a business matter. Will and I might be undertaking a new venture together . . . with my uncle's blessing, I should add.'

'Of course, dears. And the fact that the two of you make the most darling of couples is irrelevant. You couldn't do any better, Will Axford – and as for you, Clementine Grant, whatever is holding you back?' She stood, as if she did not wish for them to answer.

'Come along, dear. It's time for my afternoon nap. Thank you, Will. A delight to meet you – I hope I shall see much more of you.'

He stood and kissed her gloved hand. 'The pleasure was mine, Mrs Chattoway, and thank you – I shall visit, I promise. I would love to hear about my mother. My father rarely speaks of her.'

She tapped her nose. 'That's because he doesn't like to share her, William – not even with you.'

He turned to Clem. 'Will I see you soon, Clementine?' He kissed her gloved hand in identical fashion, but his gaze lingered.

'You shall,' she said, and he hoped she understood all of his ragged emotions.

'Until then.' He bowed slightly. 'Ladies.'

As he escorted them into the shop where they waved him off while they purchased tea, Will understood that his only chance to redeem himself would be if his research via the Kimberley Club could yield for Clementine the gravesite of Joseph One-Shoe so she could fulfil her dream to give her friend the proper Zulu farewell.

28

'Ah, there you are. Good morning, darling girl,' Reggie said from the breakfast table at Holland Park. He folded up a letter and returned it to the pile of post before turning his cheek towards Clem as she bent down to plant a kiss. 'Oh, but you smell delicious. Is that your mother's perfume?'

She leaned in to give him a hug, wrapping her arms around his shoulders and kissing him on the head. She was pleased he couldn't see the sadness in her expression, glad that he still held her mother's memory close. 'It is.'

He patted her hand. 'And what are you up to today?'

She was ready for this. 'I'm meeting a friend at the art gallery,' she lied. 'I think Mrs Chattoway might accompany us. How about you?'

'Oh, business, you know. I've got to go into the City to sort out some finances.'

'You sound very chipper this morning, Uncle Reg.'

'Do I?' he said, buttering some toast. 'Well, I suppose I'm feeling happier than I have in a while.'

'Oh? Why's that?'

'Nothing to bother you with, my darling. Business can often weigh heavily, but I think today I shall be receiving some excellent news about an investment I made many years ago. If all goes to plan, I think we should celebrate.'

She wanted to weep. 'Celebrate?'

'Fancy meeting me for dinner? I'll take you somewhere ridiculously swanky and we can set tongues wagging. How do you fancy the Criterion at Piccadilly?'

'Gosh – very swanky, then?'

'You deserve it all, my darling girl.'

She didn't know what to say. 'Shall we see how my day goes, Uncle Reg? If I have lunch with the ladies, I may not be able to fit in another meal.'

He smiled. 'Eat lightly,' he said. 'I want you on my arm tonight in all your finery so I can show you off. That Will Axford had better hurry up and get my permission or every young bachelor in England is going to be on our tail.'

She laughed, but her insides felt like a tangle of vines. Clem was not looking forward to today. The morning had begun with a lie – not her style at all – and it would likely end with the revelation of another lie: one that would change her life's course irrevocably.

'Shall I call to get you some eggs cooked fresh?' he offered, sipping his tea. 'Bread and butter is hardly enough.'

'You said to eat lightly!' She winked, knowing she wouldn't even be able to nibble the bread for the nausea she was feeling. 'I might take this upstairs, Uncle. I've realised I'm running a little bit late.'

'Off you go, darling. Have a wonderful day – I'm already looking forward to this evening hugely.' He stood to kiss her. 'See you later.'

She left the light-filled breakfast room and wondered if that would be the last time she and Uncle Reg would break bread together. Clem ran up the stairs of the London house so that no one could witness her tears.

———————

Several hours later, Clem found herself standing in the back room of a jewellery salon in Hatton Garden. Her scarlet day suit stood out in the workroom, being far more appropriate to the salon. She had needed to dress for lunch with the ladies, not her sombre mood and this task ahead. Perhaps she'd overdone it in her desire to convince Uncle Reggie that all was normal.

Will stood politely apart. His all-black ensemble, with a frock coat for the City, picked up on the black velvet trim of her lapels. She still wore her black kid gloves, although the tremble in her body had nothing to do with the cold of the December day.

This was fear.

She thought about how Uncle Reggie had taken Gillie from her, remembering that in Kimberley her ragdoll had felt heavy. By the time they had reached the shores of England he was light, and her mind had been too blurred with sorrow, anxiety and grief for her to even think of mentioning it to him. She recalled that Uncle Reggie had spent the entire voyage playing with her, cajoling her, reading with her, telling her tall tales. He had even sung her to sleep, and he had always been there when she woke up. When they had arrived he'd carried her off the ship and never let go of her hand, all the way to Woodingdene in Northumberland. He had been by her side throughout her childhood and for every important milestone – never once a harsh word, always quick with praise, ever interested in her thoughts and passions.

He had been the best and most reliable of fathers. But the whopping rough diamond known as Sirius had been secreted in Gillie, and in her heart she knew the diamonds had still been there after her father's death. She thought about the Dog Star and remembered that Joseph One-Shoe had said he would always follow her. Was he following her now in spirit?

The trap was now complete. It was a necessary evil to force the truth, or doubt would forever cast a shadow over her life. Will had likened it to toppling dominoes. They'd spoken on the telephone to finalise the details of the plan. She replayed it in her mind.

'Each domino stands on its end and must tap the next in line – you could have a dozen or more lined up and they would all fall, providing the first one was tipped over. That's what we have to do to corner your uncle into revealing the truth.'

'The truth could be the opposite of what you suspect, Will.'

'And I hope that is how it turns out, Clem.'

'What about the bank? Does anybody there know?'

'Not about what we're doing, but I did exert some pressure via my father.'

'Which he was only too pleased to provide?'

'Clem, my father doesn't dislike Reggie – he simply doesn't trust him. He prefers not to do business with him, but he is well aware of my involvement with —' he didn't finish that sentence, changing course, she was sure — 'my involvement with your uncle, and how he's pitched a new business venture.'

'And has the bank foreclosed?' she asked, cutting to the heart of the conversation.

He answered immediately and evenly. 'No. It is my understanding that your uncle's banker has spoken to him on the telephone, warning him of the dire need to inject funds or face foreclosure. It was a final warning, you could say. And it worked – he took the action we suspected he would, to avoid the public humiliation of bankruptcy.'

She nodded, gripping the receiver, hating that Will was right.

'Well, we shall find out tomorrow,' she said. 'I can't say I'm looking forward to it.'

'I can assure you I am not either,' he replied. 'There's something else I want to tell you, Clem.'

'Will, can we not . . . I mean, can it wait, please, until this unpleasant business is done?'

'Of course.' He replied as any gentleman should but he sounded disappointed. 'Except it might brighten you, and if you'd —'

'No, Will, please. Not now. I can barely face looking at myself in the mirror at the moment – I don't believe I deserve anything bright or cheerful right now, thank you. I'm better off in this mood or I won't be able to see it through.'

'As you wish. Clem . . .'

'I shall see you tomorrow, as we've arranged.'

Will murmured to her now, snapping her out of her dark thoughts, his worried expression once again softening her feelings towards him. 'Are you feeling all right, Clem?'

'I just want it to be over,' she whispered back, weary of the seesawing emotions she felt towards Will.

He nodded, glancing at his fob watch. 'Any minute now.'

Sammy Izak came over to them. 'Your uncle has just alighted a hackney, Clementine.'

'Thank you,' she said. She assumed he knew this because spies had been posted. Her ears were buzzing as though a bee were trapped inside her head and her mouth turned as dry as if she'd swallowed the ashes of her father's bones.

29

Only a few days earlier Reggie Grant had felt as though his world was opening up to its full potential. His idea of a new form of insurance for theatrical presentations was inspired. Looking beyond opera, ballet and grand orchestral performances, he could see a latent business opportunity insuring entertainment for the lower classes. Not only circuses, penny gaffs and freak shows, but pleasure palaces on the seafront and the new music halls. Now that's where real money could be made. These venues offered the masses everything from acrobats to singers for a shilling entrance fee; they were colourful, bawdy, hilarious, and worth every penny. These fun spots were becoming so popular it seemed that a new music hall opened its red velvet curtains every month.

At the beginning of the week, he had actually burst into gleeful laughter looking at his own reflection while shaving.

'You really are a card, Reggie,' he said, pointing the soapy badger-bristle brush at the mirror. 'You are a Grant who is going to be rich in his own right, and Clementine will be proud of you.'

Just three days later that buoyant mood deflated when his banker telephoned with the awkward news that his patience had run out. Reggie begged and cajoled him, even offering to double the interest on his loans, but Sir Jeremy Jones was implacable.

'It is regretful, Reginald.' He had always used Reggie's full name, which made him feel like a schoolboy. No doubt it was deliberate. 'A most unpleasant business, but we have our duty to the board and our shareholders.'

'Jeremy. You knew my father before I was born, and you've worked with me ever since his death. You promised you'd give me a few more months.'

'No, I promised you I would try. I am not the bank, Reginald. I am one of its stakeholders and we all answer to one another. I did my best for you, but the bank's tolerance has expired.'

'I can't believe they don't trust —'

'I don't know why you cannot believe it, Reginald. This has occurred before.'

'Well, quite! Isn't that the point? I sorted out that catastrophe at the ironworks, none of which was my doing!' he bleated. 'Money was forthcoming.'

'You did. But you've been drawing on the account ever since.'

'And you well know the spending has been for good reason. You know the improvements at Woodingdene. Plus my investments are not all poor decisions – they've paid dividends.'

'Even so. We accept there has been income over the past twenty years, of course, but the outgoings can no longer be ignored. Out of respect for your family we have done our utmost to turn a blind eye, essentially, but there are those calling for us to take action and I cannot hold them off any longer. We've had several conversations about the sale of some of the assets, which you assured me was underway, but I've seen no large deposits made into the account.'

Assets had been sold privately, but Reggie could hardly tell Sir Jeremy that the proceeds had been used to pay off 'other debts'.

The bank had always been so tolerant. He sighed. 'All right, all right. How much time can you give me?'

'To do what, Reginald?'

'To put us back on an even keel,' he replied, in a tone that said, *Isn't it obvious?*

'Let's not speak in euphemisms, dear boy. You're talking about an impossible situation. The bank is wishing to foreclose, do you understand?'

'That doesn't answer my question.'

The banker sighed. 'To put your account into credit and reassure the bank of your future security, you would need to find a minimum of four thousand pounds. Now, I just don't see —'

'Done.'

Sir Jeremy sounded exasperated. 'What do you mean by "done"?'

'I'll have four and a half thousand pounds in the account by Tuesday morning.'

'Four and a half . . .? But it's Friday tomorrow,' Sir Jeremy spluttered, astonished.

'I realise that. I shall journey to London and the money will be forthcoming by the close of business next Monday at the earliest, but Tuesday before midday at the latest. How does that sound to you?'

'To be frank, it sounds preposterous. You couldn't possibly raise the funds to —'

'I can, and I shall. Indulge me. Keep those wolves at bay,' he said. 'Let's have a cognac and a cigar at your club next week. Good morning, Sir Jeremy.'

Reggie replaced the receiver, and without allowing a thought to enter his head, he pulled on rubber wellingtons, put a thick oilskin over his woollen jumper, and took the snaking path down into the gardens. The steps were too treacherous on such an icy

December day. It took him half an hour of solid walking, his mind still blank, to reach the last part of the embankment. He lowered himself down, treading sideways like a goat until he hit the pathway that would take him to Louisa's Bridge.

He walked to the middle of the bridge, his footsteps creating a metallic song as they resonated through the steel. And there he stood for many long minutes, aware only that the day was darkening around him. Reggie Grant finally gazed upwards through the tallest reaches of the trees and understood that the sun would soon slip to the other side of the world, bringing a new dawn to the people of the colonies. He thought about Africa, where this new day would soon rise, shining on the grave of his beloved sister and her loathsome husband. It would light the scene of the lie of his life – the theft of their child – yet it was no lie that he loved Clementine. Everything had been for her. And what he was contemplating was for her, too.

The massive rough stone and its six remaining smaller companions would have to be sold. Although he'd taken precautions, he had hoped just the smaller stones might get him out of this jam – and they would have, if not for the bank's foreclosure. Sir Jeremy's revelation had exploded on him like a firework.

It was all manageable. There was income from Woodingdene – solid, enviable income – and there was the income from his investments, but he'd mounted the debt faster than the money could come in. The new insurance scheme had infinite potential, but Sir Jeremy and his peers didn't bank on potential – not modern, forward ideas with no track record or secure precedent. What he was proposing was so new it would be considered strange and incomprehensible, just as the telephone or the railway might have sounded to such men a century earlier.

He banged a fist on the iron railing and heard it complain across the bridge's expanse.

'I'm sorry, Louisa,' he whispered, not sure whether he was asking her forgiveness for stealing her husband's life, his diamonds, or their child. It was all wrapped up in one terrible act, the greed for Clementine and the freedom she could bring to him. He had expected to love her but not as he did. She had become his child, his reason for waking each morning and looking forward to life and its tribulations.

Now he had one more lie of which to rid himself. Selling the diamonds – including the large one – would dispose of the evidence. There would be nothing tying him to Africa once they were gone.

Finding the right dealer had taken much research. He needed someone who would not ask too many questions, who would share a similar greed and yet have the ability to transport the big diamond out of the country, perhaps to Amsterdam for cutting and polishing, or beyond. He'd seen the glitter in the Jew's eye when they had met privately two months prior and the man had finally been able to hold the rough, the size of an egg. At this stage Reggie had simply been enjoying the awe it elicited.

'This is hundreds of carats,' the diamond dealer murmured, incredulous at the massive stone winking in his hand. Even unpolished, the octahedral – that reminded him of two pyramids pressed together at their base – was mesmerising.

'I'm no expert,' Reggie said, inhaling his cigar with a helpless grin. 'I'm interested to know its worth.'

The workshop behind the salon was closed for the evening. The back door had been opened to Reggie and he'd been ushered in by the man and his son. They'd both looked stunned and, he thought, just a bit fearful at what he was offering. 'This is a private negotiation,' he insisted. 'All of these diamonds,' he said, casting an upturned palm over the display of rough stones gleaming on a velvet mat in the light of a small table lamp, 'are mine. They came into my possession in the Cape more than twenty years ago when

I dabbled in a small claim I bought from a beggared digger. They are of sentimental value – I'd hoped never to part with them, to be honest. I had wished to turn them into a magnificent piece as a gift to my niece upon my death.'

This was no lie. He had dreamed for years of leaving behind a stunning item for Clementine so that her diamonds would be returned to her without him suffering any recriminations.

'You no longer wish for that?' the old dealer said, surprised.

He shook his head, noting that the son looked unsure – he had said nothing but a formal greeting since Reggie had arrived. It seemed he did not want to be a party to this deal. Reggie didn't care. All that mattered was the price. If he ever needed to shift the big stone quickly, having a pathway for it seemed not only wise but clever.

'I've never seen such a big rough diamond. I have nothing to compare it to . . . I have to be honest, Mr Grant. I'm at a loss.'

'I understand. But I'm sure you'll agree that we are talking about a first-class stone.'

'No doubt,' the man muttered, shaking his head with awe. 'A first-water stone, I would hazard.'

'Whatever that means,' Reggie said, trying not to sneer. 'And your estimation?'

'Mr Grant, I suspect this would need a syndicate or one incredibly rich capitalist – none of whom, I can assure you, lives in England. The stone could never see the light of day in Hatton Garden – it would cause a sensation. It would have to go abroad, perhaps to America; it could certainly go into Europe. Royalty wouldn't touch it without the right provenance – there are diamond laws in Africa – and while I accept this is your stone, it has no papers, I'm guessing?'

Reggie nodded. 'Back in 1872 after several deaths in my family, with me stuck in Africa's Karoo Desert like the wild, wild

West, with madmen taking all sorts of risks, I could not let anyone know about this diamond. I was actually scared and a little out of my mind with sorrow, so I wasn't thinking clearly. I brought it home on my person.' The lie had sounded plausible as he'd fashioned it. This dealer, unless he'd been to Africa, couldn't know otherwise.

'This is not something I could handle. Twelve carats in a stone of this quality would be —' he shook his head again — 'what, er . . . fifteen thousand pounds.'

Reggie could only just rein in his glee, permitting only the smallest smile. 'Yes, well, you would know more than I would. So, if it is up to a few hundred carats?'

'An unthinkable sum, although to be honest, if they know you're in a hurry, then the price would likely halve, maybe even come to one third.'

Reggie shrugged, amazed at his self-control. He smiled like a dozing cat. 'I'm in no hurry. Well, think on it, Mr Reuben. Contact whomever you wish. I may choose to sell it sooner rather than later,' he said, keeping his options open. He knew he was confusing the dealer. 'The smaller ones are for sale, and if not through you, then I shall journey to Antwerp or Amsterdam —'

'No, no, I'm not saying it cannot be organised, but —'

'Father . . . ?'

'Hush, Benjamin. Mr Grant, I believe I know a syndicate that might be interested. Let me put out some discreet feelers.'

'Good. Discretion is everything for these stones. I do not wish my name to be attached to them. These diamonds were acquired at a time of tremendous sorrow and are a reminder of that traumatic chapter. My niece, however,' he said, before the man could leap in and ask the question, 'has little memory of that sorrow. She could have worn these as jewellery with pride and pleasure.'

'So why sell, Mr Grant?' the son asked pointedly.

Reggie was ready with a well-crafted lie. 'I believe my niece is to be married soon. And I am dying.'

Both men gasped but he maintained his smile.

'A slow death, nothing immediate, but my condition is incurable. I have come to the conclusion in recent weeks that these diamonds have brought bad luck to our family. On the day I found the stones my mother married a man I despised and my beloved stepmother died,' he lied. Reggie shook his head. 'And the night of the find, Clementine's father suffered a terrible accident, falling into the Kimberley mine. He also died, and I was left with a child to raise as my own. The day I took the stones out from where they'd been stored for two decades, I received the news from my physician of my terminal illness. Now, I don't believe in the other world, Mr Reuben, but I cannot escape the notion that these diamonds – as magnificent as they are – are harbingers of doom to our family. I think we'd best be rid of them, and I certainly don't want them draped around my Clementine's neck. She's beautiful enough anyway.' He chortled. 'Let's be done with them. Do what you can. Find me a buyer.'

Apparently, Mr Reuben had done just that, and so Reggie now found himself alighting from a hackney in Hatton Garden. He felt a trace of excitement pass through him; it was like watching the lamplighter touch his taper to a gaslight and seeing it erupt into a steadily burning flame. Inside he was burning with a mix of fear and anticipation, laced with an incredible thrill at the thought of such money, the likes of which his father had never known, even in his heyday. It was potentially more money than most of Britain's wealthiest could lay their hands on. Even at one-third of the big stone's value, the proceeds would leave him well set up for life, and Clementine would never have to consider her future again. It would be secure. And her fortune, which she was managing with care and modesty – and far too much philanthropy for his liking – would also be safe.

He was better than his father. Better than all of them, because he would leave a legacy of riches, not debt. Maybe he would have to put his name to that stone. If it couldn't be avoided, then he would source counterfeit patent papers or a licence for a claim. He knew people who could organise such things. But it wouldn't come to that. He didn't seek the glory of the stone any longer. He wanted it gone, out of the country, turned to liquid cash that could release him from his debt. Perhaps he could move to Paris for a while . . . Clementine might even agree to accompany him on a grand tour of Europe.

Reuben had sent him a telegram: *We have a buyer. Expect extraordinary sum. London, this Friday.*

He could hug himself. It was perfect timing. As much as he detested Sir Jeremy putting the squeeze on him, it was serendipitous that the bank's decision had arisen at a time when he could do something about it. He was already enjoying the thought of sitting down at Sir Jeremy's club and smiling at him, knowing the debt had been cleared – drinking a toast to himself on the old bastard's account.

He had taken the precaution of having the driver drop him off at the top end of Hatton Garden, and now he was weaving his way deeper down its narrow lanes with no concern that the man could tell anyone, if he was ever asked, where his passenger had been going. There was a lightness to his step as he thought about the future. The idea of a trip through the grand capital cities of Europe sounded more and more appealing.

'He's just moments away now,' Sammy whispered in the work-room, which had become more crowded in the past few minutes.

Clementine looked around at the men gathered there. 'Is he really necessary?' she murmured to Will, glancing towards the detective.

'It was not my idea to involve the police. I think it was Saul's son who contacted Bow Street.'

She made a sound that was a cross between a sigh and a hiss, glaring at the bulky man with his large feet and a heavy coat he hadn't removed. She could smell the rain emanating from the thick wool.

Will leaned in again. 'Clem, I wanted to tell you this earlier. But now I really do need to say something important – actually, there are two things I must say.'

'All right.' She sighed. 'Go ahead.'

She watched him lick his bottom lip nervously before he rubbed his chin, as if searching for the right words.

'Just say it, Will. I can't imagine anything could make this situation any worse than it is right now.'

He blew out a breath of resignation and the words spilled out. 'Bad news first. No one else knows of this, but your uncle may have a case to answer for the death of your father.'

The words were like a foreign language. She took half a minute to decipher what he'd said and what the accusation actually entailed.

Will looked pale around the lips, and his lovely eyes had a haunted quality. 'It wasn't murder,' he began.

'I should think not,' she said, shocked.

'But it could be what they call manslaughter, Clem.'

She was certain Will could tell it was taking all of her self-control not to unleash a shout of rage. Good manners simply wouldn't permit such a display. Maybe that was why he'd left this explosive fact until now, and in the presence of a detective?

'Will, my father died as a result of his fall,' she said, as if explaining it to a child. 'Nothing is going to change that.' She pulled angrily away as he reached out to placate her.

'Were you there?' He forced her to make eye contact with him.

She blinked with suppressed fury. 'You know I was not.'

'Well, someone else was!'

Before she could ask or he could explain, Sammy hissed for silence.

'He's here.'

They never did share the good news.

30

Reginald Grant had taken a circuitous path to the premises of Saul Reuben, diamond merchant. He'd enjoyed the narrow lanes, dodging urchins, street sellers, couples staring into the small windowpanes of jewellery stores. He watched an old piano wobbling on a cart being dragged by two men, and stepped off the pavement and onto the cobblestones to avoid it. He navigated around a small crowd gathering around a chestnut brazier. Flower girls carried baskets and well-suited men moved with long, urgent strides around it all – those, he suspected, were the diamond carriers. He felt only pride at Clem's clever idea to offer insurance to the merchants and jewellers who used these messengers.

It was quieter than nearby Covent Garden, with far fewer costermongers yelling and jostling to sell their goods, but it was busy enough that he could move with ease and not be noticed. He passed a large sign offering to buy old gold and coins for cash before he disappeared into an alley.

This twitten would lead him to his future. Within the hour he planned to become one of the richest men in Britain. He hoped his detractors were turning in their graves and dipping their respects his way.

Rot, the lot of you! he thought, but kept an inward smile for Louisa, whose love and pride in him would now be justified.

His destination was a salubrious space behind an unassuming green door, halfway down the tiniest of laneways between Hatton Garden proper and Ely Place. Passing Ye Olde Mitre tavern, he made a note to have celebratory drink within when the deal was done. He moved down the darkened alley, the sound of a corner organ grinder disappearing behind him.

It was Benjamin Reuben, the son, who answered the door.

'Ben Reuben,' he said with a wink as he lifted his hat. 'Good day to you. I believe your father is expecting me.'

'He is, sir. Come in.'

'Brr! I'm glad you have a merry fire burning, young Reuben. It's certainly a chill afternoon.'

The son, ever watchful, politely helped him off with his overcoat.

Offering to take his hat and brolly, Reggie grinned and removed a package that had been secured in the lid of his top hat. It needed no explanation as he handed the topper and umbrella to Reuben.

'Let me fetch my father for you, Mr Grant. Can I offer you some coffee?'

'That would be welcome, thank you, but only if your father will join me. No need to warm a pot just for me.' Reggie rubbed his hands together before the fire; he couldn't swear whether it was from the cold or out of gleeful anticipation.

Ben went into the back part of the premises and Reggie let his gaze roam the room. It was part salon but mostly a place to do business. He could see all the paraphernalia of the diamond trader: a counter, good lighting, magnifying tools, the usual range of tweezers and packets. Reggie unravelled the linen-wrapped parcel, in which the large diamond and its companions had travelled since he'd left the north. He wouldn't be sorry to see it go, he realised. It had been a burden in his life, growing heavier each year. The other diamonds he'd stolen he felt nothing for – merely a means to an end; they had kept his finances secure over the years. How fortunate he had been that his troubles had coincided with James Knight's diamond strike. Clem's father would have squandered the proceeds, he was sure: more hare-brained ideas, more failed projects, more alcohol. At least he'd put Knight's diamonds to their best use – and look at Clementine: she was about to come into her full inheritance and wouldn't need anyone's support much longer. Soon she would have a husband, a new life, and he could sigh with relief that he'd got her to this point. Louisa's legacy was safe. She could rest easy in her grave now that her brother had taken care of her most precious possession. Knight's death was a blessing, it really was, and once he divested himself of these remaining diamonds, he could wash himself clean of Africa, and no longer feel its fingertips reaching out towards him.

He regarded the dark timbers surrounding him and the parchment-coloured paint on the walls. He looked down at the extravagant Persian rug he stood upon. He rather liked it; it wouldn't look out of place at either Grant house. Perhaps he and Clem could go to Persia and commission a rug that somehow had their story – or at least their familial love – woven into it. It wouldn't be cheap, but then again, he was about to become one of the wealthiest men in Britain, albeit secretly so. He could buy one for each room and hardly feel the cost. The men of Hatton Garden were secretive and far wealthier than they perhaps owned up to being, he decided, testing the thick pile of the rug. He thought about how much Saul Reuben would skim off the sale price for himself. Did it matter? There was so much money involved it was going to be a problem just to stash the money. A Swiss bank account was required, and he'd already made the necessary enquiries – he planned to journey to Zurich immediately after the sale had been completed.

He took a slow, deep breath, swallowing the gloating smile that kept trying to erupt, and maintained his calm expression even despite the rising excitement. It was all going to work out.

What Reggie Grant didn't see was the long slit of a peephole in the side wall. Cunningly achieved, it sat just above a dresser and was easily missed.

Behind it was the workroom. The narrow window, concealed below a distracting mirror, allowed Reuben and his son to see a customer arriving while they were working out the back. It was from this vantage that Reggie was being gloomily observed by the assembled group. Sammy Izak glanced at Reuben and his Hatton Garden colleague moved towards Clementine.

'I'm very sorry this is happening, Miss Grant,' Mr Reuben murmured as he stepped past her to leave the workroom and greet his client.

She nodded. It was hardly Mr Reuben's fault. This had been, after all, her idea. Whatever happened next was no one's fault but her uncle's, and indeed her own. Clem knew the man on the other side of this wall better than anyone here and she could feel the buoyancy of his mood. He looked so cheerful and pleased at the world – did any of this really matter? She felt only regret and asked herself how his entrapment would change any of their lives for the better. The fact was, it wouldn't. It was about to cause pain for everyone involved. The silence as they watched Saul Reuben enter the room felt funereal. They were about to end Reggie's life as he knew it.

'Reuben, good afternoon,' Reggie said, stepping forward to shake the man's hand. 'I was delighted to receive your telegram.'

They shook hands and Reuben gestured for Reggie to join him at the counter. He obliged, and the group in the workroom was now close enough to the action that Clem felt she could reach through the peephole and touch her uncle. She could certainly make a noise to alert him.

Will touched her elbow. It was only a light squeeze, and he let go immediately, but something in his sad yet forbidding expression made her relinquish the notion of saving her uncle. Will shook his head once, as if to say, *Let it play it out as it must.* It spoke to her sense of what was right.

So be it, she thought, remembering Joseph One-Shoe's warning that Uncle Reggie loved her but was not to be trusted. It came like a peal of warning bells. This is what Joseph had meant. Perhaps he had known the truth about her father all along but had let Reggie take her back to England, where she was obviously headed towards a better life.

She swallowed her grief and returned her attention to the two men on the other side of the peephole.

———

'So, a single buyer?' Reggie asked.

'No, Mr Grant. It's a syndicate in America.'

'Excellent. How will it work?'

'They trust me and my contacts to value the stone for purchase. I will pay a deposit on their behalf to secure it. They will send their valuer to view it and then, if all goes to plan, the balance will be paid.'

'How long will that all take?' Reggie frowned, his tone urgent.

The son arrived with the coffee tray.

'Perhaps until February. But,' Reuben said, holding up a finger, 'I will make the deposit today. The Atlantic is not forgiving at this

time of year, Mr Grant, so the American representative will under-
take the voyage as soon as it is feasible. I will need ten days or so to
make a proper valuation, of course, but even I can see we are
talking about a mighty sum of money.' He smiled at Reggie. 'May
I see it again, Mr Grant?'

'Of course.'

As Reggie clutched the linen, in which the orb sat in a separate
wrap, the diamond specialist unrolled a velvet mat and brought
over a magnifying lens on a stand. Reggie admired an elegant
electric lamp Reuben was hefting to shine over the roughs. *Must be
a carbon filament*, he thought, *to be used with such abandon*, for
the light had been on since he'd arrived.

'What guarantee do I have if I leave my stones here?' Reggie
asked evenly as he unwrapped first a handful of small stones from
a handkerchief. They scattered on the velvet mat like fallen stars.

It was the son who replied. 'Our word, Mr Grant.'

'Really?' He smiled. 'Benjamin, your father is prepared to
trade a diamond that has no paperwork, no formal provenance,
despite stringent laws surrounding the exchange of diamonds.
I don't think his word cuts it – or mine, quite frankly. This is not a
gentleman's agreement. This is business, son.'

'It seems . . . shady,' the son replied, and won a glower from his
father.

'Mr Reuben, perhaps your son would prefer to withdraw from
our proceedings. I do not require his judgement.'

'My apologies, Mr Grant,' the son said quickly into the awkward pause. 'Wrong choice of word. I am more concerned than you
can imagine that we are handling a stone lacking provenance.'

'Don't worry, lad,' Reggie assured, revealing the large stone.
'The sight of it will overcome any reservations on the part of
the buyers.'

Behind the wall, Clem gasped, choking off the sound with a

gloved hand, as Uncle Reggie placed a familiar rough stone, the size of a golf ball, on the velvet. Everyone now leaned in to get a better look. On the other side of the wall, Uncle Reggie smirked.

'Brilliant, isn't it? So . . . my security?'

'We shall discuss that,' the elder Reuben said.

Clem felt the tension around her ascending. For her, it was the opposite: she was dipping in a sickening swoop as her gaze locked on to Sirius for the first time since childhood. A tidal wave of memories came roaring back. Suddenly she could hear the deep-toned songs of the Africans who dug for others. There were the smells of the dug earth of the Big Hole, the unwashed bodies of men at labour, the aroma of meat cooking in the distance. She could even conjure the aroma of Joseph One-Shoe's skin, hear his big laugh, feel the curls of his hair when he bent down to whisper to her.

'Mr Grant, just for my own reassurance,' Reuben said, 'tell me all you know of this stone, so that when I tell the Americans, I get it precisely in your words.'

Clem stared at the dull shine of what might be the world's biggest rough diamond. As she looked at it now, her heart began to pound at the realisation that it could reach over three hundred carats. There was no doubting its quality. She remembered holding it up to the light in their shanty; she'd needed Joseph to support her little palm to lift it.

'Clearwater,' Joseph had murmured all those years ago. She'd learned that as the diggers' term for perfection, while also discovering that brokers preferred 'first water'.

Her uncle's voice dragged her back into the present. 'This was dug from a claim I acquired from a poverty-stricken man. He might have been Australian, I don't know, but he was a drunk and glad to swap his claim for my money. I had no sense of what I was buying, to tell you the truth, but I got caught up with the romance of digging for diamonds. There was a sort of frantic energy in Kimberley. It felt lawless, as though anything was possible. And, it seems, that was the case. The poor sod couldn't unearth anything in his claim, yet on our first dig my team found these.'

'Did you not fear the loose tongues of those men?'

'I did, Mr Reuben. I paid them very well with cash and with liquor to make sure every last one of them was still inebriated the next day, by which time I was on my way back to Cape Town.'

'And you left your claim vacant? There could have been more stones like this,' Reuben said, incredulous. He had clearly been schooled to ask all the right questions, Clementine thought. She was amazed at how easily her uncle was weaving the story.

'I sold my claim to someone at the Kimberley Club. I had this huge diamond, so frankly I no longer cared. I needed to return to England with my niece before her dying grandmother took her final breath. Look, I'm not a greedy man, Mr Reuben. I didn't care if someone else profited from the claim. I had my prize,' he said, pointing to the small boulder before them. 'I had another prize, too. I had a little girl to care for. She was more important than anything else.' Clem swallowed to hear it. It wasn't a new sentiment, but it seemed to carry more weight today. 'I had two precious items of cargo in my care. This child was freshly bereaved and still coming to terms with the death of her mother, let alone the tragic loss of her father.'

'And now you're dying, you said,' the younger of the Reubens qualified.

Clem caught her breath and glanced at Will, who looked baffled.

'That's right. I'm tidying my affairs, you could say.'

'And Sirius, as you've called this stone, is a loose end?'

'If you must see it that way, Benjamin, yes.'

Clementine watched her uncle glance at the traders.

'Now, gentlemen, I have been candid with you and it's time you either committed to the sale or returned the diamond. I'm ready to part with it, but I shall want a down payment, a receipt, a photograph of me holding this stone, a document from you saying you have taken custody of it but not ownership, etcetera, etcetera.' He smiled, awaiting their response.

'One more question, if I may?' Ben Reuben asked. 'It's actually from the American syndicate.'

'Go ahead.'

'Sirius, the name that you've coined for this stone. The Americans wondered how you chose that and why.'

It was the first time she'd seen her uncle look unsure. He frowned. 'Oh, they can call it anything they wish. That's just my pet name for it.'

'No, they like it. They specifically asked for the origin of the name.'

She watched her uncle's smile falter. 'Do you know, I can't remember. It's Nordic, isn't it?'

The two Reubens gazed back at him, waiting.

He shrugged. 'It was a long time ago I nicknamed it that. I suppose I was thinking how strong it looked and gave it a Viking name. Or maybe it's Latin. I don't care to recall. Let them rename it any romantic title they choose – the Desert Star, how's that? Or African Light? That will create distance, too, which is preferable.'

He sounded confidently dismissive, but Clementine could tell he was uncertain. The question had caught him off guard and she could hear the anxiety in the slightly dry sound of his voice.

Clem looked down at the toes of her boots. He'd admitted long ago that he knew nothing about astronomy.

'I see,' Saul Reuben said, and nodded. 'Never mind. Er, Benjamin, can you fetch my things from the workroom? We shall get Mr Grant sorted out with his deposit.'

'Yes, of course. Please help yourself to coffee, Mr Grant.'

'Don't mind if I do. Making money makes me thirsty.'

———————

As Benjamin tiptoed into the workroom, they all moved back from the slithole and turned towards the detective. He sucked his teeth and looked to Clementine.

'Clem?' It was Will.

She could hear her uncle and Reuben senior making small talk in the next room. 'You said there was a witness?' she whispered.

'It's time to confront him, Clem,' Will whispered back. 'At the very least he has stolen your father's diamonds, correct?'

She nodded reluctantly.

He spoke slightly louder for the policeman to hear. 'Now, whether you care about that or not is irrelevant. Benjamin Reuben was so spooked by the notion of handling this mysterious diamond that he came clean to the police immediately. I had nothing to do with it, and I doubt very much the detective feels terribly comfortable about being dragged into what is essentially entrapment.'

The detective nodded, murmured softly. 'No judge would go for this.'

'I'm glad you see it that way,' she said.

She'd never been scared of confrontation and she was going to show Will Axford that she would not back down. She needed to extricate her uncle from this situation immediately.

Clem spun on her heel, and Will had to chase her down the small corridor. She entered the room just as her uncle turned around from the fireplace with a puzzled expression.

'Clem?' he said, sounding delighted but baffled. Then his gaze shifted as Will Axford arrived, followed by a stranger, a big man wearing an overcoat, and then Sammy Izak. She could see from his frown how his thoughts were turning over.

She watched as his happy, almost smug expression of just moments ago fell and his eyes dulled. A light had gone out.

'Clem,' he repeated, but this time it sounded like accusation. *How could you?*

31

Despite the warmth of the room the atmosphere was frigid. Everyone seemed to be rooted to the spot. Only her uncle looked surprised; the other players in this horrible scene had the grace at least to look embarrassed.

It was Saul who spoke. 'Miss Grant, I am terribly sorry that you are witness to this.'

'Are you, Mr Reuben?' she asked, with only a hint of sarcasm. 'I understand you have a reputation to protect, and that's why the police are involved. Nevertheless, the fact remains that my uncle chose you to be his dealer. He would not have made this decision lightly – certainly not without solid research and a strong belief in your ability to shift these stones without the proper paperwork.' The man opened his mouth to deny his wrongdoing but she continued. 'More to the point, he obviously knew he could count on your discretion . . . and your son's.' She let that sink in while she looked over to her uncle – who, bless him, gave her a rueful wink of thanks.

Will took up the reins. 'Reggie, we're here because we believe those diamonds are stolen.'

'Stolen?' he said, frowning. 'How ridiculous.'

'Clem?' Will prompted.

'Let him speak,' she replied, looking at her uncle. 'Go ahead, Uncle Reg.'

'Well, my dear,' he said – regaining his confidence, it seemed. 'These are your diamonds, of course. They were hidden in your ragdoll. Your father told me about them, told me where he'd hidden them, before he died.'

'Did he give you permission to take them?' she said, amazed by his silver tongue and oozing confidence.

'No,' he admitted, and as the men around him made sounds of outrage he held up his hand. 'I lied about how I came by them because no one would believe the truth that we carried these out of Africa in the belly of a ragdoll. But they are not stolen; I was simply their caretaker.'

'But you're trying to sell them underhandedly,' Will exclaimed, looking first at Clem and then the policemen.

'I am selling them, yes! Nothing underhand about it, Mr Axford. I simply don't have papers. There is no way to sell them except under the counter, as they say.' Clem couldn't help being so impressed by his performance; she wanted to clap when Uncle Reggie managed to sound affronted.

She was torn. Reggie was lying and she could certainly contradict him with the truth, but she couldn't be complicit in having her uncle put behind bars simply because of some diamonds. He would have spent the proceeds on her, anyway.

'Why didn't you tell me?' she asked him. She chose not to ask why he had lied to her face only days earlier.

Reggie sighed. 'I don't know. I was scared you'd judge me, think me a crook. I took them from your ragdoll when you were so little. When might have been the right time? When you were ten? Sixteen?'

'You always said I was the most mature 21-year-old you knew – why not then?'

'Because, my darling, all you left behind on that dark continent were sorrows. I wanted to protect you. Showing you the diamonds might have brought all those bad memories back. You've never been one for material things, and I didn't think for a moment you'd want to keep the diamonds that essentially ruined your father. I just didn't think you'd want to own them, parade them, wear them in any shape or form. Perhaps I misjudged that but I was doing this for you.'

Credible. Again, she could have applauded his convincing performance.

'Uncle Reggie, the stone is called Sirius, the Latin form of the Greek word *seirios*, meaning "burning" or "scorching".'

'If you say so, darling.'

'But that's not why the stone is called that. It is named after Sirius, the brightest star in our galaxy that shines over our planet. My father, Joseph One-Shoe and I named it on the day Joseph dug it out of the ground. It belonged to him, not my father and I. It was his find, but he gave it to us, and wanted no part of it. My father was bringing me home, with the diamonds hidden in my ragdoll, to sell in Europe. He was frightened by the size of this stone and knew he would not get the best price for it from the brokers in Kimberley.'

Reggie shrugged. 'Well, that's just lovely, my dear. Here you are, letting us all in on its provenance.'

She felt a gust of a nervous laugh wanting to escape. Somehow Uncle Reggie was turning this situation to his advantage. She moved over to the counter to stare closely at the roughs.

The detective spoke for the first time. 'Do you recognise it, Miss Grant?'

'Yes, of course. Uncle Reggie, this is Detective Chief Inspector Burns from the Metropolitan Police.'

Reggie, resigned, nodded to the man.

Clem continued. 'I'd hazard it's three hundred carats. I'd put my trust fund on it being what the diamond trade calls a first water.'

'I'd agree,' Sammy Izak said, nodding. 'Even a single gem from this stone, polished and set, would be worthy of royalty.'

Clementine gave him a sad smile. 'There was rock clinging to it when it was found. But that rock is fragile and when it is exposed to the air it crumbles. As you can see, there is nothing left of that, though I'd hazard there's some still in my ragdoll and wherever you kept this all these years, Uncle Reggie.'

'In my sock drawer,' he admitted, looking vaguely ashamed. 'As safe there as anywhere else.'

An awkward pause filled the room and Clem knew everyone was waiting for her.

'Detective Burns, I do not wish to press charges against my uncle. I don't care about the stones that have been sold in the past – they would have been sold for my benefit, anyway,' she said, glancing at Reggie. His expression told her he couldn't love her any more than he did in this moment. 'The showcase rough is intact, and I believe my Uncle Reggie when he says that he did not steal it in the first instance but was taking care of my heirloom.'

'Even though he was trying to sell it without your knowledge?' Will asked, keeping his tone even and without accusation.

'Yes,' she replied. 'He was not trying to harm me. My uncle, if nothing else, is a true Grant and he cares about our good name. I believe the sale of these diamonds was intended to protect the Grant empire.'

'Thank you, darling Clementine, for seeing the truth,' Reggie said.

To his credit, Will didn't give any sign of exasperation, although he did sigh, as though considering whether to raise the matter Clementine did not especially want to hear.

Their gazes met and held. He surprised her by holding his tongue.

'Well, gentlemen,' Uncle Reggie said in a freshly self-assured tone, looking around at them all, 'I think that concludes our business, does it not? Mr Reuben, I'm guessing the claim of a syndicate was a ruse?'

Reuben nodded, embarrassed.

'Detective Burns, do you have any other business with me?'

The policeman took a slow breath and shook his head. 'Not if Miss Grant is not pressing charges.'

'Then I shall gather up our property, if you don't mind, and ask everyone here to be discreet.' He quickly retrieved the diamonds, wrapping them back up in his linen squares. 'The diamonds have remained safe because no one knew about them. Clementine, my darling, shall we? Young Reuben, my hat and coat please?'

'I suggest Sirius goes into your bank vault immediately, Mr Grant,' Sammy Izak offered, with a glance at Clem that said she really must lay claim to the stones and not allow her uncle to retain them.

'We shall go directly from here,' he said, escorting Clementine to the door, his glare forcing Reuben's son to step aside. 'I can fetch my things myself, Ben. Good afternoon, gentlemen.'

And that was it. Even Clementine, who had helped him to wriggle free from the grip of the law, shook her head in wonder as Uncle Reggie walked her down the alley, diamonds in his top hat, and past Ye Olde Mitre with a bounce in his step.

'I'm sorry you had to go through that, Clem,' he said, finally finding his contrition. 'And I want to —'

'Clementine, wait!' It was Will, striding to catch up with them.

Uncle Reggie turned first. 'I'm not sure my niece wishes to speak with you right now, Will,' he said, keeping his tone polite.

'I was talking to Clementine, Reggie, not you.'

'Not here, Will,' she said, casting a glance around them. 'Uncle Reg, could you give me a moment with Will, please?'

'I'll fetch us a hackney,' he said, cutting Will a disdainful glare before stepping away to hail a cab.

'Clem, are you serious?' Will asked, dumbfounded.

'I have no intention of letting my uncle be marched off to Bow Street. How do you imagine that would help me or our family name?'

His lips thinned with the effort of suppressing his exasperation, but she knew he understood the need to protect one's reputation at all costs.

'I would prefer to deal with this situation on my own terms, and not the public humiliation that was unfolding back there.'

'What do you mean?'

'I mean this isn't going away just yet, is it? You've clearly got more up your sleeve, so let's deal with it all.'

'Clementine?' Her uncle beckoned, holding the open door of a hackney cab.

'What do you want me to do?'

'I want you to keep to yourself whatever it is you're fighting to hold back and bring it to the house. If you tell another soul before you tell me, I shall never wish to look upon you again. Your name will no longer exist in my world.'

She let all of the jagged angles of her threat pierce him.

Will cleared his throat. 'I shall come to the house shortly.'

She nodded, her expression stormy. 'Good afternoon, Will,' she said and turned away from him.

32

As she stepped from the pavement onto the carriage, Clementine made a decision that no man would ever manipulate her again. She would take full control of her life and her future.

'Uncle Reggie, I know you were preparing to make an apology to me back there, but I don't wish to hear it.'

He looked surprised by her tone but not shocked. 'You know I did this for you, though?'

'Do I?' Her tone was hard and slightly mocking.

The cab felt small and airless. She wasn't sure where this was going but she could feel the frustration simmering, desperate to spill over. They'd only just avoided handcuffs and morning newspaper headlines because Will had kept quiet, but this explosive information was still waiting to blow up. She couldn't believe where he was leading her, but now that he'd said it, she had to know – had to get to the truth of it.

'Clementine,' Reggie said, appealing to her. 'Have I ever done anything to hurt you?'

'Not physically, no, but clearly you have lied.'

'Is not telling the whole truth the same as lying – especially when it's done to protect someone you love?'

'No, Uncle Reggie, your semantic distinctions will not work this time.'

He nodded. 'You're right. I've failed you,' he said, adroitly shifting the conversation. Suddenly he was a martyr, lifting his chin, revealing his neck so she could deliver a killing slash if she chose. 'How can I make this right between us?'

'I'm angry, can you tell? So please just allow me some time to calm down. Will Axford is coming to the house.'

'Surely he can wait to see you?'

'It's not a social call, Uncle Reggie.'

She left it at that and so did he, no doubt spending the rest of the journey pondering what she might mean. Clementine was prepared for him to stew on it while she arranged her own thoughts before a new onslaught of allegations.

Will arrived when they'd been home for just over an hour, giving Clementine time to cool her face with a damp flannel and to change out of her suit of scarlet velvet. Her pale pink silk and organza dress suited the late afternoon, which already felt like evening; the light was fading by four-thirty now.

'You look very pretty.' One of her favourite maids had travelled down from Northumberland, as Clem had known this would be a longer stay than usual. 'Would you like me to re-dress your hair?'

'I suppose so.' She sighed. 'A loose chignon, please, Edith. I get a headache with that tighter bun.'

'I'm guessing Mr Axford likes your hair looser.'

She snapped her maid a look of warning. 'I'm not dressing for him.'

Edith stared back at her in the mirror, barely flinching. 'Even so, you mentioned he is coming over tonight, and looking pretty takes little more effort. Have you two had words?'

'More than that. I don't believe we're as compatible as I'd thought.'

The maid knew when to hold her tongue.

Clementine joined her uncle in the main salon, where a fire had been warming the room for hours. Reggie had clearly spent the past hour in here, pondering his future. There was no cigar burning, and the glass he was sipping from was modestly filled.

'You look lovely,' he said, standing to welcome her.

'Thank you.' She allowed him to kiss her cheek but kept it polite and disant.

'Sherry?'

'No, thank you.'

He watched her. 'I've never felt so awkward with you in all our years.'

They heard a distant rapping at the door.

'I've never had cause to doubt you in that time.'

'Clem, what is going on?'

She was saved from having to reply by the sound of the housekeeper and a light tap as she entered their room. 'Excuse me, sir, Miss Grant. Mr Axford has arrived.'

Clem stood. 'Thank you, Mrs Johnson. Show him in, please, and then no further interruptions.'

The woman withdrew.

'That sounds ominous,' Reggie said. 'I'm not at all used to you being cold and secretive.'

'Neither am I, Uncle Reg.' She turned to await Will, who stepped into the room a few heartbeats later. She knew how many because her heart was suddenly pounding so hard that she could count its rhythm. 'Good evening, Will.'

'Clementine, Reggie.' He gave a nod to each.

'Drink to warm you up, Will? Clementine won't share a sherry with me,' Reggie said.

'I won't either, Reggie. Forgive me, I need a clear head.'

'Right, well, this is all very melodramatic and clandestine, so why don't we get it over with, whatever this great secret is?' Reggie drained his small glass. His tone had an edge to it now.

'Uncle Reg, Will does have something to share with us. I am not yet privy to it, but what he has alluded to sounded so damaging that I couldn't risk it being brought out into the open in public. I am beyond grateful to Will for keeping what he has to say private so that we can deal with it between us.'

'Good heavens. Now even I'm intrigued. Go on then, Will. What is this life-changing revelation?'

Clem wished he didn't sound so cocky.

'The floor is yours, Will.'

Will moved closer to Clem but she immediately shifted to an armchair, not wishing to be part of the allegation. She looked up at Will expectantly, knowing he would have felt the snub. She didn't care right now for anyone's feelings. Her life was being unravelled and in the next few minutes she had to focus on protecting herself.

It was as though the wind had changed: the ripples of the past had reversed their direction to flow back in time. She wished suddenly she could leave the past as it was, allow history to keep its secrets, but Africa clearly wanted her back.

'Reggie,' Will began. 'I won't dance around this.'

Reggie shrugged to show he didn't care either way.

'I have a deep concern that you played a part in the death of James Knight.'

Clem closed her eyes for a second, to blot out this scene momentarily; her dread was complete. Will would not make such a statement without proof. When she opened her eyes, she saw that her uncle had snapped forward in his chair.

'How dare you! What kind of accusation is that?'

Will's calm expression was unchanged. 'One that will finally reveal the extent of your lies to the person who deserves the truth.'

'Get out!' Reggie yelled, leaping to his feet and pointing at the door. 'Don't you ever think to cross this threshold again. And as for courting my —'

'Answer him, Uncle Reg.' Clem didn't raise her voice but her words penetrated his bluster, and for just a few of her heavy heartbeats it felt like time wanted to stop. Both men stared at her and she met their gazes, unblinking. No amount of pretty hair or pale pink organza and silk could take away the ugliness of what was occurring now.

'Clem, do you really expect me to give this accusation any credence? I'll toss this whippersnapper out on his ear.'

'You can try,' said Will threateningly.

'Be quiet, both of you. Uncle Reg, I do expect you to take the allegation seriously. Will clearly does, which suggests he has evidence to support it.'

She watched his face blanch. 'Evidence?' he hissed.

'Humour me. Walk us through your memory of my father's accident.'

With fury, Reggie flicked his dinner coat, hitched his trousers and returned to his seat. He took the time to pour himself another glass of sherry. Will stood motionless near the fire; she was aware his gaze fell only on her and she studiously ignored it.

Finally, Reggie cleared his throat. 'I'm doing this for you, Clem, not because I feel the need to clear my name with Axford here.'

She lifted her eyes to her uncle and waited.

He recounted that terrible night for them.

'And then he shoved me, Clem. It was the violent act of a man out of control, out of his mind with liquor and his sorrows but —' Reggie shook a fist as though trying to touch that moment again — 'there was something else that I couldn't guess. I think it was glee. He was excited, and it was that excitement that was fuelling his drunkenness. He wouldn't listen when I said I'd come in peace to bring you both back to England and to help you start a new life. As I say, the combination of fury, alcohol and fear turned to violence that moved beyond his control.'

'So he shoved *you*,' she said, dismissing his interpretation of her father's mental state. Uncle Reggie couldn't possibly know what her father had felt. No one could. Her father had been an enigma at best – she understood that now. 'Then what?'

'Well, I shoved him back. I had to defend myself – he was threatening to kill me.'

'Kill you? My father? I find that hard to believe.'

'You weren't there, darling. There was rage and violence – the man was losing his wits.'

She sensed Will was about to drop his bombshell but she stopped him with a glance and a brief raising of her hand. 'All right, you shoved him in return – and what happened after that?'

Reggie flung his hands wide with despair. 'Well, as I recall, he weaved around and threatened me again and seemed to find new depths of rage. He was already close to the edge of that monstrous hole.'

'Did you suggest he take care?'

'Of course I did! What do you think I am? But your father had lost his mind.'

This did not gel with the person she recalled spending the day with. He had been filled with excitement, yes – excitement about their future; it had been a happy day. He'd got drunk that night out of joy, not to dampen his sorrows. 'And so are we to gather he slipped?' she continued.

'Well, the ground actually gave way at the edge and he toppled into the Big Hole. He fell to his death.'

'And that's all you know?'

'There is nothing else *to* know. He died then and there from the fall. I went straight back to the Kimberley Club and reported it – the rest is in the police records, I'm sure.'

'All right. Good. Now it's Will's turn to speak.'

Will doggedly pressed on. 'I'm going to read to you from a letter that was transcribed via telephone a few days ago. I was the scribe and what I wrote down has been verified by my father, who listened to the call as well. I will show you his signature in a moment. At the other end, the telephone conversation was witnessed by the registrar of the hospital at Kimberley, a man highly respected by all in the community.'

The atmosphere in the room was so brittle that it felt crisp – to Clem it seemed it could break with the slightest pressure, like a strand of spun sugar. In a tense silence they watched Will withdraw a sheet of paper from his inside jacket pocket and unfold it.

He took a slow breath and began.

'Greetings, Miss Clementine. I am sure you have thought me dead after all of these years. I have not wished to interrupt the good life you have made far away from Africa.'

Will glanced at her and she was frowning, waiting for a clue of who was behind this letter. 'But I re-enter it now because I am being pursued for the truth of the night your father and my best friend died.'

Her throat tightened. 'Joseph,' she whispered, her voice dry and tiny. 'He's alive?' It was half question, half accusation, but it was all relief. It was like balm to scorched skin, water to the parched, nourishment to the starved, a reprieve to the doomed. It was deliverance from private despair in just these opening lines. She covered her mouth with her fingertips to let no further shocked sounds escape.

Will continued. 'I witnessed what happened between Mr Grant and Mr James. I had put you to bed and went looking for your father. I found him walking, arguing with his brother-in-law, whom I recognised from earlier that day. Mr Grant was following Mr James. Your father tried to hurry but he had been drinking and was staggering. He led Mr Grant to the deepest side of the Big Hole, away from the town's light. You used to laugh that I could not be seen there because I disappeared into the darkness of the night.'

Clem had no control over the streaming tears now, but she pressed her hand tighter against her mouth so as not to let herself down by sounding like a hysterical woman. The sobs of relief she trapped in her chest. She would not let them hear her anguish that Joseph was talking to her, which meant he was alive and she was no longer hunting a ghost. The rage that she had been lied to diminished for now. Her mind was bubbling with the impossible joy that Joseph One-Shoe was not dust like her parents.

'Your uncle wanted you both to journey back to England with him. He offered to help. Mr James refused and told him that he had his own means now. Your father became aggressive and poked, then pushed Mr Grant, who finally shoved him, and your father fell backwards into the pit.'

'There you are!' Reggie hurled himself from his seat, emanating waves of affront. 'How is this any different to what I have said?'

'Wait,' Will said softly. He continued. 'Mr Grant knelt at the edge and lit a match to see into the pit. He stared into it before looking around. It seemed that he was trying to make a decision.'

Reggie began spluttering threats. 'That's pure fancy —'

'Be quiet, Uncle. Hear it out!' There was thunder in his expression and he levelled at her now. She no longer cared. 'Finish it, Will!' she ordered.

'After Mr Grant had left, which he did at great speed, hurrying down towards the town, I immediately climbed into the pit because I could hear Mr James calling to his brother-in-law. I have no doubt that your uncle could too.

'I lifted Mr James onto my shoulders and carried him up from the mine to the surface, which took a while because I had to find a ladder. It was too late to call for help. He died in my arms. His last words were about you: how much he adored you, that you were so much like your mother he found it hard to look upon you sometimes, and yet you were his only reason for living, and that you deserved more than he had given you. It was because of his dying words, Miss Clementine, that I didn't say anything about your uncle to the police. I want you to know my silence was not because Mr Grant threatened me later in the police house, but only because I wanted your father's hopes to be carried out, and for you to enjoy a better life than this one.

'I suspect this confession will bring you some pain, Miss Clementine, but in time I hope it brings clarity to a situation you could never know the truth about. Clarity means much to me because it also speaks of the diamonds your father and I dug for together, and the stars we used to talk about when you were a little girl. I have not forgotten my oath to you. Like the Dog Star and its companion, I have thought about you every day, Miss Clementine, and followed you in a way you could never know. I hope you have found happiness as you deserve in your life in England.' Will looked up. 'I understand he uses his proper name now, Zenzele, but the older locals still know him as Joseph One-Shoe and that's how he has signed off this letter.'

Her trembling quietened and she dabbed at her eyes with a small linen handkerchief. 'You found him.' She sniffed, amazed that she could rein in all her emotions.

'Through contacts at the Kimberley Club. Yes. He is well liked.'

'Still in Kimberley?' Her calm voice belied her despair that she had been duped for so long.

'He was. He set up a school for the African children of the miners.'

She visibly swallowed, filled with fresh emotion. Trust Joseph to be doing something so generous.

'Clementine, that could be anyone making up those lies,' Reggie pleaded.

'It's no lie.' She sniffed again . . . but these tears were the last, she decided.

'How can you possibly trust it? Will Axford wouldn't know to whom he was talking on the telephone.'

'Yes, but I do, Uncle Reggie. You see, no one but Joseph One-Shoe and I know about the Dog Star oath, or that I laughed about him disappearing when he used to sit at the Big Hole with his blanket. Only he could say those things, and that is presumably why he mentioned them, to ensure that I understood these were his words and they could be trusted.'

Uncle Reggie looked back at her aghast, and for the first time that she could remember he had nothing to say for himself: no quick rejoinder, no immediate and plausible excuse. And so she filled the silence as the atmosphere finally broke.

'Uncle Reggie,' she said, standing to smooth the crinkled silk of her dress. 'This is hard but I ask no forgiveness, as I would think less of myself if I didn't say this. You will leave this house tonight – my house; I'm sure you can find a room at your club. Please leave your key behind because you will have no further use for it. You are no longer welcome here or at Woodingdene, although I will grant you a fortnight to travel north and pack up anything and everything that is yours. Take nothing, though, that was in the house before you arrived. We have an inventory, as you are aware, so it is all easily checked but hopefully it will not come to that.'

'Clem . . .?'

'I shall make contact with Sir Jeremy and I shall pay whatever debt is outstanding to the bank from my personal funds. Are there other debts?'

He nodded miserably.

'How much is involved?'

'Perhaps a thousand pounds.'

She blinked with irritation. 'Leave details of that on my bureau, and rest assured I shall also make good on that debt immediately. I will send a reliable messenger with the cash. I need only a name and an address.'

'What do you want me to do?'

'I want you to leave, Uncle Reggie. Isn't that clear? Leave me, leave London, leave Northumberland . . . leave England, for all I care.'

'And go where?' He looked frightened.

She shook her head sadly. 'Go to Paris. Or Switzerland. You can reconnect with your mother. You've spoken about it often enough.'

'Darling, I have a terminal illness. Dr Brayson can confirm this.'

Clem's shock spiralled. She could feel trills of panic rising but still she knew she must harden her heart further. 'I feel desperately saddened to learn this now but it changes nothing.'

He looked at her as though she had just arrived from the moon. 'Clem, I'm telling you that I'm dying.'

'So was my father when you left him. I forgive you everything – the theft of the diamonds, the lies about them, even trying to sell them as your own – but not this. You left him to die in the dirt. You lied about Joseph, letting me believe him dead all these years.'

'It would have changed nothing had I raised the alarm about your father.'

'Uncle Reggie, you turned your back on his calls for help. And that's what I am doing to you. Plus, you threatened Joseph One-Shoe. I can only imagine how cruel you were to him. As we have heard, your threats had no effect. His decision was as pure as yours was clouded.'

'Clem, I don't know what to do. I'm lost.'

'That is not my problem. I am giving you a chance to make a new life for yourself instead of going to prison – I'm sure none of your sins could be categorically proven by a good lawyer anyway, so go free, Uncle Reggie. Walk away from your mess and live without fear of creditors in what time you have left.'

'You're really throwing me out of your life?'

'I am. I've always owned it all, Uncle Reg, I've just never exercised my right to that claim until now. You have no further part to play in the Grant family businesses. You are now simply returned to the status of the bastard son of my grandfather . . . and may I say, you've lived up to everything you've told me he ever thought of you.'

Clem didn't believe she had ever said anything so hurtful, or ever would again. She wanted to rush upstairs and bathe, wash her mouth, her hair, scrub herself clean of this day and its ugliness.

'You will regret this,' Reggie said, pointing at Will. He stormed towards the door, turning to glare at Clem. 'And so will you, my darling girl.'

'Uncle Reg?'

'What?'

'You still have my diamonds, I believe.'

———

Will waited with her until they heard the front door slam. She winced at the sound, which heralded the moment her life had changed once again. There was more unpleasantness ahead.

He still looked at her astonished, though none the wiser. 'Are you all right? Can I fetch you some brandy?'

She stared at the handkerchief, still folded around the diamonds. 'No, but thank you.'

'Are you all right, Clem?'

'I am. Strangely, I feel clear-headed.'

Will took his chance and knelt before her. They both knew it was inappropriate for him to remain here with her unchaperoned, but these were not ordinary circumstances. 'What can I do for you?'

She searched his lovely face and dropped her own bombshell. 'You can leave too.'

He frowned as if he hadn't heard her correctly. 'What do you mean?'

'I mean follow Uncle Reggie out of the door – and my life.'

Will blinked, shocked. 'I don't understand.'

'Well, let me be transparent, then, as tonight is all about clarity. I am grateful to you, Will, truly I am, and I admire your pursuit of the truth. In this you are honourable. However, it has made you the architect of the pain I feel this day. If you had only left well alone – as I pleaded – my life could have followed its trajectory. I was so happy. I was not suspicious of my uncle. I had plenty to look forward to and I'd just met this wonderful man, with a romantic soul and I knew he could make me content. I wanted to marry him, raise a family with him, grow old beside him looking at the stars. But he ruined all of that because his personal crusade was more important than the love that had sprung up between us.'

'Clem . . . please . . . I —'

'I know, I know, Will. This was done for my benefit, this was done to protect me . . . you sound like Uncle Reggie. You both only ever had *my* best interests in mind but all you've done is bring me pain. Uncle Reggie's a good man too, Will. He's just not as pure of heart as you are. The fact is, thanks to the two of you and your actions, all I have left is an incredibly valuable diamond and no family. That's precisely how it was when I was a child, and so the years since then have been for nothing.' She gestured around the room. 'Here I sit, as empty and dashed as I was when I was seven, except this time, Will, I'm an adult, and I am not rudderless or without means. I can make decisions and act on them as I choose. No one controls me or ever will again.'

'What are you going to do?'

'I'm going to find Joseph One-Shoe again and hug the only man I completely and utterly trust.'

Will looked entirely beaten. 'I cannot bear it that you feel nothing for me now.'

'I didn't say that.'

'But there's no hope for us?'

She shrugged. 'I don't know. They say time heals, and maybe in a year we may meet and discover that we still have much in common, including our mutual fondness.'

'I will never love anyone as I love you.'

'Oh, you might, Will. And you are free to do so, as I plan to focus on nothing but my own contentment. Right now that does not include you.' She sounded hard but she needed to be strong if she was going to leave behind the two men she loved, this time in England. Unlike the two men in Africa, who'd had no agenda but love, Reggie and Will had hurt her, and they needed some time in a different sort of desert. They both needed to understand that there was a price to pay for inflicting this pain on her.

'I shall wait for you . . . and hope you'll forgive me.'

She leaned in and kissed him gently. 'Know that I do admire your strength and the courage it took for you to follow your own path. I just cannot find the peace I need in the situation your convictions have wrought.'

He still looked stunned but a stoicism was pushing upwards within him, just as a diamond funnel had to push to the earth's surface. She could see it battling to the fore and knew he would be all right.

'Goodbye, Will.'

Part Three

33

February 1895

The attendant balanced a large tray expertly on one hand as he paused to tap the glass of the barometer. His eyebrows lifted and he nodded, glancing out the window of the first-class train carriage before continuing a dozen more steps to Miss Grant's stateroom.

He knocked at the door and waited, carefully adjusting the tea cosy so that it fully covered the pot beneath. Miss Grant liked her tea hot enough to scald and he liked to please his special guests.

'Come in,' she said from within. 'Good morning, John.' She beamed as he eased his way through the narrow opening.

'I'm not sure that it will be for you, Miss Grant. Looks as though we are aiming for nearly 90 degrees Fahrenheit.'

'Phew,' she said, fanning herself with a grin. 'Africa is punishing.'

She didn't look in the slightest bit uncomfortable to him. In fact, she appeared positively cool in her pale linen. She was a beauty, almost ethereal. Hair not Titian, like the paintings he'd seen in a book left behind by a traveller, but unmistakably coppery when the light hit it just right, as it was doing now. He had surely lost his silly heart to her during this trip – it was a wonderful warm and pleasant feeling, but she was so far above his social status that there was no point entertaining such boyish thoughts. Besides, he wanted to keep his job, but dreaming never hurt, did it?

He noticed no ring on Miss Grant's left hand and wondered why someone so lovely and effervescent was not being followed around by a pack of suitors. She made him smile every day, and had responded to railway staff with only good manners, making her the most popular traveller on this journey. He was glad she was his responsibility; he was the envy of the other private attendants.

'May I set out your morning tea here, Miss Grant?' He looked towards the small table in her compartment.

'Please do. I'm parched and you make it just how I like it. I shall miss you.'

'We aim to please, Miss Grant.'

She inhaled. 'Smells like rain in the air.'

He stood and frowned gently at her accurate prediction. 'Have you been to Africa before, Miss?'

'I lived here as a child.'

That took him unawares. 'Do you mean here, as in . . .?'

She grinned. 'As in Kimberley – yes, indeed, when it was called New Rush. I used to run around the Big Hole.'

'Good grief, Miss Grant. Then you will know what our thunderstorms can be like.'

'I love them! The Zulus believe that the Lightning Bird descends from the thundering skies and will be found wherever the lightning strikes. Some even say it will lay an egg at the exact point of the strike. To some it equates to evil, but I think of it as the bird's beautiful plumage that lights up the sky.'

He stared at her as if seeing her for the first time. 'I've never heard that before and I came to Africa nearly twenty years ago.'

She laughed. 'I was taught by a Zulu.'

He made a sound of incredulity. 'I like being surprised by passengers, Miss Grant. Let's have your tea before it cools. Would you like me to pour?'

'I'll let it steep a little longer, thank you, John. I can do it. How long do we have?'

He pulled out his fob watch. 'In just under one hour, Miss Grant, we shall arrive at the Kimberley railway station.'

'Kimberley was a camp site in the wilderness when my family first came; it was not much more than a shantytown when I left, although it was obvious even back in the 1870s that it was growing fast. I am pinching myself that a train is bringing me into an actual town.'

He smiled. 'A sprawling one, Miss Grant, with all modern conveniences.'

'I am looking forward to the surprise.' She smiled, and he took her nod as his cue to leave.

'I'll knock when we're five minutes out.'

Clem knew the train's passengers had likely been discussing her lack of husband or family chaperone. There had been some raised eyebrows on the first night – from the women, especially – as it became clear that she was travelling alone. She wanted to shake these short-sighted people by the shoulders and impress upon them that unless people like her were brave enough to flout archaic rules, women would never have escaped the chastity belts of medieval days, let alone the bustles and tight corsets of yesteryear.

Oh heavens, but she relished wearing no corset – it felt so good to climb into light cottons and linens with only a few petticoats. Clem felt helplessly smug at escaping England in its coldest of months. February could be brutal up north, but even London had been frozen to stillness on the day of her departure. There had been no one to wave her off at the dock, nor had she cared; it was surely easier to leave England's shores knowing no one would miss her, or so she'd told herself.

Will had tried contacting her several times but she had not accepted his telephone calls. His letters had been read but remained unanswered; she'd ignored them at first, deciding initially that she did not need his apologies or promises of love gnawing away at her resolve. But she'd capitulated and secretly enjoyed his letters, which she had been relieved to find were not full of ardent declarations. Instead they were affectionately chatty. It had taken all her courage to banish him, because she loved him. There was no easy way to shake that bond; only time and distance could make it recede.

Uncle Reggie, by contrast, had to all intents disappeared. She had not heard a word from him, and there had been no sightings of him in London. She had to presume he'd taken her advice and cleared off to the Continent. He had nothing to fear, though, for all of his debts had been taken care of; she had also made sure that some money was put into a private account for him so he would not want for anything.

'Is that wise, Miss Grant?'

'I think so, Sir Jeremy,' she'd said to the banker, retrieving her gloves and slowly putting them back on now that the distasteful business of settling Reggie's debts from her private fortune had been concluded.

'You really want to give him more?'

'He's family. And I love him, Sir Jeremy. I just don't want him in my life or meddling with the family's business affairs. With this money to draw upon, he can travel safely and with the security of knowing he's not a pauper.'

'Well, Miss Grant, if you want my advice —'

'I shall certainly ask for it when I do, Sir Jeremy,' she said, smoothing the last finger into her glove. 'You've been very kind, thank you.'

The look on his face was priceless. It gave her fresh confidence that in this world run by men, with all its unwritten rules that women had to follow, she was going to make a contribution to change. Not permitting Sir Jeremy to patronise her, and in making sure he understood that the bank provided a service to her and not the other way around was just another in a line of footsteps that walked her away from the domination of men. Word would soon get around the old boys' network that Clementine Grant was a woman who would not be manipulated.

Clem thought about the two young girls arriving into her care later this year. She would teach them about not fearing an independent life and to chase their dreams. She'd already made provision for Sarah, using her influence and personal funds to ensure that the Nightingale School at St Thomas's Hospital already had her enrolled. The name Dolly appeared nowhere on the paperwork and she knew Sarah would go on to fulfil the faith Clementine had in her.

Clem poured her tea, admiring the gilded china. Sunlight glinted on the rich design encircling the plate, cup and saucer, and covering the spout of the teapot. She wondered if the 22-carat gold had been mined in southern Africa. Probably. There was a new gold rush underway after two prospectors had discovered nuggets in Witwatersrand about seven years earlier. She'd read that the Cape Colony was probably going to shift its principal focus from farming to mining its mineral wealth, and it had the potential to become the world capital of gold production. She shook her head, imagining all the women being dragged to different parts of Africa as their men joined the gold rush, just as her father had leapt into the diamond rush. It had killed her mother, and more women would die for the greed of gold.

She sighed and let her mind drift. Nothing had changed in the Karoo Desert, it seemed. The wilderness was timeless. Extending to the horizon was the endless plain she remembered from her childhood, when she'd put her hand up to shade the glare of the huge and powerful sun hanging in a sprawling sky. She'd squinted, trying to pick out something, anything, in the distance. Nothing. Of course, as an adult she could now appreciate the beauty of the arid landscape, which covered almost half of the colony's surface and she'd read it yielded a wealth of unique flora and herbs, so much so that naturalists jested the meat from the animals of the Karoo was "spiced on the hoof".

Over the course of its journey the train had snaked its way through gorges that cut across a vast ancient seabed, colonnaded with towering, flat-topped hills that to her appeared blue from a distance. Heat haze made them wobble, and by night Clem had loved looking again at a sky bursting with glittering stars that lit the darkness where nocturnal animals tiptoed and highlighted the scarred tracks trodden by millions of springbok on their migration.

Time had no effect here, Clem decided. She could string together ten lifetimes and all that would have happened in the Karoo would be that the dust blew here or there. Perhaps only another Ice Age could affect it, she thought, not at all intimidated by the lonely vastness of the scenery that unnerved so many.

No, she and her adventurous parents had made a bone-shaking journey on an ox wagon all those years ago. It made her think of Joseph travelling on foot, leaving behind his tribe, everything that was familiar, everyone he loved, for the good of his people. She blinked as she thought about Joseph making the trek to the original alluvial deposits at Barkly West on foot, with no boot at all. He was the true adventurer.

Clem raised her eyes to the sky. The blue of it was so deep it felt heavy, like a solid bolt of cloth drawn tight across the dome of the earth. She hadn't remembered the African sky being so single-minded but she could smell the promise of rain and imagined that somewhere, clouds were gathering.

It had rained on the day they had arrived at the community near the river. Tent flaps, bothered by the winds, had snapped and complained while women's hair was wrenched free from pins and bonnets. Maybe heaven's tears would fall today, like a nod in the mirror to yesteryear, as she returned to Africa?

There was a gentle knock at her door and she roused herself from her musings, pulling on her jacket and checking nothing had been left out of her carpet bag. John would organise the unloading of her trunk. From the moment he knocked, the landscape began to change: from rusted brown to a first hint of green that suggested life and community, before buildings began to ease into sight. The engine driver pulled hard on the whistle, its joyful screech heralding the arrival of another trainload of passengers out of the desert and into the township of Kimberley.

The door opened and John looked in. 'All ready, Miss Grant?'

'Excited,' she answered. 'What a wonderful journey, John – thank you.'

'All part of realising Mr Rhodes's dream to have a red line on the map from the Cape to Cairo, Miss Grant.' He politely touched his cap with his finger.

'Let's hope Cecil Rhodes doesn't stop dreaming, John.'

'Indeed – I should quite like to see Cairo by train, Miss Grant.' He winked. 'Let me help you off and organise for your trunk to be delivered. It's the Queen's Hotel, am I right?'

'Correct,' she replied, following him into the corridor, where other excited travellers were gathering.

She moved to the front of the throng being disgorged onto the platform. Amid the billowing steam and the slow hiss of the train calming down after its lengthy journey, she gave a final smile to her attendant, knowing he'd be delighted by the contents of the envelope she'd left for him. 'Thank you for all your care.'

She was quick to put distance between them, suddenly eager to escape the confines of the railway station and reach the soil of Kimberley again. Nevertheless, Clem knew she should pause for a moment and appreciate this enormous building and the huge platform she stood on.

The station was built from stone the colour of the earth that had once clung to the diamonds they mined. It was extraordinary that railway lines had reached all the way here from Cape Town over the mountain ranges. The Big Hole was now formally known as the Kimberley Mine and was owned almost entirely by one corporation, the De Beers Consolidated Mines Limited.

If Rhodes, its founder, had known about Sirius, she couldn't imagine what he'd have done to acquire it.

She passed by the whitewashed arched windows to walk through the tall curved doors. It was hard to place exactly where she stood. It struck her as more of a small bustling city, with sprawling streets that wandered off into residential suburbs. Massive migration had clearly taken place as mining operations searched for those funnels of glittering wealth.

And that wealth showed. The carriage ride to her hotel passed public gardens, their verdant lawns and bright floral displays surprising for a town located in a vast desert. She asked the driver to take her on a tour of the town. There was a bowls green with manicured grass like velvet and people strolling about a proud clubhouse dressed in whites. The carriage drove past football fields and cricket pitches and even a gymnasium. The wind-ravaged wilderness that was once roughly designated as the Kimberley Turf Club had now been properly enclosed as a racecourse, complete with grandstand. Clementine wished her father could see it.

They finally drew up alongside a double-storey brick building, with the verandahs familiar to her from childhood curving around both levels.

'Welcome to the Queen's Hotel.' The desk clerk beamed at her. 'We're very busy this week, Miss Grant, but our owner insisted that we offer you our best room.'

'I don't believe I know your owner,' she admitted, signing the guest book.

'Er . . .' He frowned, checking a large book. 'Ah, yes, we received a telegram from a Mr William Axford. I gather he knows the owner, and no doubt a request was made.'

Will diligently wrote to her once a fortnight and had obviously become used to her silence, it seemed, for he addressed her as if they were having an ongoing conversation. But he'd obviously found out through other means of the timing of her journey to Kimberley. Milton probably. She had kept him on and he'd turned out to be extremely loyal and no doubt had her interests at heart in sharing this information with Will. She couldn't help but smile.

He had been looking into her plans to offer insurance to the diamond trade and they were now well advanced, awaiting her decision. He would not make a move without her – perhaps for fear of being accused of stealing the idea. *Dear Will, you really are the honourable sort*, she thought. Her fury had certainly cooled over her lonely Christmas in the north and had continued to settle over the winter until she had set sail for the Cape at the end of January. Had she been too hasty? The clerk interrupted the thought.

'And there's a letter for you, Miss Grant.'

She frowned, took it from him and immediately recognised Uncle Reggie's hand.

34

As Clem impatiently awaited the arrival of her trunk, she sat down at the small desk near the window in her room. Reaching for the ivory letter opener, she noted that the stamps were from Italy. Curiously, she realised she was pleased to finally hear from him, as there had always been a small nag of doubt that Reggie might have decided to hurry along his own death. That was another sorrow that she lay at Will's door: she wouldn't be able to spend the time Reggie had left by his side. They'd always talked of taking a grand tour together and it was something he'd become more insistent upon last year.

She slit the top of the envelope and unfolded the sheets of paper with a sense of anticipation. Clementine felt a tug in her chest to hear his familiar voice in her mind as she read.

> *My darling Clem,*
>
> *I write this to you from Elba, feeling every inch like Napoleon in exile. I am certain that I walk around this Tuscan island with a similar feeling of disgust, except in my case it is self-loathing as I have brought this all down on myself. I could mount several persuasive arguments, of course, but when I boil it*

all down to its purest form, I realise that would not assuage the anguish I have caused you.

I am not trying to be conciliatory. Please understand this. I have well and truly relinquished hope that I might mend the past in order to have a future with you. It is possible you have even done me a favour by forcing me to see myself as I truly am for the first time in my life. I am not ashamed, though, Clem, because in that reflection I do not see a bad man but simply a lonely one who wanted to earn the respect of the family that had ostracised him. I did not choose to be my father's son, and I tried daily to live up to his ideals. Your grandmother despised me for the sole reason that I was his child and not hers. I understood. I really rather admired her by the end, and we had found common ground in our shared love of your mother and thus our absolute love and commitment to you, growing up too far away from us.

Your beautiful mother was the one Grant who loved me wholly and I found in you the mirror image of her, but you are more impressive than Louisa, Clem. You are strong in ways that she was weak. I think you are the best incarnation of this family's traits, and it is obvious that your father's effervescence and loyalty run through your veins too. You are the best of all of us, Clem, and so I continue to hate myself for letting you down, while convincing myself that my secrecy was for the right reasons.

If this letter can aspire to one achievement, it is to bring you the peace of knowing that I did not kill your father. I am not a violent man. I learned early on that my brain is much smarter than my fists and I would rather argue my way out of a confrontation than fight my way through it. I don't believe for a moment that your father was a violent man either. On that night, however, he was fuelled by liquor that combined all his sorrow and defeat together with his joy at the diamond strike

389

into a mix of something most of us may never understand. It became fury and I – the Grant in front of him – represented everything in the world at which he was furious.

As you lay your lovely head on your pillow each night, my darling, be assured that your father died of the injuries from his fall. I did not help him in that moment because I truly knew he couldn't be helped and, yes, if I bare my soul to you, it is fair to admit that in those few pounding heartbeats of shock after he fell, I realised your life would be better without him. Forgive me. I had given a sworn promise to your grandmother that I would bring you home to her, at any cost, so she could give you the life your mother would have wanted for you. It was obvious on that terrible night that your father was never going to give such a life, would never let us see you or honour your mother's hopes for you. Your grandmother did not want to die without embracing you once again. I should have gone for help – yes – but I was convinced he would have been dead by the time I returned. Nevertheless, I feel only regret that I didn't act more honourably.

If you're wondering, I learned through Will Axford that you have travelled to Africa and I was not surprised to hear it.

I have decided that tomorrow I shall leave my self-exile in Elba. I don't know how long I have but I don't want this to be my final resting place. I would like to visit all those cities we used to dream about travelling to together. I want to honour that and at least leave my footprints in those places, and I shall imagine you on my arm making me feel proud and lucky as you have always done.

I am not afraid of dying, Clem. When the end comes, I think I might even be glad because there isn't much left to live for, but it will be your face in my mind and your name whispered on my final breath.

Stay safe, darling girl. And only marry when you find someone utterly worthy of you.
Yours always, Uncle Reg

She struggled to read his final paragraph because her trembling hands were making the thin paper shudder. The tremor continued until her body was shaking with fresh despair.

A demon in her mind argued that Uncle Reggie was still trying to manipulate her from afar, but instinct told her otherwise. No, Uncle Reggie's style was to pretend all was well. If he was trying to achieve anything other than to send her his love and let her know he was at peace, he would have boasted of all the wonderful sights he'd seen, his plans for where he might go next, his ideas for the Grant business. He would be aiming, through positivity and affection, to set her grudge aside – to impress her, distract her and draw her back into his arms. No, this was a different Uncle Reg: not so much contrite as resigned and accepting of her decision. He was saying the goodbye he hadn't yet had the chance to give her, in case there would be no other opportunity.

She might hate what he'd done but it could never take away the fact that she had loved him for most of her life. Here was yet another beloved lost to her.

Was she a curse on all who loved her?

Because of her decision, Uncle Reg would travel and die quietly in a place where no one would know him. No one would feel anything about his passing or would bear witness wherever they buried him. She might never hear of his death. The trembling intensified. Could she allow this to happen?

The telephone in her room jangled, making her jump, as the question loomed in her mind. She brushed away tears and took a deep breath to find her composure and steady her voice.

'Hello, Clementine Grant.'

'Ah, Miss Grant, this is Neville Moreton of De Beers here, calling from the Kimberley Club. You wrote to me?'

'Yes! Mr Moreton. Thank you for remembering I was arriving today.'

'Well, I'll get straight to it, Miss Grant, as I'm sure you're eager. The bad news is that Mr One-Shoe is no longer in Kimberley, as I understand it.'

It felt as though her world were collapsing. That she might not find Joseph had always been likely, but she'd clung to one tiny glittering hope that their deep connection would mean she'd surely sense the change in the stars if he returned to his homeland. This was not something she would ever say aloud for fear of sounding like a lunatic; it was not something she could entirely explain to herself. But deep down she'd never accepted that he was dead.

The walls of the hotel room seemed to be closing in. The demon in her mind spoke as shadows darkened around her. *No family, no lover, no marriage prospect, no best friend, no one in your life you can truly trust any more.*

'Miss Grant?' Moreton's voice banished the shadows and the room appeared normal again, its four-poster bed filling most of it, the pillows plump and the thick white linen starched and ironed so not a crease was visible. She could smell the potpourri, scented with cinnamon and anise. All her senses were intact. She must control her fears, she told herself. *Focus!*

'Er, yes, my apologies, Mr Moreton. My thoughts are scattered,' she admitted.

'I do understand, my dear. I know it must be a dreadful disappointment to you after making such a long journey.'

'Mr Moreton, can we meet?'

'Now?'

'Yes. I've been cooped up in a train for days.'

'Well, of course. Er, would you be happy for me to call at your hotel, Miss Grant? We can have a pot of coffee on the verandah.'

'Perfect. What time would be convenient for you?'

She imagined him looking at his fob watch. 'Shall we say eleven-thirty?'

'That sounds ideal.'

'I'm sorry I cannot invite you to the club, Miss Grant. Gentlemen only, I'm afraid.'

The porter conveniently delivered her trunk just as she was hanging up the telephone. The butler who followed shortly after was given instructions for unpacking and handling her possessions. Both men were tipped well.

She lingered at the dressing table to tidy her hair, not that she could ever do much with her wayward twists of coppery blonde that dodged her pins and slipped out of her hands. She had no intention of changing, having taken pains to dress appropriately for Kimberley early that morning. Glad to be in the colonies, she was able to give up her tiny waist and follow the more sensible fashion of the bell-shaped, tea-gown style. She was comfortable in light cotton, which she was sure would be seen at the seaside this coming English summer. It was perfect for the relentlessly hot days she would have to acclimatise to. She used to run around the bare earth – few pavements then – barefoot, like an untamed child. Her father had found it funny. Then she'd gone through a phase of wearing only one shoe, taking great delight in appalling Mrs Carruthers; Clem had insisted that if it was fine for Joseph, why not her? She smiled at her reflection, remembering now that she'd asked her father to refer to her as Clementine One-Shoe.

With her memories circling, Clem couldn't wait another moment within those four walls. She still had forty minutes before she needed to meet Moreton and so she decided to take a tour around the town on foot, if only to get away from the letter staring at her from the desk and the dark hulk of the telephone that had brought only more sad news.

In Kimberley nothing appeared as it had been and yet everything still felt familiar. The landscape looked wildly different with proper buildings but the air tasted as she remembered: hot, dry, crunchy from the dust all around. No more smells of latrines, though, or of dirty men. She had passed people in the hotel who wore perfume and eau de toilette. Clem had seen shanties on the fringe of Kimberley as the train drew in, so it seemed the black population lived rough while a miniature British town was growing up in their midst.

The population had changed drastically, of course, and so had the traffic – the horse and carriage, particularly the Gibson stagecoach, was now the norm rather than the exception. Dozens gathered outside the various hotels; their drivers smoked, chatted, waiting to be summoned. They clustered in their greatest number outside the Grand Hotel. She remembered it as a one-storey building, but it now swept upwards to three. It looked burnished in the sun, its brick still bright and gleaming, a rusty red back drop for the horde of black stagecoaches that were using it as a stagepost.

Clem became lost more than once due to the haphazard way the town had grown. No longer were there shops of the emporium style that aimed to sell everything a person could need. Now they specialised, and she was struck by the novelty of a store offering just ladies' shoes. If only her poor mother could see this, she thought.

The vast Kimberley sky, however, had not changed. It remained azuline lightened only marginally at its edges. The early morning had started out cloudless, with nothing to interrupt her gaze, but now she could see clouds building on the horizon. This was the rainy season; that didn't change either. And Clementine remembered all too well how this big dome of blue above her could, and most likely would, look entirely different within a few hours.

As she walked, she began to feel more conflicted; she wanted this meeting with Mr Moreton and yet she feared what he might have to say. *Don't overthink – act*, she told herself, surprised that it was one of Uncle Reggie's gems of advice that would come to her in this moment.

Briskly, she made her way back to the Queen's Hotel. As she reached the entrance, a rotund gentleman in a pale grey suit, his tortoiseshell spectacles as round as his football-shaped head, alighted from a carriage. There was a De Beers man, for sure.

'Mr Moreton?'

'Miss Grant!' he said delightedly. 'How splendid to meet you.'

They sat in wicker armchairs on the verandah of the hotel, the space cooled by leafy shrubs. Blooms of rhododendrons and azaleas blazed, and Clementine noted the strelitzia poking through like a curious listener; she had called this the lightning bird plant as a child because it resembled a crane with a fiery crown of orange feathers. She used to cut a new one each week and carry it around like a pet, chatting to it.

'Oh, this is always so reliably pleasant,' Moreton said. 'I bring my wife here regularly because of the club's restrictions.'

'You do know women will bang down those club doors sometime, Mr Moreton?'

He chuckled. 'I daresay, Miss Grant, though not any time soon.'

She gave a light shrug as if to say, *Don't be too sure*. An African man dressed in an all-white uniform arrived with a tray to pour them coffee from a tall silver pot. The waiter had several horizontal markings on his forehead; Clementine immediately presumed him to be Ethiopian. She dredged the memory from one of her long night-time conversations with Joseph One-Shoe, when she had asked him to tell her of the tribes and their rituals. Clem recalled being terrified yet fascinated when he'd spoken of the various forms of scarification, both horrified and impressed that the women followed in the practice.

'Thank you, George,' Moreton said. It showed he knew the man, but it was also a polite dismissal.

She'd been in Kimberley only a couple of hours and Clem was already finding the divide cavernous. They had been far more forgiving and community-minded at the Big Hole when black toiled alongside white as fellow workers.

'*Salam*, George,' she said, remembering the Muslim welcome she had learned as a child, before offering her best rendition of a traditional Ethiopian greeting that Joseph had taught her: '*Tena yistilin.*' She nodded, thrilled her memory was still so sharp. She wondered if poor Mr Moreton was more surprised by her use of the language or the fact that she was smiling and bowing her head graciously to the servant. She guessed it was the latter.

And George looked terrified, his gaze widening, flicking to Moreton. She leaned over slightly to attract his attention and slipped back into English. 'You are Ethiopian, are you not, George?'

'Yes, miss.' He wouldn't make eye contact, busying himself rearranging the already perfectly arranged silver milk jug and sugar bowl.

'How do you come to be all this way south, George?'

Moreton clearly didn't entertain the idea of a female guest having a friendly conversation with an African servant. Avoiding outright rudeness, he seemed to have decided it was easier to answer on the African's behalf. 'Er, George came here as an orphaned boy, as I understand it, Miss Grant. He was brought by travelling missionaries and raised not too far from Kimberley.'

'Thank you, Mr Moreton. And George, how long have you worked at the hotel?' She raised her hand as Neville took a breath, her gaze firmly on the African.

'Five summers, miss.' He bowed and stepped back as hastily as he could.

'I'm hoping the coffee is from your home country, George.'

'It is, miss. I hope you enjoy it.'

She smiled. 'I know I will.'

As George withdrew, Clem sipped and tasted the familiar exotic fruitiness that was a unique characteristic of Ethiopian coffee. She recalled Joseph boiling it for her father each morning . . . and often each night, to sober him up.

'Er, we try not to engage with the staff too much, Miss Grant.'

'Don't want to give them lofty ideas, eh, Mr Moreton?'

'No, no, I —'

'I am teasing, please forgive. As you can likely guess, because of my early childhood I am invested in the welfare of African people.' This led her to explain about her orphanage in northern England, about Sarah and about the two younger girls arriving soon that she held a particular interest in.

'My, my, that is wonderfully philanthropic of you.'

She shook her head to say that this was not her motivation. 'Joseph One-Shoe was my best friend, and to my father after my mother's death. He took care of us all, I now realise – and we all left him. I think I've been trying to make up for it ever since. Will you tell me what you know about Joseph, Mr Moreton?'

He sighed. 'I can tell you that Mr One-Shoe is thoroughly liked. I have never heard anyone speak poorly of him. He has done much good work over the years for the children of the African workers. He has excellent language skills – he speaks fluent English, even some Dutch and Xhosa. He has been a valuable go-between, and indeed mediator at times, between the African workforce and the De Beers management.'

'I am not surprised to hear this. Joseph may have been a warrior in the eyes of his people, but he was a deep thinker and a peacemaker from the moment he arrived at the river diggings. He has the sort of personality that makes a great leader.' She frowned. 'Why do you say mediator? Have there been problems?'

The space between them seemed to thicken. 'Er . . . well, I'm not involved in the actual operation of the mines. I'm an administrator, Miss Grant.'

Her forehead knitted more tightly.

'You left in . . .?'

'The early 1870s,' she answered.

'Ah, well, the mining explosion was only just occurring then, really, wasn't it?' The question did not require an answer so she remained silent, forcing him to continue. 'By the 1880s tribes from everywhere south of the Zambezi were sending their men here. It was nothing short of a mass migration for work and wages.'

'And . . .?'

He paused, looking for how to approach his knotty topic. 'You see, there's always the threat of theft, Miss Grant.' His tone was conciliatory – hopeful, even.

'I do see,' she lied, wondering where this conversation was going. 'And how did this affect Joseph One-Shoe?'

'By 1880 he'd got out of diamond digging. He'd set up a little shop that sold all manner of goods to the workers and their families, and then he used his own funds to set up his school to teach their children.' The man was hedging, she decided.

'Please go on, Mr Moreton,' she said.

'Joseph One-Shoe lived in Kimberley but was not contained in the compounds, obviously, yet he had free access to them. De Beers trusted him and so did the workers.'

'Compounds?'

'Er, well, yes. How can I explain this? You have to understand, this region sees something in the order of fifty thousand itinerant workers per year, Miss Grant. To keep track of them and to provide accommodation, the men are housed in barracks.'

'Barracks. Like an army?'

He chuckled nervously and drained his coffee. 'Yes, I suppose.'

'They are free to come and go, of course?'

'Er, not quite. These are closed compounds.'

'Prison?'

'Oh, my dear, no! Nothing like that.'

She sensed otherwise.

'It is convenient for them. Somewhere to rest, to sleep, to call their own, which puts a roof over their heads and a meal in their bellies after each day. I think the word "compound" is sometimes wrongly construed by people not from here.'

'But I am from here and I find it has a dark tone to it.'

'It's part of the *lingua franca* of the diamond diggings. In Malay the word *kampong* means "enclosure", for instance, and "compound" means much the same to us in Kimberley.' Now he was being condescending, wriggling in an effort to leap off the hook she had him on. 'Compounds were perfectly acceptable before De Beers opened its first nearly a decade ago.'

'Why did they need to be *enclosed*? Why couldn't they go home to their families after a shift?'

He shrugged. 'We are talking about native workers here, Miss Grant. They could be unreliable. They drink, they fight, they wander. For the purposes of running a business you need reliability in your workforce, and so for our part 25 acres were enclosed by a wall to look after several thousand men at once.'

She baulked, putting her cup down in consternation.

'That many need a lot of food stores, shops, a dispensary, a church, a hospital. We even have a swimming bath for our workers. They have rooms with electricity and large open areas for recreation. They are paid up to thirty shillings per week,' he said, as if that made it acceptable to shut up men behind fencing. 'I can assure you that's more than the average agricultural worker in England had at the time.' He was becoming more defensive because of her silence. 'And if a man found a large stone, he could earn a bonus as much as twenty pounds! That's akin to three months' work in one day. But . . . of course with men being accommodated in close quarters, well, there are going to be squabbles.'

'And Joseph?'

'Joseph One-Shoe was one of the peacemakers to whom we could turn. However,' Moreton said, sounding like he wanted to move on from the subject, 'Joseph – or Zenzele, as he is now calling himself – told Dr Ashe at Kimberley Hospital that his work here was done.'

'Then I must meet with Dr Ashe, perhaps?'

'He will know more. I gather they are rather good friends.'

———

Dr Ashe's head almost grazed the low doorway of the waiting room. He arrived with a cheerful smile for Clementine, full of apology for having kept her.

'I hear you were in surgery. There's no need to apologise,' she reassured him.

'I'm always on the way to or coming from surgery.' He grinned, taking off his fragile-looking rimless glasses to polish them with a large handkerchief. Despite his thin lips he had the kindest of smiles. 'I am so delighted to meet any friend of Joseph's.'

'Thank you. I know you like him well.'

'More than like him. I respect him enormously. Zenzele was important to this town. I think I would have had to perform more surgeries for the African community if not for his leadership calming many a fight.'

She bit her lip. 'I've learned about the compounds.'

'Don't visit. Don't go near them. You will not like what you see.'

'So they are prisons?'

'Of a fashion. No women or children are permitted. The men are isolated for months and forbidden to visit their families in the townships that have sprung up. Granted, it has prevented desertion and kept the men as physically fit as possible, away from alcohol and temptation. It all depends on your perspective, I suppose, as the mine owners argue most logically in their favour. There is the immediate and unforgiving presumption that every African will steal the diamonds – not *may*, Miss Grant, but will.' He waggled his finger to emphasise his point. 'And so these compounds, no matter how De Beers likes to argue its case, are about preventing illicit traffic in diamonds. The men are strip-searched at the end of each day.'

She blanched. 'Good grief.'

'I refuse to be involved in internal searches.'

'How humiliating. If no trust is given to them, why would those men feel any loyalty?'

'Well —' he gave a sad smile — 'the workers do thieve, that's the point. Not all. But it only takes one or two, and in the case of the diamond mines it's more than that. A man can make a month's wages or more from the single theft of a couple of smallish diamonds secreted about or even inside his person, if he can get away with it. It's very tempting. They have families – they have whole tribes relying on them.'

'For food?'

'No, Miss Grant. For weapons. That's where the money usually goes. The tribal chieftains like the white man's guns.'

'I see. And Joseph helped?'

'He was a voice the workers trusted when scuffles broke out or the men wanted to strike. He often negotiated better conditions for them, advocating directly with De Beers.'

'Are you able to tell me where I might begin to search for Joseph, please?'

He sighed. 'I fear he has left Kimberley. That was his plan and I haven't seen him since our last game of chess. He's quite good.'

She smiled sadly. 'My father taught him how to play, and how to box. He never lost a match, you know.'

'Had his nose broken a few times, I gather.' Dr Ashe grinned. 'He did mention your father, although Joseph is a man of few words and he did not offer up his life story willingly. I only realised how much your family meant to him when he was actually leaving.'

'What do you mean?'

'It was directly after Joseph spoke to Mr Axford about his recollections of the unfortunate incident with your father. After that it seemed our Zulu friend lost all desire to remain in Kimberley. There was an instant change, as though a burden had been lifted.'

'Dr Ashe, I was assured as a child he was dead and knew no different until that letter was read out to me by Mr Axford.'

'A terrible shock, no doubt – not just the content but the voice behind it.'

'Precisely. But it gave me back the single most important person in my life, who was essentially stolen from me.'

'I am sure he knew the effect it would have on you. I could be wrong but perhaps it was the reason he left Kimberley.'

'So that I didn't come looking for him, you mean?'

The surgeon nodded. 'He was a man of language; he could write English competently. He could have contacted you at any time, but he chose not to. Knowing Joseph as I do, I doubt he would have wanted to disrupt your life.'

'Well, he has, as you can see,' she said, but softened her words with a smile.

'I suppose he hoped you'd make inquiries and find him gone and then not make the journey. He is committed to returning to his people.'

'He should have remembered I was a spontaneous child, always impatient!' She grinned. 'He has a school?'

'A shop and a school, until recently. Both successful. He sold the shop within days of speaking to Mr Axford. There were any number of takers but he refused all offers, including a large one from De Beers, and instead sold it to a family whose father he had once dug alongside for diamonds. The sale of the shop was eight weeks or so ago, Miss Grant.'

'How would he have travelled back to his people? Ox wagon, do you think?'

He shook his head. 'No. He told me he had walked to the diggings and, wild carnivores notwithstanding, he would walk back.' It sounded so typical of Joseph. 'We had a meal together and a final game of chess. He hugged me goodbye. And I am not ashamed to admit I felt rather emotional when he left the hospital premises. I knew I would never see him again.'

'How about the school?'

'It now runs itself well, as I understand it. It has an annual fundraising effort and the support of lots of people who benefit from the work of the children's parents. Even De Beers, I might add. It is an excellent establishment – good for the community.'

'Then I suppose that is my next stop. Thank you for seeing me, Dr Ashe.'

Ashe stood, tall and straight.

'You're both about the same height.'

'Yes. We joked that we could share clothes.'

'But not shoes,' she said, smiling.

35

Afternoon had closed in by the time she tiptoed into the single class-room that acted as a school for African children, but it was empty. Tidy but abandoned. The hollow echo of her heels on the floor-boards reflected perfectly how she was feeling. Another blank. Another dead end. Another place where Joseph might be was use-less to her. She looked at the blackboard. A note written in chalk told visitors that today was a field day for the children. It was signed by Miss Londiwe.

Clem walked out onto the small schoolhouse's narrow veran-dah, from where she could see the foundations of what looked to be another classroom. Joseph's school was expanding. He would feel proud of this. The shop might have given him an income, but it would be the school that mattered. Here they were, involved in a similar endeavour to care for and educate black children. How sad that neither had known the other had taken a similar journey. She hated that Joseph had walked away from his school.

The emptiness grew. She hadn't eaten anything today but it wasn't hunger that gnawed at her belly, it was grief. She had lost him and didn't know how to look for him.

Zenzele was barefoot; he was Zulu once again and running back to his roots. So should she.

Just as Clem decided that she would leave for England immediately, a low rumble rolled across the heavens. *Impundulu is waking up*, she thought. The lightning bird would visit soon.

There was one more place she had to see before the sky lit up and opened its clouds. As she walked, her boots crunching on familiar red dust now that she was on the outer reaches of the town, she imagined the hotel clerk's expression when she told him her plans had changed. He would have to ask the butler to repack her trunk and the hotel would need to help her change her return booking on the steam train bound for Cape Town.

Clementine walked purposefully, attempting to overcome her sense of failure. She noticed that although Kimberley had become a thriving town, its sprawl of elegant suburbs comprised of large homes with sweeping, well-kept gardens, its shantytown character had not been completely driven away. Shades of the circus-like clutter of humanity she recalled from childhood were evident on its outer reaches, where the Africans arriving from across the southern part of the continent had settled. Villages had sprouted like weeds. Each family's living quarters were essentially a hut with a wooden frame, walls of sacking and a roof of iron sheets. Some had erected timber fences around their homes to enclose their chickens and keep their children safe. She felt the eyes of the township upon her as she passed.

Uncle Reggie's repeated lie about Joseph being dead felt like a bleeding wound in this moment. All of the lost years when she could have found him. Tears pricked but she walked on towards the outskirts of the shantytown to where the sprawl of humanity had not reached, and it became Africa's glorious desert again.

Clementine Grant stood on the path that traversed the lonely graves. It felt fitting that the cemetery was deserted, for it matched her mood. She walked among the haphazard sites: some mounds, most unmarked, others with beautiful inscribed headstones.

The old baobab stood plump and proud. Each tree was like a person with individual characteristics. She'd been staggered to learn that some were well over a thousand years in age and could triple that. As a youngster she'd called it the bottle tree because its trunk resembled one of her father's countless beer bottles. She recalled how she could reach around the girth of the one her mother was buried beneath, so long as Joseph One-Shoe stretched his long arms around its bark first to hold her hands. Then they could encircle it together and recite the regular prayers she said for her mother.

'It will look after Mummy,' she had observed to her friend.

'These leaves,' he'd said, pointing to the newly sprouted fingers the colour of shamrocks. 'This wise tree knows the rains are coming and its leaves await heaven's tears.'

'So even heaven is crying for my mummy.'

He nodded. 'They weep for you, Miss Clementine, that you are without her.'

She'd learned from Joseph that many of the tribes believed this tree to house evil spirits, but he admitted he'd always liked its curious shape and frantic hair-like branches. When naked it appeared like a strange creature reaching in all directions. Clementine agreed; she liked the tree and its comical shape and believed wholly that it would look after her mother as she slept.

She found the familiar final resting place of her mother, which was also now her father's. That they shared this space in death's embrace felt right, but something about the grave unsettled her. She was feeling so disarranged that Joseph was alive but would never know she'd come back for him, and she couldn't pin down the nagging thought.

She stared at the headstone. Her father's name had been added since she'd last stood here. A space had been left for that purpose, she now understood. Maybe her father had always known that he would remain in Africa. That felt like a fresh betrayal, as she closed her eyes to shut out the headstone. Had he lied to her too?

Was Joseph the only honourable person in her life?

She let her shoulders drop to drive out the tension that was forming in her neck. A fretful breeze began to blow, this way and that, tugging at her bonnet. She pulled it off and let Nature stir her hair the way it used to when she was little.

Clem knew this wind. It was an old visitor that brought with it the ever-welcome smell of rain. It was hard to describe and yet she knew it as it blew around her, carrying tiny, earthy motes of the Karoo on its breath, the smell of Kimberley itself, picked up as it passed over the mines, bringing the taste of the disgorged blue ground. The air felt heavier, damp, coming from many miles away where the rain already touched the land. She closed her eyes and listened to the wind that had chased the birds to safe roosts; they had known for some time that the lightning bird was coming.

Beyond the graves and out across the flat wilderness wildebeest were on the move; their dust was picked up by the breeze as pillars of clouds formed towering mountains over the flat landscape. A fresh faraway rumbling sounded. Normally thunder was like a warning but the storm had brought a new mood to Clementine as it began its early dance.

She felt a longing now. A yearning for her past, a wish to revisit it – a single brief glimpse. Just one chance to hold her mother's hand, to tip her head back and laugh with her father, and perhaps most of all, a chance to hear the gritty, melodic voice of Joseph One-Shoe, to see his smile as bright as the lightning and to hug him again.

'Once more,' she whispered to the wind that flicked her hair across her face and swept her skirts to one side.

The gods rumbled their discontent at her plea. The lightning bird responded to their grumbles with a gleeful crack, its plumage streaking across the distant sky.

I'm coming for you, Clementine, it threatened as the skies behind it lit and faded, lit and faded.

Africa was tuning in to her frustration, reflecting her hunger for deliverance. It wasn't atonement but she now felt only guilt for missing Joseph – only by days, it seemed. If she could just hear his voice or look upon him, she could return to her life in Britain feeling rescued somehow for seeing him alive and strong.

A thunderclap exploded; the storm had stolen closer. The whole sky brightened to a ghostly white and then returned to its brooding puddle colour as the lightning bird arched her back and danced nearer.

Rain fell in the distance, looking like a wall carried on the shoulders of an invisible army marching towards her. It would pelt her soon. It was time to leave. Clementine stepped around the grave and, using the tree for support, its bark smooth beneath her ungloved hands, she kissed the cool, pale marble of her parents' headstone.

'Farewell, my darlings. Hold hands forever.'

The rain arrived to drown her words; large drops, like glass marbles, lightly denting the dust with their long-awaited impact. It was marvellous to feel relief from the heat, but it was time for her to make a dash.

She turned and caught her breath.

Standing only a few strides away was Joseph One-Shoe. She didn't need to see his face, which was shadowed by a large umbrella. Clem knew his figure, the slight give of the hip on the side he leaned into, the tall shape that stood broad. In his hand were bright flowers, a tiny bunch, and the nagging thought fell into place. The withered flowers in a glass jar on her parents' grave were his.

'It is you, Miss Clementine,' he said, his voice thickened with the same sort of wonder as she also felt.

'It is, Zenzele.'

The smile broke. 'All grown up.'

She nodded through helpless tears that swelled and tipped over her lids to run down her cheeks, where they become indistinguishable from the raindrops.

'You are getting wet, Miss Clementine. Please?' He opened his arms and she ran to him like a child.

Neither of them cared whether it was seemly. This was love regained. This was family reunited. This was Zenzele's daughter returned.

'Oh, Zenzele,' she wept.

He hushed her and held her. 'I am very glad Impundulu kept me from travelling today,' he murmured close to her ear as he hugged her tighter.

Sitting beneath the brick shelter of the cemetery's keeper, who had graciously allowed them privacy, they listened in comfortable silence to the thrum of the rain pelting on the iron roof.

'Just like our days in the hut,' she said, smiling.

He nodded. 'You were just as beautiful then.'

They held each other's gaze and she took those moments to study the new lines in his face that attested to the passage of time, as did the peppering of grey at his temples and around his ears. To her he looked ever wiser. 'Are you really leaving?'

'Yes. And you know why.'

'Won't you miss the life here?'

'It is not good for the black man here right now, Miss Clementine. I think I must go home.'

'Will you find a wife?'

He gusted a laugh. 'Perhaps. I would like a family.'

'You deserve one. Thank you for keeping their grave so tidy. I will organise for its upkeep.'

'It is already done, Miss Clementine. The grave will be swept each week and fresh flowers will be put in the jar. They sleep soundly.'

She nodded her thanks.

'How is your uncle?'

She hesitated and then wondered why. She told him everything.

'That is a pity.'

'I know. He really was a good father to me and —'

'No, I mean it is a pity that you have cut him off.'

She blinked with surprise. Of all people, she hadn't imagined Joseph would take his side. 'I've provided for him, but I don't wish to see him.'

'Do you not miss him?'

'Every day.'

'Who benefits from this?'

She shook her head, unsure of how to answer. 'Well, I'm not sure that either of us does, but he betrayed me. He didn't tell the full truth about my father, the diamonds, his intentions. But I am angry mostly because he lied about you. This is his punishment.'

'Hmmm,' he murmured as they stared out of the hut, where they could see the rain was lessening. 'What if I told you that I have watched you grow up, in photographs and in letters? Would you believe me?'

'How could you have done that? You didn't know where I lived, or how to reach me. Will Axford has known me for only a few months.'

He waited, staring out at a sky that was promising a spectacu-lar sunset now that the rage of the storm had passed through. She sensed he was trying to make a decision and she held her tongue. He reached it with a sigh.

'I have known where you were for over twenty years, Miss Clementine.' He recited her addresses in Northumberland and London. She shivered despite the humidity of the late afternoon.

'How can you know that?'

'One of them would be on the back of the envelope that arrived from England each new moon.'

'From whom?' she asked, astonished.

'They were sent by Mr Grant. He wrote a letter each month without fail, to tell me about your life and what you'd been doing, learning, talking about. Once a year there would be a photograph or a drawing of you – he was good at drawing. So I watched you change from child to woman through pictures and his words.'

A thrill of shame coupled with disbelief traced through her. 'Uncle Reggie did this? Why?'

He shrugged. 'With who else could he share his pride in you? I think he also sensed the bond we had. I think to preserve your history he would write to me about you so someone from your past knew it all. I could tell he loved you and was raising you in a way that would have made your mother proud . . . and it made me happy.'

She was openly crying again. 'No, Zenzele, no. This can't be right. He's a dying man and I've banished him from his home. Told him I never wished to look upon him again for his treachery.'

'"Treachery" is a harsh word. Sometimes it is how you view the world that allows you to mould it in a good light. From one angle it seems your uncle has behaved in a way you can't forgive; from another, you could see him as a good man who wanted to look after you, no matter what drove him. I agree that his desire for money was part of it but it was not necessarily about riches for himself. He tried to explain many times that it was to keep your family's good standing intact – to keep your future secure.'

'Do not do this to me. Do not make me feel I've done something wrong when it took all of my courage to do what I thought was right.'

'Last year standing in your shoes that was the right approach, perhaps. Today, standing in your now very muddy shoes, knowing the whole truth, you can find it in your heart to forgive him, can you not?'

'I don't know. What about my father and Reggie's involvement in his death?'

'I felt heavy here,' he said, touching his chest, 'that you never knew the whole story of how your father died. This is why I stayed; I think I always knew the time would come when my story would be heard, but it had to be told in my words. And as soon as it was told, I felt a freedom. I did not want you to feel responsible for me. You know the truth. How you interpret it is up to you. He did not kill your father. But he did not help your father – that was his sin and perhaps you will forgive him that sin. Your father was on a path to destruction. The diamonds gave him hope but mostly for you. Without your mother he was half the man he wanted to be.'

'Who do I blame?'

'Don't blame anyone, Miss Clementine. Forgiveness is the key to a light heart.' He tapped his temple. 'And to a happy mind. There are two Englishmen who love you and I sense you love them back. Find it in your heart to move beyond the Africa of long ago. You have a life you can enjoy in the company of both Mr Grant and Mr Axford – or you can be lonely and . . .'

'And what?'

'A bit righteous like Mrs Carruthers.'

She laughed and cried at once. 'You've always known the right way. You always made sense when things felt wrong.'

'Then trust me now. You can't follow me, but you can follow my way and we can both go back to where we belong. You can make it right with the men you love.'

'I love you, too.'

'I've always known that.' He covered his heart again with his hand. 'I am secure in this, Miss Clementine, no matter where we are.' He pointed towards the sky. 'The Dog Star . . . I have always followed you, and I will continue to follow you all of my days.'

His reminder was timely. She covered her sniffs at those words by opening her bag and taking out an envelope. 'This is for you. I have carried it in the hope I could give it to you myself. Uncle Reggie didn't sell all of the diamonds. I have enough money in my own right that I will never want for anything. I've kept one for sentimental reasons, but the proceeds of the rest I want you to have.'

He didn't touch the envelope.

'You and my father dug for the diamonds together. Please allow that they be put to the best use possible. There's money in here. Build more of your school. Hire more teachers. Take on more students, buy books – whatever you need. I will help, and I will gladly send more.' Clem placed the envelope into his hand. 'Oh, and I want to give you this too. One diamond,' she said, looking for a tied handkerchief in her bag.

'I do not want Sirius,' he said, sounding alarmed.

'I understand, and neither do I. He belongs to the world. He is in a bank vault currently, but I am talking to the Natural History Museum in London about exhibiting it next year. I plan to call it the Zenzele Diamond. We'll keep Sirius as our special secret. This is just one small one because I'm sentimental and need to know you have one.'

He accepted the diamond. 'I will use your donation to build more classrooms for the children of my tribe. Maybe my great-grandchildren might study in England and visit the museum to see that mighty diamond one day.'

She opened her small bag again and took out the beaded panel. 'I have always kept this close, always felt your affection through it and always trusted that you wouldn't leave me in spirit.'

He closed a hand around hers that held the panel. 'And I have not because I threaded my promise into those beads and I will never break a promise to you. Keep this always.'

Clem smiled, her heart lighter than it had felt in many months. 'The sun is setting. We can look upon the stars together one more time.'

They returned to lean against the baobab above her parents' grave, cicadas chirping loudly into the early evening.

'Soon everything will turn green for a while. The grasses have been thirsty for a long time,' he remarked.

After all the heavenly activity a stillness settled around them; even the insects began to fall silent. The distant clouds that had been so gloomy were now fretted by a golden aura as though the ceiling of the earth was newly gilded. Behind them the sky blushed pink, dipping to violet as twilight descended. Clementine antici-pated the moon would rise through the thorn trees, which soon would be silhouetted and then they too would become invisible in the dark.

A jackal called and its mate answered. A faithful pair, just like Clementine and Zenzele. He was right. Distance did not separate them. Her heart might yearn for Africa but her life had no meaning here. Its meaning was in England, where she could change the lives of many orphans through her charitable work, and where she could gradually welcome Will Axford back into her life. Most impor-tantly, she could demonstrate her ability to forgive – the true measure of a person's humanity – and find Uncle Reggie, share his life for however long he had left. Maybe they could visit the Holy Land together as they'd always hoped.

She was grateful that she was in the presence of the one person who always shone a truth on everything – the one who had showed her the perspective of forgiveness.

Clem curled her hand into his large one and stared at his feet. He was barefoot. It spoke plenty. Tomorrow he would truly become Zenzele again but tonight they would share the velvet African sky and take heart that, no matter where she and her Zulu were, Sirius and Little Dog would never be parted.

AUTHOR'S NOTE

I grew up in a gold mining camp in Africa, and I had wonderful freedoms that few five-year-olds today might enjoy. The Africans, though segregated, were my friends. This brings me to a beautiful man who was hired in the early 1960s as a 22-year-old to look after Dad, who was busy at the mine, while we were still in England. Adongo learned to cook, tidy, organise fresh laundry, stock the pantry and generally run the household, which he did brilliantly. Then along we came – Mum, Graham and myself. We all fell in love with Adongo, especially me. No one cried harder than I did to leave him as a new decade approached, and no one missed Dad more than Adongo after our family clung to him saying farewell for the last time. He was our family – we loved him. He came into Dad's life with no English and left fluent. I spent each day helping him to learn our alphabet and numbers, and I only wish he'd taught me his.

Clementine's story is fiction, but its context is well-documented fact. *The Diamond Hunter* is set in the Cape Colony of the late Victorian era. This was a time when fortune-seekers travelled from all over the world into orgies of greed and crime, the most hateful and persistent of which, in thought, word and deed, were committed against indigenous peoples.

In this story, the relationship of Clementine with Joseph One-Shoe is inspired by my friendship with Adongo Fra-Fra. I have huge respect for all peoples from all nations, and I have a particular fondness for the Ghanaians. However, our attitudes even in the 1960s would likely still shock today. In order to keep this novel authentic, and indeed historically accurate, it's important to note that it reflects the attitudes, beliefs and language of the time and does not reflect the acceptance and integration we value today. This is a work of fiction but it rides upon extensive research based on the 1870s. Any mistakes it may contain are all mine.

I have taken a couple of liberties. First with the nutty flavoured root vegetable cassava, which was introduced into Africa from South America. I am sure I remember the Africans cooking with it when I was living in Ghana. It is versatile and prepared in many ways, but toxic if eaten raw. It is used in the story but I suspect it was unlikely to have been widely available in the Cape Colony in the late nineteenth century. Second, with the baobab tree. Although they are found in Southern Africa, they were not seen deep into the Karoo Desert. Forgive that I couldn't resist using this curious, rather brilliant tree, with all of its myth, in the story.

ACKNOWLEDGEMENTS

Plenty of generous people have contributed their time, energy and knowledge to this story, whose inception began over a pot of tea in the splendid surrounds of some hidden tea rooms in York while I was busy tying up some loose ends for *The Pearl Thief*.

A cousin I had been close to through childhood but whom I hadn't seen in maybe a score of years said he'd meet me in York as I was so time poor. After the initial rush of tumbling words catching up, we had settled down and we were onto our second pot of tea, Andrew urged me to write about diamonds. We had been in Paris together aged nineteen, discussing our futures, when we'd churned over the idea of him getting into diamonds – I had several friends involved in the diamond industry back in Brighton on the Sussex coast, where I'd been born and raised. Andrew did just that – he applied to De Beers and his excellent education and fluent French had him posted immediately into Africa, where he spent many years working for the company, before moving into senior marketing roles and ultimately head of communications. 'Write about diamonds, and I'll help. I'll meet you in Cape Town and we'll go from there.' And so I must thank my cousin, Andrew Cumine, who did meet me in Cape Town and travel with me to the Big Hole at Kimberley, organised for me to stay at The Kimberley Club – historically a gentlemen-only club – and he opened doors into several organisations, not least of which was getting into De Beers at Kimberley and sitting in its original boardroom.

I began to play with the story of a little girl from Britain growing up in a mining enclave in Africa. This wasn't so far from my own early years, as my father was involved in gold mining in West Africa, so I could touch all that childhood joy and carefree life within a camp. Plus, the Joseph One-Shoe of this tale is quietly modelled on Adongo from Bibiani . . . someone I loved enormously when I was as young as Clementine.

Alongside us were two very special guides who helped to bring the Cape Colony of Africa in the late nineteenth century to life for me. Alistair Tite, I love your Cape Town and everything you taught me from the journey of ox wagons to introducing me to the joy of warm *koeksisters*!

Steve Lunderstadt . . . wow! What a mighty resource you've been, and you were still advising nearly two years on. Thank you. I think the Big Hole might have just have remained a big hole without you there to help me build the world of diamond diggers in the 1870s. Thank you for everything, and you are one of the most knowledgeable guides I've ever had the privilege to walk alongside.

Colin Blanckenburg, thank you for your memories of Kimberley. My thanks to Alan Moss, Martin Stallion and Avril Nanton for your help in the moment of Victorian policing and orphans of African parentage.

It seems these days none of my books get written without the help of two special people. The first is Pip Klimentou, the draft reader who has been reading my raw words since book one back in the year 2000 and whose opinion for story power I rely upon. And Alex Hutchinson – a mighty influence – who meets me each year in either the south or north of England, depending on where my stories adventure, and helps me to find not only amazing locations but fabulous gems of historical interest. A trip to England would feel incomplete without Alex roaming alongside, with her endless knowledge on everything it seems, and I am thrilled that last year her debut book, *The Quality Street Girls*, went gangbusters in Britain. Hurry up with the second release, Alex. I can't wait!

The team at Penguin Random House feels like a special little club I belong to. Thank you, Ali Watts, for all your friendship and advice . . . and also to Amanda Martin, Lou Ryan, Ali Hampton, Louisa Maggio and the greater gang.

To my family . . . so glad I'm yours.

Fx

BOOK CLUB NOTES

1. James Grant hopes that a life in Africa will make his young family proud of him. Does it?

2. When Clementine is a child, Joseph One-Shoe tells her: 'Find your strength. It's always there. It will never fail you if you know where to look.' Discuss the ways in which Clementine does go on to do exactly that throughout the course of the novel.

3. In what other ways does Clementine stay true to her connection with Joseph over the years?

4. Clementine believes that 'there is always room for more compassion in the world.' How do her actions display this conviction?

5. Discuss the significance of the stars in the novel, in particular the Sirius star.

6. What does family mean to Clementine, and does that change over time?

7. Will is motivated by 'duty and honour as a man of business'. What other personality traits does Clementine find to admire in him?

8. Trust and betrayal are major themes in the novel. In what ways do you see these being explored by the author?

9. Discuss the ways in which Clementine might be considered a woman ahead of her times.

10. Clementine finds a way to forgive her Uncle Reggie. Do you? Deep down, do you think he is a good or a bad person?

11. The novel features evocative descriptions of its two main settings, Africa and England. If you had to choose, which life would you prefer?

12. Do you think this novel has a happy ending? What do you imagine might happen next to our main characters?